SISTER JANE

SISTER JANE

BY
IRMGARDE BROWN

Published in the United States by
Serey/Jones Publishers, Inc.
www.sereyjones.com

ISBN: 978-1-881276-27-2 (paperback)

DEDICATION

To my mother, Agnes Sophia Herta Elizabet Busch Berzins,
the first one to tell me to write a book when I was nine.

ACKNOWLEDGMENTS

The pandemic did its best to keep us all apart, families and loved ones, writers, and non-writers, but still, we found a way to connect. Along my convergences, I give thanks for my publishers, David and Jody, at Serey/Jones Publishers; my beta readers: Kathy Reno, Kathleen Schwartz, Pat Dickinson, Zig Berzins, Christine O'Neal, James Cameron, Erika Compton, and Lori Conway; and my writers' group: Michael Venters, Katherine Maguire, Sara K, Dan Cassenti, Mindy Elledge, Thom Hawkins, and Laura Fox. A note of thanks also goes to Dan Rodricks for insight into the world of reporting and Mark Ralston for his tips about government bureaucracy. And of course, I thank my family for indulging my dream and I thank God for sending the Muse.

1

ASH WEDNESDAY, JANE

She sprawled at the bottom of her stairs like a Raggedy Ann doll.

"Oh, sweet Jesus," she said out loud. Please God, no broken bones. She lay still for a minute to assess the pain, figuring a broken hip, wrist, or foot would hurt like nobody's business.

She had stumbled, lost her balance, and tumbled down the last three steps. Shaken, she inventoried her body as she pulled into a sitting position and leaned against the wall. Her ankle throbbed and hurt the most, but she could still move it. If she broke any bones, her family would move her into assisted living before the next new moon. How had she lost her balance?

She looked up and saw Bart sitting on a step halfway up, blithely washing himself. Had he been in the way? But then she saw several other things on the steps, items she had intended on carrying up on her next trip. Except that the next trip became the next one and so on. She saw a pile of catalogs, a People magazine or two, a sweater, and a four-pack of toilet paper. They were all hazards.

She rolled to her knees and pushed herself to standing.

"What a klutz."

She took a breath. When had she become so winded at the least bit of exertion? She limped toward the kitchen to get some ice for her ankle. Along the way, she stopped and looked around, really looked around. She lived in a pigpen. What happened to Jane the neatnik? Newspapers, junk mail, and plastic grocery bags cluttered her dining room table. Her warm jacket was lying over a chair as well as her raincoat and umbrella. As she walked into the kitchen, she found dishes layered in the kitchen drainer and a pile of dirty dishes in the sink. Last night's leftovers were still on the kitchen table as was the milk, left out overnight. She put away the milk and pulled out a bag of frozen peas from the freezer.

She looked at her teapot clock on the wall, shocked to see it was nearly 9:30 in the morning. She had never slept that late before. Or maybe she had. What day was it anyhow? She checked the calendar magnet on her refrigerator. It still showed February. No help there. She plucked the calendar from the fridge door and limped into the dining room to the telephone table. She sat down and draped the peas over her ankle, looked for her tattered address book, then called the library.

"Hello. May I speak to the information desk please?" While she waited for the connection, a recorded voice gave her a tiresome yet cheery list of all the upcoming events. Finally, a pleasant voice came on the other end.

"Information desk, this is Annie, may I help you?"

"Yes, Annie. I'm not going to identify myself because that would be too embarrassing, but could you tell me what day it is?"

"You mean the day of the week or the date?"

"Both."

"Wednesday. Ash Wednesday, March 1st."

"Oh," Jane said. "I see. Thank you." She hung up. She looked down at the calendar. Another anniversary. Three years ago, today. She could still see it.

"Jane, I am so sorry to interrupt your lesson," Dr. Landers said at her classroom door, "a friend of yours, a Dan Gillespie, is in the office. There's been an accident of some sort."

"What?"

"I'm sorry. It's your husband. Mr. Gillespie is here to take you to the hospital."

Her teacher's aide stepped up behind her and touched her arm.

"We'll be all right here. I can handle it. Call me when you know something," Alyce said.

Methodically, Jane put on her coat and picked up her handbag and tote; her mind ticked off possibilities. If this were a minor accident, they would have called her into the office by intercom. But Gillespie was here to chauffeur her, so that was a bad sign. Gillespie and Richard had left together that morning for the golf course. Wasn't that good?

When she reached the office, Gillespie stood awkwardly in his splashy lime green golf clothes that contrasted sharply with his serious expression. He took her into his arms

"What's happened?" she said into Gillespie's ear.

"Let's go. We can talk in the car," he said. "We'll come back for your car later."

Gillespie talked most of the time, she listened. He rattled on about the golf game and who was there and how everything had happened unexpectedly. Her heart pounded; she guessed the worst. She waited for him to dispel her anxiety, to say Richard would be fine.

Instead, he said, "Jane, it doesn't look good."

"It? You mean, he? He doesn't look good?"

"No, I mean his prognosis."

"Is he dead?" She had to know before they pulled into the parking lot. "I mean it. Tell me now."

But Gillespie wouldn't say, not out loud.

Somehow, she managed to walk into the emergency room, speak to the doctor in charge, and ultimately, see Richard. That is, she saw Richard's body. They hadn't admitted him into the hospital. He was DOA. That's what they said on her cop shows, DOA: Dead on Arrival. That's what Gillespie had implied. The guys had called 911, given him CPR, but there was nothing more they could do. She imagined how those boys looked, *Three Stooges* driving madly around in a golf cart.

Jane closed her eyes and held the old address book to her chest. What happened after that? She had made a few phone calls while Gillespie made the ones she couldn't bear to make. She left messages for her kids. No one picked up. Maddie was probably at yoga; Richie was in court; and Celeste never answered her phone. Gillespie must have called her "take-charge" sister Pearl in Minneapolis who insisted she would fly out the next day. And Gillespie had called Pastor Sam to put the news out by prayer chain. At least, that's what Jane assumed happened since there was already a casserole on her porch when Gillespie brought her home from the hospital.

Jane stood up to clear the memory, went back into the kitchen and slapped the calendar magnet back on to the refrigerator.

"Richard?" she said to the empty kitchen, "it's enough now, don't you think? Can we stop with the memories?"

She imagined his answer, *"I told you that two years ago. It's time to move on."* She sighed.

Jane went over to the parakeet cage, undraped it and said, "That's it, fellas. Time to wake up. Not just you tweets, but me, too."

For the rest of the morning, she experienced a vigor she hadn't felt in a long time. She became the keeper of her house once more. By early afternoon, she had tired, but it was the good kind, from a task well done. She decided to treat herself and walked down to the local bakery and bought a donut and a cup of coffee.

That night, she sat at the foot of her bed like she always did and brushed her short gray hair, or should she confess it was mostly white now? She stopped abruptly when she realized she had once again missed the Ash Wednesday service at church. As much as she loved the symbolism of dust to dust and ashes to ashes, losing Richard on this day had made the ritual bitter in her heart.

In the mirror, Jane saw herself in the same yellow nightgown. Arrayed behind her, the old oak headboard, the pillows (two on Richard's side and one on hers), the bedspread pulled down, and both cats already asleep on his side of the bed, which he always hated. They had moved on without him. Why couldn't she?

Richard was ashes anyhow. She wanted ashes, too. This time, she wanted to mark the moment, the anniversary, the loss. She looked through the dresser drawers for something she could use for ashes. Nothing. She went into the children's playroom across the hall and finally found a box of worn-down sidewalk chalk, among the pieces, a nice stubby black one. She went back into her bedroom, stood at the mirror, and drew a black cross onto her forehead. She said out loud, "Remember you are dust and to dust you will return. Repent and believe. Or don't." With that, she cried.

2

JANE, SUNDAY
IN THE SECOND WEEK OF LENT

If she left right away, she should make it to church in plenty of time. At the door, she double-checked that she had her offering envelope, her keys, and a pack of tissues. Bart and Simpson sat on the coffee table. Her cell phone chirped.

"Hey there. It was so good seeing you in church last week. You coming today? We could use you in the choir." Gillespie.

"Yes, I thought I'd try it. I'm on my way out the door now."

"Why so early? I could give you a ride."

In the last few weeks, Gillespie had started calling her almost every day. She was partly flattered, but also appalled. After all, Lindy wasn't dead, not yet.

"Thank you, Gillespie, but I've started walking again. I need the exercise."

"That's good. I'll see you there."

Jane locked her front door, stepped across the porch, and headed down the steps. At the gate, a calico cat blocked her way.

"Hello you." She was surprised the cat didn't flinch as she stooped down to pet her head. Jane assumed it was a female. "You are a very pretty girl, but where do you live?"

The cat ran up her porch steps, turned, and stared at her.

Jane chuckled. "Sorry. Not here. I've already got a pair and I don't think they want to enlarge our family."

The cat sat motionless.

"Listen, I've got to go to church. We can talk later." She opened and closed the iron gate and walked briskly toward the corner where she turned to the right and headed to church, six blocks to the south.

Jane had heard of stray animals "adopting" people by showing up on their doorstep, but this would be a first for her. She started a mental pros and cons list of keeping the cat. Not half a block later, the cat appeared on the sidewalk.

"Now kitty, you are being stupid. It's dangerous along here. Shoo! Go on. Go back where you came from."

The cat leaped into the yard next to her and disappeared. A block later, the cat was back. Jane finally gave up chastising the cat. When she reached the intersection of Federal Avenue and Benton Street, the cat sat a few feet away from her.

Jane had attended First United Methodist Church all her life, almost seventy years. God she was getting old. She stood at the corner and stared at the little red hand signal and waited for her turn to cross. There wasn't any traffic, but she thought it was only polite to wait. She had plenty of time before the 8 o'clock service and still manage to help Esther lay out the coffee and Danish for the between-services social hour.

The sun was well up and glittered through the naked trees. It was early, but she felt that spring was in the air. She heard the fast beeping of the walk/wait gizmo and stepped off the curb.

 Just then, a car careened around the corner from Benton Street and before she could catch a breath, the cat darted out from behind her and into the street. The turning car braked, and the cat leaped, but too late; Jane saw its little body connect with the car's grill, fly into the air and plop onto the asphalt with a small thud. Without a second thought, she raced around the now stopped vehicle toward the cat in the road.

A man in his early thirties got out of the car, a cigarette hung from his lips.

"What the hell? Is that your cat?"

Jane whirled on him, "What difference does it make?"

He stopped short at the tone of her voice and so did she, that force of will was unfamiliar.

"It wasn't my fault. I didn't see it," he said.

She turned from the man and gently stroked the cat's head; she said over her shoulder, "You ran a red light. It could have been me you hit."

"I gotta go. I'll be late for work." And with that, he climbed back into his duct-taped car, gunned the engine, pulled around both cat and woman in the road, and sped away. Apparently, he didn't know (or care) that the speed limit was only twenty-five miles per hour.

Jane admired the cat's beautiful tortoise shell coloring, longish hair, and yellow eyes. The cat looked to be in pain as her eyes slowly closed and opened, and then finally, seemed to stare lifelessly.

"Oh Lord, have mercy on this little creature and heal her. Give her back what that thoughtless man took away, her health, her breath, her strength, her life. Pour it back into her through your Spirit. Amen."

The eyes blinked and for the first time, focused on Jane. Very slowly, the cat moved her legs and clumsily stood, shook her body, and sauntered toward the church and into some bushes, only briefly looking back at her apparent rescuer.

Jane gawked.

What happened here? Jane was still on her knees in the street where the cat had been. There were no cars and no people, nothing but a hush as though time stood still. Then the beeping of the crosswalk signal broke the silence and seemed to say, time to move, time to walk, and time to get along. So, she stood, walked back to the crosswalk and onto the sidewalk and into the side door of the church. Her unremarkable Sunday had turned a bit extraordinary.

Had the cat saved her life? Had she saved the cat? Silly. Coincidence. Once the cat rested for a moment, she was able to walk. But something niggled at the back of Jane's brain. Had God healed the cat? Her grand-children might say, "That's mad amazing Grammy!" And Grammy Jane was thinking it was more like mad, as in regular crazy.

Jane wasn't the first one down in the church's kitchen. Esther Thyme clanked around, probably looking for the coffee parts which she never remembered were always inside the coffee urn. In fact, Esther could barely remember anything, though no one had the heart to say it.

"Esther, look in the urn," Jane said as she hung her trench coat on a hook. She went into the kitchen and pulled out the parts for Esther and started running water in the pitcher they used to fill the coffee urn.

"Where did you find that coffee basket?" Esther asked as she pulled the coffee canister over to the counter.

"Esther, why don't you wait for other people to get here to help you?"

"Henry hounds me to hurry along. I swear we get here earlier and earlier every week. One of these days, we'll get here, and the church will be locked."

"Doesn't he have a key?"

"Not anymore. Pastor said too many people had keys, so he took Henry's. I think Henry is building a case for why he should have one again." Esther finished preparing the coffee and together they lifted the urn to the counter window and Esther plugged it in. Jane pulled out the black plastic platters, laid out the doilies and started arranging the grocery store Danish and muffins. She popped a blueberry mini into her mouth before she remembered she had given up sweets for Lent. But then, she remembered, Sundays didn't count during Lent, so technically she was still good, not really cheating. Jane hoped so anyway; she was only eleven days into the season.

Jennifer Ross, Esther's daughter, scurried in carrying a huge vase of flowers. "Jerry said I could have these bouquets since no one wanted them after Miss Carolyn's funeral."

"But Jenny, they look like funeral flowers," Esther said.

"Not when I'm done with them." She pulled out the church's smaller vases, filled them with water, and distributed blossoms into each one. "They'll look sweet on our morning tables for social hour."

"Someone will notice and say something," Jane murmured.

"What? Never mind. I know you disapprove, but why waste them?" Jennifer said.

"I'm sorry," Jane said, "I'm sure you're right."

Jane finished laying out the plasticware, paper plates, napkins, and coffee cups. She found the off-brand coffee creamer and refilled the sugar packet basket. She stepped back to make sure she hadn't forgotten anything as Jennifer walked by and plopped a milky white bud vase on the serving table with a single orange gladiolus sticking out. Jane thought it looked hideous.

"Let it go, just let it go, don't say anything. It's none of your business," Richard said in her head.

From the kitchen, Esther yowled, and both women rushed in to find Esther holding up her hands in the air, one on top of the other.

"I hate cutting bagels, hate, hate, hate," Esther said.

"Oh mother, go put your hand under water," Jennifer said, "I'll get the first-aid kit."

"Please God, don't make me have to get stitches. I don't want to have to fight Medicare again."

While Jennifer went to get the kit, Jane took Esther over to the sink and put her hand under the cold running water. "You'll be fine Esther. Let's pray. Lord, have mercy on Esther and help her not to be so upset, take away her pain, and heal her cut quickly and please don't require her to go to Patient Care." Jane handed her a pile of trifold paper towels.

"Thanks Jane. Should I put my head between my legs?"

"Whatever for?"

"I thought that's what you're supposed to do."

"That's if you feel faint. Are you going to faint?"

"I don't think so. I could use a cup of coffee."

"It's not ready yet," Jennifer said as she flew back into the kitchen. She laid the battered white box with its red cross on the counter, flipped it open, pulled on latex gloves and laid out her supplies. She used to be a nurse's aide. "All righty, come over here and let's take a look," she said.

Esther walked over to the counter and Jennifer peeled away the bulky paper towels and tossed them in the trash. They stared. Nothing. Jennifer turned Esther's hand around in every direction looking for the gash.

"Mother, what are you doing? You scared us to death for nothing." Jennifer said as she pulled off her gloves and tossed them in the wastebasket.

"But I cut myself. I know I cut myself. It hurt. It bled. Look at the paper towel. There was blood I tell you."

"Well, there's no blood now," Jennifer said with a huff and left the kitchen with her kit.

Esther looked at Jane, who said nothing and shrugged, "I'd better go to choir rehearsal."

Esther wailed, "But Jane. I don't understand."

9

Jane picked up her purse and Bible and headed for the stairs up to the first floor and the choir room behind the sanctuary. She was shaken. She thought she saw blood and a cut when she put Esther's hand underwater. She had encouraged Esther to hold her arm up in the air. But the prayer. There was that prayer.

Just like she prayed over the cat. Circumstantial, right? Nothing worth mentioning. Richard would laugh it off.

Richard. She could still hear his voice. *"You're being ridiculous."*

No, he wasn't the best husband in the world. They had acclimated. But everything changed three years and eleven days ago. She was alone, so alone.

Stop it. She needed to return to life, to something recognizable, to normal. She was back in church now, she would meet with old friends, she would clean her house, she would eat better, she would volunteer, she would walk every day, she would enjoy her family as best she could. She would try it for Lent; 40 days to find normal. And if this didn't work, then, well, she would end it.

"Dammit," she said out loud and then stopped to make sure no one had heard her. She had given up swearing for Lent, too. Thank God it was Sunday.

She was one of the last to arrive in the choir room.

"There you are. Hurry up, Freedle," Gillespie said as Jane went to the robe closet.

She remembered how Dan started calling Jane and Richard by their last names when they helped at the county's emergency operations center where Gillespie volunteered. Richard was FreedleOne and she was FreedleTwo (like Thing 1 and Thing 2 from Dr. Seuss). Then Richard died, and Gillespie dropped the numbers. A little older than she and Richard, he was a tall, good-looking man and still wore a coat and tie like he was going to court. He was a good friend.

On the day Richard died, Jane had told Richard it was too early for golf, but he wouldn't listen.

He said, "Retirement has its privileges."

So, there he was at the fourteenth hole, wearing his Kelly green, with Gillespie, Mark Danforth, and Audel, when his heart stopped. All those guys looked a lot older after Richard died.

"How's Lindy?" she asked Gillespie.

"About the same. She doesn't like the exercises for her bent-up fingers. I think the therapy for her last stroke is helping her speech. Jane felt his hand on her back as they walked over to their practice area. Warm.

"Attention everyone," Gillespie said to the group. "Look who's back."

Everyone clapped and several of the ladies gave her hugs. She wasn't sure she was ready for all that, but then again, there was a familiarity to it all. Richard had loved to sing in the choir.

This morning, the choir reviewed the special music they would sing during Offering: "I Need Thee Precious Jesus." The arrangement was beautiful, although Jane thought it would sound better with younger voices. But the agreement was that the older folks would sing at the early service and the young people would run the music for the contemporary service at 10:30. Jane had heard they were going to bring in a drum set for that service, which sounded like a ridiculous rumor.

When the seven chancel choir members entered the loft in their robes, the sanctuary looked emptier than she remembered it being at the early service. Pastor Sam sat to the side of the altar and the organist played softly.

Jane checked the hymn board for the first hymn of the morning, *#793, "Oh Christ the Healer."* What would it be like to be a healer? Is that what healing felt like? In truth, she felt nothing except compassion. No drama. Her sister-in-law, Toni (was she still married to Richard's baby brother, Sid?), went to one of those full-gospel churches in the city. Toni might know something about this healing business. A few years earlier, Jane had agreed to visit Toni's church but she didn't understand a lot of the action, especially when men and women fell on the floor and the ushers covered the women's legs with large napkins if they were wearing skirts or dresses. Healing was a big thing at Toni's church along with head-slapping and group hugs. Should she give Toni a call tonight and ask for advice? That was assuming a lot, Jane Freedle.

Jane imagined herself standing in one of those auditorium-type churches, reaching out her hand over some poor invalid in a wheelchair and calling out, "Be healed in the Name of Jesus." Her hand would shake slightly, and little electrical shocks would pump out of her fingertips and gold dust would float onto the person's head. Richard was right. She was being ridiculous.

She'd better keep her morning healing incidents to herself for the time being. No Toni either. Toni was well-meaning but could be super bossy, not unlike her sister, Pearl. Besides, there wasn't much to go on. Jane refocused her mind on the back of Pastor Sam's head. He needed a haircut.

3

MONDAY IN THE SECOND WEEK OF LENT, JANE

Jane turned off her alarm, lay back in bed, stared up at the ceiling and considered how her morning routine had changed since she retired. When she was still teaching at the elementary school, there was no need for an alarm next to her bed. She rarely slept passed six o'clock. For many years, Richard worked on the Proving Ground and to beat the morning crowd going through the security gate, he left the house by 6:45. In the early years, when the kids were young, she got up dutifully to make everyone breakfast, including Richard. But as time went on, the kids left home, and she decided Richard could make his own damn coffee. Just kidding, God. She meant darn coffee of course. When the kids boomeranged back, (as in moved back to the big house) they were on their own in the kitchen as well. She didn't like to cook, not really. Had anyone noticed?

Bart and Simpson jumped up on the bed and marched across her head. They expected breakfast on time, whether she liked it or not. They were only slightly more finicky than Richard. She put on her robe and shuffled down the stairs to feed her felines and uncover Click and Clack's cage. She had always loved the NPR radio car guys and missed their live show. She chuckled to herself as she recalled the time she called into the show. God, how long ago was that? Back in the nineties? That was the most fame she had ever had in town. Fame was a funny thing. From a distance, it seemed glamourous, but while it was happening, she had felt like she was living in a glass house.

Jane was on her second cup of coffee before she looked up at the clock and realized she was running late. She had promised Maddie she would keep up her volunteering, but truthfully, she was already tired of it. Everyone wanted her to get out of the house more.

Now that her calendar was back on track, she checked off Monday. Today was her nursing home day. She went back up the stairs to get ready.

As she dressed, she reviewed her schedule for the day. She would get there around 10:30, make her rounds to the folks who couldn't get out of their rooms. She felt sorry for the poor souls who had no family visitors. Afterward, she would have lunch with the Gillespies (Dan always came for lunch with Lindy on Mondays) in the cafeteria. After lunch, she might help with afternoon bingo. It could be a long day. For dinner, she'd carry in Chinese and watch a movie on TNT. After that, straight to bed. Oh, maybe she could have a little—no, no, she gave that up for Lent. Today, a slip would count. Darn. Somehow darn was never as cathartic as damn. Oh well. Stick to it Freedle. This is the new you.

Jane still cringed at the nursing home smell. Like a hospital, but the disinfectant odor was more intense as it struggled to cover up the stench of human urine and other bodily fluids. She checked in at the front desk and got her badge.

"Good morning, Ms. Jane, you look lovely today,"

"Thank you. And good morning to you, Deztinee," she said to her favorite nurse. Here was a gal who wanted to help old and sick people. Nurse Dez loved her patients and appreciated the volunteers. It was Nurse Dez who kept Jane coming back.

"Ms. Jane, here's your visit list. We got a new intake in Room 218 who could probably use your company. She's awfully sick and I'm not sure how long she'll be with us."

"Sure. I'll pray for her, I could—"

Then she heard it. How many times had she said, "I'll pray for you" automatically throughout her adult life? But now, the thought of saying a prayer that might heal someone frightened her. Would it happen again? Was it a good idea to try healing prayers in a place like this? Her prayers could bankrupt the home. Oh, for heaven's sake, her mind was getting away from her; she wasn't a miracle worker blocking death's door. Most of the Safe Haven folks probably wanted to die anyway, if for no other reason than to get out of the nursing home.

"Room 218, you said?" Jane asked.

"That's right. May Winston: she has pneumonia and is only here temporarily. She may not even know you're in the room. Her family's from out of town, so I'm not sure if they'll get here in time; you know what I mean. They said they'd get here as soon as they can. The son said he would sign the DNR paperwork or he'll move her to a hospital closer to them. Until then, it's a waiting game."

"I understand. Yes. I'll stop by for sure."

Perhaps May Winston would be a good test for Jane, for this power or—she was at a loss for a word to call her newfound gift. Well, maybe that was the word. Gift. If it was real, then it was a gift, wasn't it? Or was it a curse? Well, whatever was going on needed testing before she said anything to anyone. Who would she tell anyway? Who would care one way or the other?

She thought about what Richard would say.

"You're talking about miracles, Jane, and we don't live in that kind of world. What? You're an apostle now?"

"I know, but –"

"Besides, why you? You still swear like a sailor if you get mad enough. You're no angel."

"I know, but—"

"And what about the real saints? Even Mother Teresa was never used like that."

"I know, Richard, but—"

"Most of the people, particularly women, who claimed to have miracle-working power or gifts or whatever you want to call it, well, they were charlatans and con artists."

"Are you calling me a fraud? Can't you once, I mean it, just once support me? I'm trying to figure this out."

"You asked for my opinion."

"Well, forget it. I'll work this out on my own. Son of a—"

"See what I mean?"

"Get out of my head Richard. You're dead." Jane grabbed onto the nearest wall. He really was dead. He was gone. God, she missed him. She even missed the arguments, sort of. No, not even that. She missed the company.

She entered Room 218. There was nothing unusual in the room. The frail dark woman was plugged in completely. The sounds of the machines, all monitoring her vital signs, were louder than the woman's breath as oxygen moved in and out through tubes up her nose. Jane was surprised they had managed to find a vein strong enough for an I.V. in those skeletal hands.

Jane walked up to the woman's bed and said, "Hello Miss May. I'm Jane. I know you're feeling poorly today. But I'm guessing you are a believer. So many of my black friends attend church here in town, Zion on the Hill, and St. Paul's AME, and what's the name of that one church at the bottom of the hill? They have the best sayings on their church sign. Maybe you go there? One of my favorites was *'SOUL' Food Served Here.'*"

She took a breath. That was probably not the most politically correct thing she'd ever said to a person. Then she remembered another one of those sayings, *"A Gift is Not a Gift until it is Given."* Her father used to say, "Shit or get off the pot." This thought was closer to how she felt. She pulled up a chair and spoke very quickly and quietly.

"So, here's the thing Miss May. I've had two weird things happen to me in the last twenty-four hours and I'm thinking it's a kind of gift, you know? But maybe I'm kidding myself. After all, that's nearly impossible, right? Ok, well, you don't know what I'm talking about and you certainly don't know me, so I'm going to take this chance and I'm going to pray for your healing. All right? I mean, I hope you want to be healed. I hope you're not a secret killer or anything. I need to know if I'm crazy or not or whether this thing will send me over the edge or whatever. My grandchildren use the word "whatever" all the time. It's an awful thing to say, don't you think? Whatever. There's nothing "whatever" about God though, is there? Are you a believer? Ok, don't answer that. I don't think that's the important part anyway. I mean, yesterday, I prayed for a cat, and she resurrected and certainly she's not a believer. Well, that may not be true, I mean, some people think all animals are a manifestation of God in some form or another. And besides, it's not me doing the healing. I get that. Believe me. I get no sensations, no nothing. OK?" She waited for an answer. "I'm talking too much. Here we go."

Jane was quiet for a moment. She gently took Miss May's hand and turned it over in her own. The woman must have been a hard worker, for her hands had calluses, even at her age. There was no telling how old Miss May was, she could be Jane's age or much older. There was the possibility that Miss May did not want to live anymore, but Jane thought about her own life and despite the loneliness and the betrayals and pain, she wasn't ready to die. She guessed Miss May might feel the same way. And what a nice surprise for her family if she was alive when they arrived.

"Dear Lord, you love Miss May. I know you do. And so, I ask you to pour your life-giving Spirit into her body and heal her. Give her body the strength it needs to breathe on her own and her mind the clarity she needs to think and the voice to speak. And if I messed up and it's her time—I mean, I just thought about that—there may be people who are supposed to die according to your timetable. So, if I'm off base, you can leave her alone. Otherwise, yes, please heal May Winston. Amen."

Jane peeked out of one eye to see if something happened. Nothing did. Well, all right. Jane felt a little stupid right then. Richard was right again. Jane stood and patted the woman's hand.

"Sorry to bother you. Have a nice day. If you're here next week, I'll come by to visit."

She walked out of Miss May's room somewhat chagrined and a little humiliated. Mostly, she was ashamed to admit she had warmed to the idea of a God-given ability to heal people. Good Lord, what an idiot. Just do your job and get on with it.

So Jane walked the halls and dropped by the rooms on her list: Amos Latimer, who liked her to sing "Amazing Grace" to him; Denise Smith, who needed her pillows fluffed and her television station changed; and Teresa Ober, who played checkers by herself and welcomed a game with a real person. Right around that time, when Jane had allowed Ms. Ober to win her second game in a row, Jane heard the patient alarm and saw nurses run past the door. This was always sad for everyone because it usually meant someone had gone into a critical state.

"Don't you worry Mrs. Ober, you're fine. Those were good games. And I'll see you next week. Would you like me to bring you anything?"

"No, I'm fine dear. I wish it didn't hurt so much to walk. I have the worst in-grown toenails."

"Time for a quick prayer then. Dear Lord, heal Mrs. Ober's toes. Amen? Amen. You'll feel better tomorrow. Now, I've got to go."

Jane rushed out because she was afraid Mrs. Ober might ask her to cut those toenails. She had a similar scenario once before and it was a grizzly job. Better to leave that task to the professionals. As she passed the nurse's station, she saw one of the nurse's aides, what was her name, Talitha or Tanita or something like that, on the phone. Jane checked the girl's name badge.

"Tanika, is everything all right? Did someone pass?"

Tanika covered the mouthpiece, "Lord no. It's a miracle. One of our patients yanked out a bunch of her lines and she's sitting up and breathing on her own. I'm trying to reach her doctor now."

Jane stood very still. It couldn't be, could it?

"Uh," Jane stuttered, "who might that be?"

"I can't say, you understand, patient confidentiality and all that."

"Of course. Of course. Sorry. Well, I'll check on the rest of my visit list. I think I'll visit that new lady in 218, Deztinee said I should try to stop by before I leave today."

"I wouldn't go down there. It's a madhouse."

Jane saw the girl's eyes get big and shut her mouth.

"She's the one?" Jane whispered.

"She's the one," the girl replied and then gratefully, returned to her phone call.

Jane folded her visit list. Her hands shook as she pulled on the sweater she had folded into her carryall and walked through the exit door to the stairs and out the building's side door. She did not say a word to anyone on her way out. She doubted anyone even noticed. But one thing she knew for sure, something big just happened.

18

4

SAME MONDAY IN THE SECOND WEEK OF LENT, TWOMEY [TOO-MEE]

Twomey stared at his screen and saw nothing. Not because the screen was blank, but because his mind had wandered again, a million miles away. He daydreamed of those early years in journalism when a story was a story, when the guys knew what it meant to investigate a lead, when they worked all hours of the day or night, when they lived hard, played hard, drank hard, and wrote hard. Twomey missed those days. He had been right at the cusp of acclaim and respect. He had almost tasted it and touched it, but then blew it. When his luck ran cold on the horses, it ran even colder in journalism. He started missing the moments, losing the string that unraveled the story, forgetting details. He could never seem to catch a break. He was a working fossil.

He had lied to his friends when he moved out to Harford County. He told them he wanted the easy life. But truthfully, he didn't have many options: retirement, transfer, or suspension. Now he was miles and miles away from any real news. He had washed up as an investigative reporter and flat broke. That was already a year ago and now he was living—no not living but dying in the boredom of petty, small-town stories. What would be next? Church news?

His phone buzzed in his pocket.

"Twomey," he said into the phone.

"You're up county, right?" the voice jumped right in.

"What do you want me to do Chuck? Pick up your laundry?"

"Don't be a shitass."

"Better than a—" he started to say.

"Take a ride over to an old folks home called Safe Haven. It's somewhere in Lafayette."

"What? Somebody died? Go figure."

"On the contrary. Somebody busted out of there healthy as a horse. The call-in said the woman flew off her bed," Chuck said. *"Take JoBeth with you and try to get a picture of this woman, wings and all."*

"You're kidding, right?"

"What's your beef, Twomey? It will give you something to do. I'm guessing you're sitting there looking at your computer screen."

"Go to hell, Chuckie," he signed off. He closed his laptop screen. He needed to get some lunch anyway. He grabbed his jacket and patted down for his keys and smokes.

On his way down the dark, narrow corridor of his building, he spoke into his phone. "Hey JoBeth, can you meet me over at the Safe Haven Nursing Home in Lafayette? Chuck wants some shots."

5

TUESDAY IN THE SECOND WEEK OF LENT, JANE

Jane's house phone jolted her out of a deep sleep. She turned her head to check the bedside clock and realized she was on the couch and not in bed. Now she remembered, she had been up half the night reading her Bible on healing. She read every example of Jesus healing people. What did she learn? He had no set technique; in fact, the writers described very few instances in detail. She had never noticed that before. The lingering question was how he picked whom to heal. Did he cherry-pick? How would that have worked?

The phone kept ringing. Jane dislodged the cats, who were uncharacteristically slovenly, and walked over to the phone table to pick up.

"Freedle! What happened to you? I think that's the first time you've ever stood us up. Lindy kept asking about you."

"What?"

"Lunch my dear. Yesterday? Remember? Are you having a senior moment?"

"Oh. Gillespie. I'm so sorry. Truly I am. Uh, I got a terrible headache and had to come home."

"You missed the excitement."

"Oh?"

"It was a circus. Some woman was skipping and dancing down the hallway saying an angel had come to her bed and healed her. They finally had to sedate her."

"Hmmm, really?"

"As far as I know, her family showed up later in the day and Safe Haven released her. She kept yelling, 'Glory, glory, glory to God in the highest' and asking if anyone else had seen her white-haired angel who glowed with the power of God."

21

Confirmed, her hair was white after all. And did she glow? That would be embarrassing. She didn't want to light up like a lightbulb.

"Freedle? You there?"

"Yes, yes. Sorry. Let me call you back later. I fell asleep on the couch, so I need to take a shower and get ready for the day."

"Sure. I'll—"

She was halfway up the stairs before she realized she had hung up on her friend. She considered calling him back, but what did she have to say? Hey Gillespie, let me pray for your wife and she'll be healed and then we'll have to stop flirting for real. Whoa! Did she think that? Stop, stop, stop.

She shook her head and moved up the creaking stairs to her bathroom. She was once again a little out of breath at the top. "Ok God, I could use a little help with this shortness of breath."

If only she could get one of those fixer-upper television shows to do her house. With only one bathroom on the second floor, Jane had begged Richard for a half bath on the first floor. But he didn't want to give up the pantry and besides, the pipes would probably freeze and who wanted to go to the john right off the kitchen? She would. But she gave up the idea. Like most things, her opinion didn't amount to much.

After a quick shower, she decided she had to tell someone about this latest experience; she wasn't ready to call it a miracle. She needed help to understand what was happening. She took a breath, picked up her cell phone, and called the church office. When the church secretary answered, she asked to speak to Pastor Sam *"He's out of the office this morning Mrs. Freedle, may I take a message?"* Cindy said.

"No, I need to speak to him in person. Will he be in this afternoon? Could I make an appointment?"

"I think so. Yes. He seems to have a 3:30 opening. Would that work for you? And what can I tell him this is about?"

She stared at herself in her dresser mirror. She had pulled her short hair back with a hot pink headband; her turkey neck was still red from the hot water. She looked more like a Carol Burnett character than a woman on a mission from God.

"Just tell him I have some theological questions."

22

"Oh. Wow. Sure. Uh, how do you spell that?"

After Jane cleaned out the birdcage, scooped the cat box, and made her morning oatmeal and hot tea, she decided to take a long walk. Her benevolent dictator of a big sister, Pearl, had sent her a workout set for Christmas and Jane got the message loud and clear: start taking better care of yourself, you can't grieve forever. Was she still grieving? Pearl and Maddie had convinced her to attend a grief group at the beginning of year two, but after three sessions, she dropped out. So many of the women called their dead husbands the "loves of their lives" and it made her uncomfortable. It was different for her and Richard. They had grown accustomed to one another. She had grown accustomed to Richard making all the decisions. And for a long while, she had let Maddie do the same. But now, she didn't like it much.

She put on her cheap store sneakers (there was no way she was going to spend more than $30 on a pair of shoes) and headed out, down Federal Avenue and then on to the walkway that hugged the river.

Jane stopped at one of the vistas. The tide was low, and the ducks were busy grubbing about for food in the shallow waters. A few sailboats were out. She had always dreamed of a leisurely sailboat-like life. But it hadn't worked out that way. Of course, she had also assumed a life of leisure would include a husband. Instead, Richard grew bored with their life together.

"Don't be such a stick in the mud," he would say.

Only she knew the real reason Richard wanted to move to a Senior community: more women and more golf. Sure, she was lonely now, but the last few years before his death had been equally lonely.

She should pray. If she was under a special touch or anointing, then she should be doing holy things. But where to start? Everything seemed different now that things were truly happening when she prayed. Go figure. She looked down and saw how tightly she grasped the rail, the blue rivers of her veins pulsed. Maybe she could pray for a million dollars. That sounded self-serving and sinful right there. She'd better keep it simple.

She murmured the Lord's Prayer and kept walking.

At 3:15, she sat in the church office waiting for her appointment with Pastor Sam. He wasn't a young man anymore, but then she wouldn't classify him in her generation either. He might be in his mid to late fifties, maybe older. His hair was thinning on top and on days he didn't shave, his beard came in white. He wasn't very tall, but he was in good shape. She had heard he played a lot of tennis and pickleball. Pastor was a kind man and very smart, but predictable. She had seen many ministers come and go in the last twenty years; most were at the end of their careers when they accepted a small-town appointment like First Church of Lafayette.

"Jane?" Sam's voice broke through her thoughts.

"Oh sorry. I was driving down memory lane. That's what we oldsters do."

Sam smiled and ushered her into his small office. The room hadn't changed much, no matter how many pastors came and went. Reference books still stood like soldiers and the house plants lived or died and were replaced by new ones. Two old, dark, red leather chairs sat facing his desk and a high-backed black one swiveled from side to side as Sam leaned back in it, relaxed.

"So, Jane. How are you doing?"

"Fine," she said with no clue how to begin.

"It was great seeing you back in the choir loft yesterday."

She didn't know what to say, somewhat surprised he even noticed.

"So, Cindy said you had some logical questions?"

Jane laughed. Cindy was the sweetest receptionist anyone could ask for but, the truth was the truth, she was not the sharpest knife in the drawer.

"Theological. Yes."

Sam laughed then too. "I was wondering if she had missed something in translation. You never struck me as a theologian. I mean, I have found you to be rooted and grounded in the faith. Surely you don't have big doubts at this stage of life?!?"

That remark was irksome. What? She was too old to think, to question? And what stage of life did he think she was in? The stage where she couldn't live by herself? That's what Maddie and Nick were starting to hint around. "Well, you know," Jane said, "they say seventy is the new sixty. I'm not ready to go out to pasture yet."

He looked puzzled. "I meant no offense. I was trying to compliment you on your faithfulness."

"Oh. Sorry."

Pastor looked at his watch. He did. He really did that. Well, if that were the hint to get on with it, she would.

"So, tell me Pastor, do you believe in miracles?"

"Of course," he smiled, "the Bible is full of miracle stories. It's foundational to our faith."

"Right, but I mean in today's world. Now. Do you believe in miracles? In healing? In dead things coming to life?"

"Whoa, Jane. That's a lot of questions that have lots of different answers."

"Not just a yes?"

"Well, no, not exactly. In essence, of course, there are stories of miraculous things happening to people. Who am I to discount these events? I do believe in a miracle-working God. And people experience healing every day, particularly by the miracle of medicine and the wonderful people who are gifted in these things."

Jane stared at him. She wasn't feeling very safe right now in her story. "And dead things? Resurrection?"

"Well, I've never seen anything that dramatic. There is something to be said for God's timing and if it's a person's time to die, praying for a resurrection might be going against God's Will."

That made a kind of sense. The same thought had come to her mind while praying for May Winston. She wasn't sure it fit the cat incident, however. But then, she wasn't even sure the cat had been all the way dead. She might want to skip that part.

"I'm wondering," Sam said, "did you hear about the healing at Safe Haven? That's a pretty dramatic expression of the supernatural, right there. But you know, the power of suggestion and the power of personal faith, can spur a lot of amazing results."

"That was me."

"I beg your pardon?"

"I prayed for her and she was healed."

25

He stared at her, patiently, as though she might explain what she meant. But honestly, what more was there to say?

"It was a miracle," she added.

"You were there when she jumped out of her bed?"

"No, not in her room, I was in her room earlier. I was in Theresa Ober's room playing checkers when the alarm sounded. But when I heard the commotion, I knew it was my prayer."

Pastor Sam steepled his fingers and touched them to his lips. Oh Lord, she was in a movie. She replayed their conversation so far in her head. She sounded like a nut case. She should leave now. Instead, she blurted out.

"I can tell you think I'm talking like a wacko, but I'm not. That wasn't the only time. On Sunday, I prayed for Esther's finger (she sliced it accidentally cutting bagels, you can ask her), and after I prayed for her, the cut was gone. And then, before church, a car hit a cat and I prayed, and it got up and walked away."

There was a longish pause. She could hear the ticking of the cheap, battery-operated clock on the wall.

"I hear what you're saying, I do. And I don't want to rain on your parade, but people often misunderstand cause and effect. You know, some people plant the seed and others tend the seed and still others reap. We never know where we are in this continuum of life, of blessings, or of healing."

He kept talking. She stopped listening. Instead, she became aware of her heart pounding and her palms sweating. She wondered if she could have a heart attack right there. She smiled at her little joke. Maybe she could pray for herself and get a healing and then he would believe her. But clearly, he didn't or wouldn't. And honestly, saying those things out loud sounded ridiculous to her too.

"Jane, am I losing you?"

"Sorry?"

"Are you getting out enough? Eating all right?"

"You sound like my daughter."

"Maddie? Why yes, I chatted with her a few days ago."

There it was. Every warning bell in her mind started ringing. Her daugh-

26

ter was at it again, but this time, working at the outer boundaries of her world.

"They don't think I should live alone. I know," she said.

"Well, it's something to think about. You might find you like living in a place where you don't have to worry about cooking or cleaning."

Jane stood up and threw out a pile of pleasantries and escaped, her freedom still in hand, the question of her sanity somewhat tabled, and the possibility that God was doing miracles through her thrown to the recycle bin. She felt thoroughly humiliated.

Before she could get through the reception area, Pastor Sam stepped out of his office and called to her.

"Listen, Jane, let's talk again. How about next week? I'd like you to know that you are much appreciated here at the church. We're so glad you're back. Your well-being and your faith walk are important to me and all of us. We're family, right?" He turned to Cindy, "Set us up for a session next week at the same time," and then to Jane, "Will that work for you too? Hopefully, your Tuesdays are not too full?"

Smartass, Jane thought. "No, fine. That would be fine. Thanks." Did her potty-mouth inside her head count as breaking Lent? Probably.

He closed the door. She watched Cindy diligently fill out an appointment card as though she was coming back to have her teeth cleaned. Cindy messed up the card and did some cross-outs and then threw it away.

"Sorry, one second," Cindy said as she hobbled over to the filing cabinet.

"What happened to your foot?" Jane asked.

"Oh, I sprained it walking up the stairs. Don't ask. I am such a klutz."

Jane's eyes narrowed, well perhaps not physically narrowed, but in her mind's eye, she could feel herself want to prove she wasn't crazy by praying for Cindy. But then, what was the point? Who was she trying to convince? Pastor Sam or herself?

Jane said, "I'll remember the appointment. Don't worry about the card," and left.

She was close to tears all the way home. The whole thing seemed preposterous after that conversation. No. Richard was right. Who was she kidding? She was Jane Smythe Freedle, daughter of a grocer and a seamstress, a retired second-grade teacher, the mother of three adult children, two cats, two parakeets, and she was a widow. It was enough.

As she walked up the old porch steps of her home, she checked her mailbox, but as usual, she found nothing but a few circulars and the town newsletter.

She replayed the scene in Pastor Sam's office again. What a mess she had made of that appointment with the pastor. How would she face him on Sunday? Maybe she could make a little joke about it or tell him she had watched too many Harry Potter movies. She could stay home and pretend to be sick. But then the shut-in team would call on her and ask to come to her house to pray for her. That would be awkward.

In the living room, she sat down heavily. From the couch, she could see through the open pocket doors into her dining room and kitchen. The dining room table, although neat and cleared off, already had a layer of dust. When did that happen? As she looked around, all the furniture needed another swipe or two. She needed to get a hold of herself. She had to rebuild her life here.

She should eat something, but she wasn't hungry. But if she didn't eat, then Maddie would think she couldn't take care of herself. She wasn't that old, dammit. She marched into the kitchen and opened the refrigerator and looked at the contents. It was grim. She had plenty of condiments, a few eggs (she was too lazy to open the carton and count), a wrapped bundle of some kind of leftover sandwich, a Styrofoam container with leftover salad from the grocery store, a half loaf of bread, butter, and cottage cheese (which was probably bad but she'd have to smell it to know and she didn't have the heart for it). In the door, she found a half quart of milk and decided to take her chances with milk and cereal. She added a little brown banana half. Later, she could boil an egg and voila, all the food groups.

When she sat at her dining room table to eat (for the novelty of it), she saw the light blinking on her answering machine. God, she hated that thing. Gingerly, she walked over to the monster and went through the steps in her head of retrieving messages before she touched any of the buttons.

"Hello, Ms. Freedle, this is Wade Twomey with the Baltimore Sun, well, really the Aegis, you know what I mean. I was wondering if we could chat about what happened over at Safe Haven yesterday. My cell phone

28

number is 410-688-7814."

The newspaper? Really? Delete. Jane couldn't understand how that could have happened. What did he know? What did he believe? How did he get her number? Granted, she was listed, but how did he get her name? She should get rid of her landline. It was an extra expense. But she liked the way the receiver fit in her ear. All the cell phones were like talking into a cigarette case.

She should call him back. Well, that was out, she already deleted his message. Back at the table, she found her cereal was soggy, so she threw it out. She checked the freezer and found a Klondike bar. Did ice cream count as sweets? Wasn't it more like dairy? Except for the chocolate. Oh, hell with it. This Lent thing wasn't working out too well. She would start over tomorrow.

She turned on the TV and navigated to Law and Order. She preferred the older episodes. She wished they would number them or, at least, play them in order. She wasn't even sure they were all on the same channel anymore. Right now, it didn't matter. Routine. That was what she needed. Watch her show, make some chamomile tea, brush the cats, and go to bed. No more flights of fancy.

Isn't that what Richard always said, *"You need to get your head out of the clouds, Jane. That's not how the world works. Just go to bed and everything will be fine in the morning."*

6

SAME TUESDAY IN THE SECOND WEEK OF LENT, TWOMEY

Monday, Ms. May Winston experienced a dramatic and generally unexplainable return to health at Safe Haven Nursing Home in Lafayette, Maryland. She claims, "A white-haired angel came to my bed and she prayed for me and she said that I was healed, and I was to give glory and praise to God wherever I went. So that's what I'm doing now." Ms. Winston attends Mt. Zion Church of the Holy Cross in Benton, Maryland. Her daughter, son-in-law, brother, and sister came to Safe Haven to take Ms. Winston back to Pittsburgh where they live. Ms. Winston had been suffering from acute pneumonia and complications.

Twomey looked at the lead and wanted to barf; it represented over two wasted hours trying to get something factual from anyone. He had interviewed the residents, well at least the ones who were aware enough to sign a release on their own (all of three, one of whom said her ingrown toenails were healed but he had no intention of following up on that), the nurses, the attending physician, and any volunteers who happened to be in the building. Of course, the volunteer assigned to Winston's room wasn't answering his calls. What was that about?

He could go to her house, but that seemed excessive for a story conjured by a sweet little old black lady who was having her day in the sun. If Chuck wanted more, Twomey would interview May Winston's minister in Benton. He certainly wasn't going to Pittsburgh. JoBeth said she got a good picture, so page three was set. He should go down to Randy's and have a beer. Or two. Or three.

He finished the story with as much fluff as he could muster and added one more line, "if anyone has additional information that could shed more light on this miracle—" he deleted the word miracle and changed it to "incident; please contact the Aegis." He hit send.

On his way out of the apartment door, he tripped over a skateboard and fell on his ass. That's it. He was out of there. He hated to move but he

30

had enough. He checked his phone, just in case Ms. Freedle had called him back, but the only message he had was from Belinda. Never in a million years did he think he would still be paying alimony after all this time. For God's sake woman, get married already. But then, who would marry her?

7

Wednesday in the Second Week of Lent, Twomey

"I don't get paid until Friday Belinda. I'll drop by with some cash then," Twomey said into the phone in between drags on his Marlboro. He could barely get in a word edgewise. "No Belinda. Yes Belinda. No Belinda." He took another drag and let it out very slowly and watched as the smoke dissipated. "No Belinda, I have not gone to the detention center to visit Arnie," he waited for the yelling to die down a little and held the phone away from his ear. *"Wade? Wade? Did you hang up on me?"* He spoke into the phone, "No Belinda, I'm still here. Your son is a two-bit criminal who passes bad checks, cheats little old ladies, and sells dope on the side. And don't tell me again 'he's your son too' or I'll get that damn DNA done and that will be that." He hung up.

Twomey tossed his cigarette butt on the pavement and sipped his coffee before heading back to his car at the pump. He had decided to look for a place here in Lafayette. Anything was better than that shithole where he was living now. Maybe he could find a little cheaper one. He was supposed to meet a rental guy who would show him a few places in town around three. On his way to the rental office, he drove by the address he had found for the Safe Haven volunteer, Jane Freedle. He wasn't even sure why he bothered. There probably wouldn't be a follow-up but he didn't like loose ends in a story. Something was off.

The woman lived on Browning Street, not far from the new restaurant on the corner of Federal Avenue. Twomey didn't care too much for the food there, too spicy, but they had a decent beer selection and three TVs. Back in the day, he would have preferred a full bar with lots of smoke and women, but those days were over. Now, he contented with a buzz on, a little political talk, and a video game or two before facing his four walls at night. As he drove down Browning, the nice early spring weather had brought out several mothers with their strollers and little old ladies power walking.

He pulled up to the address he had jotted down. It was a monstrosity of a house, painted a kind of olive green with white trim. The old porch had wicker furniture, a swing, and an old-fashioned mailbox hanging next to the wooden door. The house looked like it was waiting for the next paint job and a new roof in a big way, not unlike most houses in this part of town.

He chided himself for wasting time. But just as he was about to pull away, a fluke. One of the little old ladies walking briskly up the block pushed open the wrought iron gate and headed up the walkway and porch stairs. Bingo. Unless dear Mrs. Freedle had turned this place into a boarding house for other white-haired ladies, this was her. But now he had to find a parking place. Damn.

In this section of town, there was little to no off-street parking or garages nearby. That meant people jockeyed for a place in front of their houses or as close as possible. The street was maxed out even on a weekday. One spot had two lawn chairs sitting in it. Very tempting. In the end, he took a chance and pulled into a driveway behind the restaurant. He wouldn't be long. To justify parking there, he could get a late lunch carryout after he spoke to the Freedle woman.When he got to her front door, he took a peek through the side window panel of the door and saw a typical Lafayette 1930s home: wood floors with an area carpet in the front room (what used to be called a parlor), a wide opening into the larger dining room and a kitchen with an old-fashioned swinging door beyond, standing open. Along the right wall of the parlor was a wooden staircase to the second floor. He caught sight of his prey standing at her dining room table. She looked up and saw him peeking through the window. He waved and rang the doorbell. He put on his harmless mask.

"May I help you?" she asked through a narrow gap in the door, holding a white cat in her arms.

"Hi, Mrs. Freedle? Jane Freedle? I'm Wade Twomey, a reporter with the Aegis?" He watched her eyes, which gave most people away. She was cautious.

"Are you stalking me Mr. Twomey? If I wanted to speak to you, I would have called you back."

"I know. I'm sorry. May I come in for a moment or two? Here's my business card. See? I'm the real thing. I want to ask you a couple of questions about the incident with May Winston at the nursing home."

"Incident? Wouldn't you call it a miracle?"

"Sure. Yeah. Pretty amazing stuff. May I come in?"

There was a long pause and he wasn't sure what she was weighing in her mind, but clearly, she was considering a couple of options in her head.

"You know, Mr. Twomey, there's nothing to tell. I volunteer at the nursing home and I visit people who don't have family and friends. I went in, I prayed for Ms. Winston and I left. That was it. Now, really, I need to get back to what I was doing."

"That's great. Sure, sure. They told me you do a lot of good there. Was Ms. Winston awake when you were in the room?"

"Goodbye Mr. Twomey. It was nice to chat with you." She closed the door and the gap in the curtains.

He stood on the porch an extra moment. Nothing to the story. Let it go. She was a do-gooder and nothing more. All the same, why were her hands shaking? He turned and watched a school bus come down the street. The middle school kids must be out now. Then he remembered the rental agent and fast-walked back to his car to find a notice on the windshield. At least they didn't tow it. He headed to the rental office without stopping for food.

8

SAME WEDNESDAY IN THE SECOND WEEK OF LENT, EVENING, JANE

The cats sat on the sofa with her as they all watched Law and Order again when a key in the lock turned and the front door opened unceremoniously. In clamored Misty Renee first and then Maddie carrying the car seat with baby Mason; and of course, Nick bringing up the rear with his nose buried in his phone.

"Hello there, family. I didn't know you were coming," she said. At least, not so soon, she thought. She'd lost that bet with herself. Maddie brought the whole crew.

"I know, sorry Mother, I meant to call you, but I kept forgetting. We dropped off Mitchell at lacrosse practice and Madison at Taekwondo. We brought dinner. Hope you're hungry. Nick, take the baby."

She wasn't going to say she already had dinner, but then an egg salad sandwich wasn't exactly dinner.

"Grammy Jane, look what I have? A horse. It's an early birthday present. I'll be seven soon," Misty Renee said.

"Yes, I know. Well, that's wonderful."

"And guess what else? I get to take riding lessons this summer. Don't I, Mommy?"

"We'll see."

Jane pulled Misty Renee into her arms, their family miracle. She remembered the little preemie, born six weeks early and the long hours they all spent in NICU. She had groused a lot with her God back then. But who would know now? Misty was a healthy and happy little girl with a curiosity that never quit.

"What is your horse's name?" she asked.

"Moana."

"Well, that's a different name. Where'd you learn that?"

"It's from a Disney movie," Maddie said. "I'm surprised you haven't seen the ads on all that television you consume."

Jane watched through the kitchen door as Maddie efficiently got out plates and silverware and opened all the packages from their favorite Chinese carryout on Route 40. Nick pushed her white cat, Simpson, out of the easy chair and collapsed into it with a great huff and set the car seat on the floor.

"God, there's cat hair everywhere," Nick said as he slapped at his pants.

"You're acting like an old man Nick," she said.

"I feel like an old man." He gently rocked the car seat. His face softened as he looked down at his son. For all of Nick's negative points, he loved his kids. She had to give him that.

"I'm surprised you didn't stay for Mitchell's practice," she said.

Nick looked over his shoulder toward the kitchen and seemed to catch Maddie's eye. When he turned back, he shrugged and said, "I haven't seen Grammy Jane for a while, right? Plus, I've got a hankering for sesame chicken. Mitch said he would get a ride home with one of the seniors. I'll have to run over to pick up Madison at 6:30. She'll be starving by then."

Jane assumed Maddie had planned this pow-wow in her head and simply informed Nick in the car right before they arrived. Probably. She decided to act clueless, no reason to ruin dinner.

"Ok, everybody," Maddie called from the kitchen, "food's on. Where's Misty Renee?"

Jane looked and saw Misty Renee sitting on the bottom step having a tête à tête with Bart, the tiger female. Jane should have changed the cat's name once they discovered she was a female, but her only choice would have been to call the cat Jessica to match with Simpson and no one would have appreciated that.

"Come with me Misty Renee, let's chow down," she said and held out her hand.

The meal was good and filling and the conversation light. Misty Renee

36

asked if she could go upstairs and play in the kids' room, still loaded with toys. She and Richard never cleaned it out once Maddie started making babies—a playroom at Grammy and Grampa's turned out to be useful. Baby Mason woke up for a feeding and Jane marveled at how easily her daughter could breastfeed and still eat her supper at the same time, with chopsticks no less. Nick was on his phone for most of the dinner. Maddie asked him to put it away more than once and he did, each time, for about a minute. No change there.

Jane watched her kitchen teapot clock and longed for 6:30 when Nick would leave to pick up Madison. She dreaded the idea of having to listen to lectures from them. Nick was a bit of a schemer. She knew instinctively, if she ever fell and broke a hip, he'd have her in a nursing home and her house on the market before she could sneeze. Although he had a good job now at the city, he still did real estate on the side, and God knew what else.

"Just got a text from Madison," Nick said, "she's getting a ride here with the Smiths. They're going to stop for pizza, is that OK with you Maddie?"

"Sure, that's perfect"

No luck for Grammy though. She watched Nick's fingers fly over the keyboard. She had managed to learn how to text and even do email, but it was slow going. The phone keyboard seemed so small and she kept hitting the wrong letters. But sometimes it was worth it when her grandkids texted her back. Those messages made her feel special. Some of her other old lady friends would complain that their kids or grandkids would never call them, and Jane would always say, "Get modern. It's all about texting now." The kids complimented her for being "with it." She smiled to herself.

"So, Mother," Maddie started "Let's be honest with each other."

Here we go, she thought.

"You and I have talked before about the challenges of this house and I know how much you want to stay here, but let's face it, you really can't take care of it by yourself anymore."

"Hmmm," Jane said noncommittally. She learned a long time ago that it was better to wait until they put all their cards on the table. If she said "no" too soon, they would pounce.

"So, Nick and I were talking the other day and wondered if another idea might suit you better. Instead of moving into assisted living, maybe you would consider moving in with us?"

Jane looked at Nick, whose face was passive (he must have steeled himself for this moment), and then she looked back at Maddie. She wanted to laugh, but that wouldn't be a good idea.

"That's a very nice offer but you know you don't have enough space," she started with the most obvious roadblock, not to mention three loud children and a baby whom she loved, but in small doses.

"Well, we talked about that too. We thought the best option would be to sell this house and take the proceeds to build an addition on our house. They're called mother-in-law suites. You could even have a kitchenette. I already talked with Uncle Hank and Uncle Roscoe and they are OK with it. They never expected much of an inheritance anyway."

"How thoughtful," Jane said wryly as she thought of her octogenarian twin brothers. "And sister Pearl?"

"Oh, you know Pearl. She'll come around. Besides," Maddie added, "with some of the other things going on, you will feel safer with people around. We all miss Daddy. I just know this is what he would have wanted. But it's obvious, you need help. Please don't jump to no."

Her daughter was so intent (she must have practiced such a speech), this youngest child of hers, and up until Maddie's marriage to Nick, she had been the compassionate one. Where Celeste had been the free spirit and Richie his father's clone, Maddie used to be on Jane's team. But ever since Richard died, they were more like strangers and everything was Jane's fault. Maddie never said so, not outright, but Jane could feel it.

If only Maddie had stayed in school and finished her degree in social work. But no, the charming Nick came along. Then, Maddie had no time for anything but babies, her medical transcription work, and cooking. Jane had no idea how they managed to pay the bills. How many times had Richard bailed out Nick from one of his cockamamy ventures? But then Richard died. Nick finally got a steady job with benefits, but Maddie hardened her heart. Jane hardly recognized her daughter anymore. She seemed much more tightly strung and found fault with everything, at least, everything that concerned Jane.

She decided to address the real elephant in the room.

"I'm sorry I've caused you so much distress. I take it you talked with Pastor Sam today?"

Nick looked up at that. Maddie took a deep breath and answered, "Yes, Mother, but that wasn't the only reason we wanted to talk about this."

Jane couldn't remember when Maddie started calling her "mother." Probably since Richard died. In any case, she hated it. Maddie stood and started clearing away the takeout boxes and dishes as Nick talked.

"Jane," Nick started, as though his voice would now clear the air and make everything right. "You have been through a lot. You are still griev-ing even after all this time; we understand everyone goes through this process differently. But, you are moving into a phase of life that has a lot of new challenges for you, a lot of unknowns, and your daughter, who loves you very much, is here to help you navigate those changes. You don't need to go it alone. And when you get some crazy ideas, you can bounce them off us."

"Crazy ideas. Yes, that would be helpful," Jane said. "And did the Pastor imply that I had brought him a crazy idea?"

"No, nothing like that," Maddie said. "But he was concerned about you living alone. We all are."

"And the miracles, did he mention those?" she asked.

"He mentioned that you were at Safe Haven on Monday when that lady went screaming up and down the halls," Maddie said. "It's wonderful that she had such an unexpected recovery and I'm sure that meant a lot to you."

"I'll say," Jane smiled. "Listen, you two, I'm not ready to leave this house. I—I can't. Maybe when you get to be my age, you'll understand. I'm sorry."

Maddie turned from the sink and threw down the dishtowel.

"How can you be so selfish and stubborn? We are trying our best to help you and yet, you refuse to even consider any of the proposed options. You were the same way with Daddy. He always complained about your narrow-mindedness. He would agree with me; you can't keep living here alone!"

"What?" Jane stood up. "I won't listen to this. What your father wanted or didn't want is not up for discussion."

Maddie's mouth dropped open. Nick put his hands up in surrender. She sat and took a deep breath.

"Listen to me. I know this sounds crazy and even a little frightening. But I have been part of several miracles. Honest to God. I am not making these things up. I don't know why they are happening, but they are."

"You are not making things better this way," Maddie said.

"I suppose you could have me committed."

"You're certainly talking crazy enough," Nick said.

"Nick!" Maddie said.

Lucky for her, the baby started crying and Maddie picked him up to comfort him, then the door crashed open and Madison came running in and asked if there was any dessert left. Nick got up and pulled ice cream from the freezer and just like that, the conversation came to an end. She took another deep breath. Maybe she was cuckoo. And even if she weren't, her daughter would never believe anyway. She was on her own.

Jane heard a sharp outcry and the sound of thumping. They all raced out to the parlor to find Misty Renee crumpled on the floor at the bottom of the steps, her horse still in her hands. She was very still.

Maddie screamed which set the baby to crying, and Nick yelled, "Don't move her, anybody, don't move her. Call 911. Call 911. I'll call 911. Maddie, where's my damn phone?" He raced back into the kitchen. The baby screeched and Maddie followed Nick trying to soothe the baby as she said, "it's in your hand." Madison stood stock still, her back to the front door and stared down at her baby sister. Jane bent down to Misty and pulled the girl into her arms.

"Daddy said not to move her," Madison said, turning white.

"Get me some ice in a towel from the kitchen, Madison, quick," Jane said. And then she prayed, "Heal Misty Renee Lord, oh my God, my sweet Jesus, have mercy on this baby, on my grandbaby, on my precious Misty. You have done so much this day and, in the day before, but please, one more? Please have mercy. Heal her body, take her pain, and order everything inside her head. So be it. Amen. " And then she rocked the child.

"Damn it Jane, I told you not to move her," Nick said as he raced back into the room, phone still in hand, intermittently answering questions on the phone. "Is she breathing? Jane, is she breathing?"

Maddie followed in on his heels.

Jane looked down as Misty's eyelids fluttered. "Yes, yes, she's breathing. She's awake."

Maddie handed Baby Mason to her teenaged daughter, then bent down to Misty and pulled her from Jane's arms and hissed, "Let her go. What's wrong with you? Can't you follow the simplest directions? If anything happens to her because of you, I'll never speak to you again."

"She's unconscious," Nick yelled into the phone, "Damn it, stop moving her," he said to the two women.

"Nick," Jane said, "please watch your language."

"I do not need one of your lectures right now," then Nick spoke back into the phone, "She could be dead. Sweet Jesus. Please hurry." He hung up. "You shouldn't have moved her Jane. She probably has a concussion. What do you know about injuries like this? It's no small thing. And it's these damn ancient stairs and this God-awful house."

Jane ignored Nick. She knew what he thought about her house. She sat on the bottom step and watched Misty Renee, still praying, but silently. Maddie sat with her back against the wall, Misty in her arms. Madison, with Baby Mason, sat on the floor next to Jane. Baby Mason whimpered. Jane reached out and patted Mason on the back.

"Maddie," Nick yelled, "They're here."

Sirens came closer. Nick wrenched open the door and it nearly banged into Maddie as he rushed out.

"Mother, what were you thinking?" Maddie said.

"I prayed for her Madeline. I prayed and she is going to be fine. God heard my prayers. This is what I'm trying to explain to you."

"Mommy, what's going on?" It was Misty, her eyes open and staring up at her mother.

Maddie yelped. "Oh God, Misty? Honey. Don't move now. You fell down the stairs."

"How do you feel sweetie? Does anything hurt?" Jane said as she reached out her hand to Misty's hand.

Maddie jerked Misty away, "Don't touch her."

41

Misty looked at her mother's concerned face and then up at her grand-mother. "I don't remember."

The paramedics arrived in that instant and asked Maddie to release the child into their care. They did what all good EMTs do and checked her vital signs, investigated her limbs, and checked the girl's head for a wound.

"You say she fell down the stairs?" one of them asked? "Did you see her fall?"

"No," Nick answered, "but we heard her scream and the sound of thump-ing and then we found her at the bottom of the stairs. She wasn't moving I tell you."

"How do you feel?" the female EMT asked Misty. "What's your name?" She asked a few more probing questions about the accident. Misty couldn't remember falling, except maybe a little, she kind of remem-bered the feeling of flying.

"Did I fly Grammy?"

"No, I don't think so. I think you tripped. But you are OK now."

"I think you should take her for x-rays," Nick said. The medics rolled their eyes in response to the obvious and gently placed Misty on their stretcher. At first Misty looked frightened. "Daddy and Mommy will be with you honey," Nick said. "Maddie, follow us in the car."

"No. I will go with Misty," Maddie answered.

"All right, all right. I'll take Mason and Madison. Right? Right?" Nick was still screaming and repeating everything. He was in a panic.

"Madison, put Mason in the car seat," Maddie said and then screamed out the door, "Nick, wait for Madison. She has the baby." Maddie grabbed the diaper bag and her purse.

"I'll clean up. Misty's fine. I'm sure of it," Jane said to thin air.

As Maddie raced down the porch steps, Jane heard her say to no one in particular, "Why does everything have to be so damned complicated?"

As she closed the door, she said aloud, "I couldn't agree with you more."

9

Thursday in the Second Week of Lent, Jane

Jane Freedle would heal no one today. She didn't care; someone could fall over in a fit right in front of her and she'd call 911. Whatever calm she had felt the night before, was gone. Her family thought she was bananas, her pastor thought she was senile, and her friends thought she was delusional.

Shortly after breakfast, the house phone rang, stopped, and rang again. She didn't answer it. Then her cell phone started up. Why did she still have two phones? She sighed. She assumed the calls were Maddie and Jane finally picked up to hear the news about Misty Renee and inevitable rebuke.

"She's fine, right?" Jane said into the phone without bothering to say hello.

"Yes. But not without a lot of questions. Mother, you must listen to me. You have gone too far. I swear they'll send out a social worker to our house next."

"That's ridiculous. Did you tell them that you were almost a social worker?"

"Mother."

"It's true. You should go back to school and finish up that degree."

"Mother. Stop. Do you understand that you could have hurt Misty? You have got to face reality. You are not an agent of God. You did not heal her, she was lucky."

Jane took a deep breath or two. Neither spoke for several seconds.

"You are not the only one who misses Daddy."

Jane finally said, "I'm sorry--."

"Quit saying you're sorry," Maddie said.

"I was going to say, I'm sorry but I don't believe in luck. Another thing, none of this has to do with your father, except that you are acting like him. He treated me like an idiot too."

"Daddy would want you to listen to me—"

"Stop telling me what Daddy would want."

Maddie hung up.

Jane needed a diversion; a little work in the garden might help. That's what she used to do to get away from that terrible feeling of inadequacy. Back upstairs, she changed into her work clothes, padded down the steps again and into the kitchen and grabbed Richard's old jacket she wore when she worked in the garden. Bart and Simpson danced around her legs trying to come outside with her, but she shooed them back inside.

On the deck, she stopped short. The yard looked grim. When was the last time she had gardened? She frowned. Two years, maybe even the full three? Was it possible? Had any of her roses survived? And what was that leggy thing? She didn't remember seeing it among the lilies before. The boards around the raised vegetable bed had collapsed and her gnome was face down in the overgrowth. More weeds camouflaged the flat stone path to the shed.

The truth was right before her. She had deserted her flowers, her bushes, her vegetables, even her birdbath. Although spring had continued to appear every year despite Richard's death; she had ignored it. Before he died, Jane had thought of spring as the announcement of new life, color, and hope. Now, spring was just another anniversary full of sad memories.

"I told you this yard was too much for us," Richard said in her head.

"Not today, Richard, I have enough on my plate."

She vaguely recalled the first summer after Richard died when her old neighbor, Louise Kornacki, had made a valiant effort to keep the yard in shape, but then Louise moved away. Who lived in the Kornacki house now? Not just the garden and house had gone untended, everything and everybody. She had been in a fog all this time. She should find out where Louise moved to, probably Florida.

Maybe her kids were right about the house. She stared. Too bad a healing prayer wouldn't cut the grass or trim the weeds.

"Lord, I could use a little strength and energy right now. Can you heal a limp heart and brittle joints?"

The day was almost warm for mid-March. Could she make a dent? Could she uncover what her sorrows had buried in the anarchy?

"We should move," Richard had said the Christmas before he died.

"Move where?"

"Into a condo. Into senior living. Anywhere I don't have to mow the damn grass or clip the hedges anymore," he said.

"I don't want to move. I grew up here."

"Blah, blah, blah," Richard said, *"your father worked hard all of his life to move from the top of the store to a real house. I get it. Come on, Janie. It's time to move on. I'm tired."*

"Then go to sleep. Call it a day. I'll do it myself."

Go to sleep. And so, he did, three months later. Good job, Jane. Curse the guy. Way to go. But in the end, that's where she was now. Alone and faced with doing it all by herself.

She checked her watch. Thursday was reading day at her elementary school, but not until after lunch. She had at least three hours to work.

What the hell. She slogged to the shed and pulled out the rake and her old work gloves, dusty from lack of use. Later today, she would drop by Wal-Mart on the way home from the school to buy new ones. She started raking in the closest corner to the deck, the least overwhelming part. With each pull of the rake, she felt better and stronger. Perhaps this work was an answered prayer.

When she finally put away her tools and stood on the deck surveying her work, she was a little disappointed. It wasn't much. Despite her hard effort, she had barely tamed one corner of the jungle. And yet, she had found the crocuses coming up and the snowbells, all hiding under the leaves. More than likely, she would be sorry tomorrow for all this en-thusiastic labor.

Her brain had worked too. She didn't know how the gift worked or to what extent. She needed to do some tests, some research, something more systematic. Time to go pro-active. Wasn't that the phrase of the day? Go big or go home. Or, in her case, go to "the" home.

After a hot shower and a quick reheat of last night's lo mein, she headed to her old elementary school to meet her little readers. Most of them were struggling but getting better. After months of weekly visits, she could finally see improvement in one or two. This was one volunteer job she never suspended. The kids loved her unconditionally.

By the last bell, Jane was already out the door to the school parking lot and on her way to get those garden gloves from Wal-Mart when she passed the lacrosse team warming up on the high school field. She thought about Mitchell and wondered if he was playing. She pulled over and walked over to the gate.

"That will be $4 ma'am," the woman in the ticket booth said.

"What? Oh, I wasn't planning to stay."

"I've got it," a voice said behind her. It was Nick who rarely missed one of Mitchell's games.

She should have escaped right then. The last thing she needed was a tirade from her son-in-law. He led her by the elbow to the home side of the field.

"Well, this is a good way to kill two birds with one stone," Nick said.

"Kill?"

"You know what I mean. I need to speak to you and watch Mitch play. Let's find a seat."

They climbed up a little higher than usual which she interpreted as away from prying ears. She sighed heavily as they sat.

"I'm not mad, Jane. I mean, I was furious. But I'm not now. I have some questions." He was talking to her, but he looked straight ahead. He waved. Jane looked out on the field. She had forgotten how the players all looked alike in their helmets and gear. When Mitchell waved back, she marked his number, 09.

"Are you going to ignore me?" Nick said.

"No, no. Well, maybe. I wasn't listening. I've told you everything I know."

"Does it work every time?" he asked.

"It? You mean does God heal the person every time? So far, yes."

"How many?"

46

"Six."

"Does power flow out of you or something? Do you feel drained or lightheaded?"

She looked at him and he finally turned to face her.

"That's what happened on Star Trek," Nick said.

"I don't think I can have this conversation right now. I need to go to Walmart and buy new garden gloves." She stood to go. He grabbed her arm and pulled her back on to the bleacher. She stared him down and he let go.

"Just for a minute. Please," he said

"What do you want?"

"Misty Renee, she's good. She's fine. She's a good kid. I'm just sayin' thanks, I guess."

She studied this man carefully. His forehead beaded with sweat, the dark hair hanging down over his forehead was also wet. His jaw was pulsing. He turned back to the game.

"My mother is Catholic, you know." Nick said. "When I was a kid, she went to Mass every day, never missed. I was an altar boy on Sundays, the early service. Father Tony was the priest back then. Another good Italian boy, my mother always said. My mother believed in miracles. She would order holy water from the Jordan River and medals of Mary from the gift shop in the Vatican. When she was a little girl, her grandmother was sick, and her mother took them all down to the Basilica in Baltimore to some shrine there. My grandmother lived another fifteen years, that's what my mother said." He lapsed into silence and they watched the opening face-off. Her grandson, Mitchell, was near the goal.

Jane wasn't sure where Nick was heading with all of this. But it was the most he'd ever said to her voluntarily. He got out his phone and she assumed that was the end of the conversation.

"The family doesn't get to see my mother much since she moved back to Baltimore," he said.

"Yes, I know. I think the last time I saw her was at Richard's funeral. Or maybe last Christmas."

"Yeah. She still prays for Richard. They liked to flirt a little."

47

Jane turned to her son-in-law. She wanted to say it was news to her, but truthfully, Richard flirted with all the women. And Nick's mother, Rosalie, was very pretty, that is, until she became ill. And there it was. Jane figured it out.

"You want me to pray for your mother?"

He was silent.

"She only has a few more months. She's at Stella Maris." Nick said.

"I know. But—" she started to say.

"But what?"

She wasn't sure what the "but" was about either. Just that she had not, so far, prayed on-demand or had anyone directly ask for prayer. And from Nick, of all people. Her daughter had gone the other way, nearly accusing her of being bonkers. But here was Nick, asking for prayer. Would God answer?

"All right Nick. But I need to be there. Go there. I'm guessing. Touch her."

"Here's a picture of her," he held up his phone to Jane. Rosalie was a skeleton of her former self. She had always been a robust woman who served homemade pasta at every meal. Her laugh was like rolling thunder, coming from deep within her. Nick had five siblings, or six as Rosalie would say, and she would pull out her locket with her stillborn baby's picture, the first one.

"Sunday," Nick said, "we can go on Sunday. I'll pick you up."

"All right Nick, after church."

"If this works, you'll be famous."

"Nick, this isn't about that. Just help me out in the garden sometimes."

"I don't do yard work."

"And that's part of the problem."

48

10

SAME THURSDAY IN THE SECOND WEEK OF LENT, TWOMEY

That idiot, Watson, never bothered to mention the rental was on the second floor over a restaurant. The good news, he had the front two rooms while the tenant in the back had the restaurant kitchen directly under him. Of course, both tenants had to walk up the back stairs right past the garbage cans. It was an odd arrangement. At the head of the outside flight of stairs was their entrance. Once inside, a landing with a door opposite the entrance that he guessed went to the restaurant. With a turn to the right, a shorter flight of stairs led to the true second floor and apartments. The back-tenant's entry door was on the right and Twomey's rooms were down a short hall to the left, past the kitchen they shared. This is what his life had dropped down to apparently.

He'd like to blame everything on Belinda, but she was only one part. Besides, he had to admit, they had had a few laughs along the way. That is, before the cards and the ponies took over. He would never forget that one lucky streak. Pure fire. He couldn't lose. Thousands of dollars flowed into his hands that year. But now, this is what he had to show for it. His luck had to turn eventually. Didn't it?

Two hours later, he had moved all his stuff into his new apartment. His other place was cheaper, but someone robbed him within weeks. He lost his TV, his desktop computer, and about anything else that plugged into an outlet. Thank God he had his laptop with him that day.

The new place held several surprises; decorated like Watson said, in a rustic modern style. Lots of wood, little comfort, but not half bad. There was even art on the wall, quite modern. The best part was the comfortable bed, a real surprise. But the oddest thing was the shared kitchen down the hall. The entire floor used to be a single apartment, and someone did a funky renovation.

He sat in one of the straight-back chairs and looked out the front window. His front view: an antique store, cleaners, skateboard shop, and a tarot card reader. Pretty sad offerings for the main drag through town, of course this was the north end. Out the side windows (he'd never had a corner apartment), he had a view of the houses across the street, and to his surprise, old Mrs. Freedle's house was one of them. Was that serendipity? But to what end?

He needed a smoke and a drink to commemorate his new digs. But, on his way out, he hit his knee on a corner nail of the wood-framed couch and swore up a blue streak. When he looked down, he had torn his pants and was bleeding.

"What the --!?" Whoever repaired the arm had done a crappy job and left a nail sticking out. He heard a blender going in the kitchen and assumed it was his neighbor. He limped out his door toward the opening of the kitchen to ask for help.

"Dude, you got any Band-Aids?" Twomey asked.

The guy yelped, his hands flew up and so did the blender lid; green stuff flew everywhere. Twomey pulled back.

"Holy Mary, Mother of God," the guy cried.

"Hey, man, sorry," Twomey said from the hallway. "I need a Band-Aid."

"Sure, sure. Of course. I can oblige you. Just a moment," the guy said as he removed his disposable gloves and put on a second pair. "I'll be right back," he flattened himself as he passed Twomey in the doorway to avoid making contact. Twomey took another look in the kitchen; it was immaculate. Most of the stainless-steel surfaces untouched by green goop gleamed, no stray jars or dishes or glasses anywhere. Every counter was completely clear except for the items the man needed for his smoothie. Had Twomey walked into some version of The Odd Couple?

"My name is Vasquez, Maurice Vasquez." He did not offer to shake Twomey's hand. Instead, he had a Band-Aid clutched in a pair of tweezers which he offered to Twomey.

"Uh, thanks."

"I'm sorry I can't assist you in any other way. It will take me some time to bring order back to the food preparation area. In the future, please be aware that I am in this area between 4 and 6 p.m. I hope that will work out for you. I can negotiate a fractional change to that time, let's say give or take twelve minutes, but any more than that and my daily schedule would turn upside down. You understand?"

"Sure. Whatever. I have a microwave and a coffeepot."

"Excuse me, but the lease clearly states that no appliances may be added to the kitchen. Microwaves are extremely volatile and produce radiation. They also zap all the nutrition out of one's food. What you do in your space is up to you. But this area has rules that I must insist upon."

"Are you for real?"

"I beg your pardon?" Vasquez said wide-eyed.

"Never mind. I get the picture." Twomey started back to his room.

"Mr. Twomey—"

He stopped and turned, surprised the guy knew his name.

"I agreed to this rental on a probationary basis. This is my home, you see?"

"Of course, it is."

"No, I mean, your rooms were part of my place as well. But I needed additional funds."

"I get it. Sure, man."

At that point, Twomey didn't bother to go back to his rooms but turned and headed down the stairs, tried the odd door and discovered it did indeed bring him into the back of restaurant below. Handy. He went through the storage area, passed the restrooms, and on to the bar where he ordered a scotch neat and looked at his leg. The blood had dried in a long stream under his pant leg. He'd be making another trip to Goodwill.

"What's with Vasquez?" he asked the bartender.

"Who's that?"

"Never mind." Twomey checked his watch. It would be another hour before Vasquez vacated the kitchen. He ordered a hamburger rare, fries and a beer. "Could you turn the channel to a real sport?"

"You don't like bowling?"

Twomey stared at the guy without answering. The bartender changed the channel to a sports network. A little while later, as he finished his sandwich, a couple of guys, worker types, came in for a drink and sat around the corner from Twomey at the bar. It wouldn't be the first or last time

Twomey eavesdropped a conversation.

"What kind of bullshit is this Roy? That asshole doesn't know his head from a hole in the ground."

"You don't have to tell me. I can't believe they even won that contract."

"How many times did I tell them in that meeting we couldn't do it that way? How many times?" the guy complained as the bartender gave them both beers from the tap. They were regulars.

"They weren't listening," Roy said, "They never listen."

The conversation rambled for a while and then the other guy, Gordy, or something like that, got back onto his original grievance.

"I'm gonna file a complaint. That's what I'm gonna do. Hells Bells," Gordy said.

"To who? They're probably in on it," Roy rubbed two fingers together to indicate that money was involved.

"S'cuse me," Twomey slid over a couple of stools. "I might be able to help you."

"How's that?" Roy said.

"You guys work for the city or something?" Twomey asked.

"Wastewater treatment," Gordy said.

"You know," Twomey shook his head, "it doesn't seem to matter how big the city, there are always cheaters."

"You got that right," Roy said.

"You know the best way to catch a cheater? Get it out to the public," he said.

"What? How? Like a letter to the editor or what?" Gordy said.

They both signaled for another round and included Twomey.

"Let's go over to a table. I'm Twomey, Wade Twomey. I've been a reporter for thirty years and I know stink when I smell it. You guys give me the dirt you know, and I'll blow the thing out of the water. Your jobs are safe, and we get rid of one more corrupt government official."

Roy and Gordy looked at each other. They hesitated for a minute and he added, "What have you got to lose? I'm the one putting my neck on the line if you're wrong. I'll never mention your names. Sources are sacred, man. You know what I mean?"

"You gonna go undercover?" Gordy asked.

Twomey smiled. "Nah, believe it or not, the old saying is true: just follow the money."

11

FRIDAY IN THE SECOND WEEK OF LENT, JANE

Whatever garden enthusiasm Jane had the day before went out the window as a cold wet morning greeted her when she poked her head out the back door. The cats didn't even try to get out. How did they know it was raining?

She filled their dishes with dry food and then took the cover off Click & Clack's birdcage. What a ruckus they started into right away.

"All right, boys. Settle down. I am moving as fast as I can. Quiet down."

She smiled all the same. The parakeets always cheered her up. Everyone asked if the cats bothered the birds, but she didn't think they cared much. Of course, she always wondered if it was like the movies where great havoc took place once she left the house.

As part of yesterday's plan to explore the extent of her gift, she intended to make a direct attack on the unsuspecting sick. This would be like guerilla warfare, quick in and out. The local hospital was probably the best place to go incognito. Hardly anyone ever asked for credentials. She would spread out her visits so the nurses couldn't see a pattern of her slipping from room to room. She would bring flowers. Then she could say she had wandered into the wrong room. If this worked, she'd have a broad range of illnesses and people to assess afterward.

She started after lunch. She dressed in her most inconspicuous old lady outfit of a dark green velour tracksuit and sneakers. She wore her beige raincoat and fold-up rain hat. She carried her reusable "Think Green" bag and drove to the grocery store to pick up three bunches of cheap flowers. She was on a mission for God. She'd had it with asking for advice. She was on her own.

Every step of the way, she kept a running list in her head of what to watch out for: enter by the side door, bypass the gift shop where one of the Young at Heart gals volunteered, take the elevator to the fourth floor, avoid the nurses' station, and go into the first patient door that's ajar. Once inside, check the whiteboard for the patient's name, give a brief explanation, and go.

First one: Mabel Archer.

"Hello Mrs. Archer? I am here to pray for you." She gently touched the elderly woman's hand and prayed. It didn't take long. After all, God knew what the problem was. God had given her the idea to do it this way. When she finished with "Amen," she found Mrs. Archer looking at her.

"Is it time? Am I going to heaven now? Are you here to take me?"

"No dear, I'm here to pray for your healing."

"Oh no, I don't want that. I don't have anyone anymore. I don't want to go back to the old people's apartment house. I'm ready to die."

"But I already prayed. I'm sure you're healed."

"You had no right to do that. You should mind your own business."

Jane stared at Mrs. Archer. How could she have gotten it so wrong? "I'm sorry. I assumed—"

"Who gave you the right to play God? What do you know about me? Nothing. I used to have a beautiful house and a family. But they're all gone. In one accident, everyone gone but me. I lost everything. And finally, I'm sick enough to die. So, take it back. Whatever you did, take it back!"

"I—I can't. Maybe God won't hear my prayer. Maybe you'll still die. I don't know. But maybe God wants you to live."

"I'm going to call the nurse and tell her about you. You're a menace to society, barging into my room like this," Mrs. Archer said as she grappled for the buzzer.

Jane fled the room. In a moment, the nurse would respond to the call, she slipped into the next room and closed the door.

"Hello?" a woman's voice said from the bed.

Jane turned and saw a young woman stare at her.

"Sorry, I made someone angry and thought I'd better hide."

The woman laughed, "Oh, that hurt."

"What hurt? Laughing?"

"Yes, I have a big incision and it hurts to laugh or cough, but they want me to do that anyway, so maybe it's a good thing you made me laugh," the woman said.

"Right," Jane looked back at the door. "May I sit down for a few minutes?"

"Sure, I could use the company. My husband couldn't stay with me today. He said he'd bring the kids by later tonight after work."

They were both quiet for a moment. The woman was plain, but also pretty in a simple way. She had pulled her light brown hair back into a ponytail, and a book lay open before her. A picture of her family stood on the bedside table. She wore a cross around her neck.

"Would you like to be healed?" Jane asked.

"Thanks. But I think I already am. The doctor said they got it all."

Jane nodded. This was not turning out like she thought it would. She needed to rethink. First, she had someone who didn't want healing and now she had someone who didn't need it.

"Would you like some flowers?" Jane asked.

"But aren't they for a friend?"

"You can be my friend instead. I'm Jane."

"Susan. Thanks for the flowers, new friend. I think there's a vase in the closet."

Jane got out the vase and put all three bunches of flowers in it. All together they looked quite lovely.

"There, not bad," Jane said. "So, how about I pray for you anyway, so you can be up and around sooner. You and your husband can go out dancing."

"Well, sure. But I won't be dancing." She pointed to a wheelchair in the corner. "That's my next best friend over there. Don't be embarrassed. I'm used to it. I was in a swimming accident when I was a teenager. I'm in the hospital today for a mass they found in my stomach."

Jane walked up to Susan's bed and took her hand. Without a second thought or permission, she prayed for her wheelchair-bound friend. Jane would not remember the words she prayed, just her desire for this young mother to have everything she needed to be whole and healthy. She sensed God's pleasure.

"Do you believe in miracles, Susan?"

Susan shook her head. "Not generally, but I do believe in God. Thank you."

"I'd better go. Please don't try to find me or look for me. OK?"

God had done something huge in that room. On her way out, she turned, "If you want to try something challenging, make friends with the lady next door here. She has no family and no reason to live."

Jane left the hospital with a little swing in her step. All right, she thought, that had not gone perfectly, but she had helped that Susan woman. And maybe old Mrs. Grouchy too. She decided to treat herself to lunch at the little 1950s café in town. They made sodas from scratch and the best grilled cheese sandwiches.

When she walked in, the room was full of people, which was rare. She saw one stool at the small counter, or she could ask to sit with someone she didn't know.

"Excuse me, is anyone sitting here with you?" Jane said to a woman reading a book at a two-top table.

"No. Please. I could use a little company," the woman said. She was a little younger than Jane, and prettier. Her short brown hair peppered with gray, her glasses were rimless, and she wore a simple skirt and blouse with a poncho thrown over her shoulders.

"Thanks so much," Jane said. "My name is Jane, Jane Freedle."

"Nice to meet you. You can call me Sister Bernie," the sister said and extended her hand.

"Oh, you're a nun. I'm sorry. I didn't mean to disturb you."

Sister Bernie laughed. "Please, not at all. We generally like people."

Jane blushed. "Of course, you do. I'm sorry."

"No worries. Please order and I'll have a second cup of coffee. It's so good here and terrible back at the convent."

"Where is that?"

"Catonsville. The other side of Baltimore. I come up here once a week to visit a couple of my hospice friends," Sister Bernie said.

Over the next hour, they covered a lot of topics, from Orioles baseball to Star Trek to Law and Order, her favorite TV show. They lapsed into silence.

"Tell me," Jane said, "Do you believe in miracles? Specifically, healing miracles?"

"Absolutely, I do. I've known a few people who've had such a gift."

"You have? You do?" Jane looked down at her empty plate. "Do you have that gift?" she asked.

"No, not in the least bit. But do you?"

"I think so. I pray, and people become well." She looked up at the nun's face, an unchanging serene expression, just like Jane imagined nuns were supposed to be.

"Ah. that's wonderful," Sister Bernie said.

"Is it?"

"Of course. For how long?" the sister asked.

"A week, no, not even a week yet," Jane said.

"I have no plans today. Would you like to talk about it? I'd love to hear your story."

Jane told her everything. A stranger, who became Jane's anchor in just under two hours.

12

SUNDAY IN THE THIRD WEEK OF LENT, NICK

He told Jane he would pick her up around 10:30, right after her church service. Checking his watch, he had time for a cup of coffee. He didn't tell Maddie about his plan to test Jane because he knew she would object, vehemently. Up until last week, he had been ready to put his foot down and place his grief-crazed mother-in-law in a home (and not his home, no matter what Maddie imagined). But then, when Misty Renee was fine after that terrible fall, he started to wonder. What if? What if it was all true?

"Black coffee and two sour cream donuts," Nick said to the speaker at the drive-through.

"Anything else?"

"That's all." He rolled up his window and didn't bother to listen to the rest. He bought the same thing every time he came here.

If she were for real, she would need representation. She would need someone to protect her from the charlatans. She would need a manager. He could do all those things. Besides, he was family. His mind started to reel with the possibilities. They would need a website with a dedicated email address and an 800 number. And a PayPal account, they would need that. He could probably get business cards made quickly online. And they would need scheduling software. He could probably use the same software they used at the city. Oh, and maybe the best part, eventually, he could give up working at the city altogether. He was sick of the politics. Yes, if this thing played out right, they could all make a fortune.

His phone started playing the Star Wars theme. He snatched it up.

"Fabriani."

"Hey, Mr. Fabriani? This is Gordon Thomas over at the wastewater plant. I've been tryin' to reach Del Keithly, but he must be at church or something."

"What's up?"

"Well, we got a problem. Yes sir. I was afraid this would happen. I told you. So, now there's a major leak in that new pipe setup those turkeys installed last week, and the flow meter is showing all kinds of weird readouts."

"I don't know what that means."

"Well, it could mean one or two things, but they're both bad."

"I'm saying," Nick spoke very slowly, "that I can't help you. Text your supervisor. Or call Amos."

"I talked to Amos, he said I should call you."

Shit, shit, shit, was all Nick could think. "All right, let me call A&M. They must have an emergency line and I'll get back to you."

That's all he needed, another headache. Zach had promised him that nothing would go wrong and now, this was the second time Nick was getting an SOS from the plant. Damn it to hell. It all started with Maddie totaling the Chevy. Just like that, savings gone, insurance skyrocketed, and she insisted they get an SUV.

He looked up Zach's number and hit the autodial. It went to voice mail, of course.

"Zach, this is Nick. Get your people over to the Lafayette Wastewater Treatment Plant and I mean today, as soon as possible. The flow meter is bad or something like that. Call me."

He pulled out of the donut shop parking lot and onto Route 40. If only Maddie wasn't always such a Debbie Downer. He should have gone ahead with that Financial Advisor Test Prep course. He could be making bank now instead of dealing with this shit, literally.

"I don't want you to be disappointed," she had said.

"What? You don't think I can do it. Is that it?"

"I never said that, but you know how much you hate taking tests. You have a good job now. We don't have to be so stressed out all the time. I want you to think about a Plan B."

Maddie was always about Plan B. She couldn't run for the golden ring without a plan for the silver. No risk, no glory, that's what he always said. So, what the hell, this would be his Plan B: Sister Jane, Lafayette's miracle healer. But first things first.

He wouldn't jump on the Sister Jane idea until he had all the proof. And what better way to do that than to give Jane a shot at his mama. If it didn't work, well Ma was already dying anyway. If she lived, we'd celebrate. The only real downside, if his mother recovered, was the wait for Dad's inheritance. That's when he could start investing some serious money.

He pulled up to Jane's dumpy house and honked. She promised to be at the door so he wouldn't have to park. Nick had to smile when he saw her come out. What was it with old women and bright colors? Was it their eyesight? She wore a flowered jacket (where did she even find such a thing to buy), bright green pants pulled up high, a yellow polo and a yellow scarf. She looked like one of his tent sales of Easter flowers.

"Good morning, Nick." Jane sniffed as she got into the car. "I can tell you've been smoking again. I thought you gave it up?" she said.

"I did give it up. I never smoke in the car. Whatever. Let's not start like this, OK?"

"You're right. My apologies."

They were silent as he pulled away and headed up the hill toward I-95. He watched Jane from of the corner of his eye as she looked outside.

"What do you see," he asked.

"Change. I can remember when this was a country drive up the hill and now it's one house after another. Richard's oldest brother worked on Uncle Stan's farm right off this street. I had begged for us to get married on that farm. It was so lovely and charming with a beautiful view of the water."

Nick waited, but she quieted. "What happened?"

"Oh, we married in the church. Our mothers got together and decided it was best."

"I don't remember Richard having an older brother."

"Randy died young, not long after that, in a training accident. He wanted to be a Green Beret, but he didn't even survive boot camp."

"Wow. Did the Army pay out on that?"

"What?" Jane turned to him. "I have no idea. Is that the only—" she stopped.

Nick could sense the conversation might go downhill. He changed the subject. "Uh, do you still see any of the other in-laws?"

"Occasionally Sid, the younger brother, and his wife Toni; they take me out to dinner when they come up to see her family. They live in Baltimore. Your mother knows Toni."

"How's that?"

"Toni grew up Catholic, went to Rosalie's church."

"Wait a minute, you mean Antoinette Lancaster? I dated her daughter at St. Joe."

"She's a Freedle now. Married Sid on the rebound."

"She was always nice. How about that? I wonder if Ma knows." he said.

"Maybe we should talk about your mother's health instead. How long has she been in hospice?"

"About six weeks. We've been taking turns going down to spend time with her. It's lung cancer, you know. She's on oxygen."

"Which is why I don't understand how you can keep smoking," Jane said as she turned back to the window.

How similar Jane and his wife could be. No matter what he did or tried, it was never good enough. His mother was not much better. Ma complained all the time. He didn't visit her enough, he didn't buy the right gift at Christmas, he didn't get on the honor roll in fifth grade, he didn't block that pass in football, he didn't score. He never seemed able to score.

They were silent.

Finally, Nick said, "How was church?" Not that he cared, but it seemed like a safe subject.

"I don't know. I didn't go."

"Really? Why?"

"It's too hard to explain. I feel like a different person somehow and I couldn't imagine myself going through the same Sunday morning routine. I don't want to talk about it."

They lapsed into silence again.

Traffic was relatively light for a late Sunday morning. Had he made another mistake? Now that Jane had gone quiet on him again, he wasn't sure how to fill the space. He turned on the radio. She asked him to turn it down. He offered her one of his donuts, she said no and something about Lent and making up days, which made no sense to him since it was Sunday. Of course, Nick hadn't given up anything for Lent in years. He hadn't been to church in a long while. If he did go back, he'd be in confession for a week. He made a couple of calls. He left another message for Zach and set up a pick-up basketball game with the guys. He texted Mitchell to get on his homework.

"You really shouldn't text and drive," she said.

His phone rang. It was Zach. Finally. He turned to Jane, "I've got to take this."

"What's up, my man?"

"Don't ask me what's up. That's what I want to know. Did you send someone?"

"No, listen, man. We're slammed right now. Besides it's Sunday. That would cost you double time."

"What do you mean? It shouldn't cost me anything. The system isn't working. It's leaking, it's doing all kinds of shit."

"We'll send someone out Tuesday or Wednesday."

"That is insane." He looked over at Jane, knowing she always commented on his language. Her eyes closed; she shook her head slowly.

"Unacceptable, Zach."

"It is what it is, man. I gotta go. My old lady's calling me."

"Zach? Zach!" The asshole hung up on him. He hit redial.

"Nick! This is our turn." Jane shrieked.

"Shit." He careened around the corner and almost jumped a curb. "Son of a bitch." He pulled into the lot, which was full of course, and drove to the farthest side to park. He backed into the spot and just sat there. His heart was racing. Jane said nothing but he could tell her body was tense.

"Are you OK walking from here?" He asked.

"I'm not an invalid—yet," she said.

"I meant—"

"I know, I know. Let's just go."

As they walked, she seemed more agitated than usual.

"Look, I'm sorry about the driving. I've got some trouble at work and—"

"It's not that. I'm just nervous about praying for Rosalie."

"Why? You don't think it will work? We don't have to go in." Once again, he wondered if this was going to be a wild goose chase.

"You don't get it. This is new to me. I don't know how or why these things are happening the way they do. I'm a little old lady most of the time. I'm a nobody. So, why me? And yes, what if it doesn't work? What will you and Maddie think of me then? Or, the opposite, what if it does work? Maybe your mother wants to die. Have you thought of that?"

"Uh, no. But I don't think anyone wants to live in pain."

Jane said nothing.

They arrived at the front desk, signed in, and took the elevator to the third floor.

"One more thing, Nick," Jane said, "We may not see an immediate result. I mean, she may not jump out of the bed. You understand? It took May Winston about two hours before she started proclaiming her healing. I wasn't even in the room. I don't know why there's a gap or if there is one every time. I—" she hesitated, "I don't think I could bear to sit around and wait."

He hadn't anticipated that. He figured miracles happened instantaneously.

"Well, we could eat in the cafeteria and then come back up and check."

Jane looked at him with an odd expression that he couldn't interpret. "No. I want to go home and get back to work in my garden or rest."

They arrived at his mother's door and he tapped before entering.

"Well, I'll be a monkey's uncle," Ma said, "look what the cat dragged in."

"Hi Ma. I brought you some company."

He watched Jane's reaction to his mother's appearance. It was different looking at her through Jane's eyes, the wires, the lead line of her IV and morphine pump, the nose clip and the monitors all beeping in step with her heart and breathing. Ma was still reading those trashy entertainment magazines and tabloids which she had stacked on her bed. The television was blaring, so he turned it down.

"Hi Rosalie. It's good to see you," Jane said.

"Jane, Jane, Jane. Who woulda thought it would be me here and you there?"

"Ma—"

"It's all right, Nick, I know what she means," Jane said. "Rosalie, this is no punishment, you know that don't you? Cancer is a roulette wheel, that's all."

"I always hated that game," Rosalie said. "Come on in then, sit down, and keep a sick woman company. Any good gossip?"

Jane smiled. "I see you haven't changed a bit. Well, let me see, Joyce Murdoch is divorcing her husband."

"After all those years? Well, I always say, once a cheater, always a cheater."

"And Eloise Grafton's house had a fire."

"No! What happened?"

"She was running a séance kind of thing with some gal who convinced Eloise her house was on sacred ground and they'd be able to speak to her dead husband if Eloise would let her light lots of candles."

"Oh my God."

"The candles caught the curtains, and poof. Eloise was heartbroken of course. But she managed to get the dogs out and some of her precious photographs. There was a lot of damage."

"Who's Eloise Grafton?" he asked.

"And," Jane ignored him, "I have some personal news."

"Are you going to be a grandmother again?" Ma asked.

"Actually, it's one of the reasons I'm here. Things, well, rather people, I mean, have, uh, gotten better, well, I mean, they've—"

"God's given her the gift of healing Ma. She raised some other woman from the dead at the nursing home in Lafayette," he said, to move things along.

"She wasn't dead," Jane corrected him. "She had pneumonia. She was dying."

Ma looked from him to Jane, her mouth slightly open, the swishing of the oxygen in and out of her nose, the only sound in the room.

"That's not funny, you know," Ma finally said.

"I'm going to go ahead and pray for you. OK? I mean, you do want to get better, right? I mean, you want to live?" He watched Jane step closer to the bedside.

"Wait a minute. Wait a minute. Jane, you're not Catholic," Ma said.

"No, but—"

"You got something with you like holy water or something? Or a cross? Or a rosary? I mean, what are you pulling here? You could be puttin' my soul in grave danger."

"Ma, let's not split hairs already, for Christ's sake," he said from the foot of the bed.

"You can go right to confession for taking the Lord's name in vain, young man," Rosalie said.

"Come on Ma, she's had some good luck with this thing, and I think it's worth a try," he said.

"Luck? You call the things of God Almighty, luck? Did you go to Mass this morning? You didn't, did you? See what happens when you fall away, when you cheat God? You start bringing the separated brethren into a Catholic institution. It's not right."

With that, his mother started to gasp. She was having a hard time catching her breath. Her eyes began to bulge a bit.

"Ma? Ma? You OK?"

She waved him away. He ran out to the nurse's station. When he returned, Jane had crawled up onto his mother's bed and held Ma in her arms. Ma was no longer breathing heavily or maybe she wasn't breathing at all.

"What are you doing? What are you doing?"

But before Jane could answer, the nurse came in, followed by a team of resuscitators. They asked them both to leave the room.

He leaned against the wall outside the door and Jane leaned next to him. Neither spoke. His mind raced. Once again, he had screwed things up. What the hell was wrong with him? And if this took his mother over the edge? If she died now, it would be his fault. He was trying to help, wasn't he? But Jane, she jumped the gun. She should have waited for the doctors. She was the one who didn't listen. "If she dies, it's going to be your fault," Nick said.

"OK, but that was not a nice thing to say. And if she recovers?"

He stared at her. "You prayed for her in there didn't you? After she told you not to?"

She shrugged. "I guess. It all happened pretty fast."

He rubbed his face with both hands. "We're gonna wait."

"I don't want to."

"Find your own way home."

He walked down the hall to a sitting room, she followed. On his way, he heard singing in the patient room next to them. It wasn't particularly good.

"You should have let me handle it. You jumped right in. She wasn't ready," he said.

"You may be right. But I didn't want to do any more small-talk."

The TV in the corner of the waiting room had one of those fixer-upper shows on. They both watched the screen. Only three other people sat in the room: a man sleeping in a wheelchair while his daughter or caregiver buried her face in her phone; and an African-American woman in a spectacular purple hat and flowered suit who sat like a statue, she must have just come from church. The singing next door stopped. The woman got up and met the women coming out of the patient's room.

He watched them hug and cry. The one that seemed to be in charge was a very blonde woman who had styled her hair in a big poufy way. She also wore a hat, but smaller, like the Brits wore, and a very red dress. He couldn't see her face.

"Let's get out of the hallway and go in here to pray for you, Dolores. God is here, I tell you, and Brother James is fine, just fine, and ready to go home," the blonde said. They all trooped back into the waiting area. One of the women in the group turned down the TV.

He watched as the women surrounded purple hat Dolores and prayed for her, heads bowed, while their hands either patted the woman or reached up in the air. Some of the prayer was in English but a good portion of it was gibberish. This must be tongues. He looked at Jane to see how she reacted. She had closed her eyes. Was she praying for Brother James healing? What nerve.

The women finished and hugged again. Group hug. As they pulled apart, the blonde turned.

Jane said, "Toni? Toni Freedle?"

The woman looked at Jane and then at him. "Omigod. Jane! I was thinking about you the other day. And is this who I think it is? Nicky!" He stood and she pulled him into her arms. "I was always sorry my Emily didn't snag you. You are still quite the hunk," she gripped his biceps. Then she hugged Jane.

"He and Maddie are married, they have three children," Jane said.

"Of course, he is. But why are you here, honey?" Toni said to Nick.

"My mom, Rosalie."

"Oh Lord, Rosalie's here? I'm so sorry, I didn't know. I will be lifting her up." She turned to her friends, "You all go on, I'm gonna sit here with my sister-in-law and my daughter's ex-boyfriend."

Before they left, she introduced them all.

He only told Toni the essentials about his mother. Jane said nothing. Toni nodded and added short appeals to God throughout his explanation.

"I will be keeping you in prayer, Nicky; you and your mama. And Jane, we need to catch up soon. You look good, honey. I'll call you next week."

When she finally left, the room quieted again. The man in the wheelchair never did wake up.

13

St. Joseph's Day, Monday in the Third Week of Lent, Twomey

"I'm telling you, Chuck, I'm about ready to put this story to bed. There is corruption at City Hall in beautiful downtown Lafayette, a little sleepy town with a secret or two."

"You better have strong sources buddy."

"I wasn't born yesterday. I'm doing my due diligence. I've got all the public estimates for the work done at the wastewater plant and I've got witnesses to the ineptitude and negligence of the company that got the bid for twice the price. I've got to ask a few questions to find out who the ultimate sign-off was on this and then, Boom!"

"Ok, Twomey. Send it down to me when it's ready. You got pictures?"

"I will. But listen Chuck, I want this in the main paper, not just the local edition. And I want it broken at the right time online."

"We'll see. I'll run it by Rudy. But no promises."

Twomey wanted to chew the guy out, but he hung up with a polite good-bye. He had to curb his temper, or this story would go nowhere. He knew he wouldn't win a Pulitzer or anything, but at least the story had some meat to it. And he might get a shot at something bigger or maybe there would be a follow-up. He needed this.

He leaned back in his chair and looked out the windows. Nice day. He checked his phone for a return message from one of the water treatment guys. They were supposed to meet up that night at the restaurant down-stairs. Nothing yet. He wanted to eat something, but he was running short on cash, again.

He thought of Vasquez's side of the fridge. He opened his door and a note fell to the ground.

"Dear Mr. Twomey, it has become apparent that you are intentionally removing items from the refrigerator that are not yours. Cease and desist

or I will have to take more drastic measures. Maurice Vasquez, Esq."

Twomey rolled his eyes and walked into the kitchen, still pristine. Everything in him wanted to pour ketchup all over the counters and spit on the floor. Instead, he checked the refrigerator for food, his or otherwise. What the hell could a twerp like Vasquez do to him anyway? He bent to peer inside and noted how ridiculous it looked. His shelf had three items: eggs, bread, and margarine. Vasquez's shelf had lots of green leafy things, yogurt, a pasta concoction in a clear plastic container, fruits, and some high-end cheese from Wegman's along with other things he didn't even recognize. Twomey thought he might try the pasta.

"Don't even think about it," Vasquez said from behind him.

Twomey stood, the pasta container still in his hand. "I was admiring your handiwork."

"That's a lie. You were going to steal it and eat it."

"So, what are you going to do Vasquez, call the noodle police? Lighten up. I'll put it back."

"No, you have already introduced unsanitary conditions to the container. Take it and be done with it."

"What is your problem?" He leaned up against the counter and started picking at the pasta with his fingers.

"I am trying to stay alive."

"What?"

"That's right, Mr. Twomey, I am dying, and I am on a strict regimen. So, take your nasty habits and your cavalier attitude and return to your private rooms."

Perhaps for the first time, Twomey took a hard look at his "almost" roommate and could see the signs of a ravaging waste. The man was very thin and his skin like paper. His eyes were deeply set, and the bones carved out his face. Twenty years ago, Twomey would have assumed the man had AIDS, but credible treatments were available for that nowadays. He couldn't exactly ask what the hell he was dying of, not while eating the man's food, which made him stop. Was it safe?

"Don't worry, I'm not contagious," Vasquez said.

Twomey brushed past his neighbor, then turned, "Sorry, man. Yeah. Sorry. No more food swiping."

Finally, around 4:30, Twomey went down to the restaurant and sat at the bar. He hadn't heard from the workers, Roy and Gordon, but he figured they might show up soon. But by 6, he knew they had stood him up. He fumed. Finally, a text came through from Roy. "The deal is off. They fired Gordy today. I'm out." Twomey swore to himself. He should have known better. These guys were total boneheads. He texted back, *"Whoa buddy. Take it easy. Let's talk."* He received nothing for some time, but finally the little dots started to signal typing. Then nothing, the dots disappeared.

Twomey tried again, *"I can protect your identity. You got to trust me."*

Finally, Roy texted back, *"Let me think about it."*

And this is how it would go. Nothing in investigative journalism was ever easy, even in a podunk little town. He looked at his watch, damn, he had to get over to the city council meeting, another yawner. He threw back his beer, tossed a couple of bills on the bar, and headed out.

Attendance at the Council meetings was generally sketchy, maybe twenty people on a big night if they were giving a "student of the month" award or swearing in someone to work on the July 4 parade. Really hot stuff. He scanned the agenda and was surprised to see a matter related to the wastewater plant. Now that was interesting. Maybe something happened over there today that was a precursor to firing Gordon.

Twomey was not disappointed. There had been an accident at the plant and the Council members were asking the mayor to put together a team to investigate the causes. He hedged and said they would handle it. They tabled the item. Food for thought. He texted Roy, *"I know about the accident. Just give me some details."* The shit was about to hit the fan.

He nearly left when they started open comment time. A little old lady, who knew how old, came up to the microphone and introduced herself as Mabel Archer, 410 N. Juniper Street, Havre de Grace.

"I think I should be taken seriously. I have already filed one complaint, and nothing happened. I called the police, and they don't care. I have lived in this city all my life, and I think it's outrageous that I am being treated like a goofball."

The mayor said, "Do you want to tell us what happened?"

"Well, I didn't sit through this boring meeting for nothing. I was in the hospital last week, perfectly happy to finally be dying when a crazy white-haired woman came into my room unannounced and said she would pray for me to be healed. I didn't want to be healed."

Mrs. Archer put air quotes around the words "to be healed" as though it was a cliché.

"My rights were violated, and no one seems to care. Now, I want you to find this woman and tell her to cease her activities."

"But are you saying you were healed?" the mayor asked.

"Yes, I was healed, and I downright resent it!"

Twomey wrote down her name and address. The Safe Haven/Freedle story just opened back up.

14

Tuesday in the Third Week of Lent, Jane

Jane sat at the volunteer reception desk at the library. She had tried to get out of this shift, but they called and begged her to cover the desk for someone who had called in sick. She was still out of sorts. Ever since Sunday at Stella Maris, she no longer knew what was normal and what was not.

The entire episode with Rosalie had been a nightmare. By late afternoon, Rosalie's condition remained unchanged, so they suggested Nick come back the next day, but to call first. The drive home was even worse since Nick alternated between yelling at her or bruising silences and dramatic sighs.

"That's my mother you were practicing on," he said at one point.

She didn't answer. Everything in her wanted to say she wasn't practicing, that it was his idea in the first place, but honestly, nothing she said would make a difference. She was afraid Rosalie would die too. Was God letting her down? Had she let God down? She had no idea why Rosalie would be any different from anyone else she had prayed for so far. Unless it was the denominational bomb. Did it matter? Wasn't God the god for everyone?

Nick finally called her Monday night. Rosalie was stable and her vitals were back to normal. She seemed better than she been for some days. Jane was relieved.

"Excuse me," a voice interrupted her ruminations at the front desk. She looked up to see a young woman with a baby in a sling carrier.

"I'm sorry. My mind was a million miles away. Welcome to the library, how may I help you?" she said.

"I need a restroom with a changing table."

Jane walked her to the restrooms and returned to her desk to meet the next guest.

"Hello, Mrs. Freedle. It's Wade Twomey, remember me? What a nice surprise, eh?"

"Mr. Twomey, honestly, how did you find me here?" She could feel her face flush as she sat down, putting the counter solidly between them.

"I'm using the library. Honest. Some jerk stole my printer from my last apartment. Who knew I'd see the lovely Mrs. Freedle at the information desk?"

"This is the reception desk. Information is upstairs."

"OK. So, tell me," he leaned on the counter," have you been in touch with Ms. Winston?"

"Who?"

"You know, May Winston, the woman you healed at the nursing home?"

"No. She left the area— "she stopped abruptly. Did he catch her in something? She studied his face, but his eyes betrayed nothing. "I don't know her."

"What else do you do here besides show people where the johns are?"

"Mr. Twomey, I have other customers to help."

She watched him turn around and of course, there was no one there.

"I get the impression you don't like me, Mrs. Freedle, and honestly, I'm harmless, passing the time of day. I might even check out a book while I'm here. I heard this great podcast on faith healers yesterday and I wanted to get some more information. You know much about faith healing?"

Her teeth clenched. She had to relax. But the idea of a reporter asking lots of questions gave her pause. What if he wrote an article about her? What would happen then? Once again, her mind whipped up a football stadium where she stood on the platform sprinkling holy water on the sick while everyone screamed her name. Then, as she left the stage, they'd grab at her clothes, she'd fall, and they'd inadvertently trample her to death.

"You'll have to ask a librarian upstairs. At the desk. The real information desk. Upstairs," she said.

"Thanks Mrs. Freedle. I will," he said. "Smile," and then he took her picture with his cell phone. He leaned over her counter again, closer this time, "Do you believe in that healing stuff?"

Saved from an answer, an irate man needed to speak to the manager immediately. She excused herself and went into the staff area without looking back. She informed the manager and then slipped into the staff restroom and locked the door. She rinsed her face at the sink and avoided looking in the mirror. She was acting like a criminal, like she had something to hide. Well, she did. Or did she? What exactly was she afraid of? All she had to do was tell the truth. What's the worst that could happen? The first picture that came to her mind was Joan of Arc burning at the stake. Jane was not inclined to become a martyr.

She told the assistant branch manager that she didn't feel well after all (a white lie, she hoped) and escaped.

The rest of the day proved blessedly uneventful. By evening, she had settled on the couch with a TV tray table holding her pot pie with the cats sniffing around, and cable giving her 254 choices of mind-numbing viewing when her cell phone rang. It was Nick.

"Sister Jane, you may be on to something."

"I beg your pardon," she said.

"It worked. You worked. God worked. Whatever. Mama is sitting up and breathing on her own. Everybody's in shock. You did it. God did it. You're the real thing."

"Oh. Well, that's good news then. I'm glad I didn't kill her."

"Yeah, well, sorry about that. I apologize. I was not myself."

More irony, she thought; she said nothing, although Nick apologizing was a change.

"So, listen, we need to sit down and do some planning."

"I have no idea what you're talking about, Nick."

"Yes, you do. You and I both know that you can't keep this thing under wraps for much longer. You'll be eaten alive."

Her mind conjured cannibals dancing around her as she boiled in a large black cauldron. Her dread and fear were overtaking reason.

"Jane? Are you listening to me?"

"What? I'm sorry. What did you say?"

"I said, sooner or later, someone's gonna talk and as soon as one person leaks, others will come forward. And then the press will grab it and God only knows what else."

"You make me sound like a sexual predator."

"What?"

"Never mind. Have you talked to Maddie about this?" she asked.

"Not yet. I mean, I think we need to plan our reveal so that we can control the message. I took a course on marketing, so there are a lot of questions we need to ask ourselves before we go public. We need to set some goals, identify our ideal client."

"Sick people, Nick. God heals sick people. Besides, you keep saying "we." And "our." Since when did you take ownership of this?"

"We're family. I'm here to help. I don't want you chewed up. I know we've had our differences Jane, but honestly, I want to help"

"You're giving me a headache."

"Hey, no problem, you can pray it, away right? Kidding. Just kidding."

Jane hung up and turned off her phone. She also pulled the jack from the wall of her house phone.

"Damn it," she said to the cats. "If he's right, I'm in some deep trouble."

15

WEDNESDAY IN THE THIRD WEEK OF LENT, JANE

At her kitchen table, she drank hot tea and wrote in her journal. What had started as a mere list of people and their healings by date had grown into a more detailed examination of the "gift" and its negative ramifications. She should stop. Just stop. After all, she was only one person; what was God thinking?

And what should she do about Nick? What would Richard say?

"Nick is a wannabe con artist."

"But he's family. And he seems genuinely interested. He's being more supportive than Maddie. Maybe I should call Toni after all. She seems to know about these things."

"You should talk to a doctor. Talk to Pastor Sam again. Get some reliable authority."

"But this is different. It's miracle stuff. It's not normal."

"Exactly," Richard said.

She dismissed him. She had to do this on her own. With God. Somehow. But things were happening faster than she expected.

Rosalie's healing would have repercussions for sure. After all, how many people walk out of an end-of-life care facility? Would there be an investigation? And then there was Nick's insistence that they "organize," as though it was a union thing. And yet, Nick might be better at fielding questions from officials and the like. She could barely tolerate talking to a policeman at a traffic stop much less a judge. She stared out the kitchen window. What do all the Christian books say? Let go and let God? How does that even work?

Click and Clack chirped merrily. One of the cats sat in Richard's kitchen chair snoring, probably Simpson. He never got the purring thing down. Life was simple for them. When Richard was alive, her days had been simpler too, more straightforward. Richard always knew what to do. She missed that. Or did she? Had she secretly hated all that predictability? His control? Tears sprang up. Was Richard commanding her or advising her? Perhaps it was time to stop the train, move into senior living, play pinochle all day, and eat three square meals.

The doorbell interrupted her reverie.

A UPS truck pulled away and she found a small package at her door addressed to her. But, before she could close the door, something ran in. A cat.

And not just any cat, the cat: the long-haired calico from the street. The stray cat she had prayed for outside the church. That same tortoiseshell now sat in the middle of her front room as though nothing unusual was happening. Jane crept up to her slowly, "All right. Be still." She held out her hand. "Take a sniff."

As Jane gently picked up the cat, she said, "So, the miracles keep coming. I guess you figured I wouldn't toss you out since we have a history." The kitty jumped from Jane's arms when a knock came at the door and then the doorbell rang, twice. The cat leaped from the floor onto the mantle of the fake fireplace.

"Good morning, Jane."

"Esther! What a surprise. And Henry! Do come in. Can I get you anything? A cup of coffee?"

"No, no," Esther said. "Come on in Henry and stop being such a doubting Thomas."

Jane watched Henry shuffle in behind his wife and collapse into the recliner next to the fireplace. The cat stared at him and Henry stared back. Henry was one of those men who had little awareness of what he was wearing. His open collared plaid shirt did not match his pants and he wore black socks with sneakers; his baseball cap advertised a deep-sea fishing charter boat.

"I don't like cats," he said.

"Sorry. It's a stray that adopted me," Jane said.

"What?" Henry said.

"Which is exactly why we're here," Esther said. "Henry is losing his hearing and if things don't change, I'm going to kill him. He runs the TV as loud as possible and says, 'what?' to me about 300 times a day. Now, Jane, you and I both know that something happened Sunday a week ago, and I don't care what my daughter says. You prayed and my cut disappeared. Now, do the same thing for Henry."

"But Esther—" she started to say.

Esther would have none of it and walked her over to Henry, placed her hands on his ears and commanded, "Pray."

Jane whipped through a quick prayer and almost hoped it wouldn't work so Esther would leave her alone.

"It may not work the way you think it will, Esther. Not everyone is healed right away."

"Who else is there?" Esther asked.

"I beg your pardon?"

"Who else have you prayed for?"

"Here and there. People. I mean, it's not for me to say," Jane said.

"What? You have people signing a HIPAA paper?"

"Don't be silly. I'm . . . people you don't know. Okay?"

"Oh. Fine. If this works, I'll send MaryBeth over. She's another one that can't hear worth a toot. All right. God bless you, Jane. Henry, let's go."

"All right," he said as he pulled himself slowly from the soft chair. Esther looked at him and then at Jane.

"Hallelujah!" Esther said, "He heard me." Esther squeezed Jane's hand and left a twenty-dollar bill rolled up in it. "Thank you, dear," Esther said and waved.

As they left, Jane wondered if Henry's hearing was an actual physical problem or a matter of self-defense. She put the twenty in her jeans pocket; she would decide what to do about that later. She headed for the kitchen to clean up a bit and have a second breakfast. She pretty much lived on eggs. It was a good thing she didn't have cholesterol problems. She had forgotten about the new cat until she heard it and one of her own exchanging dangerous yowls; she rushed into the front room.

"You two stop it this minute! Bart, this is our new friend. Her name is, uh, what should I call you?" Her mind was a blank. "Bart, this is kitty without a name. Kitty, this is Bart. And over there? Simpson. All cats must get along," she said as she stroked them one by one. "Kitty, you started this whole thing. We'll have to give you a name that fits. Something miraculous." She chortled. "Would that work? Sure, I'll call you Miracle. Done."

She heard the mail carrier step onto the porch and quickly opened the door. She greeted the woman as she often did over the years but had no idea what her name was.

"What should I call you?"

"Priscilla. But my friends call me P.J. Here's a circular for you. There's still something in your box from yesterday," Priscilla said as she left the porch with a wave.

Jane looked through the decorative holes of her mailbox and saw a white envelope.

"Thanks, P.J." she said as she pulled it from the box; no postage was on the envelope. Someone had dropped it in personally. Jane was in postal heaven, an actual letter and a package on the same day.

Before she had a chance to open them, she heard her house phone ring and ran back into the house to pick it up. Gillespie.

"First you skip out on lunch with Lindy and me on our regular Monday last week, then you skip choir on Sunday, and you missed Young at Heart again this morning. What is going on Freedle?"

She had completely forgotten about the Young at Heart meeting at the activities center. Her life was changing fast.

"Nothing is going on. I mean, it's complicated," she said.

"You sound like an ad for a movie. I assume you've skipped lunch altogether."

"Well, I—"

"Exactly what I thought. I will pick you up in eight minutes and we'll go to the diner on Route 40. Wait for me outside, your street is murder on parking."

She grinned. "All right, Gillespie," but he had already hung up. She considered her next dilemma, "to tell or not to tell about the miracles." She had no one to ask for advice. Richard would be embarrassed. She couldn't count the number of times Richard had called her embarrassing, either because of what she wore, or what she said, or how she laughed, or what Christmas cards she bought.

She shook him off and pulled out the letter from her pocket.

The letter had no return address. Inside she found a fifty-dollar bill. No note. Nothing. Just the cash. A donation? It felt wrong to accept money for something God was doing, assuming that was the reason it was there. Or maybe someone thought it was a drug house. If it were a donation, how would she handle this at tax time? She'd have to declare it as income. Were donations like tips? With Gillespie on his way, she couldn't sort it out now. She put the money in her old cookie jar in the kitchen, "*The first place a burglar would look,*" Richard murmured in her ear. A car horn beeped.

At the diner, Gillespie propped the menus behind the condiment tray after he ordered a BLT from Kim, the regular lunch waitress, and Jane ordered the soup of the day with a half tuna sandwich. Someone had selected a Frank Sinatra tune on the old jukebox. Gillespie put his straw hat on the bench beside him and pulled off his parka. No tie today.

"How long have we known each other, Jane?"

Using her first name meant this would be a serious conversation. Gillespie was a good-looking man even in his mid-seventies, his salt and pepper hair now whiter than gray, his skin barely touched by liver spots, and his beautiful hands, free of any arthritis. He was strong and carried himself with confidence wherever he went. He was a Democrat, which was always a source of argument for him and Richard, and yet they continued to be friends until the end. The last time she remembered Gillespie calling her Jane was right after Richard died. Gillespie would often replay that day with her.

"*Richard had hit a ball into the rough. We didn't realize he had collapsed there. I think Richard died at the golf course, but who knew for sure? I wanted to tell you that day in the car. I didn't know how to say it.*"

He always felt guilty, she knew, as though he should have been able to do something to prevent Richard's dying. She had a feeling he was going to warn her again now.

"Yes, we've known each other a long time. Are you trying to make a point?" she asked.

"A little of both, I guess. I talked to Esther on Sunday, or rather, she

81

talked at me on and on about God using you for miracles. She kept holding up her hand in my face as though it proved something."

"Yes, that would be Esther."

"I'm also guessing that you think you had something to do with that Safe Haven woman." He waited for her to answer. "Did you? Is that why you left? I saw you run out the side door."

Nothing to say.

He continued. "Do you know how many people have called me to ask what is going on with you? Of course, I don't have anything to tell them because you, dear friend that you are, haven't considered confiding in me, or for that matter anyone else. Instead, we've got a lot of fake news bouncing around the church."

"I talked to Pastor Sam."

"Well, he's not addressing this situation unless you call a sermon on false prophets a hint."

"You're kidding?" Her temper flared as she thought about the implications. "I know eight people who might disagree with you and Pastor Sam. I am not a fraud. I'm still me. And God is bigger than all of us."

"Eight? What the hell?"

Their food came, but she wasn't hungry. Gillespie seemed to have lost his appetite as well.

"Maybe nine," she said, "Look, I don't think I want to talk about this with you. Either you believe me, or you don't. I'm not going to try and convince anyone anymore."

"What exactly is it that I'm supposed to believe? That you're an angel or something? That you're an apostle from God? That you're the next Aimee Semple McPherson?"

"Who's that?"

"She was a popular faith healer in the 1920s. She also married three times, milked Hollywood for all it was worth, and ran away with the sound man while her people thought she had drowned in the ocean."

"How do you know all this?"

"I read biographies."

"Did she heal?"

"What?"

"Did she heal? Despite all that other stuff, were people healed?"

"I dunno. I guess. Doctors substantiated some of the reports. Look, that's not what I'm trying to talk about here."

"I am. Look at me, Dan Gillespie. I am telling you that everyone, not one or two, but all the people I've prayed for, experienced a healing. 100%. I don't know why; I don't know how. But it's real."

"Are you a doctor that you can verify these claims?"

She looked away, her mouth set.

He continued, "I'm telling you that miracles don't happen like that. Cuts to the skin do not heal over spontaneously. And if it were true, then you should be sitting at Emergency and simply laying hands on everyone who comes in with a gunshot wound." Gillespie breathed heavily.

"I'll call a cab." And she pulled out her cell phone.

"Don't be ridiculous but I think you need to be evaluated." He called Kim over and asked for carry-out containers. They sat in silence until Kim had stored the sandwiches and Gillespie paid the bill.

"May I pray for Lindy?" Jane asked.

"No."

"Then, I have nothing more to say. You and Richard, you're both the same. You think you know everything, understand everything. But you don't. Not this time."

They left the restaurant.

Later that evening, she was still upset about her encounter with Gillespie. Why was it important that he believe her? She remembered how frustrated she used to get when Richard wouldn't believe her stories at dinner.

"You're exaggerating Jane," he would say. *"That's not how the world works. Quit trying to make the world fit into what you want to see through those rose-colored glasses."*

No one in her family took her seriously. Her dreams, her hopes, her abilities were inconsequential. She was a mother, a wife, a grandmother, and a second-grade teacher. Nothing more. Except now. She could be famous, just like Nick said. She could turn the world upside down.

She was tired and decided to go to bed early. On her way up the stairs, the front door opened. Had she forgotten to lock it? In trooped Nick, the teenagers Mitchell and Madison, and Misty Renee.

"Hey Jane. Sorry to bother you but Misty needed to use a bathroom and the one at the field was closed up."

"Hi Grammy, I gotta go real bad number two," Misty said.

"All right dear, come on up," Jane said from the stairs as Misty passed her.

"Hey guys," Nick said to his older two, "why don't you dish out some ice cream for all of us. I bet it's still here from the other night. Is that all right, Jane?"

"I guess. I was about to call it a night."

The teens ran for the refrigerator, arguing over who would serve and what would be fair.

"Have a seat," Nick directed her to the couch and then he sat beside her. "Please accept my apology for the way I treated you at Stella Maris. I was wrong, OK? But I need you to believe me, to trust me, I get it. You are the real deal. God is doing something huge here. But your life is about to change in a major way, and I think you need your family behind you. I want to help, to handle the details while you are doing the big stuff, with God, you know? I respect what is happening to you."

"All right Nick, I'll try."

He went on, evidently not hearing her. She had thought about Nick quite a bit and realized she did not want to have another conversation like the one this afternoon with Gillespie. If she could direct people to Nick or Maddie, then things would be better. They had all the proof they needed. And for that she was grateful. And evidently, she was getting some support this time. She needed a little dose of that right now. If she didn't trust family, who could she trust?

"So, what I'm saying is that people are going to hear about you, and I know you want to do good, but you're only one person. You need a manager."

"I said all right, Nick."

"What? You did? Hey, that's great. That's perfect. You won't regret this Sister Jane."

"Do you have to call me that?"

"It's easier that way. That's what they call people in Toni's church, right?"

"You told Toni?"

"Mom called her. They put it on Facebook. We'll give you a page soon."

"I have Facebook. Madison set me up with one at Christmas."

"Well, that's different. You'll see."

Nick was so enthusiastic and happy. She hadn't seen this in her son-in-law for many years. But a part of her was frightened. Was it all one enormous mistake? Or worse, was she a fake? Were all these events mere coincidences? And Sister Jane? Really?

"And Maddie?"

"Sure, sure, Maddie's in."

"Really? I find that a little hard to believe."

"She's just mad right now. You'll see, blood is blood. She'll come around.

"But Nick, can we revisit this Sister Jane name? It's a bit over the top for me."

Nick was already on his phone. But this time, apparently, on her behalf.

"Grammy, can I take this blanket home to my horsey?" Misty said as she came down the stairs.

"Of course," she said." I think your sister and brother have ice cream waiting for us in the kitchen."

Nick slipped his phone into his pocket. "By the way, did our business cards come in?"

"Business cards? There was a small package today. You're not serious?"

"Overnight delivery. Love it." He grabbed Jane around the waist and led her into the kitchen, "Come on Sister, we're about to change the world."

Jane was quiet. Was she ready to take on the world? Was God?

16

Thursday in the Third Week of Lent, Nick

Thank God he was able to move his meeting with Voorhies to another day. The Roy situation at the wastewater plant was starting to blow up even more and he didn't want to think about it today. He should have known Zach wasn't telling him everything. The deal was supposed to be a win-win for everyone, but of course, he had assumed that Zach and his company would do the work right. When that shit poured out into the river, his phone was burning up. Then, Zach's people didn't show up until Tuesday and who knew how much the cleanup would cost now. His ass was grass. And worse, Voorhies told him a reporter was snooping around too. God, what else would happen? He needed his own miracle this time.

Shouldn't God take care of it? After all, he was in God's army. That's what Toni said this morning.

"Nicky, Nicky, Nicky, God's hand is on you for the greater good. You're a soldier in His army and we'll be out there together fighting Satan. I am so proud of you. I keep givin' glory to God for his miracle touch on Rosalie for her complete healing. She is such a fine woman. I remember going through first communion with Rosalie. I know it's hard for her, now that I've got a personal relationship with Jesus, but I'm believing she's gonna come around. Amen? Amen. Let's pray for God to be here in our meeting today."

He tried not to cringe under her blast of praises and amens. He met Toni at the Panera near Towson about an hour before he had to pick up Mama, released today. The hardest part of today would be telling Ma about some of the end-of-life decisions he had made on her behalf, like selling the house and storing her things. He was so sure it was the right thing to do. She was dying, for God's sake. He'd think about that conversation later.

"Amen," she said. He missed her entire prayer.

"Yes. Amen. So, tell me, what is the best way to introduce Jane, I mean Sister Jane, to the faith community? How will people know to come to her for her gifts?"

"It's just one gift, isn't it? I mean, she's not prophesying or anything, is she?"

"Uh, I don't think so." He had no idea what that even meant.

"Well, we could host her here at Glorious Presence Christ our Savior for a Sunday night healing service. I'm sure Bishop Bones would be more than willing to have her preach and teach and heal."

"Uh, I don't think so. I doubt Jane is interested in preaching or teaching. But tell me how a healing service goes in general. What is it like?"

"Usually, there's a lot of music and then preaching on the power of God to heal along with some famous examples from scripture, and then there's the first offering for the church. After that, the anointed healer will call up the sick, one by one, for prayer while the choir or the congregation sings worship songs, giving thanks to God and encouragement to the sick person to believe. The words to the songs are projected on a big screen behind the stage."

"Is everyone healed?"

"Oh heavens no. God has three answers to prayer: yes, no, or wait. But we must not hesitate to ask. Jesus said, *'Ask not and you shall receive not. James 4:2.'*"

"Then what happens? How many people come forward? Who decides who gets prayer?"

"Usually, that goes on for an hour or so. If it's a big crowd, the ushers pass out numbers ahead of time. In some cases, Bishop might know someone he believes is ready for a healing miracle and he'll start with that one. And of course, there's a final goodwill offering for the healer and a big healing at the end."

"Goodwill offering?"

"Yes, people give from their hearts to support the minister of healing. Scripture says, *'Do not muzzle an ox while it is treading out the grain, a worker deserves his wages.'* That's in First Timothy, I think. I can look it up."

Nick's mind reeled with possibilities. If they had a healing service at the high school auditorium, let's say 500 people showed up and if everyone threw in $5, that would be $2,500. But most would probably do more, maybe $20 or even $50. And what if they maxed out the place, like 950 people? They could make $20,000 easy. And then, he could move her to the Arena. What would that hold? 2,500 people or more. Plus, the online donations. She could use extra income, and so could he. Sooner or later, she would need to move out of that house. She deserved it.

"Yep, I was right. I Timothy 5:18."

"Let's do one of those services in Lafayette, Toni. Will you help?"

"Praise the Lord. Let's bring Jesus to Lafayette. I'll talk to my brother's son, he's in the band at the church. And of course, Sid is an usher. I'll talk to the bishop too."

"You're still married to Sid Freedle?"

"Third time's the charm, honey. When should we do the service?"

"I don't know. Sooner the better. Let me check with the school."

They discussed the service for a little longer and then he had to leave to pick up Ma. As he drove to Stella Maris, he remembered the things he had to confess.

"OK, God. Do your thing here," he said to the roof of his car.

Ma waited in the lobby when he arrived. He had to admit, despite the weight she had lost, she still looked beautiful to him. He let her talk as he wheeled her to the car and strapped her into the passenger seat. She was on Cloud Nine. He hated to bring her down, but he had to tell her what he had done.

He started the car but didn't pull out of the parking space. "So, Ma, we need to talk."

"I know. So much has happened. My mind is spinning. First thing I'm going to do is take a long bath in my own tub."

"Ma, try not to be mad at me."

She looked over at him and he could see her eyes narrow.

"What did you do?" she asked.

"I wanted to get out in front of the eight ball. You had enough on your plate, and we were all worried; I figured the best thing would be to take care of some loose ends early."

He turned to her then as best he could on the driver's side. She pressed her lips together and gripped her discharge bag. She said nothing and looked straight ahead.

"So, I sold the house, well it's on contract, and we put your things in storage. All the money will go into your account and everything I did was to help. So, now, Praise the Lord, you're healed, and I got you on a waiting list for a great place at Seven Oaks. It's a retirement village right close to Stella and Spencer. It even has a pool."

"I want my house back."

"I can't. I'm sorry. I—"

"And what about my car? Tell me you didn't sell my car?"

"Gone. But we can rent you a new one until we find something better."

"And where am I supposed to sleep tonight? In a motel?"

"You could stay with us—"

"Never."

"I didn't think so. Rita said you could stay with her in Dundalk."

"Great."

"That's OK then?"

"Oh sure, Rita the hypochondriac and Earl, the chain smoker. Perfect."

"Ma, God is in the driver's seat—"

"What? You talk like Toni now? Tell me, you think this pleases God, this disrespect you show for your mother?"

"Ma, we thought you were dying. Everyone agreed. It wasn't just me."

"Fine, just put me in another nursing home. I'll die a second time. Is that what you want?"

"It's an apartment. It's nice. It's close to everything."

And on and on and on it went. Finally, Nick put the car in gear and headed for Rita's house. He half-listened. He had too many women in his life, and they were choking him to death.

When they arrived at Rita's, she said, "Don't get out Nicky, you've done enough. I want to talk to Jane, in person. And I want a prayer cloth from her."

"What's that?"

"If you went to Mass like a good boy, you would know. I want her to bless one specifically for me so I can hold it with my rosary when I pray. You bring Jane to see me or bring me the cloth, or both." She slammed the car door and then opened it again, "I want my house back."

"Ma, I can't—" she slammed the door again. "Son of a bitch." He pulled away. What was a prayer cloth? He vaguely remembered television preachers who would sell things like that. That could be another income stream. When she wasn't as mad, he'd have to ask her about other things they sold on TV. He hoped Ma would be all right at Rita's. He was doing the right thing.

When he got home, Maddie was nowhere, but her actions spoke loudly enough with the "single place setting left on the dining room table" routine. This was how she made the point he had missed dinner without letting her know. Again.

He went into the kitchen and found everything put away. He foraged in the refrigerator and found lasagna, still warm. He dished up a huge piece. He heard the kids running around upstairs. He sat in the dining room to eat.

Maddie came down with Misty Renee about thirty minutes later.

"Oh, you're home," Maddie said.

She knew damn well when he got home. The garage door made enough racket opening and closing that everyone knew exactly when Dad got home.

"Hi Daddy. We finished my homework; do you want to see it?" Misty Renee said.

"Sure baby."

He took Misty's notebook and slid his plate away. Maddie picked it up and took it to the kitchen but then, mysteriously, came back into the dining room with the same plate and plunked it back down in front of him.

"How is Grammy Rosalie?" Misty Renee asked.

"She's good," he said and looked at Maddie. "She's staying at her sister's house for a while until we get her settled into a new place."

"I told you not to list her house," Maddie said quietly.

"What's done is done. Good job Misty Renee. But I think it's your bedtime, right?" he said.

"Oh, all right," the girl said as she kissed both her parents and ran up the stairs.

Maddie sat opposite him, holding a beer, not her usual choice.

"Are you still mad at me about your mom?" he asked.

"What do you think?"

"I think your mom is a miracle worker and deserves to have her family support her. This thing is going to get bigger and bigger and you're in denial."

Maddie took a long swig from the bottle and then slammed it down on the table; a little beer flew from the opening onto the wood. She wiped the table with her hand.

"I've gone along with every one of your cock-eyed plans. You've been a knife salesman, a computer repair guy, and a Realtor. We've moved three times in five years, we flipped a house that no one wanted and now we live in it, we bought a timeshare that no one wanted, and we planted bamboo to sell that no one would buy. You finally get a real job at the city and now you want to ruin everything by running a faith healer business with my mother of all people. I'm done. I will not be a party to this."

"You're making a mistake," he said.

"They've all been mistakes. I mean it, Nick. It may be time for you to move out."

"Maddie, you don't mean it. Your mother is counting on you to be there for her. I told her that you were all in."

"You lied. I am not in at all. My mother is suffering from dementia or even worse, bipolar disorder with symptoms of grandiosity. You and she will make our family a laughingstock."

Maddie pulled her long hair out of its ponytail and cinched it back up again tighter. She wore no make-up and her eyes were red, he assumed from crying. He had not seen her quite this angry in a long time. He had to convince her.

"My mother was discharged from Stella Maris today. How many people

91

do hospices release without dying? And there are others she has healed. Your mother's got a record of every person she's prayed for since this started. Talk to Rosalie. Talk to any of the people she's helped. Or even better, come to Jane's house and watch. It's real. She's real."

Maddie sighed. "I'm going to call in the big guns. I'm calling Aunt Pearl."

Nick groaned. Jane's oldest sister was a force to reckon with. She was the kind of person who could put a kibosh on the whole thing. Hopefully, he could get things rolling before the colossus arrived.

He got up and walked around the table and kneeled beside Maddie. He put his hand next to hers on the table, not touching, but close.

"You are the most amazing wife a guy could have. I love you. I can make it up to you." He gently placed his hand on hers.

She turned to him. "Not this time, Nick. It may not be enough this time. You can sleep on the couch." She got up and left him there. He took a swig from her unfinished beer. This may be harder than he thought.

His phone rang. Madison changed his ringer again, this time to "who let the dogs out?" He checked the caller ID. It was Voorhies from the office. He let it go to voicemail. If he heard one more thing about the wastewater plant, he would snap.

17

SAME THURSDAY IN THE THIRD WEEK OF LENT, TWOMEY

"Good morning," Twomey said as he shook hands with Tom Voorhies, the Lafayette city manager. "I appreciate you giving me some of your time."

"No problem. Twomey, is it? Am I pronouncing it right?"

"Yeah. You're close. It's like the number "two" and then "me.""

"Sit down, sit down. How can I help the press today?"

"I wanted to ask you a few questions about the wastewater treatment plant."

Voorhies shifted in his desk chair a bit. "We sent out the information on that little accident. We're glad no one was hurt, and the system suffered no long-lasting negative effects. It's just a clean-up operation now."

"Yes. Thanks. I got that info, but I was a little more interested in the original contract the city signed for the upgrade that kind of started this whole mess. I discovered some contradictions between the work proposed and what's actually been done along with cost overruns?"

"No, no. There was a misunderstanding. We're working that out in-house."

"Who signed off on that contract? Did you?"

"Well, not really. I mean, we all worked on this project. I'd have to talk to the mayor. Give me your number and I'll give you a call tomorrow."

Twomey checked back in his notes. "Who is Nicholas Fabriani? Does he work here?"

"Yeah, yeah, he works with me. What are you insinuating? Really, let me get back to you."

"Sure," Twomey said evenly. "Just wanted to get a response from you before we go to press on this Fabriani guy. Looks to me like he may have cut a deal with the contractor. Is he here today?"

"No, he's not. I think I'd better ask you to leave now," Voorhies stood.

Twomey stood. "One last thing. Do you know anything about this Archer woman who complained at the city council meeting this week?"

"What? Oh, that's a civil matter. She'll have to litigate that on her own."

"OK. Thanks."

He felt like his younger self. He had the city nailed on this contract thing and sooner than later, it would get ugly. Woohoo! He decided to try his luck on the Archer woman. It could be a two-bird day.

He stood at the door of the senior housing unit in town, buzzing Mrs. Archer's bell. When she finally answered, she was quite irritated.

"Who is this?"

"Hello, Mrs. Archer. My name is Wade Twomey, I'm a reporter with the Aegis."

"What do you want?"

"I was at the city council meeting and heard your complaint. I thought you might like some press coverage on your situation."

"What good would that do?"

"Could you buzz me in so that we could talk in person?"

"I don't know you from Adam. You could come up here and rape me."

"I wouldn't do that Mrs. Archer. How about we meet here in your lobby?"

He didn't know where his patience came from, but it paid off. She finally came down and they sat in the building's lobby for about twenty minutes. She told him the whole story and more. Then he showed her Jane Freedle's picture on his phone.

"Is this the woman?" he asked.

"Why yes. It is. I'm going to sue the heck out of her. What's her name?"

"Jane Freedle. She lives here in town."

"Of course. I know that name. Well, she's a menace to society, that's for sure. Goodbye." She headed to the elevator, on a mission of revenge and terror.

"Oh, Mrs. Archer, just to confirm, you were healed?"

"What?

"The healing was successful?"

"Yes, yes. And that's the point isn't it? The doctor said I would probably live another ten years with my heart back to being as good as new. I'm stuck in this crappy life, alone, in a one-bedroom at an old folks' apartment building. It wasn't supposed to be like this."

Twomey stood silently for a moment as he watched the elevator doors close. He had to think about that. Mrs. Archer had a bad heart and now she didn't? How was that possible? No way to corroborate it either; no doctor would speak to him. Funny, the Archer woman wasn't questioning the healing part of this story at all. She was mad she wasn't dead like she planned. There's one for the books. He headed back to his place.

As he drove past Jane's house, he noticed a small crowd of people standing on her porch, some looked like they were holding up the walls. He drove around the block and finally found a place to park on Jones Way. He grumbled about the walk but then figured he could get a better look at the Freedle house. Was she having a party?

He stood at her iron gate and hailed someone on the steps. There was an odd mix of people around, but mostly women.

"Hey, what's going on?"

"Praise the Lord, brother. We're from Glorious Presence Church here to pray for Sister Jane," a woman in her forties answered.

"Mrs. Freedle?"

"Why yes, the Lord has a mighty hand on this sister. Scripture says, *"Is any sick among you? Let him call for the elders of the church; and let them pray over him, anointing him with oil in the name of the Lord: And the prayer of faith shall save the sick, and the Lord shall raise him up; and if he has committed sins, they shall be forgiven him. James 5:14-16."*

"You've got quite a memory there. And you are?"

"Sister Earnestine Bones. I'm the bishop's sister-in-law."

95

"Nice to meet you. Is Sister Jane here?"

"I don't think so, but we've been anointing the house and praying protection over this place. Would you like to join us?"

"Thanks, I'll pass."

18

FRIDAY IN THE THIRD WEEK OF LENT, JANE

When Jane came down her stairs, she could see through her front window that people stood on the porch, but they weren't like the ones from Toni's church who poured oil all over her house. She had never heard of such a thing. She had been on her way to a lecture at the Lockhouse when they arrived; they were all full of joy and music. She left them to their anointing. But these folks were different. When she opened the door, she could tell they were mostly sick or had a sick person with them. One of the women carried a toddler. They stared at her.

"Are you Sister Jane? Can you help my little girl?" a young woman said.

"I'm not sure what to say. I mean, how did you all know to come here?"

A woman in her 40s with horn-rimmed glasses and a cane said, "My daughter goes to Glorious Presence Christ our Savior Church in Baltimore. She posted it on my Facebook page."

The mother of the toddler added, "That's where I saw it too. My husband thinks I'm crazy, but we're desperate. Our little girl has leukemia; we go back to the doctor tomorrow. Please pray for her."

And one after the other, they recited their needs. She wanted to weep. A scripture about the poor came to mind, something Jesus said about always having the poor with us. Evidently, that held for the sick as well. She couldn't send them away.

"Just give me a few minutes to take care of my pets and make a cup of coffee. Um, maybe, you could all fill out a 3x5 card for me with your basic information like name and address and your prayer need?" As she turned to go inside for the cards, Miracle followed. The toddler stroked the cat as Jane handed out the cards and a few pens. She told them she would speak to each person individually.

She started a pot of coffee and then wondered if she should offer her guests anything to drink. That was absurd, she didn't have enough cups.

She popped a piece of bread in the toaster when her house phone rang. Not even nine o'clock; she needed a secretary.

"Jane? It's Sam Goodson."

"Oh, yes. Hello Pastor." There was a pause.

"Just checking in on you. We, uh, had an appointment day before yesterday? On Wednesday?"

"Right, right. I am sorry. Just so busy. You understand. Things have been hopping…, —," she wasn't sure how to finish that sentence. Things were hopping in the miracle business? That sounded crass.

"Would you like to reschedule?" he asked.

"Sure. But listen, I have a few people here right now. My son-in-law, Nick? You've met Nick, right? Of course, you have. I'll have him call you and set up an appointment. All right?"

"Excuse me?"

"I've really got to go. My toast popped up. Bye." And she hung up. That worked out. Sort of. She headed back to the dining room with her coffee and toast and pondered the arrangement of chairs. If there was more than one person, they could sit on the couch by the window. The recliner might work for her, but it was getting harder and harder to get out of it. Instead, she pulled over her dark blue barrel chair to the mantel. That way, she could see everyone coming in and seat them. She also carried over two dining room chairs just in case. If children came, they could sit on the old Persian area rug.

She went to the kitchen and found her TV tray and set it up next to her. She pushed the low coffee table into the dining room so it wouldn't be in the way. She remembered she had some paper cups left over from Misty Renee's last birthday party, so she put those out, along with a pitcher of water, on the end table near the door. She sat in her barrel chair and surveyed the effect. Should she put on a CD? She didn't have that many Christian ones. She'd ask Nick about that. She was ready for her first customer or patient or client. Yes, client. That sounded better.

She stood up and then sat back down again. Was she crazy? Well, if she was, then they were all crazy with her. She prayed. "OK Lord, I'm counting on this being the true thing to do," she felt the cat rub up against her leg and then settle in next to her chair. That seemed fitting.

"All right Miracle, you ready?"

She invited the first client into her living room and began, in earnest, to pray for total strangers. At first, she came to the door and invited the next person, but after a while, it was more efficient to have the person leaving the session to call in the next person. She thought only eight or nine people wanted prayer, but the parade was almost non-stop. She prayed for the toddler's leukemia; she prayed for a knee that was not healing properly after surgery; she prayed for heart disease and liver disease and a gall bladder; she prayed for allergies and skin cancer. And then, she was surprised to see Cindy limp in.

"Hi Mrs. Freedle. Surprise."

"Yes, I am. Are you coming to see me about your ankle? I should have prayed for you the other day at church, but I was a little confused after my appointment with Pastor Sam. How did you know to come here?"

"I eavesdropped on Mrs. Thyme telling some of the knitting ladies about her hand and your powers to heal. I have all the addresses in the church directory."

"Now, Cindy, you know this is isn't me healing, right? I pray and ask God to heal. That's it."

"Yeah, yeah. Sure. But I have a question. Can you heal a broken heart?"

She wanted to laugh but quickly realized this young woman was serious. Jane wondered if it was possible.

"I don't know," she said. "All I can do is pray, to ask. But it's not the same as a sprained ankle; feelings are complicated by character and memory, hopes and disappointments. Sometimes, we say we want our heart healed but really, we don't because of what it might take to do it. That's me talking, not God, because I'm old enough to have had a broken heart a time or two."

Cindy smiled. "Well, I'm desperate. I loved my boyfriend so much and, well, he dumped me."

"I'm sorry, but—"

"That's not all of it. Please don't tell Pastor Sam. I'm pregnant. Can you pray that away?" Cindy looked at her with such a pathetic expression. Jane begged God to help her say something wise. But no easy answer came to her.

"Cindy, being pregnant is not an illness and neither is a broken heart. They are all part of life's challenges, with sorrow and joy, mistakes and successes."

The girl looked crestfallen.

"Nonetheless, let's pray and see what God chooses to do, all right?"

When Jane opened her eyes, she could tell Cindy had cried through the entire prayer. She doubted the girl heard anything from that prayer. Jane almost forgot to pray for the ankle and threw that in under her breath at the last minute.

Cindy thanked Jane although she was disappointed that baby unmaking was not within Jane's ability. Before she left, Cindy said, "By the way, you'd better get a basket or something for the money out on the porch."

"What money?"

"There's a bunch of dollars and change on the little table next to the swing. Someone plopped one of your plants on the bills, but somebody might steal it."

Jane thanked her and walked out to the porch with Cindy, who had not yet realized that she no longer limped. She found the bills and some coins under a pot of pansies. She told the people assembled that it was unnecessary to give her money. She carried the cash to the kitchen and added it to the other bills in her cookie jar. Then she had a most extraordinary idea. She made a quick sign on one of her 3x5 cards, "*Take some or leave some*" and put the jar outside. That felt right.

By lunchtime, she was exhausted. Since only a handful of people were on the porch, she said, "I'm sorry to make you wait longer, but I really need a short lunch break." They smiled and said they would wait. Her pile of contact cards on the TV tray table was already an inch high. She found a basket to put them in.

Just as she finished making a grilled cheese sandwich and a can of tomato soup and sat at the kitchen table, the front door opened.

"Hello whoever it is, but I need a lunch break."

Maddie answered, "It's me, Mother. Who are all those people on the porch?" She came into the kitchen carrying baby Mason in his car seat.

"Oh, I'm so happy to see you honey. Those are my clients. They have all come for help. For prayer. For healing prayer. Didn't Nick tell you?

They just started showing up. The trickiest one was a young woman who wanted healing for a broken heart, among other things, I'm not sure how that will go."

Maddie stopped mid-stride. She set the car seat down right where she stood and walked back to the front door. "I'm sorry everyone, but I'm going to have to ask you to leave." Maddie pulled the door behind her so Jane couldn't hear what else she said to them. When she returned to the kitchen, her face flushed with anger; she carried the cookie jar with her.

Jane stood. "You had no right to do that Madeline."

"No right? My mother is behaving insanely. She has strangers on her doorstep and she's giving away money. It would only take one phone call for me to get an ambulance out here and take you to the fifth floor for an evaluation."

Jane wanted to scream, but instead she sat back down. That would solve nothing. If she did scream and shout, her daughter might take that next step. Frightening. Nothing with Maddie had been the same since Richard died. Jane had assumed it was her daughter's brand of grief. She knew how much Maddie loved her father but now the girl was becoming more and more like him. That likeness included a growing disdain toward her. Nick had lied about Maddie.

"Nick said—" she started to say.

"Don't talk to me about Nick. He's the one that has made this whole mess worse. Nick is very persuasive. He could convince someone to cut off her own foot."

"Forget about Nick then. What would it take for you to believe?"

"Believe what? That you're an angel from God passing out sugar cubes?" Maddie sat at the kitchen table then and began crying. The baby woke and started crying as well. "Where is Dad when we really need him? He would never have allowed this to happen," she said as she wiped her face with a cloth diaper and picked up the baby and proceeded to nurse him.

"That's true, which is another reason why I need to follow through on this– this phenomenon. I used to think you understood me, at least a little, but now I see that Richard's practicality runs hot through your veins," she said.

"It's the only thing that has kept my marriage together. And the kids."

Jane paused. Was it true? Was it practicality or control?

"Maddie, I don't know what's happening between you and Nick. But I do know something extraordinary is happening to me. Please, give me a month. Give me until Easter. It's a little like Kris Kringle in "Miracle on 34th Street." No one believed in him either."

"O dear Lord," Maddie said as she rolled her eyes.

"Please. See what God is doing here. Watch. Stick around today and watch, for an hour or so. Please?"

"I have to pick up Meredith at 2:30 for her piano lesson."

"Fine, until then."

She led Maddie to the recliner, where she set the baby down beside her in the carrier. Jane looked out the front door to see if anyone remained after Maddie sent them away. Two men and a woman with a boy in a wheelchair waited for her. She went out and chatted with them before inviting them in. Miracle sat on the arm of Maddie's chair. Maddie rocked the baby back to sleep in his car seat. Jane watched Maddie's eyes widen.

"Mother, you can't—"

Jane held up a hand to still her daughter. Jane asked the boy a few questions.

"I was in a motorcycle accident with my dad. He, uh, he died. This is my Uncle Joe and Uncle Smitty, his brothers."

"I tried to tell him—," the mother started to say.

"You are very brave," Jane said to the boy. "Let's trust God," she said to the mother.

When she finished praying, the boy's legs appeared straighter right away.

"Can I walk now? Can I stand up and walk?"

Jane heard her daughter's intake of breath.

"Most healings are not immediate," Jane said, "but if you'd like to try to stand up, I think that would be all right."

Maddie stood to interfere, but Jane blocked her approach. The boy, Sammy, focused on getting out of his chair all by himself. They all stood around him as he pulled his body up and finally stood, albeit a bit unsteadily. He wrapped his arms around Jane.

"I did it! I did it!" the boy said.

"You did well Sammy, you did very well. God loves you so much," she said to him. Then to the mother: "Please be sure to take him to your specialist as soon as you can."

"Thank you. God bless you," the mother said and gushed on and on for some minutes as Sammy sat back in his chair. Jane watched as they wheeled him out and the men carried him down the porch stairs.

She turned to Maddie, "You see? It's wonderful!"

Before Maddie could speak, another voice interrupted, "Hello, Jane."

She turned to find Sister Bernie standing at the door. "It seems you have brokered another miracle of God," the sister said as she crossed herself.

Jane introduced Sister Bernie to Maddie, who shook her hand but then left for the kitchen, ostensibly to retrieve the diaper bag. Sister turned to Jane. "So, I came by to see how you are doing, but it appears you are fine."

"Yes and no. I still have lots of questions but few answers. My daughter is unhappy with me, as you can see; my son-in-law thinks I'm to be a celebrity; my pastor thinks I'm senile; and most of my friends are keeping me at arm's length. It's confusing." Jane looked at her daughter whose jaw clenched as she reentered.

Maddie picked up the car seat. "I've got to go and pick up Meredith."

Jane touched her daughter's arm and looked for something, anything, that might indicate her daughter was coming around.

Maddie left without a word.

"She'll be back," Sister Bernie said.

"Yeah, one way or another."

"There's another reason I've come. I have a proposal for you. How would you like to disappear for a few days and come to the convent? No one will follow you there and you'll have some time to commune with the Father and contemplate some of your questions and maybe get some answers."

"But I'm not Catholic."

"That doesn't matter in this case," Sister Bernie said. "You'll be our guest at the retreat house. We'll feed you and we can talk privately. We'll pray together. And no healings are necessary, unless one of the sisters breaks a leg."

Jane laughed. "When?"

"As early as tonight. I have to go up to the hospice house now, but I could swing back through town and pick you up." Sister Bernie turned to Miracle, who was back on the mantel, "Sorry, no cats at the convent." The cat began to wash herself.

"I'll do it. Let me text my granddaughter to see if she'll take care of the fur babies," Jane said.

19

SAME FRIDAY IN THE THIRD WEEK OF LENT, TWOMEY

What a day! He couldn't wait to get home, drop his stuff, and have a beer. For the first time this week, the garbage cans didn't smell foul as he went up the back stairs. One piece of good news. When he was through the outside door and turned to head up the inside stairs, he saw Vasquez's feet, only one in a slipper, hanging over the top step. Was he dead?

Twomey took the last steps two at a time, set down his computer bag, and bent over Vasquez, putting two fingers to his carotid to check for a pulse and put his face near the guy's nose to check for breathing. Twomey pulled out his phone to call 911 when Vasquez's hand shot up and grabbed his wrist.

"Holy shit. You're like some zombie," Twomey said.

"Don't call an ambulance. Please. Can you help me to my rooms?"

"Uh, yeah, OK, sure." He started to help Vasquez to his feet, but that proved impossible. In the end, he picked up the man, lighter than he had even imagined him to be, and carried Vasquez inside. The rooms were immaculate and sparsely furnished, with utilitarian, but expensive-looking pieces. Twomey assumed it was Danish or Swedish or some such style. The room was all neutral tones except for the artwork. Spectacular splashes of color covered the walls. Near the window sat an easel and paint cabinet. Damn, weird Vasquez, was an artist. No wonder.

"Put me on the settee, over there," Vasquez said.

Odd white fabric covered all the upholstered furniture, and he was beginning to understand it was all about allergen protection. He laid Vasquez down as gently as possible. He had to catch his breath.

Vasquez pulled himself up a bit, not quite to an angled sitting position, but not quite prone either. He dragged over some pillows to support his weight. "On the counter, over there, bring me the container with purified water. Please put on gloves. They're in the basket by the door."

Twomey dutifully headed toward the basket but kept his eye on Vasquez, who unhooked a tube and inserted the prongs into his nose and turned on a machine parked next to the sofa, probably oxygen. Then Vasquez waved him over, clearly impatient for water. Vasquez uncovered the jug's mouthpiece and drank deeply.

"You should see a doctor," Twomey said.

"I have discovered unseemly consequences upon seeing a physician. Generally, in my condition, it means a hospital stay of some length and I am no longer interested in spending my days in that manner. Death is inevitable. But then, so is yours. And if you don't stop smoking, it may be sooner than later."

"Thanks, Dr. Vasquez, I'll tell my mother you cared." Twomey paused. "So, like, what is it?"

"It? My dis-ease? It's not AIDS, if you're wondering. So, you can rest easy in the kitchen. But it's a form of SCID. I will assume you are un-familiar with this acronym. The letters stand for Severe Combined Im-munodeficiency Disease. Perhaps you remember the story of the Bubble Boy?"

"You have that?"

"Not exactly. They thought I did when I was a child, but it's similar. It gives the term 'allergic' a whole new meaning. Anyway, that is inconse-quential now. I simply choose to live out the rest of my life in my way. When necessary, I get an injection or a blood transfusion, but generally, I have controlled my environment and my food sufficiently to sustain myself. Unfortunately, your presence here in my room will need to be cleansed, when I have my strength back."

"You're disinviting me?"

"Correct. Please use the sanitized wipes to close the door behind you. Both booties and gloves are always in the basket at the door if you need to enter a second time." The conversation had taken most of Vasquez's energy and very slowly, he lowered his head down onto one of the pil-lows and closed his eyes.

Twomey left, picked up his computer bag, and headed to his apartment. As he passed the kitchen, he could tell Vasquez had been in the middle of food preparation. What the hell. He played housemaid and cleaned up everything. He threw out the concoction in the blender, assuming Vasquez would do the same, and used Vasquez's cleaning supplies under the sink to wipe everything down. While working, he wondered if Vasquez would be a good human-interest story. Not that those were Twomey's forte. Would Vasquez even permit it? Doubtful.

He picked up his computer bag again and stepped toward his side of the apartment. As he was about to unlock the door, his phone buzzed. It was a text from Roy, the wastewater guy, *"Meet me at the plant, the back door of the main building, in ten minutes. Bring a camera. Or forget it."*

The only camera he had was his phone, but it would have to do. On his way out the building, he saw a package addressed to Vasquez at the top of the steps. Twomey recalled seeing packages there almost every day. It made sense; the guy probably had everything delivered. He carried it up the inside steps and set it outside Vasquez's door. He was being quite the Boy Scout today.

The plant was on the other side of town, so he had to retrieve his car. He hated losing his good parking spot but assumed it would be worth it. He drove through the area that locals called the projects and followed the signs to the plant. It was quite dark by then. Roy stood outside smoking.

As he approached, Roy tossed his cigarette. "I'm gonna show you some of the things we were tellin' you about. You can't use any pictures in the paper, but you may need 'em to understand how this works and what's wrong with the system now. If somethin' doesn't change soon, we could end up poisoning people. I'll be giving notice soon."

Twomey said, "Let's roll."

20

SATURDAY, THE DAY OF ANNUNCIATION IN THE THIRD WEEK OF LENT, JANE

She woke a little disoriented. A bell rang slowly and sonorously, not unlike the Catholic church near her. And yet no cats walked on her bed demanding their morning meal. She recognized birdsong out the window but not what she normally heard. The bed was lumpy and when she opened her eyes, all she saw was an off-white plaster wall. The convent. She examined the room more carefully in the light. Above the single, lace-covered window on the far wall was a wooden crucifix and, on the right, a small writing table. In the left corner was a dresser perpendicular to the foot of the twin bed and a small vase of flowers sat on a doily. Her mother had used doilies on all their wood furniture.

Sister Bernie had encouraged her to sleep as long as she wanted to, but added, "if you want breakfast, it's only served until 9 a.m. in the lunchroom, on the second floor below you at the end of the hall."

She had no idea what time it was but got up all the same. She wasn't even sure why she had agreed to come here or what to expect. As she padded out of her room in slippers and robe across the hall to the communal bathroom, she heard singing, but distant. She brushed her teeth and washed her face but skipped a shower and dressed in her little cubby of a room. Sister had said jeans would be fine, but Jane had to wear a little white doily as a head covering. She felt a little ridiculous.

When she found her way to the lunchroom, it was empty, but a coffee pot was on, so she helped herself. About fifteen minutes later, several women of varying ages entered (also wearing white doilies), greeted her with warm smiles, but remained silent. She recalled another instruction; the great silence would be in force through breakfast. Soon, a sister brought their food, and everyone ate soundlessly. She was about to jump out of her skin. She imagined clicking her shoes like Dorothy in "The Wizard of Oz" to whisk herself back home.

She walked back to her room alone and considered packing up and going home. But if she did that, she'd have to call Maddie to come and get her and undoubtedly endure nearly an hour of Maddie's lectures in the car, with an emphasis on "what were you thinking?"

She heard a gentle tap on her door. Should she say, "Come in" or would that break the silence? She opened the door and Sister Bernie came in smiling, dressed in a traditional nun's habit.

"I'm sorry to be so late in getting to you. Let's sit down," Sister Bernie said. Jane sat on the bed and Sister grabbed the only chair in the room.

"It's all right to talk now?"

Sister Bernie laughed. "Of course. Besides, you're not a sister here. It's all right for you to break the rules a little."

"And you?"

"I work with many people outside the convent. Grace abounds in attending to the needs of others. In other words, no worries." She smiled. "I know this is all a little awkward. I've brought you some information about our order and how we normally spend our days here. But Jane, you are our guest. You can choose to participate or not participate as you would like. The main thing is for you to have some time to think and pray. Right?"

"I suppose so. The last three weeks have not been easy; some days have felt good when I'm sure I'm doing the right thing, but then other days, not so much. It's all happening so fast. My daughter thinks I'm psycho."

"I can imagine. But, under the circumstances, I think you're holding up well. Give yourself some time to contemplate this gift, to accept it or not."

"Is it a gift?" Jane said, "Or is it a curse?"

"I believe we all have free will. You can always choose not to exercise it," Sister Bernie said.

"And if I don't exercise it, as you say, will it go away?"

"I don't know. I've never encountered boundless capacity of this kind before."

"And why me?"

"I don't know that either. But there's a pretty popular response to that question."

Jane waited.

"Why not you? Every saint has asked these questions," Sister said.

"I'm no saint."

"Me either. But God is using both of us, just in different ways. Now, I've got to meet another client. Will you be all right? Feel free to walk the grounds. Sleep. Listen for the food bell and if you like, listen for the bells that call us to chapel during the various hours of prayer. It's all in the booklet. In the chapel, sit in the back row; it's a better view of what's going on."

When Sister Bernie left, Jane felt a little better about staying. It was a retreat, that's all. The only difference between this and a women's weekend at Calm Waters was that she was retreating alone. And until last week, she had been mostly alone anyway. She decided to take a walk.

The flower beds were beginning to sprout and after a while, she grew accustomed to the nuns in their black and white habits and light gray aprons toiling in the dirt and wheelbarrowing away the yard waste and twigs that littered the grass. The paths wound around the property and at one point, she turned around and got a better look at the building, three stories in stone. It reminded her of a New England private school (or what she imagined one would look like).

Around the next curve was a bench with a vista of several fields; she stopped to sit. She breathed in the scents and clean air and prepared to ask God several questions. In the end, only one question kept bubbling up: "How long will this gift last?" If it was forever, then she would have to make some serious plans. But if it was temporary, then she could limp along the same way she had been. Another question surfaced, would there always be pushback from her family, especially from her youngest daughter? Her mind wandered.

Back in the day, when she and Richard argued, it was Maddie who helped make the peace. When Jane had her cancer scare, it was teen-aged Maddie who sat beside her hospital bed while Richard took breaks to golf. And it was her daughter who encouraged Jane to get her hair cut into a pixie. Richard was furious, of course. As her hair turned gray, Richard wanted her to dye it. He said her gray made him look older. She colored her hair for several years, but she couldn't stay on top of it and hated the telling row of gray roots when she parted her hair. She gave it up, despite his peevish comments.

Richard. He was a good father and provider. And he was friendly and funny and much respected in the community. But with her, he was more withdrawn. She believed his time in Vietnam had changed him, too. The strangest things would infuriate him, like the cats pooping outside the litter box or the guy across the street who parked in "his spot." Richard could be a little scary when he was angry. Not that he ever took a hand to her. But his fury filled a room. Once, early on, she forgot to flush the toilet and Richard marched into their bedroom, took hold of their antique bed frame, and shook it so hard she had to hold on to the headboard not to be tossed onto the floor. He could be a volcano.

She returned to the present at the sound of the bell for midday prayer and decided to join the sisters as they trooped toward the chapel. She didn't realize until she was inside that the nuns sat separately near the altar while visitors sat in the back behind an arched wooden divider. Several women from breakfast sat there and one, a young African American woman, guided her through the service. The best part of the service was the sisters singing. She looked for Sister Bernie, but couldn't make her out from the sea of black and white.

Lunch was a simple fare of soup and sandwiches, not unlike what she would make herself. The next time Maddie complained about her eating habits, she could claim she ate like a nun. To her disappointment, none of the sisters ate in the visitor lunchroom. For all she knew, they were having steak and fries. When she returned to her room, she decided to take a nap. She had overheard another woman refer to their rooms as cells, but that seemed uninviting. She preferred to think of her little space as a sanctuary, a secret place.

Jane woke in a panic, her heart pounding as the dream hovered at the edge of her mind. The man in the dream morphed back and forth, first as her father and then as Richard. The father/husband was drowning kittens in a washtub in their backyard. Jane was little, maybe six or seven. She had begged her father not to do it, but he was resolute. Her mother had dragged her back into the house but turning back, Jane saw him thrust his hand and the first kitten under the water. That memory had lain dormant. And here, it returned to her as a dream. But why was Richard in the dream as well? Had she ultimately "married her father" as psychology books would say? She had never planned on marrying Richard Freedle. He was fun to date and drive around with in his mother's little Nova. In Richard's mind, after six months or so, they had dated long enough to have sex. When she got pregnant with little Richie, they "had to" get married. She was a little disappointed by all that sex part and back then, she wondered why all the magazine articles and talk shows talked about sex incessantly. Nothing much to it. Later, she understood that many couples enjoyed this intimate act and women could have orgasms as readily as men. Richard thought it was crass to discuss bedroom activities out loud. It never occurred to him to ask what gave her pleasure.

One of their biggest disagreements was about Jane going back to school to finish her college education.

"Why do you need to go back to college?"

"I want to be a teacher. I've always wanted to be a teacher," she said.

"You need to be with our son. Who's going to take care of him while you go to classes? Your mother? That's out, she's got enough on her plate with your dad now that he's had a stroke. No. And who's going to pay for it? No. End of conversation."

She loved being a mother, but Richard kept crushing her dream to make something more of her life. Only after she had all three kids and they were in school did Jane, on her own, sign up for classes. She paid for the first semester on her own, but then Richard relented, mostly because he realized they would need a second income to raise three kids. He was that practical.

She sat up when she heard the bells ringing for prayer. She hopped out of bed, straightened her little head doily, and walked to the chapel. As she listened to the litany of prayers, she found herself weeping. All along, throughout her marriage, she had been drowning, like those kittens, and she didn't even know it.

21

SAME SATURDAY, ANNUNCIATION DAY IN THE THIRD WEEK OF LENT, TWOMEY

Twomey looked out his side window toward the Freedle house. Once again, people were on the porch, but this group seemed different than the holy rollers he had encountered on Thursday. He decided to walk over and ask a few questions. He'd only been up for an hour or so after working late on the wastewater plant story until almost three in the morning. He was tired but pumped. Maybe he could be a big fish in a small news pond for a while before he retired.

When he strolled through the iron gate, he watched a guy on the porch, maybe in his late 30s, dark and handsome, and quite energized by the Freedle phenomenon, explain things to the small crowd.

"Ok, folks. As I said, Sister Jane is not here right now. But, if you'd fill out this registration card, we'd appreciate it," the man said as he passed out the cards. A dozen people sat on the porch rails, on the swing, in the Adirondack chairs and on the chair arms. Twomey stood at the bottom of the steps. The guy handed him a card but Twomey slipped it into his pocket.

"My name is Nick, everyone, and I'm Sister Jane's son-in-law. We're family and we're all excited about what God is doing here. And if you want to help Sister Jane in her ministry, then we also have a little donation container right here. Sister will be back soon."

Twomey saw a little sign on the cookie jar that said, "Donations Here, God loves a cheerful giver, II Cor 9:7."

As Nick turned back into the house, Twomey decided to find out more about the people who were here. He contemplated whether to start up a casual conversation or reveal upfront that he was a reporter. He opted for casual. He could go the next step later if he needed names and permissions.

For the next fifteen minutes, he hung out near the door and asked folks what had brought them to Sister Jane. Most of them were more than willing to share how someone's brother, sister, or uncle had heard about the miracles she had performed. These people had a full range of ailments, from cirrhosis of the liver to Hepatitis C. One lady had a broken finger and an older man said his wife was forgetting things. One mother had a child diagnosed with juvenile diabetes. And in all those cases, he could not help asking, do you believe this woman can heal?

The woman said, "Don't you? Why are you here?"

"Uh, I've got erectile dysfunction," he said.

The woman stared at him and turned away. Twomey heard Nick's angry voice through the front door, still cracked open.

"What do you mean you don't know where she is? We've got people here." There was a pause, then, "Dammit. Fine. Fine. Please call me back as soon as you know something." With that, Nick came back out and apologized to the small crowd. "I'm sorry folks but it appears that Sister Jane has taken some time off for prayer and fasting."

"God is good," a woman said.

"Based on the contact information you give us on the cards, we will give each of you a call or email and make an appointment, all right?" Nick said.

There was some murmuring, but in the end, everyone turned in their cards and left. Twomey remained.

"I'm sorry brother, did you have another question?" Nick asked.

"Well, actually, my name is Twomey, Wade Twomey. I'm with the Aegis."

"Oh, you're gonna do an article on Sister Jane? That would be great. Yeah, that would be great."

"Can we go inside?"

"Sure, sure. I don't know where she got off to. Usually, she's a homebody, you know?" Nick said.

They sat in the living room. Twomey noted the arrangement, particularly the single chair set by the fireplace mantel. A cat sat as still as a statue on the mantel and stared at him. He didn't like most cats and he could tell this cat didn't like him. He heard birds chirping in the kitchen.

"Can I get you a cup of coffee or something?" Nick asked.

"That would be great. Black for me." As Nick left for the kitchen, Twomey looked around the room. On a TV tray table, he saw a stack of 3x5 cards in a basket. A glance told him they were like Nick's registration cards. He grabbed the stack and slipped them into his pocket. He used to have a little white angel on his shoulder who would warn him about bad behavior like this, but he had kicked her to the curb too many times. Black angel cooed, "You're only borrowing the cards anyway."

"Here you go," Nick said as he came in with a porcelain mug emblazoned with *Best Grandma Ever.* "I love these single-serve coffee makers. Quick and easy," Nick sat on the barrel chair at the mantel while Twomey parked on the couch. "So, what would you like to know?"

"Whatever you can tell me. You know, the who, what, when, where, and why."

"Well, no one knows the why. Toni, Jane's sister-in-law, says it's a God thing. So, yeah, that's all we know about why. It all started—"

And Nick told all he knew as Twomey took notes. Nick said he hadn't met all the people she had healed so far, he was honest about that, but he did tell the story about his daughter falling down the stairs and his mother at Stella Maris. Twomey tried to appear neutral but it all sounded like an amazing fairy tale.

"I know what you're thinking," Nick said, "that we're nuts and so is Sister Jane. I thought the same thing, but you can ask at Stella Maris. How many people check out of hospice?"

"It happens more often than you might expect. But that's beside the point. Tell me, you know for a fact that Mrs. Freedle claims to have healed May Winston, the woman at the nursing home?"

"You can call her Sister Jane. Absolutely. She did it. Without a doubt. I'm telling you, she's the real deal."

"That's wonderful," he said drily. He asked a few more questions about Jane's family and church and if Nick had any pictures of Sister Jane.

"I don't have any of her doing her healing thing, but we do have family pics. Will that work? I could email them to you."

They exchanged emails. When Twomey looked down at the email, he said, "Fabriani? Wait, you work at the city?"

"Yeah. Yeah." But before Twomey could ask more questions, Nick's phone rang, and he ushered Twomey to the door as he listened on the phone. Twomey couldn't believe his luck. Not only could he follow up with Nick on this looney faith healer crap, he had direct access to the wastewater case. This guy was a real loser. Twomey would drop by later.

Before walking back to his apartment to write up his notes, he made a visit to the Methodist church to get an interview with Sister Jane's pastor, Sam Goodson. As he approached the stone building, he was impressed by the enormous stained-glass window facing the street. He followed the signs to the church office around the side, only to find a young woman locking up.

"Oh, hello," she said. "I'm sorry, but we are only open till noon on Saturdays."

"So, Reverend Goodson is not here either?"

"No. He tunes up his sermons at home. Can I help you?"

At first, he was going to leave a message, but then took a chance on a few questions since he was on a roll.

"I came by to ask him about Jane Freedle, the new faith healer in town."

"They are calling her Sister Jane now," the girl said.

"Yes, I know. Do you know her?"

"She's come to this church all of her life. She's a widow, you know. So, she's been a little sad lately, but now, this is huge, you know? These are real miracles. Do you need a miracle? I can tell you where she lives."

"No, no, I'm good. I was over there today, but she seems to be out of town or something."

"She healed me."

"Really?"

"I'm sorry. I didn't catch your name," the girl said.

"Twomey, Wade Twomey. I'm with the Aegis," he gave her his card.

"Is that why you wanted to talk to Pastor Sam?"

"That's right, but tell me about your experience with Mrs.—Sister Jane?"

"She prayed for my sprained ankle and see? It's perfect. And she even

116

prayed for my broken heart."

"Fascinating. What was your name?"

She hesitated as Twomey pulled out his notepad. "Is there a problem?" he said.

"No, it's just that, I work here, you know. And well, Pastor Sam is not a believer, you know?"

"He doesn't believe in God?"

"No. No. God no. I mean," she laughed nervously and took a drink from her plastic water bottle. She wasn't pretty in the traditional way. She had very curly hair and small teeth, but a nice figure. "What I meant to say is that he doesn't believe in Sister Jane's miracles."

"I see."

"I'd better go. I've got to meet a friend at Jiffy Lube. It's a beautiful day, isn't it?"

He watched her walk to her old Sentra and pull away. Despite her ditziness, she was likeable. More importantly, he found it interesting that the Freedle woman's pastor was not on board the hallelujah train. He would come back to chat with the good reverend for sure.

As he walked home, he noticed the girl was right. Although it was still chilly as March usually is in Maryland, there was a fresh scent to the air and the sun shone brightly through the tree limbs. A nice day. He pulled out Sister Jane's cards from his jacket pocket and read through the names as he walked. He could probably pretend to be a volunteer and ask people how they were doing. Who would suspect foul play? He smiled. Oh yeah, he was in the zone.

He got to his apartment stairs behind the restaurant and found another box addressed to Vasquez. He carried it up the rest of the way and knocked on the apartment door.

"It's unlocked," came the answer from within.

Twomey opened the door and showed Vasquez the box.

"Put on booties and gloves if you're coming in," Vasquez said.

Twomey hesitated.

"Fine. Don't come in then if you're fearful."

"I'm not afraid," Twomey said.

"I saw you across the street earlier. What's going on? Why the crowd?"

As Twomey put on the booties and gloves, he said, "That, my friend, is a story you will not believe."

22

SUNDAY IN THE FOURTH WEEK OF LENT, NICK

Nick couldn't park in his garage because Misty Renee had left her bike in the driveway along with a very intricate sidewalk chalk creation. The last time he drove over her artwork, she didn't speak to him for hours. As he walked up to the house, he noticed the grass needed cutting. God, he hated yard work. Just as he was about to go in, Mitchell met him at the door.

"Dad, you promised to take me out driving."

"What? Yeah, well, can't your mother do it? I've got a lot on my plate, Mitch."

"Daaaaad. It's not the same with Mom, she keeps stomping the floorboard. Come on, please. Just for an hour?"

"OK. I get it. Give me a minute. I gotta speak to your mother first. Is she here?"

"Yeah, I think she's helping Madison with her homework while Mason takes his nap."

"Where's Misty Renee? She left her bike out again. Someone's gonna steal it and she'll be cryin' about that. I've told her a million times—"

"She's up the street. I'll be in my room when you're ready," Mitchell said as he bounded up the stairs.

Nick stood in his foyer for about ten seconds considering how to tell Maddie about the upcoming newspaper story. The upbeat approach would not be the right tone with her. He didn't understand why she was so obstructive in every conversation about her mother. But he had to get her buy-in before the article appeared in Wednesday's edition. Somehow.

He walked into the dining room and both Maddie and Madison were bent over a math book.

"Something sure smells good," he said.

"Hi Daddy," Madison said.

He loved it when his teenagers called him Daddy, especially Madison. Every time she said it, he would remember the little three-year-old girl running and jumping into his arms, "Daddy, Daddy!"

"Hi sweetheart," Nick said to Madison and kissed her forehead. His wife, on the other hand, did not even look.

"Mitchell wants to go driving and I said I could go with him, but I need to speak to your mother first. Are you two almost done?"

They both answered. Madison said "yes" and Maddie "no." Maddie looked up and he put up his hands in surrender.

"I can do these problems by myself, I think," Madison said.

Maddie sighed and stood up. She looked at Nick then and said, "What now?"

"Let's go in the kitchen," Nick said. He liked their kitchen with its marble looking counters, wood cabinets, and black appliances. They designed it themselves. In the end, he wasn't sorry they didn't flip the house. He liked it. But Maddie said it was dated. The HGTV renovation shows were giving her the latest lingo and must-haves.

"So, did you find your mother?" he asked.

"I didn't look."

"Maddie!"

"Don't 'Maddie' me. She went on a retreat of some kind. It was probably a good idea to get away from all the craziness. That, at least, makes sense. She left me a voice mail."

"Was there a message for me?"

"On my cell phone? No."

His voice mail was full of messages from Voorhies. He didn't want to know about that. He sat at the island while she stood at the sink. He looked through the patio doors but instead of finding encouragement saw more long grass as high as the first step to the deck.

"When I get back from driving with Mitchell, I'll cut the grass. Although I think Mitch should start doing the grass more often, don't you?"

"We had a deal that you two would alternate. It's your turn. You forgot that part?"

"Grass got long fast for this time of year, don't you think?" She stared at him. He said, "Did Jane say when she was coming back?"

"Nope."

Nick took a deep breath. His phone rang. He checked to see if it was Jane. No luck. Voorhies again. Not now. Not now. He took a breath to try again with Maddie, the oven timer went off. She put on oven mitts and opened the door. The sweet smell of pie filled the room.

"That smells amazing. What's the occasion?"

"I usually make something sweet every Sunday. If you were home more, you might notice the pattern."

"I'm sorry, OK? Look, I'm sorry about everything. I'm sorry about our argument on Thursday. I'm sorry."

She said nothing as she put the pie on the front burner of the stove.

"Things are breaking open with your mom's—" he hesitated, "—with her abilities. A lot of people are asking for her help. And she wants to give that help. And I want to help her help them."

Maddie put her hands on the sink and looked out the window to the back yard. "What exactly does this help of yours look like?"

"I'm her manager."

"What?" She whirled to face him, eyes flashed anger.

"Mom," their daughter called from the dining room, "would you guys go into the family room, it's kind of hard to concentrate."

Maddie marched into the family room and sat on the end of the couch. He followed but opted for the ottoman in front of her.

He spoke quickly. "Just give us a few days to prove it to you. Please. People are talking. There's even been a reporter who wants to tell her story. We've got a special healing service in the works. It's going to be great." Maddie said nothing, so he kept talking. "A lot of people are on board like Aunt Toni and my mom and a bunch of people from Toni's church. This isn't about me anymore."

"It's always about you." She said, then paused and rubbed her forehead, "So, tell me, Mr. Manager, what if this thing gets picked up by the national media? It would be a feeding frenzy. You think my mother would be able to handle that?"

"That's what I mean. That's why I'm there to be a buffer. An article is coming out in the Aegis. Sister Jane handles the miracle stuff and I handle the business end."

"What business end? Sister Jane? What article? No, never mind. No more. I don't want to know. I was there the other day. I saw enough." She walked back over to the kitchen and picked up her cell phone.

"Who are you calling," he said.

"I can't cope with this alone. I'm calling in the whole family for real this time. It's got to stop. And you, Nick, you need to move out."

Madison stood at the door to the dining room. "Mommy, Daddy? What's going on? Are you getting divorced?"

"No, no, baby." he said as he moved to his daughter.

"Madison go upstairs now. We will talk later."

"Maddie! Stop it! I can talk to my daughter."

But Madison bolted and ran up the stairs sobbing.

He took a breath. "Here's what I think," he said.

"This should be fascinating," Maddie said, rolling her eyes.

"I get it. Things are tense. So, I was thinking I'd move in with Jane for a couple of weeks, long enough to get over this initial transition time."

Maddie put the phone down and stared at him. "Just get out."

"I'll pack a few things after I drive with Mitch and cut the grass."

"Just go. Please. Go. I will take care of it."

As he drove away from his house, he fidgeted and turned up the radio. Things had not gone well. The only good sign was that Maddie wasn't screaming. Or maybe that was worse.

His phone rang, still the "Star Wars" theme. He answered it without thinking.

"Fabriani," he said.

"Nick. I've been trying to reach you for days. What the hell is your problem? Why haven't you called me back? You can't put in for leave by

email during a mess like the wastewater plant. What is going on?"

"Tom. Hey, yeah I am so sorry."

"I need you back in the office tomorrow morning. You understand? And I want an explanation about this A&M Methodologies company and how they got the contract. I made a few phone calls and every one of my contacts says they are bad news."

"Sure Tom. I'll clear all this up. Everything will be fine. Look, I gotta go."

"Tomorrow, Nick."

Nick hung up, pulled over, and rifled through his glove box for antacids.

He pulled into the lane behind Jane's house where she usually parked. He was surprised to see her car sitting there. It never occurred to him that she hadn't driven to where she was. He lucked out and found a spot around the corner on Federal in front of the antique place. When he got to Jane's, he found a handful of people on the porch again and several notes taped to her front door.

"Hello folks. May I help you?"

A woman in her 20s spoke up, "We heard there's a healer that lives here. But nobody's opening the door."

"That's right. Sister Jane is on retreat, spending time with God. You'll be able to check out her schedule on Facebook tomorrow. Just look for, uh, Sister Jane of Lafayette. Yeah."

"She won't be back today?" an older woman with a walker asked.

"No, I'm sorry. But we'll have a newsletter on the porch here starting tomorrow about all the upcoming events including a healing service. Now, everybody can fill out one of these registration cards and we'll contact you soon. Be sure to include your email."

"I don't have an email," the walker woman said.

"Just give us the information you do have. God will provide the rest," Nick said, thinking that sounded like something he should say. Then he added, "Now, I'm going inside to prepare the way for God to move through Sister Jane. I hope you will all pray for her too."

"Amen, brother," a man said from the porch swing, although Nick didn't think he looked like one of the faithful, with his black leather jacket, sunglasses, and day-old beard, but who knew. The man stood up and flipped a business card at Nick as he walked past. "I'll be back," he said in a heavy accent. The card read, "Ivan Kravchenko, Exports and Imports" along with a phone number. Nothing else. Nick looked up in time to see the man step fluidly into a black SUV and drive away, the windows tinted very dark.

Nick put the card in his pocket, pulled the taped notes from the front door and let himself in. He went straight to the dining room table and set up his laptop. Belatedly he remembered that Jane had no Internet so he would have to use his phone as a hotspot. The main thing was to get Jane's Facebook page up and running, announce the healing service, and get a first draft of their "Sister Jane Speaks" newsletter.

23

SAME SUNDAY IN THE FOURTH WEEK OF LENT, JANE

By late afternoon, she got the rhythm of the convent. She attended all the services, wore her head covering without feeling awkward, and even managed to sing some of the songs. She sat in the library reading a book about the miracles of the saints when Sister Bernie found her.

"How are you doing Jane?"

"I'm all right. I'm still confused but it's peaceful here. I like it."

"That's wonderful. Stay as long as you like. I recommend you stay until you are truly ready to go back."

"Yes, that's the question. Will I ever be ready and what will I be going back to? I'm not sure I can handle this healing business."

"It doesn't have to be a business," Sister Bernie said. She reached out and pulled Jane up from her chair. "Let's walk." They left the library and took the winding path outside to the right; the one Jane liked the best as it snaked through a grove of old sycamore trees. "I recommend you keep things simple. This is God's problem more than yours."

"How do you figure that?" she said.

"You didn't ask for this any more than someone asks to get cancer or experience injury in an accident. These are things that happen in God's goodwill."

"God's goodwill?"

"God is good and everything that happens is within God's sovereignty. We must figure out how to respond to the challenges of our lives. Does God speak to you audibly?"

"I don't think so. If I started hearing voices, I'd have to check myself into a looney bin."

Sister Bernie smiled. "You're not crazy. But you are an instrument of

God. And eventually, perhaps, we'll learn why."

"But not today? Maybe I should stay here and be a nun."

Sister Bernie chuckled. "Are you too chilly to sit down?" They sat on the same bench with the view of the fields Jane had discovered the day before.

"Do you grow anything in those fields? They belong to the convent?"

"They do, but mostly they're cut for hay. Our leadership team makes arrangements with a local farmer."

They were both quiet for a couple of minutes. It would be dark soon, but for now, the sun was throwing golden beams through the trees. A breeze was picking up as well. There was a good chance of rain soon. Sister Bernie broke the silence.

"You will always have the freedom to stop. You need to remember that. Do good until you cannot do good any longer, and then stop."

"The gift will go away?"

"I don't know. Perhaps. Or not. But it's always up to us to exercise our gifts, to act or not act, to give or not to give."

"That sounds too easy. So many people are already involved."

"Of course. But we have the model of Christ Jesus to follow. In the end, it was better for us that He stopped. But who understood that back then?"

Jane had another question. "What about people I know who really need prayer? For instance, a family friend, Lindy Gillespie, she and her husband Dan have been friends for a long time. But she had a severe stroke along with other issues and lives at Safe Haven. I know God could use me to heal her, but her husband refused my help."

"Your help? Or God's help?"

"Both. Either. I don't know."

"Is Lindy able to ask for help herself?"

"No. Not really. I mean, she would not be able to understand what is being offered," Jane said.

Sister Bernie went quiet. "Have you ever felt restrained to pray for someone?"

"Once. The church secretary had a sprained ankle, but I wanted to pray for her to prove a point. I got the bad motive message pretty loud and clear."

"But I believe your motives are sincere here. Go to her and allow God to direct you."

Jane looked up as she felt droplets fall on her hands. "Oh boy, we're going to get soaked."

"Let's run," Sister Bernie said as she grabbed Jane's hand and they ran up the path, laughing like two school girls: the sister in her black and white habit flying in the wind and Jane in her sneakers and blue velour tracksuit.

"Come, let's sit in my office," Sister said. "Tell me more about Richard. Were you happily married?"

"We were happy at the beginning, I think. When we were just starting out. I remember running with Richard once at the beach, right after we were married. I was only four months along, not showing too much and the family had chipped in for us to take a long weekend honeymoon in Ocean City. One of those days, we drove over the bridge to Assateague Island and walked the beach. And not unlike just now, a storm came up and we had to run back to the car and laughed all the way. That was a happy time. I'm not sure when we changed.

"It's hard to entertain negative thoughts and memories of a loved one who has passed away," Sister Bernie said.

"Yes. But somehow, those are the thoughts coming up. It's like God is trying to pull away a veil. All along, it was easier to play the part of the happy wife and allow Richard to make all the decisions; anything to avoid rocking the boat. I thought he was good at being the head of our home. Now I'm not so sure."

"Do you trust yourself?"

"Ever since his death, I've had to do more on my own, make decisions. It's uncomfortable. I'm never sure my choice is the right one. Richard was always sure.

"And when he was wrong?"

"He never was."

Sister looked at Jane and said nothing. The silence was heavy in the room.

"For a while, I did my best to keep everything the same. I'd ask myself, what would Richard say or what would Richard do? But this? This faith healing stuff would never meet Richard's approval. He would have put on the brakes from the very beginning. Can I tell you a secret?"

Sister Bernie smiled and put out her hands in welcome.

"I hear Richard's voice. You asked me if I heard God's voice, instead, it's his."

"I thought as much. You can mute that anytime."

She looked at Sister and shook her head.

"I've tried. And now, Maddie has taken on Richard's voice too."

"Your daughter?"

"My youngest. It's her husband, Nick, who is trying to help. He believes me. Maddie, not so much. No. Not at all."

"And your other children?"

"Funny, I haven't even asked them or told them what was going on. Celeste, she's the baby, became a total stranger to the family after her divorce when she moved to Philadelphia five years ago; my oldest, Richie, he's a workaholic at a law firm. His wife is Vietnamese; her name is Hang; she's lovely, but incredibly quiet and submissive. It's like Richie married an idea of who a wife should be. I guess our marriage taught him that."

Silence descended again.

"Should we take a break?" Sister Bernie asked.

"No, I'm OK. I was just thinking how I have allowed my children to treat me like Richard did, or simply ignore me. When Richie and Hang come to visit, it's as though I'm not even in the room. I tried to call Celeste occasionally, but she only offered monosyllable answers to my questions. Once I asked her if she was dating any nice men and she laughed hysterically."

"And Maddie?"

"I think she blames me for her father's death. Like I was not good enough for him or held him back, like a heavy weight. I don't know. After he died, she tried to take over everything, like I was an invalid. The more I pushed back, in the last year or so, she became angrier. She keeps telling me what Daddy would want me to do."

Jane looked down at her hands and saw the wedding ring. She began working it off her finger. Tears poured down her face. When she finally got it off, she handed it to Sister Bernie.

"I'm not Richard's wife anymore, am I?"

"Who are you then?" Sister asked.

"Just me. I'm Jane."

"It's a good start, a very good start."

24

Monday in the Fourth Week of Lent, Twomey

"Chuck, what is the problem?" Twomey said as he sat across his assignment editor's desk, in an office with one window facing the parking lot and one into the newsroom. Twomey looked through the interior window and remarked how quiet the room seemed.

"Back in my day, this place would have been full of smoke and copy editors screaming for their stories," he said.

Chuck grunted, "Whatever," his eyes were on his computer screen.

Twomey remembered writing those stories on a Selectric typewriter. He loved that little machine with its white correction ribbon, what an invention. Typewriters were part of the din. Today, everyone buried their faces in the online headlines, pecking silent computer keys, as one news cycle ran into the next one.

"There's no problem," Chuck said, "I just want to be sure we make the right choice on which story to drop first. I gotta admit, you've got two good ones, the exposé, and the healer story. What exactly is your angle on her?"

"She's a charlatan of some kind, but I can't figure out how she does it. The son-in-law is a real piece of work, and I found out yesterday that the two stories are connected."

"What?"

"Yeah, the son-in-law/Sister Jane manager, is neck-deep in the wastewater plant shit."

"Hmmm. I'm not sure that's a good thing. Look, let's post the wastewater plant story first and then let the chips fall where they may on miracle lady. We'll go with Wednesday's Aegis, maybe let it spill into the Sun, but edited down."

"Ok. That'll work. First draft is done; I'll send it to Stephens later today."

An hour later, he sat opposite his ex-wife, Belinda, at a hotel bar. He wondered if their marriage ever was salvageable. She was hot, in that Hooters kind of way, but older, like him. He knew she hated the aging process and was doing her best to look 40, which wasn't working out that well. She still wore her bleached blond hair high and collared shirts that gave men a glimpse of her breasts, which were still splendid. She wore short skirts and four-inch heels which made her legs nice and curvy. Yeah, she could turn a head or two, until they got a good look at her neck. That was always the giveaway for women over 60, or 50 for that matter.

"You look good Belinda."

"Yeah, well, I was doin' better when I had a trainer, but, thanks to you, I couldn't keep up the payments."

"Right. So, here's your money, fresh from the bank."

Belinda took the envelope and proceeded to count it.

"You know, Bee, if you didn't act like such a bitch, you might meet somebody nice."

"Shut up. I'm not taking any chances. The last time you handed me an envelope, you shorted me a hundred bucks."

"I made it good. I always make it good. Who's your new boyfriend?"

Belinda looked up from her counting, "What makes you think I have a boyfriend?"

"The little rock on your hand is new."

"eBay." She put the envelope in her oversized black bag, took her martini, downed it, and stood up. "You know, Arnie's probation hearing is day after tomorrow." She stood by the table waiting for him to respond.

In the old days, he would have lit his cigarette and blown smoke at her. "So?"

"Why don't you at least visit him?"

"We've had this conversation a million times. He's a cheat, a junkie and probably a dealer. He deserves to be in there. I told you. Leave it alone."

"You are cold, Wade Twomey, very cold."

He finished off his beer as she left the restaurant. Of course, she didn't leave him any money for the bill either. He threw some cash on the table and headed out. He had asked Belinda to meet him downtown since he had the meeting with Chuck. But now he had some time to kill. He thought of Vasquez and decided to walk over to the Pratt library to use their Internet.

He sat in the Business, Science & Technology room up the steps from the main hall. He used his laptop to look up Severe Combined Immunodeficiency Disease. He read, "*Severe combined immunodeficiency (SCID) is a group of rare disorders caused by mutations in different genes involved in the development and function of infection-fighting immune cells. Infants with SCID appear healthy at birth but are highly susceptible to severe infections. The condition is fatal, usually within the first year or two of life, unless infants receive immune-restoring treatments, such as transplants of blood-forming stem cells, gene therapy, or enzyme therapy.*"

Holy shit, he thought. The guy is a walking miracle. Twomey spent the next hour researching the disease and finally found a specific article written about one survivor, Maurice Vasquez.

He checked his watch and, realizing he was only minutes away from rush hour, threw his stuff together and walked quickly from the library to the parking garage. Despite his rushing, when he merged onto I-95, it was already bumper-to-bumper traffic. He stewed. He switched on the radio and flipped through channels. The talk shows were all about politics, which made him angrier, and the little music he could find was punctuated by ridiculous DJ chatter. He was about to turn it off when he caught the word miracle. A woman had called in to a local Christian talk show.

"*I give all the glory to God. My daughter had leukemia. We took her to the doctor the next day, and he was shocked. God is a miracle-working God and He's using Sister Jane to touch lives. Amen?*"

"*Where is this healer?*" the host asked.

"*Up in Lafayette,*

"Dammit," he said as he flipped off the radio. How many times had he lost a scoop to inexplicable timing? If Jane Freedle's story were on the radio today, someone else could pick it up. He had to get that story posted now. Without a second thought, he pulled from his lane onto the shoulder of the road and focused on reaching the next exit. Cars beeped and some even tried to pull out in front of him, but he sped up. He was within yards of escape when he heard the siren and saw the lights behind him as he drove onto the ramp.

The next thirty minutes were fraught with a lot of waiting as Baltimore's Finest looked up all his details and issued him a multi-point ticket and fine. As he pulled away from the cop, he let out a stream of expletives. Whatever had made him think his life was looking up, just blasted out of the water. He drove back to the Sun building and finished Sister Jane's story there and walked it through. Chuck might push back, but Twomey's gut told him to move on the story and get it in by deadline today for the Wednesday edition.

Back in Lafayette, after a long day, he slammed his car door and once again complained to himself about the ridiculousness of a small town having a parking problem. Tonight, he was a full two blocks from his apartment. The only bonus was the new downtown liquor store where he grabbed a twelve-pack and stopped for a sandwich at the 7-Eleven. He had to juggle his stuff when he found Vasquez's daily delivery at the top of the steps, but he managed to stack everything up and slog up the indoor stairs. When he got to his neighbor's door, he dropped the box and then walked on to his door.

He let himself in, put the beer and sandwich on his multi-purpose table, and set up his laptop. Out of habit, he checked the activity at Jane Freedle's house. He watched a couple of hopefuls walk up to Jane's door, read the note on the door, chat with others encamped on the porch, fill out one of Fabriani's registration forms, drop it in the basket, and leave. Someone had put up a tent in her front yard. On closer inspection, it looked like there might also be people sitting in their cars, waiting. This was the result of word of mouth and social media and maybe that damn radio show. What would happen after his story on Wednesday? How long would this Freedle woman continue her charade?

25

WEDNESDAY IN THE FOURTH WEEK OF LENT, JANE

Sister Bernie said it was no problem to drive her back to Lafayette that morning after the breaking of the great silence. Jane had wanted to stay longer at the convent, but felt she needed to get back to her fur babies and parakeets. As they drove up to her house, she was shocked to see so many people on her porch, a tent in her front yard, and a line of people standing on her walkway, and then along her fence on the sidewalk. At her front door, she saw Nick waving forms and what looked like raffle tickets. She asked Sister Bernie to drive her around to the back.

"Are you going to be all right?" Sister Bernie asked as she pulled up behind the house.

"That's a good question. I thought I was clear about the way forward, but I didn't expect to find a madhouse."

"Remember, Jane, you have freewill. There is no compulsion in the things of God. And God is always at work, always present."

"Yes. All right," Jane said as she climbed out of the car and pulled her overnight bag from the back seat.

Sister Bernie rolled down the passenger window. "You can always leave a message at the convent if you need me or want to talk," Sister Bernie said and then waved as she drove away.

Jane stood in the alley for a minute and pondered her next move. She wasn't ready to go inside. Instead, she rummaged in her tote for her car keys, threw her bags into the backseat, and pulled off the pad. She looked back to make sure no one saw her. Jane had been thinking about Lindy and Dan on the way home. She would visit Lindy and do as Sister Bernie said.

When she walked up to the desk at Safe Haven, she found Deztinee at the nurses' station.

"Well, you're a sight for sore eyes, Mrs. Freedle," Deztinee said.

"Hello dear. I'm sorry I haven't been able to volunteer. That's a long story. I'm here to today to visit Lindy Gillespie. May I go in?"

"I don't see why not. Here's a badge for you."

Jane walked down the hall to Lindy's room where she had visited many times, usually on Mondays when Dan was there. They would eat lunch together, Dan feeding her as it was too hard for Lindy to coordinate the utensils.

Lindy sat in a wheelchair facing the window. She had always loved the outdoors and it was a bright day with redbuds in bloom outside her room.

"Hello Lindy, it's Jane."

Lindy turned her head and gave Jane her crooked smile. She made a sound close to "hello" and Jane sat beside her.

She didn't know what to say. In the end, Jane told Lindy her story from beginning to end. Lindy sat and appeared to listen, but Jane had no way to know for sure what Lindy understood. They held hands while she spoke. Finally, Jane wrapped up with a question, "May I pray for you? I believe God would answer that prayer."

Jane barely had the words out when Dan walked in Lindy's room.

"Hello Freedle. What are you doing? It's not Monday."

Lindy turned and made several sounds that Jane could not interpret. Dan frowned. Then a few words came through like a version of her name, "Jay," and maybe "hep" for help.

"Now Lindy, my darling, don't you fret. Everything is fine. Jane came to visit you but now she needs to leave." He looked pointedly at Jane.

"Let me pray, Dan."

"Lindy is not an experiment."

"I'm not experimenting."

"Don't make me call the nurse."

She leaned down and kissed Lindy on the forehead. "You're making a mistake," she said and left.

Her mind reeled as she drove home. She had been so sure God wanted her to be there. When she pulled onto her parking pad, she asked God to heal Lindy from afar. Nothing.

She needed to be home. She slipped through the back gate and onto her deck. She let herself in the back door and found the unexpected smell of pizza. She hung up her coat in the little mudroom nook and re-entered her kitchen, which was not the way she had left it. The sink was full of dirty dishes, a pizza box with a half-eaten pizza sat on the kitchen table (the source of the smell), and a carton of cokes were on the counter with a few empties beside it. The place looked like the morning after a teen overnight. She scanned the dining room and found the table covered with papers and a laptop. She dropped her bag by the stairs and pulled out her cell phone to call Nick, who finally picked up after several rings.

"*Jane, where are you?*" Nick said.

"What have you done to my house Nick Fabriani?"

"*What?*"

"Don't what me, young man. Come inside right now and explain to me what is going on," she said.

Jane could hear Nick say to the crowd, "Hold on folks. This could be good news. I'll be right back."

She marched back into the kitchen to wait for him. She uncovered the birdcage and fed them, apologizing the whole time for being gone so long. They cheeped.

"Sister Jane," Nick said as he came toward her with open arms. "You are a sight for sore eyes—"

"Don't call me that. What happened here?"

"It's people Jane. People who need your touch, your gift. It's amazing. So many people, and so generous."

"I'm not talking about the people. I'm talking about my kitchen."

"What? Oh," he said as he looked around. "I'm sorry. Yeah. I've been so busy. I had to take off work. We've got a pile of registrations and I'm trying to figure out how to take care of everyone. Their stories, Jane, are heartbreaking. I had no idea. We've got to help these people."

"Nick. I just walked in the door."

"Where were you? Maddie said you were on a retreat. I mean, what was that all about? Never mind. I get it. You're tired? You want to change clothes? What do you need?"

"Clean up your mess."

"Sure, sure. OK. But listen," he said as he put the pizza box on the counter and threw away some of the cans. "I had to do some triage, you know? I mean, some people are super sick, so I gave them the red tickets. You know, so, after you're dressed or ready or whatever, I would start with the red tickets today."

"Red tickets? This isn't a show, Nick."

"Don't I know it? But what would you recommend? These people are dying."

She wasn't sure what to think. But she had to do something. Sister Bernie's words rang in her head, "Do good until you cannot do good any longer."

"All right Nick. I will go upstairs and freshen up, but I will not have strangers in my house with this chaos. Clean up. Straighten the dining room table. Make some ice water. Paper cups are in the cupboard in the pantry. I'll be right back, and we'll see what God has in mind here."

As she walked past the table in the dining room toward the stairs, she glanced down and saw a flyer with her picture on it and the words, "Sister Jane Touched by God," across the top. She grabbed it off the table and walked back into the kitchen. Nick was washing dishes.

"You need a dishwasher," Nick said.

"I need you to explain this," she said as she waved the flyer in his face.

"People need to know how to find you."

She sighed and shook her head slowly. This was not what she had in mind, at all. Although moved by Nick's sincere concern for the sick, she had to remind herself that he could swing from compassion to folly from one minute to the next.

"Please don't distribute this flyer anymore."

"But if we want Sister Jane—"

"Don't call me that." She tossed the flyer into the trash can and left the kitchen. She headed up the stairs to her bedroom. Why was she so angry? She unpacked her overnight bag, put her worn clothes in the laundry basket and put her toiletry bag on the dresser. She glimpsed her

SISTER JANE | IRMGARDE BROWN

reflection in the mirror and stopped short. There were no mirrors at the convent.

So much had happened in the past few days; she didn't know what she expected to see, but certainly not the face she saw. She looked different, yes, she looked younger, maybe? How was that possible? And yet, her eyes no longer looked so rheumy and her skin looked suppler. Perhaps she was getting a by-product from all the prayers after all. She smiled. Ridiculous. She sat and tried some of the practices Sister Bernie had shared with her, like breathing and silencing the clamor.

After about fifteen minutes, she headed back downstairs and took a deep breath as she looked at her living room, still set up from her first healing prayer sessions. Nick put a pitcher and cups on the cleared dining room table. Jane stepped to the front door.

"I can do that part," Nick said.

"I know. But I want to say hello."

When she opened the door and stepped out, the people stopped talking amongst themselves. She heard someone call out, "Praise the Lord," and then they all began applauding and even cheering. She nearly wept at the ovation. She lifted her hands to encourage them to stop; it was all too much. Instead, she heard a man cry out, "Bless us, Sister Jane, bless us." Jane hesitated, but then made the same cross sign she had seen Pastor Sam make a thousand times. The crowd quieted. She wasn't sure what she should say next, so she improvised.

"Bless you, in the name of the Father, the Son, and the Holy Spirit. Thank you for coming. Please come in."

Nick stepped in front of her at that moment. "What she meant was red tickets first please. Red tickets first, five at a time."

She wanted to object, but then she looked at the expanse of needy people. They wouldn't all fit inside. Maybe Nick was right after all. She went back in and sat in her barrel chair by the mantle. Only then did she notice the tortoise-shell cat she had named Miracle sat on the TV tray table Jane had set up earlier. Jane rubbed her head and ears.

"Hello Miracle. It's good to be home, I think. Are we ready to get to work?" Her other cats were nowhere to be seen, but more than likely, hiding upstairs. They were not good with strangers and probably angry with her for being gone so long.

As the first people came in, Jane directed them to the sofa and incidental chairs. Nick carried in more dining room chairs. Jane asked the children to sit on the floor, much as her second-graders had done at school. Nick handed her the stack of registration cards. These were a little bigger than the 3x5 cards she had started to use. She looked at the basket and wondered where those were. Nick probably moved them.

She called out the first name and so it began. At first, she was a little embarrassed to have an audience, but soon, she could feel their support in prayer. She experienced a presence of power and love. She was with God and God was with her. God sighed with contentment.

26

SAME WEDNESDAY IN THE FOURTH WEEK OF LENT, TWOMEY

He knocked at Vasquez's door on his way out around ten in the morning. The same boxes Twomey had brought up the last two evenings were still outside his door. He didn't want to jump the gun, but this did not seem good. No answer. He knocked again, a little harder.

"Vasquez, open up."

Nothing. He knew Vasquez would be furious if he called 911, so his only option was to break down the door.

A couple of foot kicks and the door lock broke from the jamb. When he entered, he saw Vasquez at his easel, his back to the door, his ears covered by bulky headphones and the music so loud, Twomey could hear it. Vasquez turned and stared. Twomey mouthed "sorry" and pointed to the two boxes. Vasquez sighed and turned back to his work. Twomey dragged in the boxes and then called the rental company and left a voice message to send someone to repair the door. Not a great start to the day.

He was on his way to the 7-Eleven for the morning papers when he saw the crowd outside Jane's house, even bigger than the day before. He chuckled again at the folly of the general public. Just as he was about to move on, Jane came to her door. He had to admit, she looked almost radiant. She must have been a pretty woman back in the day. He watched as she symbolically drew a cross in the air. He was too far away to hear what she said, but the crowd cheered and within moments, Nick shuffled people through the doorway. Her appearance changed his plans. He would pick up the newspapers, but then he wanted to get inside Jane's house. With this development, he could easily create a follow-up to his story today. He called JoBeth.

"Hey JoBeth, it's Twomey. Got a shot request for you here in Lafayette."

"Where? You got the go-ahead from Chuck?"

"Sure, sure. It's 505 Browning Street, right off Federal. You'll see the crowd."

"What's the story? I'm booked till noon."

"That'll work. I'm following up on my little faith healer."

"Whatever." She disconnected.

He bought two copies of both local papers as well as the Sun. He stood by the coffee machine and flipped through the papers quickly. Gratified to find Ms. Jane Freedle on the front page of the People, Places & Things section of the Aegis, he found a shorter article above the fold of the Maryland/Around the Region page in the Sun. Pay dirt.

He walked directly to Jane's house and pushed his way through the crowd on the sidewalk claiming to be her brother who flew in from Florida. The waters parted. When he got to the front door, someone pulled him back.

"Excuse me," a man said from behind and gave him a registration card and a donation envelope, "You fill this out first. Sicker people get red tickets."

"I'm a neighbor. How much you pay for a ticket?"

"You don't pay for a ticket. It's a freewill offering. It's more blessed to give than receive. Then you wait and pray some more."

"Why do you have a red ticket?"

"I'm dying, brother, you know? It's like an emergency room; the sickest ones get in first. You got to ask Brother Nick to give you a red ticket. But we all keep the Sister in the light while she's doin' God's work. What's your ailment brother? I tell you, the Lord is moving mightily here," the man said.

"What's your name?" Twomey asked.

"Ransome, Lionel Ransome. Stage Four lung cancer. And you?"

Twomey evaded an answer as Nick came to the door.

"Hey there Nick. Can I come in? I've got something for you," he held up the newspapers.

"Oh, great, great," Nick said, and then leaned into Twomey's ear. "Could you come around to the back, we're really busy in here."

"Sure. That's fine."

Before he walked around back, Twomey detected three important things:

Nick controlled who entered Sister Jane's sanctuary; Nick might be taking money from people who wanted a red ticket; and out on the street, the first of the local news vans were pulling up. That Sister Jane would dominate the local news cycle, now that his story was out, was a given. But he wanted to be the one with the next big reveal. Best case scenario? He'd uncover her technique.

He found the back door unlocked. Amateurs. In the next few hours, reporters would be looking for any way inside, from unlocked doors to windows to Bilco doors to the basement. He locked the door behind him as he stepped into the kitchen. He saw a pizza box on the counter and snuck a piece of pepperoni. Two birds tweeted at him amiably. He stood just inside the dining room door eating his slice. Eight or more people crowded into her living room, some sat on the floor, a few stood around the perimeter. He couldn't see Jane, who must have sat in the fireplace chair. He inched around the dining room table to catch her words.

"Now, remember, Rebecca," Jane said to the mother of a child who sat on Jane's lap. "I have not seen any pattern in the healings. Some are quick and some take time. In any case, when you see signs of improvement, please go to a doctor right away."

"Yes. Yes ma'am. We will. God bless you. Tell Sister Jane, thank you, Aisha."

"Thank you," the little girl said.

The small crowd applauded. As the mother and child moved to the front door, Jane called the next name from her stack of registration cards. Nick met the woman and child at the door and appeared to encourage a donation; the woman reached for her wallet. Shysters, all of them. Sure, he thought, tell the saps that it might take a while before any healing happens but be sure to drop your coin before you leave. He commended himself for the right tone in his article: skepticism with a large dose of reality. Besides, most people who looked for healing in a setting like this couldn't be that sick in the first place. They probably manifested what they wanted to believe.

Twomey had given up on God a long time ago. He would never forget his high school basketball team dying, or his army buddies in Vietnam. As far as he was concerned, human beings created God to explain away the things they did not understand or fear. Their belief in a god gave them license to ignore facts and science.

He felt something against his leg, that cat. Why was it that the very people who hated cats attracted them? He tried as gently as possible to push/kick the animal away from him. "Get," he said. The cat stared at him. A woman who stood in front of him turned and shushed him. He rolled his eyes and signaled Nick to meet him in the kitchen. Jane, who had been praying for a woman wearing a blue turban, stopped in mid-sentence, and looked over at him. He smiled and wiggled his fingers at her. She closed her eyes and returned to her prayer; he retreated.

"Here it is, Nick," he said and handed Nick copies of both papers. "You understand that I had to take a more distanced point of view. I never did get that picture from you."

"Sure, sure. Yeah, sorry about. Listen, we're pretty busy now, I'll read them later."

"What are you going to do about the TV crew out there?"

"I'll take care of it. I'll speak to them. No problem," Nick said.

"So, Nick. What can you tell me about the problems at the wastewater plant?"

Nick had turned to leave the kitchen then stopped. "What?"

"The wastewater plant. I'm doing another little story on the problems over there. You have any comments I can add? I spoke to Voorhies the other day, but you were out. I guess you were working here at the house."

"It was you? You're the reporter?"

"That's right," Twomey smiled in his most engaging way.

"No comment. You'd better go. No comment. What the hell!" Nick said.

Twomey was about to press in with a few questions when one of the porch guys opened the front door and said, "Sorry to interrupt Sister, but the police are here to talk to you."

Nick went into overdrive and strode over to the door, "I got it, Jane. You keep doing the Lord's work." Jane appeared a little nonplussed. He guessed the neighbors had complained. That crowd had started spilling into the street and now, with press vans, traffic was probably at a stand-still.

Twomey helped himself to the last of the pizza, closed the box, and slipped it next to the trash can under the sink. He also poured himself a

Coke from the fridge. He wanted ice but he would have to fight ice trays and decided against it. He pulled a kitchen chair over to the dining room table where he could see better into the living room. He also turned the open laptop around so he could see the screen. The cat jumped up on the table between him and the laptop.

"Get out of here. You're not allowed on the table," he tried hissing at the cat.

The cat meowed and lay down on the keys.

"Very funny, cat."

Nick had come back in with two local cops. They introduced themselves to Jane and once again, asked to speak to her directly. She apologized to the group and asked them to wait outside while she spoke to the officers. Nick escorted everyone out and took back the cards from Jane, apparently to return them to the people for their next visit.

"Mrs. Freedle, you probably don't remember me, but you were my second-grade teacher. Tommy, Tommy Hancock?"

"Oh, of course. And look at you now," Jane said.

He smiled to himself. With that look, he was sure Jane Freedle had no idea who Tommy Hancock was then or now.

The other officer continued, "Mrs. Freedle, we can't have these crowds on a residential street like this. Have you looked out your window?"

"Why no, I haven't," she said and leaned over her couch to pull the curtains aside from her front window. "Oh dear." People still packed the porch and across the street, and the officer noted that a second van had arrived. Jane turned to the officers, "I had no idea. But didn't Nick explain what is happening here?"

"Not exactly," Officer Hancock said, "But in any case, we still have to insist that people stay on the sidewalk without blocking the right of way. We've already told the television crews they must move their vans as soon as possible. Some people are spilling over into other people's yards."

"We've had complaints," the second officer said.

Nick came back in.

"Nick?" Jane said. "The police are saying that we've had complaints."

144

"What exactly are you doing here, Mrs. Freedle?" Officer Hancock asked. "Do you have an event permit?"

"It's a little like a house church. I work for the city, Officer. I'm Nick Fabriani," he offered a handshake. "I work with Tom Voorhies. No worries, we're in compliance here. We didn't expect the crowds, but I'll manage them better from now on." His phone rang. He silenced it without looking.

"Oh, sure, Mr. Fabriani, I remember you. But listen, have you thought about moving all this to a bigger venue?"

Twomey got up and moved in closer toward the partially closed pocket doors to hear the conversation better. Jane stood with her arms crossed as though she was holding herself together. She looked over and saw him again. He gestured for her to sit. She made a face at him. He shrugged. Nick explained to the cops that he was working on that very thing. He looked over to Jane and said, "You see what I mean, Jane? We're going to have to move to a bigger space sooner or later." She shook her head slightly and looked down.

" We'll help you out with the crowd today; we'll get everyone off the porch, off the grass, and onto the sidewalk." They left the house and Nick followed. Jane sat and the weird cat jumped into her lap. She buried her face in its fur.

Twomey approached Jane, the cat growled in his throat.

"You don't like cats, do you Mr. Twomey?" she said into the fur.

"They don't like me."

"They are usually very good at judging character."

"So am I."

"And what do you judge so far?"

"About you or the cat?"

Jane looked up then and smiled at his small joke. Her eyes seemed to pierce his veneer. And unlike the woman he had met the first time, at her front door, or later at the library, this woman was much more calm and serene. He could see how people might fall under her spell. She almost made him uncomfortable, which was rare.

"I think you've pre-judged us both," she said.

"I'm practical," he said as he sat on the edge of the recliner beside her.

"You remind me a little of my husband. He died three years ago. He never believed in me either. But that was then, and this is now."

"I believe in truth. You're asking me to believe in Santa Claus."

"I don't care if you believe or don't believe. It changes nothing," she said.

"Then let me tell your story. You have nothing to hide?"

"Not really. Unless I'm a lunatic, but that doesn't speak well of God's judgment."

"Are you a saint then?"

Jane laughed.

"How long have you been able to do this?" he asked.

"First of all, let's be completely clear. God does the healing. And God has been in the miracle business more than five thousand years."

"And you?"

"Since May Winston. But you knew that already. What do you want?"

"I want to tell your story from your point of view. I want exclusive access," he said.

"I don't have journalists lined up at my door."

"On the contrary," he got up and pulled the lacy curtains aside. "You seem to have forgotten what is waiting for you out there."

"And how did they find me?" Jane asked.

"Your son-in-law mostly, on Facebook and such. But I did write an article about Sister Jane. It's in today's paper. You're trending, as they say."

"What more do you want then? You already have your article."

"I want to follow-up with your point of view. I'll be a silent witness. Plus, I can work the press. I can keep them at arm's length."

"You want to be the one who exposes me."

"I didn't say that."

"I'm not a fool. But I'll make you a deal. You tell the truth, even if it's outside your wheelhouse. Prove me wrong, crazy, or lying. Or admit I'm being used by God for miracles."

He looked at Jane for a long moment. Her sheer confidence was astounding. "No other interviews but mine? You follow my lead."

"Agreed."

"You have a deal, Sister Jane."

"Do you have to call me that?"

"But I thought—"

"Nick's invention. But that's another problem. By the way, Nick won't like this arrangement."

"Nick will be busy. He can work the crowds, I'll work the press," he said. "Besides, he has other problems brewing."

"Really, like what?"

"You don't know?"

"I don't think I want to know right now."

Jane walked over to the end table by the door, poured herself a glass of water and drank deeply. She turned to him. "When I was a little girl, I wanted to be a nurse. After I saw my brother break his leg, the bone sticking out, I threw up and changed my dream to become a teacher. Funny how things work out."

The front door flew open. "Jane, there's a woman who collapsed out here. Please come," Ransome, the same man who had stopped Twomey on the porch, said.

"Wait, don't go outside," Twomey said.

It was too late. She was out the door before he could stop her. He followed her onto the porch, and they found a woman crumpled onto the steps. Without thinking about the cameramen or women running up to the wrought iron fence, Jane sat beside the woman and lifted her head into her lap.

The woman gasped. "So much pain. Inside. Please help me."

"I will. God will." Jane said. And then she prayed quietly into the woman's ear. He would have sworn, on another day, they had orchestrated the scene. Even Nick appeared spellbound and others lifted their arms into the sky praying in all sorts of ways. A man, undoubtedly someone related to the collapsed woman, kneeled at her feet. Someone else started singing and several joined in. The cameras rolled. He looked out over the crowd and saw JoBeth, the Aegis photographer among them, snapping away. That was good. He thought about the laptop on Jane's dining room table. He could start right now, throw something together about this incident and beat everyone outside. He'd get some Sister Jane quotes too.

The woman on the steps quieted as he heard Jane say, "Feel the presence of God within you. The Holy Spirit is filling you with peace. The stones are disintegrating. You are under the grace of God. Just breathe. Breathe. What's your name dear?"

"Advika. Thank you."

"It's not me, Advika. Really, this is God touching you within."

"But Allah—"

Reporters were screaming questions at Jane and the couple, the wife in her hijab.

Twomey touched Jane's shoulder, "You'd better take her inside now before all hell breaks loose. Trust me on this."

Only then did Jane look up and see the cameras and journalists pressed against the fence. She rose with Advika and turned to go inside; reporters kept screaming questions. He passed Jane and stepped down the stairs toward the frenzy.

"All right guys, that's it. Um, uh, Sister Jane is not doing interviews or answering questions any more today," Twomey said. "Go file your stories; the Sun will carry an exclusive interview later today."

"I thought you retired Twomey," a man yelled from the back of the crowd.

"Not yet, Charlie, not yet." He turned to Jane and the Muslim woman before they entered the house, "Should I call an ambulance? "

"Why? The pain is gone," Advika said.

Jane rolled her eyes at him; they continued into the house.

Nick grabbed his arm and hissed into his ear, "Who put you in charge?"

"Why, Sister Jane did."

"I told you to leave, you're an opportunist."

"Well, that's the kettle calling the pot black. Keep it simple Nick. You do the mumbo jumbo crowd and I'll control the press."

"She told you she would give you an exclusive interview?"

"She did and that, my friend, was the smartest thing she could do, unless you want her eaten alive. Keep your head." Some of the people were still praising God while the reporters continued to shout questions, now at him. He asked Nick, "Is that your laptop on the dining room table?"

"Yes."

"I need it. What's the password?"

Nick said nothing.

"Don't buck me Nick; I still have the wastewater plant story to write once Sister Jane has blown through the news cycle," he said.

Nick paled. Then he spoke slowly, "Fabriani6."

"Twomey!" someone called. Twomey turned at the door and saw JoBeth waving.

"I'm writing now. Turn in your best shots to Chuck at the Sun. Tell him my copy is coming."

"Will do," She yelled back and ran off with her cameras bouncing on her hip. Other reporters ran for their cars.

27

THURSDAY IN THE FOURTH WEEK OF LENT, NICK

He walked into the kitchen, anxious for his first cup of morning coffee. Jane stood at the screen door looking out onto her deck and garden. Two of her cats made figure eights around her legs. The third one, the newest one, sat on the refrigerator. The parakeets were under cover, thank God, they made a hell of a racket.

"Jane, why did you give Twomey exclusive rights to your story?"

She jumped and yelped. "Have you never heard of 'good morning' before creeping up behind someone?" She closed the back door and poured kibble for the cats and uncovered the birds.

"Good morning. Now, how did that happen? Did you even read his first story? He might as well have called you a con artist."

"I read it, after he left. But honestly, Nick, he interviewed you. I assumed you trusted him."

"Well, I don't. Not anymore. Don't do that again. Please. Promise me, talk to me first. I'm your manager, remember?"

"It's not like I'm a rock and roll star."

"Not yet," He said and went back into the dining room to open his laptop and search for Twomey's latest story online. He had no idea how long it would take to appear.

From the kitchen, Jane said, "In that case, I'll get out my old guitar and start practicing my Peter, Paul, & Mary songs."

"What?" he said. What was she talking about now?

"Never mind. I would have made coffee," she said, "but someone replaced my old pot with this newfangled thing. You know anything about that?"

"Yes, Jane. I'll show you." He sighed and walked back to the kitchen.

He had to remember he was dealing with someone a lot older. Patience, he told himself, be patient.

Before the water finished dripping through the coffee pod, someone knocked on the front door.

"I'll get it," he said and left Jane in the kitchen watching the coffee flow. "What a surprise. Nice to see you, Pastor Sam. Is Jane expecting you?"

"I don't think so. I hope it's not too early. We wanted to get a jump on the day." They shook hands. "This is my wife, Stella. This is Nick, Jane's son-in-law."

"Nice to meet you," Stella said as she looked around.

"Jane!" Nick yelled, "You've got company."

Jane stood at the kitchen door. "Hello Pastor, . . . Stella. It's rare to see you two together, you're both so busy."

Nick glanced out the front door as they walked through and saw a small crowd already and it was barely eight in the morning. "Hey, folks," he called through the open door, "you gotta line up along the sidewalk. No one on the porch till nine, OK?"

Someone called back, "What about those two?"

"No worries. It's her pastor. They're having a quick conference. Here, pass around these registration cards. Weren't you here before?"

"Yeah," the man said, "but I've got somethin' else."

"Fine. Fine. Just be sure to check off that you're a return customer, I mean, client." he said, and closed the door quickly as he saw photographers run up to the fence. When he looked through the door curtain, he could see one of the vans from a local station had managed to snag a parking place right across the street.

Sam and Stella sat with Jane at the dining room table. He heard Jane say, "I don't understand."

"Can I get anyone a cup of coffee?" Nick said. All three of them looked up at him with an incredulous expression. Then Sam turned to Jane.

"It's all right to talk," Jane said. "Nick has been helping me with the crowds and such. You were saying you're worried? Don't tell me, one of my offspring called you again?"

"Well, yes and no," Sam said. "I planned to drop by in any case. Then

151

Stella said she could come with me before she headed to the office. I hope it's not too early. To be honest, I did get a phone message that Maddie called."

"I see," Jane said and then looked directly at Nick.

He shrugged. He had avoided a Maddie discussion ever since Jane got back. He checked his phone. Damn, he missed Mitchell's lacrosse game last night. He'd better call Maddie later today. He still hadn't picked up two voice messages from the office. He was out of personal days and forgot to call in sick this morning. Now, there was an irony. But he just couldn't face the office right now. Stella's voice brought him back to the meeting at hand. She folded her hands on the table as though she was praying.

"Do you find all of this extraordinary?" Stella asked Jane.

"I do," Jane confessed, "we're still working on the best way to handle everything."

He took this as an opportunity to speak. "You know, Sam, what we need is a bigger venue. Since Jane is one of your people, wouldn't it make more sense for her to use the church?"

Sam turned to him, "It's a bit premature."

"What do you mean?" he said.

"Jane," Stella interrupted, "Have you been reading biographies or other sources of information about faith healing?"

"A little, toward the beginning. I read all the Christ passages on his healings."

"And are you trying to replicate those experiences?" Stella asked.

"No, not really. My gift works differently. After all, Jesus was God. Or is, right?" Jane looked from Stella to Sam expectantly.

Nick discerned these two did not believe in Jane's abilities. "It's real, you know," he said to them. "I've seen it with my own eyes."

Stella ignored him and took one of Jane's hands. "We've known each other for a while now, don't you think? I have always respected you and Richard and all the time and energy you have put into the church. Sam feels the same way. But when we lose someone we love, that time of grief will be different for everyone. We all respond in unpredictable ways. When we enlarge our personal experience and draw other people into that world, however, I'm saying that a lot of people are out there on the street who are placing a great deal of hope in you. That's a tremendous responsibility."

"I agree," Jane said.

"Absolutely," Nick said. No one looked his way.

Jane said, "And how terrible it would be if it wasn't real; if it didn't work; if it was a figment of my imagination or a delusion."

"Exactly," Stella said.

"But that's the point. It is real. God is working through my prayers. And if I can do this good thing, I will. I must," Jane said.

"Praise the Lord," Nick said reflexively, clearly the Toni influence was getting to him.

"How do you know it's working?" Sam asked Jane.

"We're keeping records," Nick said. "Ask the people. Invite us to do healing in your church. If you want more people to come to your church, this will do it." He smiled, thinking he had hit on a great idea, an appeal to the administrative side of the pastor.

"I spoke to my district superintendent and both of us believe it would be unwise to invite this kind of sensationalism into the church," Sam said.

Jane sucked in a breath. She said, almost tearfully, "Are you saying I am no longer welcome at the church?"

Nick watched Stella look at her husband balefully.

Sam continued, "I didn't mean that, no, not exactly. We need to calm things down. We can't have television cameras and reporters hovering around the church. Honestly, Jane, you know I, well, we, all of us, want what is best for you. I strongly suggest you spend some private time with Stella or someone else, but I think you need help. I would be remiss if I weren't honest with you."

Jane was about to weep, and Nick did not want them to see that; he resented their smug disbelief. "I think you should leave now," he said.

They looked surprised.

"We'll be back in touch," he said.

As the couple got up, Jane pushed back from the table and headed to the kitchen, but then stopped and turned. Her eyes no longer looked filled with tears. She said, "Pastor, let me know when you would like me to pray for you. Don't you still have ulcers?" She let the kitchen door swing shut behind her.

28

SAME THURSDAY IN THE FOURTH WEEK OF LENT, TWOMEY

"Damn it to hell, Twomey. You are damned lucky your little religious nut story worked out. But next time, give me a heads up. Holy shit," Chuck said.

Twomey held his cell phone away from his ear. He had just finished his lunch at the Waterside diner near the promenade, enjoyed a smoke and watched the sailboats on the river. He never understood the appeal of a sailboat, too much work just to make it go forward.

"Sure, sure. But it's good stuff, right? I think I can squeeze one or two follow-ups out of this thing," he said. He flicked his butt to the parking lot.

"Fine, but what about your regular obligations? Stephens told me he hasn't gotten a single local sports story or a report from local government from you in a while."

"City council only meets every other week. I'm on it. I'm on it," he said.

"And what is happening with the corruption story? I want to run that no later than next week. You said it was done."

He didn't want to bring up the real reason for his delay. He wanted to keep Nick Fabriani on a string in case he needed quick access to Jane. He punted," I've got an appointment with the mayor this afternoon."

"What's that going to do?"

"Trust me Chuck."

"Never. I've got access to your complete file, remember? I know you."

"Suck it up, Chuck." He disconnected and smiled at his little rhyme.

But the kid editor had the power to ruin everything. Power was wasted on the young. He sent a text, "Sorry about that Chuck. I will catch up." No reply.

The woman at the city government reception desk, Ethel Peterson, according to her nameplate, was having a busy moment: two phone calls and two customers standing in line. Her slightly blue-silver curls swathed her head while her glasses hung from a cord around her neck.

"Hello, Ms. Peterson, I'm Wade Twomey. I was wondering if I might see Mayor Reynolds?"

"I'm not sure he's here yet. One of his boys has a junior varsity game after school, but let me check with Gloria, his assistant." She picked up her phone and dialed an internal number. "Have we met?" She said and he thought she might be flirting with him.

"Uh. No. But the pleasure is all mine," he said and reached out his hand to shake hers. She dropped the receiver and had to re-dial Gloria.

Finally, Gloria came out. "I am so sorry Mr. Twomey. Did the mayor set up an appointment with you? He didn't tell me about it. Anyway, his son is starting today, and Scott didn't want to miss it. Lacrosse, you understand. I could re-schedule you."

"No, no problem. Is he at the field here in town? Maybe I could just meet him there?"

"I suppose so, although you'll have to buy a ticket. The far side of the field is the home side. I'll text him to let him know you're coming."

Small-town America had a whole different set of rules for running a city or a business. Family life, school sports, and the marching band trumped everything else. He walked passed the school, the police station, and across the street to the field. The entry fee was only $4. He saw the mayor standing in the bleachers, wearing the school colors, and waving a cowbell. The home team scored.

He walked up the bleacher stairs and stood next to the mayor. "Which helmet is yours?"

Reynolds said proudly, "Number 18. Same number I had in high school."

"You went to school here?"

"Yes. Great school. Really great. Go, Jimmy, go, go, go. Check him!"

Eventually, the mayor sat and Twomey with him. The mayor turned to him, "I was wondering when you would be around. Can we keep this conversation off the record?"

"OK," he said.

"Any chance I could ask you to drop this wastewater plant story?"

"I'm not sure that would be in the public interest. Sir."

The mayor looked around to see who might be within earshot. "Look, we've started an internal investigation. It's not like I'm pushing this thing under the rug; I don't want the bad publicity for Lafayette. We depend on two things here: the loyalty of our residents and tourism. This story could undermine both. Last year, we had a huge fall-out over one of our seafood festivals. Parents walked up and down the street with placards. It was a nightmare. It's the appearance of evil, you understand? I mean, this is not Flint, Michigan, where government people intentionally looked the other way. This was an accident."

"I appreciate everything you are saying Mayor, but the story is less about the accident and more about the contract being given to an incompetent company at a higher rate. I'm trying to confirm if the person who signed that contract got a kickback."

Mayor Reynolds jumped to his feet as the boys scuffled for the ball. His son got a hold of it and passed it to a teammate. "Yes, Jimmy. That's how to play it," he yelled. They were both standing again. "He's gone, the signer."

"Does he know that?" he asked.

"You know him?"

"Fabriani? Yeah, sort of. But shouldn't he be prosecuted under the law?"

"He's a good guy. Family man. Losing his job will be enough of a hit," the mayor said. "He'll get his notice today. What about the story?"

"Let me think about it," he said. Although, he wasn't even sure he could stop the story with Chuck asking about it every day. And honestly, did he even want to? But he could make quite a formidable enemy of the mayor and any future story could be dead to him. The good-old-boy network was alive and well in beautiful downtown Lafayette.

"One more thing," the mayor said as Twomey started to leave. "We're not fond of any kind of sensationalism here. Do you know *Good Morning America* called me about Jane Freedle after the AP picked up your story? Richard would be turning over in his grave."

"You know the family?"

157

"Sure. His son, Richie, and I went to school together. He was a couple of grades ahead of me. His dad was great, a good guy."

"You have a lot of good guys in this town."

"We do. Listen, take it easy on Jane. She taught second grade right here in town. I was her principal for a few years. But I'm thinking this widow thing took her over the edge."

"You think she's deranged? Is that on the record?"

"Hell no."

"Con artist then?" He asked.

"Not a chance. Jane is good people. Maybe she's delusional, I don't know. But her family will take care of her. It doesn't have to be all over the news. Quite an embarrassment to the kids."

"Don't worry too much Mr. Mayor," he said. "It's a news cycle. Another story is probably waiting right around the corner."

"Just as long as it isn't the wastewater plant story," the mayor said, and looked Twomey in the eye and then laughed. "Don't know why, but I like you Twomey. You're a—"

"Got it. A good guy."

As he walked back to his car, the mayor's comments about the morning talk show gave him a different idea. What was keeping him from offering his story about Sister Jane to one of the cable news channels? If he had to, he could even drive up to New York. When he got to his car, he drove over to the library to sit in their parking lot and use their Internet.

158

29

SAME THURSDAY IN THE FOURTH WEEK OF LENT, JANE

She must have prayed for at least twenty-five people since she started sessions that morning. The illnesses were starting to blur into one another. How did doctors do it, meet sick people every minute of every day?

Nick bought her one of those "be right back" door signs that looked like a clock. She put it on the door with the big hand showing 30 minutes. He ran an errand and told her Toni would be there soon to help handle the people. But she wanted a break now. She needed to pee, and she was hungry. For some reason, people randomly brought food in casserole dishes and take-out containers. The largesse reminded her of the days after Richard died when dish after dish came into the house along with packages of paper towels, napkins, and toilet paper. That toilet paper had lasted almost a year.

She made herself a tuna salad sandwich and sat in the kitchen. The cats lounged nearby, hoping for a treat. She still had one client on her heart: Junie. The girl couldn't have been more than nineteen or twenty. (Should Nick add age to the registration card?) Junie came in looking very shy and very pregnant.

"Hello. Junie. How can God help you today?" This was the line she had started using for each person.

"It's my baby. Something is wrong with her. Something with her DNA. I can't handle it," Junie said, tears brimmed. "When my boyfriend found out, he said no way he would stick around for a deformed kid." She began to cry in earnest. "It's too late for a legal abortion; please help me."

"I'm sorry, Junie," she said. "I can't ask God to terminate this pregnancy."

"I know that. But can you heal the baby inside me?"

Now, here was a new question. Up until today, all she imagined were bones that came together, internal organs returned to their original state, and cancers eradicated from a body. But a child, a fetus, whose altered DNA would cause inexplicable change, was that child sick? This was an ethical question she did not want to ponder, not one bit.

"I'll pray. I don't know the answer to your question, I don't."

She had prayed as best she could, leaving a wide berth for God to re-fashion the course of this unborn child's life, or not. In her mind, each person has challenges, some people have terrible parents, and some have learning disabilities, and some have brilliance. Each one must choose how to react, to respond to their circumstances. Was this any different? She didn't know.

"Is she healthy now?" Junie asked.

"I can't say. You will have to decide what is healthy after she is born."

"That's not fair. All of these other people are healed, but you can't heal this?"

"I don't heal anyone. It's God who does the healing."

"Well, it's God that made this mess. I think you're a fake," Junie said and left, crying again.

Jane had made a note on her card. She would follow up in a few weeks.

She finished her lunch when her back door flew open and Toni came in like a windstorm, followed by a stranger. They were laden with all kinds of bags and boxes which they dumped on the dining room table. Toni wore a bright blue jumpsuit along with a big chunky necklace, a knee-length yellow sweater and boots with extremely high heels. How in the world could she walk in them?

"Good morning Sister Jane, or is it afternoon already? This is Sister Rovanda from my church. We have been shopping all morning looking for the perfect outfit for you."

Rovanda was the opposite of Toni. Where Toni was tall in her high heels, Rovanda was quite short and had some weight on her. Her hair was in perfect cornrows with long extensions but pulled back into a kind of loose ponytail. Her nails were long, and each nail had a different decoration. Her earrings swayed and brushed her shoulders. Rovanda wore a very tight dress, in Jane's mind, particularly for someone that size. She couldn't imagine what the two women would pick out for her, style-wise.

"Outfit? What on earth are you talking about?"

Rovanda smiled, "It is such a blessing to finally meet you Sister Jane. I can see God all over you." Rovanda gave her quite the bear hug.

"I beg your pardon?" she said. She had no idea what it meant to have "God all over her."

Toni pulled clothes from her bags, "Look at this! Isn't it adorable?" It was a white dress that had one of those odd hemlines, longer in the back than in the front. "Rovanda does beautiful handwork. She's going to embroider a magnificent gold cross right across the chest."

"Yes ma'am. Do you think we got the right size, Toni?"

"Come over here, Jane, let me hold this up against you."

Jane stood beside them, but a bit dazedly. "I don't understand what you are talking about. Why would I need such a dress?"

"For the healing service on Palm Sunday. We're so excited." Toni said.

"I didn't agree to that."

"It will be fine. You don't need to be nervous one bit. And you will look gorgeous," Toni said.

"I think it will be perfect," Rovanda added.

"I'm not wearing that," she said.

She watched their expressions. Hurt. But then Toni brightened.

"Don't be silly. You must wear something. You can't keep wearing these velour tracksuits."

She looked down at herself. She loved this suit, the turquoise color brought out her eyes.

Toni said, "I'm starving. How about you, Rovanda? Nick said the refrigerator was full of yummies." The two women flounced into the kitchen.

The doorbell rang. Jane looked at her watch and realized her break time was up. Had she even gone to the bathroom? She couldn't remember. She needed fifteen more minutes, if nothing else, to clear the air with Toni and Rovanda about the dress.

"Hello. I'm sorry but—" Jane started to say.

"Hello Mrs. Freedle? It's Susan, from the hospital?"

"Oh, my heavens, of course it is. Oh, my dear girl, come in, come in." Embracing Susan, only then did she realize the full weight of this woman's visit. Susan walked in. Susan, the one with the wheelchair, walked.

"I didn't look for you, honestly," Susan said quickly," but then I saw your name in the paper and well, I wanted to thank you. I don't know what else to say but that. Thank you so much."

"I see, of course, I see. God is so good." She grabbed hold of Susan and hugged her again. Both women cried in joyful tears. When Jane pulled away, she grabbed some tissues and wiped Susan's face and then her own. They laughed at each other. She felt so warmly toward this young woman. Susan said, "The newspaper article wasn't exactly complimentary to you, I'm deeply sorry. I could tell my story to the press if you would like?"

"No, no. It's not necessary. It can be our secret. People who don't believe God can heal won't change their minds with one more story. I'm learning that truth each day."

"I'm so sad for you," Susan said.

"Don't be."

"You look amazing, really beautiful and glowing."

"Oh no, glowing? Like a nuclear accident?"

Susan laughed, "No, like an angel. But tell me, can I help in any way? I owe you so much. My family is in awe every time I walk into a room."

"That's wonderful."

The doorbell rang and Jane brought herself back to obligations.

"I'd better get back to work, as they say. Just come and visit me again. Any luck with Mrs. Archer?

"I'm working on it," Susan said, her eyes twinkled as though she held a secret.

"I want to meet your family," Jane said. "But really, I'm fine. Would you mind going out the back door? I think it will be easier for you. I don't want reporters on your case. Come, I'll introduce you to my sister-in-law, Toni. She's a real go-getter," Jane said as she gently directed Susan to the kitchen and once again, pulled the swinging door closed.

"Toni? Rovanda?" Jane said, "You two will love this story. This is Susan."

On her way back to the living room, she pulled shut the pocket doors between the living room and the dining room. She didn't usually do that, but Toni and Rovanda had big booming voices. The doorbell rang again, quite insistently. She opened the door.

"Here's my registration card," the woman said as she pushed past Jane. "My name is Minerva James."

"Hello. Nice to meet you. I was going to take—"

"You've got to help me. My back is killing me, and I've got arthritis so bad that I can hardly walk sometimes. I've been to doctor after doctor and I can't get no relief. Where should I sit?"

"Right here on the couch is fine," she sighed, and headed toward her chair by the fireplace. Miracle, who had been quite absent for the last hour or so, appeared out of nowhere and sat on the end table next to the new client.

"I don't like cats," Minerva said.

"Perhaps you'd be more comfortable in one of these chairs?" Jane indicated one of the dining room chairs. The woman sat heavily in the proffered chair.

Jane was about to ask a few questions when Minerva launched into a very long-winded description of her ailments and how long she had been suffering. Jane felt an uncomfortable stirring within, something she had never felt before. Finally, Minerva finished.

"Can you help me or not?" the woman asked.

"This process is really up to God. I'm more like a pipeline. God is the miracle worker, not me. Right?"

"I wouldn't know."

Jane began to pray, then paused. Only one time before had God stopped her prayer for someone and that was back in the church office when she wanted to pray for Cindy's ankle. But then, her motives were fuzzy. This time felt different. She tried again.

"Lord, I'm asking—" Nothing. No words would come. She could not speak. Was it over? Had the stream dammed up?

Jane pulled her hands back from Minerva, leaned back, and opened her

163

eyes. Minerva stared at her, eyes hard and challenging.

"Ms. James. I am sorry, but I cannot pray for your healing."

"Why not?"

"I'm not sure, but I cannot. Your pain may be of your own making." Jane knew that sounded harsh, but she didn't know how else to say it. She didn't want to say God told her not to pray.

"What are you saying? Who made you the judge and the jury?"

"Uh, no one. I'm—"

"I deserve the same healing as anyone else. Is it the money? Is it because I don't have enough money?

"No, I—"

"My sister warned me. She read about you in the paper; you're a crack-pot!"

Minerva rose, her face splotchy with anger.

"You're a phony. I should have known. And I'll tell everybody. What are you gonna do about that? Uh? Uh?" Minerva James yanked up her large purse and swung it hard and hit Jane directly in the side of her face. And again. The whole time, Minerva screamed and called her names.

Jane cried out and fell to the floor; the woman hit wherever the bag would land. Jane heard Toni and Rovanda yell on the other side of the doors, those damn old sticky pocket doors. Finally, someone pulled Minerva off. Jane rolled over as best she could and saw Minerva's foot nearly kick her. She rolled again and bumped into the couch. When she heard a cat yowl, she forced herself up into a sitting position, just in time to see Miracle leap from the couch to Minerva's sweater draped over her shoulders.

"Miracle, no!"

Too late. The woman screamed and ran out of the house calling for the police. Minerva's sweater was now with Miracle, claws trapped in the fabric on the floor. The cat growled and tore at the sweater.

"We need to call 911," Toni said.

"No, please don't," she said.

"We have to Sister," Rovanda said. "That woman assaulted you. Plus, you're bleeding."

Nick appeared at the door, "What in the name of God happened here?"

30

FRIDAY IN THE FOURTH WEEK OF LENT, TWOMEY

In his disposable gloves and booties, he drank a glass of water, no ice, while Vasquez sipped on a green drink.

"How is it?" Twomey asked.

"Because of your efforts, I would like to commend you, but I must be truthful, it's not exactly what I had hoped for."

"I could try again."

Vasquez held up his hand in refusal. The hand shook and he brought it back to the settee arm. An open book sat beside him, but Twomey seriously doubted the man could read anymore.

"Sorry about the door. Looks like they came right away?"

"Yes."

"I brought your mail up, but I didn't see a food delivery today," he said.

"There's not much point, is there?"

"I never marked you as a fatalist."

"You barely know me," Vasquez said. "I speculate you may be reconnoitering for a story anyway. I suppose I could invite you to write my obituary."

"Human interest stories are not my strength, but I am curious about you. I did some research. You have quite a reputation as an artist."

"Had a reputation."

"How did you end up in Lafayette of all places? People don't usually move from New York City to beautiful downtown Lafayette."

"Would you please get me a glass of pure water from the bar over there?"

Twomey obliged and said nothing, letting Vasquez decide if he wanted to talk. They were amiably quiet for some time. Twomey fell into a different version of himself around sick people and death beds: his basket-ball team, his mother, his cousin Andy, and his beloved dog. And then, all the wounded guys who died in his arms in the rice paddies, all shot from afar and shot without warning. All of them had brought out a sub-dued version of Wade Twomey, a grieving witness formed as a teenager when he wrecked that car and destroyed the lives of four families. That younger self who sat by each bed and watched his friends die, one by one.

"Travelling was always hard for me," Vasquez said at last. "Lots of pre-cautions and preparations. But I had a friend, a former lover, who had an art show here and I wanted to attend. It was folly to travel in the winter. And I suffered for it; I had a severe relapse and ended up in the local hospital. Long story short, I decided to end it here."

"How long ago?"

"Longer than I expected, obviously."

"And your friend?"

"He died a couple of years ago. He was probably the one who exposed me to the virus that took me down that year. Doesn't matter. Most people assume I am dead already. I will accommodate them soon enough."

Vasquez took a sip of water and leaned his head back.

"Tell me the gossip from across the street," he said, his eyes still closed.

"Well, yesterday, Sister Jane had her first reality check when a woman assaulted her because the healing didn't work. But the Sister refused to press charges. An ambulance came and Jane resisted going to the hospital, but to no avail, her fan base insisted. Then, while prone on the gurney, a sheriff showed up and gave her a subpoena. Old Mrs. Archer is suing her. "

Vasquez chuckled. "You're making me laugh. What a circus."

"Yeah, the real joke? Sister Jane can't heal herself."

"What a surprise."

"But if she wanted more news coverage, she got it. I'm getting most of the firsthand stuff, but to get the whole shit-show, I'd have to almost live there."

"I believe it."

"Hey, I've got an idea. When she gets out of the hospital, I could ask her to work her magic on you."

"Very funny, Twomey. No thank you. I'll go gentle into that good night."

"You're misquoting Dylan Thomas. He wouldn't like that sentiment."

Vasquez smiled.

Twomey said, "Despite all the believers who swear by her authenticity, Sister Jane is starting to get pushback. I have a gut feeling she won't be in business too much longer.".

"What kind of pushback?"

"Well, more like this woman with the handbag or people holding up signs calling her a witch, and so forth."

"Oh, the Wiccans won't like that."

"My other problem? I can't find enough data to expose her. I didn't tell you the other day, but I pilfered a stack of some of her registration cards."

"And?"

"I called everyone. Out of that group, not a single naysayer. They give her all the credit, or God, or whatever. Some of them even went to a doctor for an affidavit. It's quite the operation."

Vasquez was fading. Twomey decided to leave and let the man sleep. Long hours of sleep were one of the signs near the end. He wondered if he should write the obituary after all. He could probably get a discount on the insertion if he did it locally. Would anyone care? He considered a visit to some of the art galleries in town in case they had any additional information on Maurice Vasquez. He checked his watch. After lunch he might peek in on Jane at the hospital.

31

SAME FRIDAY IN THE FOURTH WEEK OF LENT, JANE

When she woke up, the room was dark. She registered the sounds of monitoring machines and beeps. Was she dying?

"Mother?"

She turned her head and found Maddie at her side. Her head hurt a little and she tried to touch it, but her arm tangled in the sheet.

"It's a bandage. It's OK. You're going to be fine. Don't try to touch it," Maddie said.

"Oh. I've never been hit by a purse before."

"It was the buckle that did the damage."

Jane wanted to sit up but felt groggy. "What time is it? Why is it so dark? Is it night? Where are the kids? Where's Nick?"

"No, it's nearly noon, I can turn on a light. The lady on the other side has the window curtains closed."

"I need to get home. People are waiting for me."

"No one is waiting. We sent them all home. You need to rest."

"Maddie. You can't be in charge."

Dr. Sheldon, stethoscope around his neck and several pens and pencils poking out of his lab coat pocket, came in. Amos had been the Freedles' internist as long as she could remember. He looked as old as she was.

"Good morning, Jane."

"Hello Amos. Isn't it about time you retire?"

"I could say the same about you. I understand you have a small business out of your home?" He chuckled.

She looked at Maddie and then the doctor; she didn't find that funny. "When can I go home?"

"Shortly. I'm waiting for the test results. I doubt you have a concussion, but we wanted to be sure which is why we kept you overnight.

He checked her records on a laptop and then her head and eyes. After a few more routine questions, he said, "You need to take it easy Jane. Neither one of us is a spring chicken anymore."

"Do you believe in healing miracles?" she asked.

Maddie jumped in. "Mother, let's not get into that with Dr. Sheldon."

He took her hand, "Do you?"

"I don't have much choice but to believe. It's happening every day," she said.

"This whole thing," Maddie said, "is totally out of control. These are grandiose delusions, probably brought on by dementia. It may even be a Jesus Complex."

"Maddie!"

"I'm not trying to be mean here, Mother, but this has got to stop."

Dr. Sheldon said to Maddie, "Perhaps you should initiate an investigation. The Catholic Church has very rigid guidelines to identify and substantiate miracles. Something concrete like that may help the situation. It would take the emotions out of it."

"We're not Catholic," Maddie said.

"Doesn't matter," Dr. Sheldon said. "They investigate miracles in general."

"But doesn't that put credence to the preposterous?" Maddie said.

"Possibly." He turned back to Jane, "Tell me, I'm curious, was it you that entered Mable Archer's room a week or so ago?"

"It was. I confess. But that was early on. I don't do hospitals anymore."

"She's suing the hospital, you know."

"I'm sorry to hear that," Jane said. "She's suing me too."

"What?" Maddie said.

"But her heart is as good as new," he said. "I've got to continue my rounds. You should be discharged by two o'clock or so."

"Thank you, Amos. You still have that hernia? I, uh, you know, could pray for you?"

He turned to her at the door. "I'll let you know, thanks." He smiled and waved as he left.

"What is he talking about?"

"He has a hernia."

"Not that, the lawsuit."

"It's nothing really. Well, I mean it's something, but I'm not sure what to do about it. Nick said he would pass it to Richie."

"That must be why Richie is burning up my phone. I told him I'd call him back later. Of course, he's too busy to come to the hospital." Maddie said.

"It will work out. Where is Nick?"

"He has the kids, at your house. Madison is packing up a bag for you."

"What for?"

"You're coming home with me."

"No."

"At least for the weekend. Everyone's coming. Aunt Pearl is flying in, Celeste and Luke are coming, and so are Richie and Hang. Everyone is concerned about you."

Jane had a string of swear words on the tip of her tongue, but two things stopped her. One, she imagined herself on the fifth floor of the mental health ward, only two floors up from where she was now and two, there was a tap on the open door. Twomey. She wanted to be angry at him too, but for now, he would be a distraction to Maddie.

"Come in," Jane said, more loudly than necessary.

Maddie turned to the visitor. "Hello, may I help you?"

"I heard Sister Jane landed in the hospital and thought she could use some cheering up," he said.

"Please don't call her that. This is not a good time," Maddie said.

Jane had never noticed before how tall he was, which seemed silly considering how many times she had stood next to him. Perhaps it was because Nick was tall too, but where Nick was lean and dark, Twomey was pudgy around the middle. He had unruly salt and pepper hair and hadn't shaved. His eyes were very gray. He must have been quite the catch in his younger days. He held out a small bunch of flowers to Maddie.

"Those look like grocery store flowers," Jane said.

"But of course, nothing but the best for my girl," Twomey said.

Jane cocked her head.

"Kidding, just kidding," he said.

Maddie set the flowers down without putting them in water. Jane spoke quickly to Twomey, "You and Maddie have something in common."

He looked at Maddie questioningly.

"She doesn't believe in miracles either. This is Maddie, my youngest daughter, Nick's wife."

She thought she heard Maddie say under her breath, "For now."

"This is Twomey, I forgot your first name. He's a reporter."

"Wade. Wade Twomey," he reached out his hand to Maddie.

"Reporter? You're the one who wrote those terrible things about my mother?" Maddie glared.

"Wait a minute," he said.

Jane should have been upset by their little argument, but for some reason, she wasn't. It kept Maddie occupied and distracted her from discussing Jane's God-given gift. Jane didn't think anything could stop the gift, particularly not her daughter's opinion. But one thing struck home. Did Jane have a Jesus Complex?

A nurse walked in. "Sorry, folks, but Mrs. Freedle's bedmate is trying to sleep. Would you mind taking your conversation out in the hall?"

She watched them leave and heard the woman on the other side of the curtain thank the nurse. When the nurse closed their door on her way out, Jane said aloud, "Sorry about that roommate."

"Why were they arguing about miracles? I could sure use one about now," the woman said.

"Hang on, I can help with that," Jane said, Jesus Complex or not.

32

SATURDAY IN THE FOURTH WEEK OF LENT, NICK

They sat at Jane's dining room table to work on the healing service. Toni, Rovanda, and his Ma shared sub sandwiches he brought in with him. They reviewed all the graphics and handouts and social media posts. He asked Toni if there would be enough volunteers on board.

"We're covered," Toni said. "I've got eight male and four female ushers and two security. Do you think we need parking attendants? Rovanda got some nice baskets for the offerings and Bishop said he would come for the blessings and share a Spoken Word."

"That's great, but let's keep the preaching part down to a minimum," he said.

"Twenty minutes?"

"Twenty? Hell no, maybe five."

"I don't think he'll come for five minutes," Rovanda said.

"That's all right. The focus is on Jane anyway."

"But Nick, if we want the people to come out, they're going to expect a man of God to be on hand," Toni said.

"Fine. Fine. We'll need ticket-takers."

"Tickets? I thought this was a service?" Rovanda said.

"Yes, free tickets. I want people to register to get their tickets online. It's all there on Facebook. We need those emails."

"Good luck with that," Toni said.

Ma had been quiet most of this time. She finally asked, "Does Jane know about all this?"

"She knows about the service. It will be fine," he said. "Here's the thing. We have already raised about $3000 here at the house. I think we can pull in $20,000 next Sunday to cover our next service at the Arena."

"God will be glorified," Toni said. "That's why we're doing this, Rosalie."

"But how is Jane going to pray for all those people?" Rosalie asked.

"It will be like a lottery," he said. He checked his watch. "Crap. I gotta go. Maddie's got a big family meeting planned. Can you ladies finish up folding these mailers? I'll put them in the mail tomorrow. Thanks for everything. Ma, you ready?"

"I'm going to the meeting?"

"I could use your story," he said.

"Testimony, that's what we call it. Your testimony to the power of God," Toni said.

"Hallelujah," Rovanda added.

"I'll pass. Just drop me off at Cousin Sally's; she's on the way," Rosalie said.

He explained to Rovanda and Toni how to lock up and then escorted his mother out to the porch. Despite Maddie's huge sign that they had suspended healings until further notice, several undaunted people sat or stood on the sidewalk. He hated to discourage them, but he hated to give up his parking place even more. He had to get going or be late for the meeting. His mother was uncharacteristically quiet.

"Ma, are you OK?"

"Yes. Well, no. I'm a little nauseous."

"Mama, what is it?"

"I'm going to be sick." She vomited on the sidewalk.

33

SAME SATURDAY IN THE FOURTH WEEK OF LENT, TWOMEY

Twomey thanked Pastor Goodson for coming in on a Saturday morning to meet with him.

"I want to be clear, Pastor Goodson, I am, in no way, out to damage Jane Freedle's reputation or to endanger her in any way. But I do think it's important for the public to be somewhat careful when dealing with phenomena of this sort."

"Of course, of course. I believe, if we can all maintain the right tone, it will be easier on her when things become clear. I've been invited to a family meeting today at her daughter's home."

"An intervention then?"

"Of a sort," Pastor Goodson said. "Her family is concerned and hope to get her the help she needs. My wife is a psychotherapist and believes Jane is suffering from hyper religiosity. This sometimes occurs in people experiencing deep grief over the loss of a loved one."

"So, you're taking the mental health route? You've known Jane for a long time then? Did you know her husband?"

"Oh sure. Richard Freedle was a great guy. His heart attack came out of nowhere, a widow-maker. He and Jane were heavily involved in the church. Richard was on the Pastor/Parish Relations Committee. And before that, he was the treasurer and on the Administrative Board."

"And Jane?"

"She sings in the choir I think, or used to, and serves with the United Methodist Women."

"Have any of them reached out to her?" he asked.

"Well, yes and no. Unfortunately, Jane has done this prayer thing with a few of them and you know how it goes. These women can be impressionable."

"How many are we talking? One, two?"

"I don't know. Maybe a dozen or so."

"Jane Freedle healed more than twelve people in your church? Successfully?"

Twomey was frustrated. The more people he interviewed, the less useful evidence he found.

"How does one measure success in this situation?" Pastor Goodson asked.

The obvious answer was "not being sick," but Twomey didn't want to go there. They discussed some alternative ideas and a couple of people who might be willing to talk to the press.

"You might want to speak to Dan Gillespie; he's a family friend," Pastor Goodson said.

"He's on the healed list?"

"No, but he and I have talked, and he's concerned."

Twomey considered attending church on Sunday, but then thought better of it. For all he knew, lightning might strike. All right, he was being overly dramatic. He had checked out of religion when God checked out on him and his abusive father. If God couldn't answer the prayers of a ten-year-old boy, why bother?

He wrapped up the interview, then stopped at Cindy's desk. She was on her phone playing a word game.

"Hey," Twomey said. "How's the ankle?"

"Still great. Perfect."

"Pastor Goodson said you could help me with contact information for these people?"

He gave her the list. She scanned the names and then looked back at him.

"Why is it so hard for people like you and Pastor Sam to accept miracles?"

"Who said we don't?"

Cindy furrowed her brow, scanned her directory for the names and handed him the paper. "Mrs. Freedle is a wonderful and kind woman. She would never make this stuff up. So, go ahead. Interview the first couple on your list, Estelle and Henry Thyme. Estelle was the first, she told me

176

so. But I'll tell you this. Everyone, and I mean everyone I know, who Sister Jane touched, has renewed their faith in God. And here's something you may not know. Some of the people that were healed, they're starting to pray for people too."

"What?"

"For healing. Not at 100% like Sister Jane, but it's spreading."

"Oh, great."

He took the list and thanked the young secretary. The whole thing smacked of mass hysteria. But wasn't mass hysteria when large groups of people became ill, not well? He had a headache. Before he called the church list, he decided to follow up with his old friend Mabel Archer now that she had hired a lawyer, which he discovered while eavesdropping at the hospital outside Jane's room.

At the senior high rise, he rang Mabel's buzzer and waited.

"Hello?" she said, in a much kinder tone than before.

He introduced himself and asked if he could follow up on their previous conversation with a question or two. She hesitated and then he heard her speak to someone else.

"All right," she said, and buzzed him in. "Apartment 304."

When Twomey got to the apartment, he was surprised to find the door already open a crack. He pushed the door open and found Mrs. Archer had company, a young woman in her mid to late thirties and two children whose ages he couldn't guess, but probably under ten. The four of them played Mexican Train Dominoes, a game he played as a child. The younger woman looked up and smiled. She was a nice-looking woman and unassuming, with no make-up or jewelry except for gold crucifix at her neck.

"Hello, Mr. Twomey," the woman said. "My name is Susan. These are my girls, Edna and Rose."

"Hello. Nice to meet you," Twomey said. "I didn't mean to interrupt your party, Mrs. Archer. I can come back another time."

"No, no. It's fine," Mrs. Archer said as she laid down a tile. "Susan wanted to meet you face to face."

"Yes, Mr. Twomey, you see I am also a product of Sister Jane's prayers. However, you will not find me on your list because she asked me to

177

remain anonymous."

"And why is that?" he asked.

"Because of people like you, I would imagine," Susan said.

Mrs. Archer cackled.

He could sense this interview was not going as he had intended. He was already on the defense when he should be on the offense.

"And your illness, if I may ask?" he said.

"Nothing too serious; I had stomach cancer and several crushed Lumbar vertebrae," Susan said, and smiled.

"She's a walking miracle," Mrs. Archer said. "Get it? Walking?"

"That was funny Mabel," Susan said.

"You know," Mrs. Archer said, "I wanted to do stand-up comedy when I was in my twenties. But then I met Harold and had kids instead. We all did the family thing back then."

"What's a stand-up?" one of the girls asked.

"It's when you tell jokes in front of an audience," Susan said. She turned toward Twomey, "Was there something specific you wanted from Mrs. Archer?"

"It's your turn, Mommy," the other child said.

"Just a minute, sweetheart," she said.

Twomey put away his notebook. "I was curious about the lawsuit. Your lawsuit, Mrs. Archer? Just for the record?"

Mrs. Archer drank from her iced tea glass.

"It's a matter of public record, anything you would need to know." Susan said.

"Are you representing Mrs. Archer?" They laughed. This was going nowhere. He finally threw in the towel with one last question, "Will you both be at the big healing service next Sunday afternoon?"

"What service?" Susan asked.

Ah, so there was something they didn't know.

"It's a matter of public record on Facebook," Twomey said. "I'll let myself out."

Smartasses, he thought, as he took the elevator down. He wondered if this Susan character was telling the truth. Was she a lawyer? She would be the most dramatic testimony of them all. But what was the connection between the two women? He had not seen that coming. And what made Archer change her spots? He headed home with little information to add to his follow up-story. He might have to invent something. He would call the list again and see if anything budged.

He grabbed a late lunch from the restaurant below his apartment. At the top of steps, he was glad to see a package for Vasquez, small, but encouraging all the same. Why was he hanging around Vasquez? Was it the fantasy of Sister Jane laying hands on the man and having him rise in perfect health? That reverie had no legs. He dropped the box at Vasquez's door and tapped three times, their most recent and unobtrusive signal.

To his surprise, Vasquez opened the door. He looked a little stronger today.

"Is it over across the street? The crowds have thinned." Vasquez asked.

"Not yet."

"Tell me this, why aren't you castigating this woman in the press? I read your article; all quite accommodating. Where is the science? You are equivocating. I'm somewhat disappointed in you."

Twomey continued to unlock his door and tossed his laptop on the sofa. Vasquez followed and stood outside the doorway. "Easy for you to say," Twomey shot back. "I'm working with a bizarre combination of facts and fantasy. Just today, I met a woman who claimed Sister Jane cured her of stomach cancer and several lumbar vertebrae, which means she can walk. Another witness told me that other people are performing the same magic as Sister Jane."

"Did you see the woman walk?"

"No, not exactly. Look, I'm working on it. You want to help me out? Make yourself a guinea pig."

"That would give the appearance of hope."

"Or defiance," he said.

"No. Good day."

"Fine!"

34

SAME SATURDAY IN THE FOURTH WEEK OF LENT, JANE

The weather was extraordinarily warm for the first of April, so they congregated on Maddie and Nick's screened-in deck, a ceiling fan whirred, and a pitcher of lemonade sat on the side table. There was a nice view of the town below. Through the pale green of spring leaves popping out on trees, she caught glimpses of the glinting waters of the Bay.

If only someone would jump up and yell, "April Fool." She certainly felt the fool. Whenever she was around her family now, it was difficult to inhabit the "new" Jane called by God. Here, she was under the power of habitual behaviors, theirs and hers.

The only family members missing from this Maddie-inspired meeting were Nick and her twin brothers. Since the boys moved to Bela Vita Acres in Tampa, she doubted they were even invited or if they were, forgot about it.

She turned to her glass of lemonade as they continued to discuss her in the third person as though she wasn't there. She wanted to slip out, but big sister Pearl, who sat next to her, kept patting her left hand unconsciously.

"Can we get back to the here and now?" Pearl said. "Whatever happened before today we cannot change."

"Why can't we trust Mom? It's not like she has a history of weird behavior. What if—" Celeste tried to continue.

"You haven't been here Celeste, you don't know how difficult it has been to cope," Maddie said.

Celeste sat on Jane's right, the epitome of a middle child, but of course, not a child at all. She was the free spirit and more artistic one of the siblings, but her brother called her "new agey" and seldom treated her seriously.

"I'm here now and I have an opinion," Celeste said.

They stopped talking when Madison came out and complained that Luke was playing a violent video game with bad language. Celeste followed Madison back into the house.

"No surprise there," Richie said.

"I heard that, asshole," Celeste said, holding up her middle finger overhead.

"Celeste, please!" Maddie said

Richie sat with Hang. Jane had always felt sorry for Hang, who seemed to disappear in plain sight. They married ten years ago, but still no children. She wondered if she should pray for Hang one day. But was that a healing? What if they didn't want children? Richie kept checking his phone in between comments to the group.

"Why did you even bother to call Celeste?" Richie asked Maddie.

"She's still family and has the right to know what's going on. Besides, I didn't think she would come."

Maddie sat opposite Jane and next to Richie, a united front. Even when they were little, Richie would take Maddie's side and vice versa. Poor Celeste was always the odd man out. Funny, Jane felt the same way. Maybe she and Celeste were more alike than she knew. Celeste was trying to take Jane's side, but they needed back-up.

"Where's Nick?" Jane asked.

Everyone turned to her as though they had forgotten she was there.

"He's late, of course," Maddie said.

"Let's pray. I think we've started off on the wrong foot." Pastor Sam said.

Pastor was the surprise guest. What could his role be? The voice of authority on the spiritual nature of her gift? Or something else? Had his wife schooled him in what to say? She didn't want a psychological assessment.

"Should we wait for Celeste?" Pastor asked no one in particular.

"No, go ahead," Pearl said. "She doesn't believe in God anyway."

As everyone settled into their prayer poses, Jane considered Pearl's re-

181

mark about Celeste. Was it possible her daughter didn't believe in God? When did that happen? And yet, Celeste was the only one who appeared to be on her side. Where was Nick?

Pastor Sam prayed: "Dear Lord, give us strength, patience, and wisdom as we discuss this complicated situation. Give us open eyes and open hearts. Keep us mindful of your presence—"

She stopped listening. She fidgeted. She wasn't a crackpot. And yet, whether she liked it or not, her family could lock her up in a mental health hospital. It didn't seem to matter to any of them that she had proof. She wished she had called Sister Bernie in as a backup.

"Jane," Pastor Sam said after the amen, "the main thing we all want you to know is that you are loved, and everyone here cares about you deeply. We are concerned, yes, but no one wants to do you harm in any way."

If he thought that was reassuring, he couldn't have been more wrong.

He continued. "We have talked offline and all of us agree that you have been through a difficult three years ever since Richard died. Everyone misses him terribly, of course. And although you are a very capable woman, no one begrudges you this time of grieving. It is not uncommon for people in grief to become fixated on something. For some, it can be very destructive, like alcohol or even drugs. But because of your deep faith, it's been on things religious."

"Thanks everyone, but—" she started to say; Pearl cut her off, again with a hand on her left wrist.

"Hold on little sister. Give us a chance to tell you what we see and how this activity of yours has been affecting your family," Pearl said.

"I'll start," Richie jumped in. "I've already had people come up to me at work to ask about you. My boss called me into his office and told me this situation must be affecting my work. He said I seemed distracted, especially after I bungled a case last week. That's not me."

Maddie added, "I'm worried about the kids. They ask questions I can't answer. Why is Grammy acting so different? Why are there people at her house all the time? Is Grammy a saint? Really, mother, how should I answer that? The kids adore you but I'm not feeling comfortable having them around you like this. I'm sorry."

Jane held back tears. My God, she had no idea.

"I got here last night," Pearl said, "but the stories of your escapades are quite chilling. My dear little sister, I work with the sick and ailing all day long. I work with doctors. What you claim and what Maddie and Rich described to me, is bonkers."

Celeste returned with Nick in tow.

"Hello everyone, sorry I'm late," Nick said.

Nick looked like he had slept in his clothes. Did he have a hangover? He hadn't shaved that morning and his hair, normally perfectly styled, was messy. The family might send them both to the funny farm.

Jane got up and refilled her lemonade from the side table while Nick pulled up a chair next to Pastor Sam, completing the circle. Pearl brought Nick up to speed on what was going on. Jane purposely stood by the table and didn't return to the circle. She shivered. In the dogwood tree beside the deck, she saw a beautiful red cardinal. Right after Richard died, a cardinal had made nearly daily appearances outside her kitchen window on the crape myrtle. Somebody once told her it was a spirit messenger from Richard, letting her know he was nearby. She looked at the bird now and wondered if it was Richard again. Was he there to support her or condemn her along with the rest of them?

"I'm telling you, people, this is the real deal. I know it sounds nuts, but Sister Jane is not your mother or your sister anymore. She is an instrument of God," Nick said.

"You're not helping," Maddie said.

Nick went on to describe the many people who had visited Jane and the illnesses that her prayers cured. He talked about the joy in people's faces when their loved ones healed. He told stories about the sick little children and mothers who came to the house.

"None of those people returned to complain. If anything, they told their friends and those friends told their friends. Jane is a phenomenon."

"But Nick, why would God do this? What possible purpose would it serve for a woman like Jane Freedle, however worthy, to be given such a task and disrupt the normal flow of people's lives?" Pastor Sam said.

"And what happens when another case like the one yesterday comes along? When Jane is unsuccessful? What harm will the next disgruntled person do?" Maddie said.

Jane walked back to her chair and stood behind it. "I was not unsuccessful. That woman was not sick."

"So, what are you saying? You are judge and jury for who is sick and who is not? Should we call you Doctor Jane?" Richie asked.

"You are being mean," Celeste said.

"I'm being realistic. Mom. Look. I'm sorry. I love you. OK? Hang loves you. But people, intelligent, college-educated people, our friends and colleagues, do not—cannot—believe this is real."

"What will it take for you to believe?" Nick asked the group, turning from one to the other. "And what are you implying there, Richie, that just because I didn't finish college, I'm stupid enough to believe in miracles? You can be such a jerk."

"Says you? The ultimate screw-up?"

"Richie!" Jane yelled. This whole thing was going nowhere, she thought. Lord, help me.

"Whoa, guys, guys," Pastor Sam said as he stood between them. "Let's take a little break."

Jane watched Pastor pull the two men aside and talk with them quietly. She went inside and up the stairs to the kids' bathroom.

On her return, Pearl met her at the bottom of the steps.

"Let's go out on the porch," Pearl said.

Pearl wore a denim dress and her hair was in the same French twist she had worn for the past half-century along with her mandatory sensible shoes. Pearl was the same no-nonsense person she had been all their lives. Their mother had leaned on Pearl when Pop had his stroke. It was Pearl who arranged for the twins to move to Florida and into assisted living. It was Pearl who handled the burial service for their mother, without a tear. Yes, Pearl was a rock, which was great until that rock was about to drop on her.

Maddie's porch was typical of all the mix-and-match development homes on the hill outside of Lafayette's city limits; it was big enough for two chairs and not much else. Maddie had added a few hanging plants which warmed up the setting and a small table between the chairs with a metal rooster for decoration.

"Nice day," Jane said, putting off the inevitable lecture.

"You can't kid a kidder," Pearl said. "I'm not just anybody, you know. We've been sisters forever; I changed your diaper when you were a baby. I know you."

"You're not that much older than me. And I know you changed our mother's diaper too. So what? This is different. This is bigger than all of us."

"We are ordinary people, Jane. We live small lives. We get up in the morning, we go to work, we cook meals, we watch television, and we raise children when there are children to raise. We do the best we can with what God deals us. We endure."

Jane thought about their traditional, nearly humdrum lives, and she couldn't disagree. Up until a month ago, she felt the same way. She had been a cog in a very simple machine and like the little engine that could, she had kept going up and up an endless hill. But her life changed. Even though it was stressful and a bit strange, even though she had odd bedfellows in this journey, like Nick and Toni and Rosalie and Rovanda, even though some of her clients were unpredictable, she liked it. She believed in her mission. She had a purpose and she had her God and Jesus too. Jesus was her red cardinal, her spirit messenger. She could not stand down. If she had to, she would go it alone.

"I endure, but in this new life," she said.

"Don't you hear yourself, this grandiosity that God would choose you to be a faith healer or whatever you call it. Look at me. I love you. I have always loved you. But I am afraid for you. This is crazy talk, even delusional. If you keep going like this, I may have to do something radical."

"Are you threatening me?"

Pearl took a deep breath before she went on, "I'm warning you, yes. Don't you trust anyone in your family? Try turning the tables a little. What would you do or say if this was happening to one of us instead of to you?"

She pondered this question and had to admit she probably wouldn't believe it either. But what did she fear the most? Losing her family's goodwill or losing the gift of healing? She needed more time, a way to delay their determination to stop her work.

"You make a point, Pearl. What do you recommend?"

"Finally. All right. Let's go back into the meeting and discuss that very thing. What did Dr. Sheldon say when he saw you at the hospital yesterday?"

"Nothing much." The last thing Pearl needed to know was that Mable Archer, a faith-healing catastrophe, was suing the hospital and her. Maybe, if her family thought she was open to seeking help (whatever that might look like), then she could try to work something out, a compromise of sorts. She needed more time. She'd better get to Nick before Pearl made the announcement.

As they walked back out to the deck, Jane stopped and pulled Nick down to her level and said in his ear, "Follow my lead for the next ten minutes."

"What's going on," Nick said.

"I know this family better than you. Trust me. Hold your tongue."

As she sat down, she saw Pearl in a side conference with Pastor Sam, who was nodding. Her plan must be working.

"All right everybody, let's settle back in," Pearl said. "I know people are getting hungry, especially the kids, but pizza is on the way. Thank you, Maddie. Now, I had a private conversation with Jane, and she has agreed to take the next reasonable step in this process."

"That's wonderful news," Pastor Sam said. "We believe the easiest step forward would be for Jane to have a few conversations with a professional who would be sensitive to her faith values as well as her—well, state of mind and heart. I spoke to Stella this morning and she would be quite willing to take on this task."

"Who is Stella?" Celeste asked as she took hold of Jane's right hand. Jane squeezed back.

"She's a psychotherapist and Pastor Sam's wife," Maddie said.

"Excuse me," Jane said, "No offense to Stella, but I would prefer to see someone who doesn't know me, if you don't mind. Perhaps Dr. Sheldon would have a recommendation." Amos Sheldon was terrible about returning phone calls and she figured she could pick up several days playing phone tag with him.

"That's a wonderful idea," Pearl said.

186

"But Jane—" Nick started to say; she gave him a withering look and he stopped.

"What about in the meantime?" Richie asked. "Mom, can't you take a little vacation from this activity until you meet with someone?"

Her answer was blissfully bypassed when Mitchell came out yelling that the pizza had arrived. Everyone stepped into food mode. Pastor Sam came up to her and gave her a big hug.

"Everything's going to be fine. We'll bring everything down under the radar and you'll see, you'll be right as rain soon enough. Now, I've got to head out and do some edits to my sermon for tomorrow."

He said his goodbyes to everyone else and left out the side gate.

Celeste came up to her, "Mom? Are you OK really? I mean, I think it's very cool that you're able to step into an alternative state of being and manipulate reality. How did you learn to do that? I believe we should all be able to do what you're doing one day."

Jane kissed her on the cheek. "I love you, honey. Thanks for making the drive down. Where are you staying?"

"I have a friend with me from Philly; we're staying at her friend's house across the river. Luke asked to stay here and hang with Mitchell."

"That's wonderful. Let's eat."

Maddie pulled out an additional plastic folding table for the pizza. She brought out a large green salad for the adults and cookies for dessert. For the next hour, Jane allowed herself to enjoy the best parts of her family. The kids bounced around on the grass in the yard between bites, everyone passed around the baby, and no one mentioned the meeting or her gift within her earshot.

Nick seemed agitated when she finally got him off to one side and told him to relax. He kept talking about a lot of loose ends and he needed to head back to the house soon. She noticed his hands shook as though he was coming off a drug. Surely that wasn't possible, was it?

"Is there something you're not telling me? I could go with you to the house."

She didn't realize Pearl stood right behind them.

"Now Jane, I came all this way to see you and you want to leave? Come on, let's take a walk like the old days. I want to tell you about my retirement plans."

"So, you are going to go through with it?" she asked.

"I really am."

"All right," she said, "Nick? I guess you're on your own. But don't forget to feed the cats and cover the birdcage when you get back."

He smiled. She had grown fond of Nick over the last week or so. He could be so heartfelt and enthusiastic and loyal. Perhaps he had really changed. But then, she remembered his terrible history of poorly planned ventures. Was she just one more? She watched him attempt to talk to Maddie, but her daughter was having none of it. Once again, Jane wondered if God would answer a prayer for a broken marriage. Unfortunately, in this case, Jane was part of the problem.

Nick's phone rang; it sounded like the theme from the old "Jaws" movie. He turned away from everyone and stepped over to their privacy fence, and although he was trying to keep it down, she heard him say, "You gotta give me a chance to make this right. I'll call you back." He left the yard. Maddie stared. Jane had a bad feeling.

35

SUNDAY IN THE FIFTH WEEK OF LENT, JANE

When she woke early Sunday morning in her granddaughter's room, she groaned out loud. First, the bed was terrible; she didn't know how Madison could stand it. Second, her mind immediately revisited her late-night conversation with Maddie and Pearl.

"Here's the best part," Pearl said. "I already have my house on the market. As soon as it sells, I can move back here; we'll sell the family house, pool our money, and move into a condo. Won't that be great? Just like old times."

"Oh, Aunt Pearl, that's fantastic," Maddie said.

Jane became furious again, just thinking about it. But arguing with Pearl was like arguing with Richard, and worse, living with Pearl would be like living with Richard, too. Pearl would be in charge.

After begging off from Maddie and Pearl to go to bed, she had called a taxi to pick her up by 6:30 in the morning. She would live this day her way. She found her overnight duffle and repacked it quickly. She put on the same beige pants and then borrowed a Hopkins sweatshirt from Madison's closet.

She crept down the stairs and out the door to meet the cab at the curb. He drove her home and although it was a relatively short ride; she gave him a nice tip. Her plan was to change clothes, have a cup of coffee, go to church, and prove to Pastor Sam that there was no reason for her to skip church just because of a little notoriety. Afterward, she would enjoy a breakfast at her favorite café.

She reached the church a little late on purpose and went straight up to the balcony where no one sat for early service. All the same, Pastor Sam saw her right away; she gave him an innocent wave. He nodded but looked around to see if anyone else saw her arrive.

She stood to sing the first hymn, found the right page, and sang lustily.

189

When she sat down after the hymn, she caught Gillespie's stare. If only he would allow her to pray for Lindy. She waved to acknowledge him, but he merely crossed his arms. Not a good sign. As she perused the rest of the congregation from above, she saw Esther Thyme flap a bulletin to get her attention. Jane put her finger to her lips and closed her eyes. Hopefully, Esther would get the message.

At the midpoint, during announcements and before the sermon, Jane had a start when Esther stood up and interrupted Iris Barnhart's reading.

"I'm sorry to interrupt," Esther said, "but I would like to recognize Jane Freedle, who is here with us today, sitting in the balcony. Her prayers to God are healing people. In fact, several people right here in our congregation have experienced God's grace through her prayers. If God healed you through Sister Jane, please raise your hand. Oh, come on. I know people are here who went to see her. Let's give God a clap offering." The small congregation applauded weakly. Esther persisted.

"We should be proud that one of our own has been touched by God," Esther said.

Pastor Sam stepped up to the podium. "Why thank you, Esther, thank you. Perhaps we should continue—"

"Is that true, Pastor?" a voice called from the congregation. "Are these miracles from God or the devil?"

Jane held her breath. She knew very well that this was not how things rolled at First Church. People didn't stand up and speak spontaneously. There was an order to the service and anything out of that order was a shock.

Pastor Sam cleared his throat. "God is sovereign, and all things fall under his purview. Now let's pray and return to our order of worship," he said. "If anyone would like to speak to me after the service about this subject, I would be happy to discuss it with you."

And with that, everything went right back to the way it had been. Normal. She recognized the pivot immediately. The same thing had happened to her at Maddie's. Everyone had a routine and their expectations of others were based on the familiar and the ordinary. But her gifting was anything but normal and she could see now how uncomfortable it made people.

The next hymn was "*Trust and Obey*," a favorite. She looked down at the bulletin to check the sermon title Pastor had paired with the hymn: "*God Delights in Obedience.*" With no prior knowledge that she would be there, this message was not for her. No. This message was for people who might follow her, who might disobey. But disobey who? Would Pastor forbid or discourage his flock to visit her for healing? She felt a flutter of unease. Was this what Jesus felt as he swam upstream, against the norms of the day, against normal?

She waded through the sermon but bristled at his final point about people chasing after false Christs. Perhaps he would have been more direct if she weren't listening. Did he, like Maddie, think she had a Jesus complex? Pastor asked for a time of silent prayer with all heads bowed; he signaled her to meet him downstairs. Usually, after a service, he greeted people at the front door. Was he offering to have her shake hands with his constituents? Not likely.

"So good to see you this morning, Jane. But I think it might be better if you slip out ahead of everyone. You understand, don't you? We didn't discuss your plans to attend services today. It might cause more disruption than necessary at the crossover time when the 10:30 people are coming in."

"Sorry to be a bother," she said.

"Not at all. Just give me a heads-up next time," he said, and gestured for her to head down the side steps as the narthex doors opened.

She walked toward the café.

What if Maddie, Sam, and Stella were right? She pondered the possibility of having a Christ complex. She could be just delusional enough to believe God would choose her to do miracles much like Jesus. Would that be enough for the prayers to work? Aren't Christians supposed to believe that miracles are real and possible? That Jesus rose from the dead, was born to a virgin, made blind people see, and deaf people hear? Wasn't that the point?

"*You're being too literal. Many of these stories were metaphors,*" Richard said.

"But I'm not living a metaphor. I believe—"

"*Give it up, Jane. Stop now, and it will all go away. You're embarrassing the whole family.*"

191

"Go to hell."

She jerked open the café door and sat at one of the window tables. She wept and prayed. *"Show me, God. Speak to me with someone else's voice."* The 1950s jukebox played "All Shook Up" by Elvis Presley. God had quite the sense of humor.

"Are you OK Mrs. Freedle?" the server asked.

"Yes, yes. Sorry. I'll just have the western omelet and coffee, thanks."

"Look. Someone dropped this off yesterday. Is this for real? It's you, right?"

Jane looked at the flyer: *Palm Sunday Healing Service with Sister Jane, the Healer of Lafayette.*

"Ah. Yes. That's me." She didn't realize how far Nick had taken things.

"That's awesome. I'm gonna bring my aunt, she's got throat cancer. Can you heal that?"

"I don't heal. God heals. Listen, just skip the order. I think I need fresh air." She left the café and headed for the park.

She pulled out her phone to call Nick, but as soon as she turned it on, it rang.

"Mom? It's Celeste. Where are you?"

"I went to church. I plan to take a walk in the park. Tell everyone to stop worrying, I'm a grown woman for heaven's sake."

"Aunt Pearl is on a warpath. She sent Nick out looking for you. Can I meet you at the park?"

"What? Why? Never mind. Sure, fine." Jane turned off her phone. She would speak to Nick in person.

At the park, she sat in the gazebo and enjoyed the magnificent view and balmy spring weather. She loved it here; the river and bay stretched out before her and the city dock filled with visiting boaters. The park had early spring picnickers, not unusual on such a beautiful Sunday. Behind her, she could hear children laughing and giggling in the playground.

Richard slipped back into her thoughts. *"You know, you are taking on a serious responsibility here. I mean, anything could go wrong; people could sue you or even have you thrown into jail. You seem to think you can heal everyone. Even Jesus didn't do that."*

"Gotcha. According to Matthew and Mark, Jesus did heal ALL the sick. So there."

"Well, we know that didn't end well," he said.

"Very funny." He always had to get in the last word.

"Excuse me. Are you that faith healer? Are you Sister Jane," asked a man who stood at the rail of the gazebo.

She felt like Peter, who Jesus asked three times if he loved Him. She took a breath, was she, or wasn't she? "I suppose I am. Yes. That is who I am." There was no turning back now. So be it. She would walk out this new normal. She watched him walk the park and tell picnickers that she was there.

Celeste arrived shortly afterward and brought a friend with her. They stepped into the gazebo. Celeste hugged Jane.

"I don't have much time, I had to tell them where you are. But I need you to meet someone. This is Abigail Jacoby. She's my partner. And, well, we live together. We're a couple."

"What? Oh. Well, that's nice," Jane said.

"Nice to meet you, Mrs. Freedle. Or should I call you Sister Jane?" Abigail said.

"Hello, of course. I mean, whatever you like. Wow, you really caught me off-guard." She shook Abigail's hand and then hugged her and then shook her hand again. "Aren't we the modern family? I didn't have any idea. I'm sorry. I don't mean to sound so dense." She was prattling. "I suppose you didn't come here to ask for healing then?"

"Healing from what?" Abigail asked.

"Oh Mom, you're kidding, right?" Celeste said and gave her a sideways hug.

"Right. OK, that came out wrong," Jane said.

Like Celeste, Abigail appeared a bit arty; she highlighted her short hair with bright pink while her face and ears sported numerous piercings and her arms bore tattoos from shoulder to wrist. Her clothes were unremarkable.

"Can we go now," Abigail asked Celeste.

"Sure, sure. You'll be OK, Mom. I'm proud of you. We'll have you up

193

for dinner soon."

"All right." Celeste hugged her and the two women left. Jane stood on the steps and waved. "I love you, Celeste."

Jane hadn't handled that well. Sure, Abigail had a chip on her shoulder, but who could blame her? They were swimming upstream, too.

"Excuse me," a tall stately man said who stood before her. "My name is Calvin Dobbs, a man just told us that you are the faith healer I read about in the newspaper. This here is my mother, Mary Brown Dobbs, and this is my wife, Marian, our children, LaShon, Chastity, and Samuel."

"How do you do," Jane said as she shook hands with the family. People around the park stared and passersby slowed to see what was going on.

"We are asking you," Mr. Dobbs said, "as a family, to heal my mother. She says she doesn't want to be healed, but she is in a mighty amount of pain."

"Mrs. Dobbs, I am happy to meet you. I'm Jane Freedle," she said as she reached out to the old mother in the wheelchair.

The woman could have been eighty or a hundred. She was frail and her mouth drooped in a perpetual frown. She wore a flowered hat.

"I don't want to be healed. I want to go home and be with Jesus. I'm tired. I'm very, very tired," Mrs. Dobbs said.

Jane turned to her son, "I appreciate you wanting your mother healed, but really, it's not up to you. Or me, for that matter."

"Are you sayin' she has to want to be healed before it will work?" his wife asked.

"No. Not exactly. But I have prayed for people who did not want healing and it caused a lot of problems afterward. If she allows me to pray, I will, but in the end, it will be up to God, and her, whether she lives or dies or even gets better. Can you understand that?"

Other spectators came closer to the gazebo and sat on the grass behind the family.

"Please, Miss Jane, please pray for Grama," little Chastity said.

Jane turned back to Mrs. Dobbs and bent down to her level. "Mrs. Dobbs, I need your permission to pray. I can ask God to release you from the pain, but I can't promise there wouldn't be a request in my prayer for healing, too. It's kind of a package deal."

In a quiet voice, Mrs. Dobbs said, "I can remember when white folks couldn't wait for us to die. Now I got a white woman who wants me to keep on going."

"Please Grama. We love you so much," Chastity said at the arm of the wheelchair.

"All right, child. All right. But, Sister, whether I heal today or not, I could die tomorrow. And when I do, I'll be going home to my Jesus. I will not live forever. God don't want that."

Jane prayed. She recognized the voice of God through Mrs. Dobbs. Yes, this was Jane's time, but it was only a season of healing. When God achieved His purpose, she would stop. But, on no account, would anyone live forever through her prayers nor would she hold someone back if he or she was ready to die.

36

SAME SUNDAY IN THE FIFTH WEEK OF LENT, NICK

After driving around town for nearly an hour looking for Jane's car, he found it in her parking pad behind her house. What an idiot. Wherever Jane went today, it was either on foot or with someone else. He gave up the search and went back home.

When he got there, all the women were in an uproar. For some reason, they decided to take their fury out on him.

"Where is she? Where in the hell did she go?" Pearl said to Nick.

Then Maddie, "If you hadn't encouraged her on this cockamamie lark, none of this would have happened."

He remained silent. Maybe he had learned something from Jane after all. The more he tried to convince the family, the more upset they became. In fact, they were the worst ones.

"We should probably call the police," Pearl said to no one in particular, and yet, to everyone.

Maddie's phone rang and she punched it hard.

"It's Celeste," she mouthed to Pearl. "She's what? Where? Oh, for God's sake," Maddie disconnected. "Celeste reached Mom. Apparently, she went to church in a cab, and then walked to the park and has started praying for people.

"What? Dammit," he said

"Isn't that what you want her to do?"

"Not in the park," he said.

"I'll go get her," Pearl said.

"I'll go with you," Nick said. He told Jane a million times not to do spontaneous healings out in public because it would cause a storm wherever she was. Plus, it would take people away from next Sunday's healing service.

"Can I drive?" Mitchell said at the bottom of the stairs, having eaves-dropped.

Three adults answered simultaneously and not a single answer matched. "Sure, why not?" Nick said, "Maybe next time," replied Maddie, while Pearl said, "Absolutely not." In the end, Mitchell prevailed since they were only going downtown.

Maddie pouted a bit about staying at the house, but then the baby woke up from his nap and that was all there was to that.

When they arrived at the park, Pearl said, "Mitchell, stay in the car."

Nick didn't care if Mitchell followed. "Be sure to lock the car if you come."

His main concern was the size of the crowd and the lack of registrations. He couldn't get Jane to understand that they had to use basic business sense here. If she had kept him in the loop, he could have redirected this mess before it happened. Now they would have to deal with a crowd as well as Pearl.

The crowd was about five or six people deep, sitting on the grass around the gazebo with Jane standing up inside it, at this point, talking with a man. Some of the younger kids and teens were hanging on to the sides of the gazebo or sitting on the railing. People waited in a line too.

"Oh my God, is this happening?" Pearl asked out loud.

"Yeah, pretty much," he said to Pearl. When they reached the crowd, he said, "Hello folks. What a wonderful day for the hand of God to touch the people of God."

Several people, who sat in the grass around the gazebo, murmured "amens".

He worked his way up the steps of the gazebo, leading Pearl by the hand, repeatedly saying they were family. When they got up close, he could hear Jane use her simple prayer style. He wondered if Toni could coach Jane in ways to fire up the crowd with more dynamic exclamations and petitions for God's mercy.

"Thank you, Sister Jane," the man said as he held her hand and then kissed it. "God bless you."

"Thank you, Thomas. But that's not necessary. God is right here with us. It's God's power not mine."

"Yes, Sister. Thank you all the same. My knees feel better already."

Nick saw Pearl roll her eyes. She whispered into his ear, "How do we get her out of here without causing a riot?"

He smiled. "I got this." He started to say something more but then Jane turned to them and held up a finger for them to wait. Maybe it was a good thing for Pearl to see Jane in action.

At that point, a woman, accompanied by a young man, maybe her son, walked up into the gazebo in front of Jane. The woman carried a white, red-tipped cane. She and Jane chatted for a minute or two and then Jane put her hands on the woman's eyes.

"Did I hear that woman say she has macular degeneration? That's irreversible," Pearl said.

"She looks blind to me," he said.

"We have to stop this. It's cruel to that poor woman." Pearl stepped over to her sister. "Jane, please."

At first, he tried to stop Pearl, but then decided to let things fall where they may.

Jane opened her eyes and removed her hands from the woman's face. "Mrs. Anderson? This is my sister Pearl from out of town. She has never experienced a supernatural healing."

"Neither have I," Mrs. Anderson said. The woman was short, maybe 5'2" or so and a little overweight. She had dyed brown hair with a pretty healthy salt and pepper stripe down the middle. She wore no make-up, but she did have a pearl necklace over a simple print dress. She probably went to church that day.

"I was telling Sister Jane that I was at the early morning service at the Methodist Church this morning when one of the women of the church introduced the Sister to the congregation. I'm visiting my son, Tony, here, who works at the city dock. He has been my eyes and has described what everything looks like in this lovely town and the beautiful church. You see, I started losing my sight when I was in my early fifties. I can still see a little light on the edges, but mostly it's black."

"And you believe that a prayer can bring back your sight?" Pearl asked.

"Maybe. Maybe not. But it's worth a try, don't you think?"

Jane returned her hands to the woman's eyes and started to pray again.

Nick couldn't believe how different Jane and her sister were. Where Jane was slight, Pearl was stout. Jane was mild-mannered, Pearl was a little sharp and more severe. Where Jane was conciliatory, Pearl was somewhat combative. Right now, his biggest concern was that Pearl would stop the prayer in the middle and yank her sister down the stairs and stuff her into the car.

"Dad, what's going on?" Mitchell said from behind him.

He held up his hand for quiet. From the crowd, someone started singing Amazing Grace. A few minutes later, Jane removed her hands from Mrs. Anderson's face. Nick had been around Jane's prayers long enough to know that most people didn't usually experience an immediate healing. But as soon as he looked at Mrs. Anderson's face, he could tell she had.

"Oh, my sweet Lord," Mrs. Anderson said.

"Mom?" the young man said behind her. "Mom, are you all right?"

Mrs. Anderson dropped her cane and took Jane's face into her two hands. "You are truly an angel from God." Then she turned to look out over the crowd and out over the Bay. She cried out in great joy, "I can see. I can see!"

The crowd went wild. They lifted phones to take pictures and videos. Some people praised God and still others fell to the ground. He watched people phone their friends and family, while some looked like they were posting their pictures to social media. He looked at Pearl and she was as pale as a ghost. She had backed up against the railing as though she needed to steady herself. He smiled.

"Good stuff, right?" he said to Pearl.

Jane stepped over to her sister, "Are you all right, Pearl?"

Pearl stared; her mouth opened to speak but nothing came out.

He seized the moment and addressed the crowd. Jane could take care of Pearl.

"All right, folks. All right. We are so glad you could all witness this powerful demonstration of God's hand touching others through Sister Jane. Next Sunday, from 2 to 6 p.m., Sister will be at the high school auditorium for a city-wide, well no, a county-wide healing service. Get your free tickets on our Facebook page. But right now, Sister Jane needs to rest." He took his baseball hat and put it on the bottom step. "If you would like to support Sister Jane's ministry, in whatever way you can, drop your offering in this hat here on the steps.

Some people in the crowd grumbled, but in the end, they began to disperse and not too soon, as a local policeman strolled up to him.

"You folks have a permit to assemble here like this in the park?" the officer asked.

"No, sir. But we're not assembling. This was one of those spontaneous things. We're all done. See?" He indicated the people moving away from the gazebo.

"What kind of spontaneous thing?"

"Why, this is Sister Jane, the faith healer. Would you like to meet her?" He said.

"You don't say," the officer said as he came up the stairs. Nick was a little worried about leaving the hat unattended, but to his surprise, Mitchell picked it up and walked through the crowd.

"Sister Jane, there's someone who would like to meet you," he said. "This is—what's your name?"

"Banes, Ted Banes," the officer said.

"Sister Jane, this is Officer Ted Banes and this, sir, is Sister Jane."

Jane smiled at the officer, "Nice to meet you Officer Banes. I'm Jane Freedle. Is there something God can do for you?"

"Naw. I'm fine. Of course, I wouldn't mind a promotion," he said.

That was an interesting idea. Nick had never considered the possibility. Could Jane pray for jobs, or outstanding debt, or a new car? He could use that himself. He hadn't told anyone yet, but he didn't have a job anymore. Voorhies said it was the mayor's decision. What the hell. Whatever happened to second chances? Not to mention the investigation and Twomey breathing down his neck. He had tried to call Zach a dozen times, but the guy wasn't picking up. His only hope now, for any income at all, was Jane.

Jane laughed. "Well, Officer Banes, God has given me a very narrow scope. Are we in any kind of trouble?"

"No. You're fine. Sometimes the neighbors across the street from the park get agitated when there's a large unscheduled crowd," Banes said.

"We're leaving," Nick said as he gently took Jane's elbow. They walked through the crowd and several people reached out to touch her, not in a grabbing way, simply a tap or a gentle pat on the arm like a cat or dog. Some would reach out their hands and she would shake them quickly or touch their heads. He didn't think Jane was even thinking about the motions. Pearl, on the other hand, was in a different kind of daze.

When they got to the car, Mitchell was already in the driver's seat. He pushed open the front passenger door from inside for Jane.

"Come sit with me, Sister Jane, aka Grama Jane," Mitchell said.

Jane leaned down to look inside the car. "It can't be, you're driving already. I am so proud of you, Mitchell. Absolutely, you may take me home, driver."

"Aren't you coming back to the house?" Pearl asked.

"I need some alone time now." Jane said.

Pearl looked around the park, at her family, and then at Jane. "I think I'll take some vacation days this week. Do you mind if I stay in town with you?"

"I think that will be fine. Why don't you go back to Maddie's with Nick and Michell to get your things and Nick will bring you back in the morning," Jane said.

Pearl sat quietly in the back seat of the car.

Something important happened to Pearl in the healing of the blind woman. In all the time Nick had known Pearl, he had never heard her ask permission for anything.

37

MONDAY IN THE FIFTH WEEK OF LENT, JANE

She was barely through her morning ritual with the cats and parakeets when her house phone rang. She glanced up at her teapot wall clock to discover it was only seven in the morning. She considered letting the call go to voice mail, but what if it was an emergency. She answered.

"Hello, Jane Freedle?" a stranger's voice on the other end of the line said, *"this is Jill Ann Brown, guest coordinator for Fox & Friends. Are you familiar with our show?"*

"Yes, but—"

"We have been reading about your amazing gifts of healing and our producers are anxious to have you on our show. Naturally, all your travel expenses would be covered."

"No thank you," she said.

"This is such a wonderful story about faith and hope. Our audiences will resonate with you. Our people will believe you."

"No."

She hung up the phone. She liked watching that show sometimes in the mornings, but all she could imagine was more people stretched out in front of her house. She didn't need any more publicity. How did celebrities stand it?

"Did you hear that girls?" she said to her fur babies. "Your Mama is starting to believe she's a celebrity." Bart and Simpson didn't even look up from their kibble, while Miracle meowed.

She should have known the Fox phone call was only the beginning. In the next two hours, she heard from Sonya James at *Good Morning America*, who promised to respect her story, particularly Robin Roberts, who was looking forward to their interview; Thomas Alton with the *Washington Post*, who wanted a rebuttal from her about the allegations that she was duping the public; Jack McIntyre, who was the guest coordinator for Lester Holt and *NBC Nightly News* (they wanted her response to the Center for Inquiry assertions—she wondered what those were exactly); and Judy Ebel, from MSNBC's *Rachel Maddow Show,* who wanted to give her a chance to react to another guest reporter who would be appearing on the show: Wade Twomey, from the *Baltimore Sun.* Jane ground her teeth on that one.

At first, she was polite. But by the time she spoke to the Post reporter, she said, "I stand by every healing that God has done" and hung up. The last straw was the cable news request and their mention of Twomey. She slammed the phone down and seethed. She thought he was moving to her side, a little, or at least respected their agreement. What a fool she was. She unplugged her phone and turned off her cell. If she hadn't sent Pearl home with Nick and Mitchell yesterday, he could have handled these calls. The only problem was she couldn't be sure Nick would say "no" to these people. And what about Twomey's promise to handle the press? Perhaps she should go on the offensive and call him. Yes, after she calmed down, she would.

She went back into the kitchen and found three cats sitting quietly and staring at her. When she bent down to pet Bart, she ended up with a trio of purring cats rubbing up against her. They seemed to know she needed comfort. She also needed some downtime. She went out on the front porch and turned the hands on the "be back soon" clock to 1:00 p.m. and put the cookie jar back on the little table. She and Nick were still at odds about the signs for the jar. Since he wasn't there, she made a new sign: "Take what you need." Several people were already standing outside the gate anticipating a 9 a.m. start time.

"Hello everyone," she said. "I'm sorry to disappoint you, but I won't be having any prayer sessions until after lunch today. Please come back if you can."

She noticed the news trucks had left, which was a good thing. Only then did she see a dozen or so people on the other side of the street with placards; one sign said *"Beelzebub Lives Here"* and another, *"Black Magic is a Sin"* and still another, *"God will not be mocked."* They stood ramrod straight and silent, but their eyes drilled into her. She covered her heart as the words pierced. A stronger, more confident Jane would cross the street and speak with them. But she wasn't there yet. She felt her skin crawl. Those people didn't even know her.

Jane went back inside and up the stairs to get into her gardening clothes, intent on subduing her rebellious garden out back and prayerfully lamenting the protestors across the street. When she stepped outside, she remembered her decision to call Twomey. She went back inside and retrieved her cell phone and carried it outside. She scrolled through recent calls and found the only one without a name attached. She dialed.

"Mr. Twomey? This is Jane Freedle—"

"Hello Sister Jane, to what do I owe this morning call?"

"You should damn well know."

*"Whoa there, **Sister** Jane—"*

"Don't mock me. I am boiling mad right now."

"And why is that?"

"Stop interrupting me." She took a breath to check if he would speak again. Silence. "You still there?"

"Yes, Jane."

How did he manage to sound so disingenuous and sincere at the same time? "I'm talking about our agreement. Is this how exclusivity works? I tell you my story and you sell it around to the cable news networks?"

"I'm not selling your story; I'm selling my story that happens to include you."

"That's splitting hairs and you know it."

"Besides, how do you even know about that?"

"I was invited to be on the same show with you," she said.

"Nice, maybe you should do it."

She wanted to growl. "As a rebuttal! Rebuttal! That means you would be calling me a fake. You agreed to have an open mind and to tell the truth. Tell me, what proof do you have that people have NOT been healed? Tell me that. Go ahead."

There was silence again.

"Just what I thought. This sounds like something Nick would do." She hung up, stuffed the phone into her jeans pocket, grabbed the rake, and attacked the fallen leaves and twigs with it.

She looked up sometime later, when two people came out her back door.

"Ms. Freedle? My name is Corporal Meyers, and this is Specialist Thompson. Sorry to startle you. The front door was open. We have been instructed to be your escort officers today and to accompany you to a classified location. Here is our identification."

She stood very still; her garden rake braced in the crook of her arm. She couldn't gather her thoughts or put them in any semblance of order. She looked at their badges quite blankly, barely registering their affiliation.

"I don't understand," she said. "What are you talking about?"

"We have an order to escort you, ma'am. You are in no danger. Please remain calm. It's simply protocol. Would you please retrieve your identification, like a driver's license, and then we can be on our way?" Corporal Meyers said.

How often had she admired young officers with their close-cut hair and ramrod straight posture? But somehow, in person, and standing in her yard, they were intimidating. Even the young woman soldier was all business. What kind of specialist was she?

"I'll go inside with you, ma'am," the woman said. She gently took the rake from Jane and handed it to the corporal. "Everything's fine," as she put her hand under Jane's left elbow and got her moving.

"I'll pull around to the back here," Corporal Meyers said to his partner.

Jane stopped, "I need to call someone. I should call my daughter or my son-in-law, my sister, my manager, my neighbor. They'll be worried."

"I understand your concern, Ms. Freedle," Specialist Thompson said as she tugged at her elbow, "but unfortunately, we've been instructed that our movements are classified today. That means we can't tell anyone where you are going. But please understand, you are not under arrest or anything like that. It's more like a national security matter."

"National security? You've got to be kidding," Jane said.

"We do need to move along. Would you like to leave a note?"

"I'd like to change clothes and take a shower." But as soon as she said it, she could tell that Specialist Thompson was about to nix that request.

"I just don't understand what is happening." Her hands shook, which always gave her away. For the second time today, she was afraid. "I'm not a criminal. I think you've made a mistake. Maybe you meant the house next door?"

What made her throw her unknown neighbor under the proverbial bus? That was a desperate move. The soldier shook her head. Jane walked mechanically over to the armchair where she normally left her handbag. Miracle was sitting on it.

"I can't take you with me," she said and gently stroked the cat's head.

"May I pet the cat?" Specialist Thompson asked.

"You like cats?"

"Love them." She put her hand out to Miracle and much to Jane's surprise, the cat didn't hiss or eagle-eye stare at the woman. This made her feel better.

"All right, then. I'll write the note. What time should I say I'll be back."

"I don't know for certain, but by this evening since we weren't instructed to bring along anything for an overnight stay. By the way, do you have a cell phone? I'll hold it for you."

Jane retrieved the cell from the kitchen table and handed it over and then sat to write a note. Her hand shook and she tried to take a deep breath. Specialist Thompson turned off the phone.

"I promise, Mrs. Freedle. You will be perfectly safe. Are you ready? We'll leave out the back way. I think it will cause less of a stir."

38

SAME MONDAY IN THE FIFTH WEEK OF LENT, TWOMEY

There's was something about a second cup of coffee in the morning that was most satisfying. He stood at his side window and watched Jane's house, a habit now, since there was always something happening. The latest addition to the scene was a group of protestors. That would play well on the evening news once they heard about it. He had told Jane he would handle the press, but he hadn't anticipated this little twist. Despite himself, he had to admit they were a little creepy in their silent vigil. He wondered if Jane knew. He would go down soon and ask a few questions, but he needed to wait for the interview prep call from MSNBC.

When his phone rang, he assumed it was them, only to hear Jane's voice. She got the better of him. When she hung up after comparing him to Nick, his conscience via the little white angel on his shoulder squealed. Maybe he shouldn't do the interview after all. He hadn't checked with Chuck either, just rode out like the Lone Ranger he liked to be. The coffee tasted bitter in his mouth; he walked to the john and poured it down the sink. He grouched, *Fine, Mr. Higher Power, but if I do this right thing, you owe me one.*

He texted Jane, "*All right. You're right.*" Then, he erased that and wrote, "*All right, you win,*" erased that one too and finally wrote, "*All right, I'll wait.*"

He went back to reading the online news. The next time he looked outside, a heavy-duty black Chevy Suburban pulled up to Jane's and double-parked. Two soldiers climbed out and walked up to the house. When no one answered the bell, they tried the door and entered. The sick and needy, who normally lined the sidewalk had dwindled, and the press vans had disappeared. Two minutes later, the corporal came back to the car and pulled away.

He called Jane's cell phone, but it went to voice mail. What kind of trouble was this? It made no sense. He grabbed his stuff and headed down the stairs. He walked through the protestors, across the street, and through Jane's front gate.

He tried the front door and found it still unlocked. He closed the door and locked it behind him and called out for Jane. No answer. He walked through the house and into the kitchen. He looked through the back door in time to see Jane helped into the back seat of the Suburban; the female soldier sat next to her. "Shit." In a perfect world, he would "follow that car" but he was low on gas. When he turned, he saw the note and her cell phone on the kitchen table.

Dear Nick, Pearl, and Maddie, I am being taken to a classified location by two Army escorts. They say I am not in trouble but won't tell me anything else. I should be home later this evening. Please pray for me. J.

He wrote on the bottom of the note, *"Call me when you get back. 2-me"*

Nothing more to do here until Jane came back. He had learned a long time ago that worry accomplished nothing. On his way out, he stopped at the bookcase next to the fireplace. Along with a wide variety of books, she had many family photographs: the young bride with her dapper husband, another with both families lined up on either side of the newlyweds, a huge family photo at the beach somewhere, probably Ocean City. Twomey was an only child and had been jealous of large families. But as he grew older, the idea of chaotic special occasions left him cold. Her family looked like a cacophonous nightmare. Tucked behind her kids and grandkids, he found one small picture of Jane in her twenties, wide-brimmed hat in one hand, while her other hand had pulled her long brown hair out of her face. She looked resplendent. He pocketed the picture.

He shook off the nostalgia and headed back out the front door.

He walked directly across the street to his apartment building and up the stairs; he stopped at Vasquez's door and knocked his agreed-upon rap. The door clicked open.

"You need anything? I'm heading out again soon," he asked.

"There's a list on my counter, next to the water purifier."

"Sure, boss, let me fetch that for you."

He wiped the doorknobs with the hand wipes and then put on his gloves and booties before entering further. Vasquez was painting again, but no longer in bright vibrant colors, but in blacks and grays.

"What's that, your death wish?"

"It's my death reality burgeoning forth from my soul," Vasquez said.

"Poetic. But dark. Do you even want to live?"

"Of course, but not enough to trust my fate to a charlatan or stand on a sidewalk waiting for the breath of God to breathe on me."

"You believe in God?" Twomey asked.

"Of course. But my God may not be like your God. My Savior may not be like your Savior."

"I'm sticking to my higher power, that's the extent of it."

Vasquez went silent. Twomey watched Vasquez place a very thick, very vibrant red splotch in the upper right quarter of the dark mire.

"What is that? The Angel of Death?" he asked.

"Maybe. Or an Angel of Light."

Twomey glanced outside and saw Nick's 4x4 pull up.

"I'm gonna run. I've got some questions for Nick," he said, and removed his sanitary gear.

"Why are you getting so entangled with these people? I ascertained that your interview on cable news this evening was of paramount importance. I will be watching by the way."

"I'm rescheduling."

Vasquez turned. "Why?"

"I made a deal, that's all. Oh, hey, I forgot to tell you about the military escorts who came to pick up Jane. Her story is far from over, so I'm keeping all my options open. Don't worry, I got this," he said and waved away his friend's concerns.

"You're losing clarity of purpose," Vasquez yelled as a parting shot.

Once across the street, he found Nick fumbling with the front door key.

He grabbed the jar of money and pushed open the door.

"Jane?" he called.

Twomey followed him into the house through the open door. "She's not here. There's a note for you on the kitchen table."

"Who the hell asked you to come here? What the hell is going on? I'm gone for a few hours and all hell breaks loose again. What are you talking about?"

"Two military types, an escort of sorts, came and put her in a car and drove away. They were in uniform. I'm guessing the feds are getting involved."

"What? Why? What for? She hasn't done anything. This is the freakin' United States of America. What's happening to our country?"

"Maybe they want to interrogate her or test her?" he said.

"What the hell for?"

"Think about it. She claims to heal. The army has sick soldiers. Who knows? I've got to go and send in some copy and then head to a city council committee meeting."

"Wait a minute. What are you saying? The government is interested in her healing gift?"

He shrugged and left as Nick started a string of curses that would curl anyone's toes.

39

Same Monday in the Fifth Week of Lent, Jane

One officer drove while the other sat with her in the back seat. No one spoke for the longest time. Her leg jiggled. She didn't know for sure why they were secretly abducting her, but she assumed it was because of her gift. It certainly felt like an arrest since she was going "who knew where" against her will. Perhaps she should have put up a struggle instead of being led like a lamb to slaughter.

"Baaaa," she said under her breath.

"I beg your pardon?" the woman said.

"Oh, sorry. I didn't mean to voice that. Honestly," she leaned over to look at the officer's nametag, "Officer Thompson, I thought we lived in a free country. Since when are God-fearing, flag-waving citizens taken by force to a secret location? You know, I'll be contacting my Congresswoman as soon as I get back. I'm sure my rights are being violated this very moment, Officer Thompson."

"Specialist. I'm Specialist Thompson. It happens more often than you think," she said.

"What does?"

"Taking people to classified meetings. It just means you're valuable."

"That's not very reassuring, Specialist Thompson." she said.

Another silence descended.

"I don't understand why I couldn't make one phone call. Even criminals can make one phone call," she said. "You have my phone. It would only take a moment. You could listen. I can be discreet."

Thompson shrugged. "I left your phone behind."

"I should have called the police."

"I'm sorry, ma'am, but our authority outstrips the local police."

"Where are we going? Can't you tell me now?"

No answer.

"I don't understand what is happening to our country. I am a citizen and I have rights. I'm not a bad person. Do you know why I'm in this predicament? I know. It's because of the gift."

Specialist Thompson looked at her and started to ask her something.

Her partner turned his head, "Thompson, let it go. Ms. Freedle, we are only the messengers. We have our orders. Everyone will treat you with respect and no harm will come to you."

She gave up and stared out the dark windows. She decided prayer would be her best option. She murmured a few words to calm her fear.

As they drove straight through Baltimore, she determined they were heading to Washington. Would they be going to the Pentagon? When they hit I-495, they headed to the right toward Silver Spring and soon, she saw the Mormon Temple rise above the beltway. She wondered what the Mormons would think of her gift. Did they believe in miracles? But then she shook off that question. What difference did it make? So far, she hadn't witnessed God make a distinction between believer or non-believer, saint, or sinner, Baptist, or Muslim. She thought about the story of the Canaanite woman who had asked for healing for her daughter; Jesus demurred and said the woman was not of the House of Israel. But then, the mother reminded him that even dogs received crumbs under the Master's table; He relented and healed the girl. Jane believed in that space where Jesus extended mercy without boundaries and healed them all. And if that was true for Him, then she would rest in that truth more intentionally. Again, Sister Bernie's words echoed, "Do good as long as you can, and then don't."

They were on city streets now, somewhere on the southern side of D.C. It might even be one of those outlying communities like Arlington or Alexandria since she saw a lot of office buildings. When they pulled into a driveway underneath a glass and steel building, she saw no sign out front. Was it the NSA? They parked underground and her escorts took her up the elevator to the fifth floor, into an empty conference room, and then offered her a cup of coffee or a soft drink. She shook her head and sat down at the conference table. Her escorts didn't leave, but stood by the door until several people came in. She sat on her hands.

She heard all the introductions of the half dozen or so who entered, yet the names flew through her brain. There was a Colonel Michael something who was also a doctor and chief of something, Dr. Landon Light, an assistant director who appeared to be in charge of the meeting, a couple of other scientist PhD types, one in a lab coat and the other, a lovely Asian woman whose name sounded like Miko or Mikado or something like that (she was in a uniform), and a couple of older men in traditional suits and a younger one in a light-colored jacket and bow tie. Everyone did a lot of smiling and handshaking before they settled around the conference table.

"Mrs. Freedle, allow me to apologize for all of the intrigue. But this is a unique situation and we wanted to fly under the radar if possible," Dr. Light said.

She inadvertently let out a little "ha" but then added, "Sorry."

"You are sitting in one of the most important agencies in the U.S. government called DARPA. Have you ever heard of us?"

"No, sorry."

"That's fine. DARPA is an acronym for the Defense Advanced Research Projects Agency. Our mission is to discover innovative and breakthrough technologies to maintain our national security and to restore and maintain our warfighters' abilities and health. We have studied all kinds of capabilities, capacities, and skills. But we are not the only agency interested, which is why Colonel Deina is here from MEDCOM and Baxter, from the NSC. We have heard about you and wanted to meet you."

She looked around the table. Stunned, she said, "How?"

"That's not important at the moment," Light said. "But we would like to ask you a few questions."

"And if I refuse?" She had no plan to refuse; she just didn't want to roll over. Would they put her in jail or solitary confinement?

Mikado spoke, "Ms. Freedle, of course, you could choose not to cooperate, but we hope you won't do that. We are scientists and researchers here. We are curious. If it's true, that you can do the things we have heard about, then we want to know more about it."

"Tell me your name again," Jane said.

"Emiko. Dr. Fujihara. I am a clinical psychologist. My specialty is preternatural phenomena, telepathy, and clairvoyance."

"I think there's been a misunderstanding somewhere. I don't do these things. I'm not clairvoyant nor do I teleport people. I'm more like a tool that God wields. There's no science to it," she said.

Another man spoke up. He was young, like Dr. Fujihara, and had a scar from a cleft palate operation that made him somewhat endearing. He shaved his hair short on the sides like a soldier but kept it long on top. She assumed it was a trendy style.

"My name is Baxter. Emiko, I mean Dr. Fujihara, and I are colleagues. We're hoping you would want to tell us your story. We are here to listen without judgment. Honestly. I mean, you must admit, what is happening in your life right now is quite special. Aren't you a bit overwhelmed? I know I would be."

"At first. Yes. But I got some counsel from a nun friend of mine. And it's better now. Well, it was better until your cavalry arrived. Could I get some water after all?"

Baxter smiled, walked over to the credenza, and brought over a mini water bottle and a cocktail napkin. She closed her eyes and threw up a flash prayer for God to give her the right words. What the hell, she thought.

She launched into her story, nearly the same story she had told Sister Bernie not ten days earlier and to Lindy on Wednesday. Had it only been that long? She told them about the cat and Esther Thyme (and of course, Henry, who came along later), and she went ahead and told them about May Winston and later how people came to her door. She explained about the registration cards since she couldn't keep all the names straight in her head. She did not tell them about Susan, to protect her from further inquiry. She explained how one thing led to another and how Nick got involved and how she was no longer going out and looking for people, but they were coming to her. She didn't mention the healing service since she was still uncomfortable with that whole thing anyway. And she certainly didn't mention the lawsuit.

Dr. Fujihara spoke first, "How does it feel when you are healing?"

"I'm praying. I don't feel anything."

Mr. Light said, "What is your success rate?"

"I beg your pardon?" she said.

"He means how many people are successfully healed?" Baxter said.

"All of them."

"What?" the colonel said and then the room erupted into a bunch of side conversations. She took a swig from her water. Baxter winked at her and smiled. She saw him look at Dr. Fujihara and mouth the words, "I told you so."

"Are you telling me that you say a prayer over these people and they simply jump up as if nothing is wrong with them?" the colonel said over everyone's talking. The room silenced.

"Well, not exactly. Some people experience immediate healing, but others seem to have a delay. I don't know why. It's not mine to know."

"Tell me Ms. Freedle," Dr. Fujihara said, "Is this something you can do at will? Anytime? Anywhere? For anyone?"

"Yes. I suppose. It's not like I go around tapping people on the head or anything. We usually have a conversation first and then prayer. I think the person has to want to get better."

"What do you mean?" Baxter asked.

"I've had a couple of unfortunate circumstances when one woman was healed but she wanted to die. I felt bad about that one. And then another woman came for healing, but she wasn't sick, so she beat me up."

"Holy shit," another man spoke under his breath.

"Baxter," Dr. Light said, "would you please take Ms. Freedle to the cafeteria. I'm sure she would like some lunch. We're going to have a talk (we'll pull you in later) and then we'd appreciate it if you and Mrs. Freedle would join us again after lunch. We will have you home again by this evening. Now, if you can promise not to mention where you are, I'm sure Baxter can find a phone for you to call home and you can let everyone know you are all right."

When she and Baxter were out of earshot, she asked, "Am I in trouble?"

"Not at all," he said. "You are amazing. I think you are handling yourself like a pro. The cafeteria's in the basement. Here's the elevator."

Since lots of people were around, she didn't say much until after they picked up their food, cafeteria style, and sat down to eat.

"What will the rest of them do for food?" she asked.

"Upstairs? They have assistants who will order in sandwiches so they can have a working lunch."

"And why were you picked to be my babysitter?"

He laughed. "I like you Jane Freedle. You were my idea."

"What? How?"

"You see, I'm Susan Baxter's brother-in-law. Small world, heh? I noticed you didn't mention her in your story."

"Oh. Yes. Well, she's special, that's all."

"She is indeed. My brother is a lucky man."

"But wait, Baxter is your last name and not your first name?"

"Yeah. It stuck from my service days."

In his late thirties, she guessed, Baxter was one of those men who always seemed comfortable in his skin; no matter where he was (office or cafeteria), he appeared confident. She didn't know many other young men who could look sexy while wearing a bow tie on a pale blue shirt tucked into khakis. He was also a fast eater and consumed his hamburger in short order. She wanted to kick herself for ordering an egg salad sandwich; after all, she ate eggs all the time. One of these days the cholesterol would catch up to her.

"Tell me, Jane, may I call you that? I'm curious, have you seen God heal someone with mental illness?"

"No one like that has come to me so I don't know the answer to that question. Same with open wounds although Esther's cut was bleeding or addictions."

"Do you get tired or drained?"

"Not really. If anything, a little energized. My turn to ask a question. What happens next?"

"I don't know for sure, but I can make an educated guess. If there's time today, they'll ask you to pray for some folks so they can see the process for themselves and then test the people afterward."

"What are you saying? They have a room full of sick people waiting for me to pray for them?"

He laughed. "No, but a hospital is nearby. Would you be all right with

216

that? To pray for some of our military people?"

"I guess so. But it makes me nervous to ask God to prove a point. It's like testing God."

"You focus on the person, like you normally do. If anyone's testing God, it's the U.S. Army and DARPA. Now, how about that phone call? Whom would you like to call?"

She thought through all the possibilities and opted for Pearl. After witnessing the healing in the park, her sister had changed her attitude. Jane guessed this new Pearl would not yell at her on the phone either. She used Baxter's phone. The call went as she expected with Maddie in the background demanding more information and the baby crying.

"I'll let everyone know that you are OK. Hey, Nick keeps complaining about a man who lives across the street and says he's butting into our business," Pearl said.

"That would be Twomey. He's a reporter for the Aegis. He lives over the restaurant on the corner. I run hot and cold with him."

"Hot?" Pearl asked.

"Not that kind of hot. For God's sake. I've got to go."

Baxter acted like he was reading a brochure about the nutritional value of food in the cafeteria, but she knew he was monitoring her conversation to make sure she didn't say anything that would cause a problem later.

"How'd I do?" she asked.

"Great, but now I'm interested in the hot and cold journalist."

"Stop it. What is your role here anyway?"

"If I told you, I'd have to kill you," he said and smiled. He took his phone from her and checked for messages. "They're ready for us. You need a restroom first?"

"I do, thanks."

When they got back to the conference room, only Dr. Light and Dr. Fujihara remained.

"I hope you had a pleasant lunch," Dr. Fujihara said.

"I'm very good company, very entertaining," Baxter said and smiled at

217

the good doctor who rolled her eyes.

"Mrs. Freedle," Dr. Light said, "would you be willing to use your talent on some of our patients at Walter Reed?"

"Gift. I prefer calling this work a gift since I don't do anything but pray and believe."

"Gift, then," he said.

"All right. Walter Reed? Isn't that where they take presidents and other government dignitaries?"

"Yes," Dr. Fujihara said, "but I doubt you'll be meeting any of them today."

"That could be interesting," Baxter added.

"No," Dr. Fujihara said directly to Baxter.

"Excuse me," Dr. Light said, "can we take that conversation offline? Mrs. Freedle, can we move forward with a visit to the hospital?"

"All right, but please remember, I don't control the timing."

"Yes, you mentioned that before," Dr. Fujihara said. "I think that's a fascinating twist."

The four of them went back down the elevator to the garage and climbed into the Suburban with the same driver, Corporal Meyers. She was glad Baxter was with them, despite him being so top secret; he knew how to make her laugh.

She rode in the middle, between Dr. Fujihara and Baxter, while Dr. Light rode upfront. Dr. Fujihara had changed into civilian clothes during the lunch break. Jane was glad; the doctor looked less formidable. Dr. Fujihara was not a conversationalist, more the quiet, introverted type, or perhaps she couldn't slip any words into Baxter's rambling commentary. Jane wondered again if they were an item. That thought made her smile.

They parked in the staff garage of the hospital and Dr. Light directed the driver to several reserved spaces.

"Are you all right to walk a bit, it's about two blocks to the Arrowhead building," Dr. Light asked her.

"Do I look that old and decrepit? I think I can manage."

Baxter leaned in and whispered in her ear, "You tell him."

She gave Baxter a good-natured thwack on the arm the way she used to do to Richie.

As they walked, someone ran up to Dr. Light and gave him a sheaf of papers. She guessed it was the patient roster. She felt her heart skip a beat. Wasn't this what she had wanted all along, some corroboration? Respect? If the scientists confirmed her healings, then she could mollify Maddie and convince Twomey. But was it ever about the science? Or was it about faith? Should it matter to her who believed or who didn't?

In the first two rooms, the patients were unconscious, but their doctor met the group there to tell her about their ailments. When he stepped back and gave her access, she focused on doing what she normally did. She talked to them as though they could hear and understand her. She told the patients what she was doing but asked silently if God permitted her to pray (she had added that ever since the terrible experience with the purse lady). When she finished, she thanked the patient and God. That was it.

After about ten patients, Dr. Light said, "That was our last scheduled patient; perhaps this would be a good time to sit down and talk. I believe Dr. Fujihara and Baxter are in the conference room waiting for us.

Once seated, Dr. Fujihara spoke, her voice calm and soothing.

"Thank you, Ms. Freedle, for sharing your gift with us. I have to say, this has been an extraordinary experience. And although we will need several days for follow up and testing, we have an additional proposal for you."

Jane looked from Dr. Fujihara to Dr. Light to Baxter and back to the Dr. Fujihara. "I don't want to stay here if that's where you're headed with this. I want to go home."

"We're concerned about your safety, Mrs. Freedle," Dr. Light said.

"Safety? What? Why?"

"I'm not sure you understand the implications. If these healings are certifiable, you could become an asset to our national defense," Dr. Light said and then added, "We have an apartment nearby that is completely secure. You would be our guest."

"You mean a prisoner," she stood. Her voice cracked, her hands shook, and she clenched them together. "I'm not a dog or a monkey you can

219

train to follow your orders. I'll call my Congresswoman. I'll call my lawyer. I'll call the police."

"Hold on. Hold on, Jane, you are absolutely right. It's OK. You're right. I think there is a better way for us to work together," Baxter said. Dr. Light started to speak, and Baxter held up his hand. "Please sit down. Jane. Please?"

Dr. Fujihara touched her arm. "Yes, Ms. Freedle, please sit down. Baxter and I have discussed an alternative while you were finishing up your rounds. Dr. Light, will you indulge us?" She gave him a look that seemed to say, "let me handle this." Dr. Light crossed his arms.

"Here's the idea," Baxter said, "you go home but we go with you."

"We who? Those escort officers?"

"No, no," Dr. Fujihara said, "but if you would allow it, I would like to come and spend time with you, to watch how you work in your own space. In that way, when I have questions, I could ask you in person. I won't be in the way. I promise. I'll be like a fly on the wall."

"Be careful, lots of spiders live in Lafayette," Jane said. "Listen, I don't understand what you are all talking about; you're acting like something bad could happen to me." She watched as Dr. Fujihara and Baxter exchanged glances again.

"Not yet. No danger yet; we want to keep it that way," Baxter said.

Dr. Fujihara added, "It's not about that for me. I want to learn from you. Perhaps there's a motel or B&B nearby where I could stay?"

Jane laughed. "You wouldn't want to stay in any of our local motels, you might get propositioned. The B&B's are nice downtown, but usually booked this time of year. How long are we talking about?"

"A few days, maybe a week, while they monitor the patients here; they'll keep me posted on their progress and I'll update you," Dr. Fujihara said. "We want to be transparent here. You deserve that."

Jane wasn't sure if she should start laughing hysterically or crying. The whole day was like a very strange dream. If Richard was in the room, he'd be saying "yes sir" and "no sir" to all these important people, but once they got home, he'd have her hide and tell her she was wasting everyone's time. What would her family say?

"We'll come up with a good story to tell your family," Dr. Fujihara said.

Jane wondered if the woman could read her mind. "How did you know I was thinking that?"

Dr. Fujihara smiled. "It's logical that you have those concerns. Honestly, I do not read minds."

"I can vouch for that," Baxter said.

Jane laughed. "If you say so. Should I call you Dr. Spock? All right. I give in. When can we leave?"

"A Star Trek fan? I knew I liked you, Jane Freedle," Baxter said.

"Baxter, please be serious," Dr. Fujihara said and then to her. "And may I call you Jane? You can call me Emiko."

"Of course," she said.

"We're agreed then?" Dr. Light said.

Baxter said, "So it appears. But I have a twist we could make to these arrangements. How about the doc stays in your home, Jane? I bet she and Nick would get along beautifully."

Emiko gave Baxter a look. Jane was sure of it now. They were friendly on the side.

"Wait a minute," Jane said, "how do you know about Nick?"

Baxter put his finger to his lips, "If I tell you —"

"Never mind," she said and shook her head. "But Emiko — did I say it right — you'll have to sleep in the children's playroom on a bunk bed and we all share the same bathroom."

"I could sleep on the couch," Baxter offered.

"No," Emiko said, "you will stay at your brother's place."

"Fine."

40

TUESDAY IN THE FIFTH WEEK OF LENT, NICK

His brain was in high gear as he clomped down the stairs at Jane's. Maddie had made it clear he was not welcome in her bed. (When did that expensive king-size bed become hers?) It was just as well. He only had a few more days to promote the healing service on Sunday. This event had to be successful and he meant financially above all. He needed something good to happen before he told Maddie about losing his city job and the upcoming investigation.

He smelled bacon frying; Jane was up and cooking in the kitchen. As he crossed into the dining room, he saw the new girl come out of the kitchen and prop open the swing door. She had taken over part of his workspace on the table already. What the hell?

"Uh, hi," he said as he reached across the table to shake her hand. "We didn't get a chance to meet last night. I'm Nick."

"Yes. Nice to meet you. I'm Emiko."

"Great. And what's your first name?"

"That is my first name. My last name is Fujihara."

"Sorry. Sure, of course. So, where you from? Vietnam?"

"No. I'm from Los Angeles. My grandparents emigrated from Japan."

"Oh. My sister-in-law is from Vietnam. I thought, maybe—"

"I understand. We all look alike." She smiled amiably.

He wasn't sure if she was slamming him or not. "So, uh, what brings you here?" He went to his side of the table and sat opposite her as though they were desk mates.

"I met Jane yesterday, like many people do, and I offered to volunteer some time for the cause. She's letting me stay here, the kids' room. Is that a problem?"

"No, of course not. I mean, it's Jane's house, right? So, she healed you? No, I mean, God healed you, of course. That's great, just great. Look, we have these contact cards we ask everyone to fill out. Sister Jane doesn't always remember to pass them out, but we want to stay in touch. Let people know about upcoming events, that kind of thing." He handed her a card and a pen. She set it down next to her laptop but didn't fill it out.

"Nick! You're awake," Jane said as she carried in two plates with eggs, bacon, and toasted English Muffins. She placed one in front of the girl and one for herself. "I'd offer you breakfast but I didn't realize you were up. I think there's still some bacon."

The newest cat jumped on the table.

"Jane, could we keep the cats off the table, please?" Nick said.

If such a thing was possible, the cat looked at him with disdain and jumped off on her own.

"I'll just have coffee. Maddie is bringing Pearl here after the kids get on the bus. I asked them to stop and pick up something for me to eat." His stomach growled. "So, Mikimo, we appreciate your offer to help. We could sure use some extra help posting flyers around town."

"Emiko. E-M-I-K-O. I think I'd rather do something here at the house. Help with the—"

"Clients. Yeah. I usually do that face to face stuff. Warm up the crowd, that kind of thing. Get them ready to meet Sister Jane."

Jane said, "Maybe Emiko could enter the cards into the computer. You were saying the other day that you were behind."

"Yes, but we do have to think about privacy and all."

"Of course," Emiko said, "but I think Jane trusts me."

"Yes. It will be fine," Jane said. "Have you been checking the voice mail, Nick? I noticed the machine is blinking."

He walked over to the machine and ran it back for messages. "We were worried about you, Jane, you know. Why didn't you call us sooner and let us know what happened? Jesus Christ, if Twomey hadn't seen those army guys, we wouldn't have a clue."

"Everything is fine."

The machine played back, "*Mrs. Freedle? This is Officer Hancock. We*

223

met last week. We are trying to track down Nicholas Fabriani. We under-
stand he might be staying there, according to his wife. Could you give us
a call back at 410-939-6200? Thanks so much."

"What's that about?" Jane asked.

"It's all under control. I already called them back. Nothing to worry your head about." He deleted the message and needed to distract Jane. "We've got a big day ahead and a stack of people to reschedule. You're doing sessions today, right?"

"I could reschedule clients," Emiko said and then sneezed.

"Oh, dear. Don't tell me you're allergic? I'll put Bart and Simpson in my room for the day. But I'm afraid Miracle insists on being at the sessions."

"I'll be all right; I'll just take some Benadryl®," Emiko said, but Jane was already halfway up the stairs. Emiko turned to Nick, "Give me the numbers, and tell me what you want me to say."

He pulled out yesterday's cards from his file box and told Emiko, "Appointments are spread out over the day, four to five people every fifteen minutes, but only on the hour so we can fit in the walk-ins. Jane usually eats lunch around 12:30 or 1 p.m. so no appointments then. After the appointment is set up, you can enter the names and email addresses into Mail Chimp®.

"I'm familiar with it," she said.

"Great, being a quick learner is a plus."

He was about to go outside and greet the morning rush when Pearl and Maddie, who carried baby Mason in his car seat like a permanent appendage, trudged in through the kitchen.

"Where's Jane?" Pearl said, and he pointed upstairs; she followed his direction.

Maddie handed him a McDonalds'™ bag and he went into the dining room. She put the car seat on the table on top of his papers.

"People are lined up outside again and there's nowhere to park," Maddie said.

"That's what they do," he said. "It's morning, our busiest time of the day, Sister Jane will be starting soon. I told you it was like that. You

224

want to stay?"

"I still have a house to run, clothes to wash, rooms to vacuum, floors to clean. Adult stuff," Maddie said. "By the way, when are you going back to your real job? Or do you even have a job? Did the police call here for you? They called me looking for you but wouldn't tell me what they wanted. That was lovely."

"Everything will work out. You'll see. I appreciate you holding down the fort, Maddie. I do. But this is a big week. I need to get the registrations started," he said.

"You still insist on doing this event on Sunday? My God, everyone's insane," Maddie said.

"I'll go out front and hand out the cards for you Nick, so you two can have some privacy," Emiko said.

"And you are?" Maddie said to Emiko.

"She's a volunteer, Maddie. She experienced a healing and now she wants to help. That's what happens here. Healing changes people's lives. They see the world differently," he said.

"You've all been drinking the Kool-Aid," Maddie said.

The sisters came down the stairs and Jane went right to Maddie to hug her. Maddie's arms never left her side. Jane cooed at baby Mason on the dining room table and picked him up to sway with him.

"Hello, I'm sister Pearl; you must be Emiko."

"Nice to meet you," Emiko said.

"Listen up everybody, this is all fine and good, but we've got clients outside and we need to get to it," he said. Jane handed the baby to Pearl and walked over to her seat by the fireplace.

"Mother, where is your cell phone? I've been trying to call you all morning," Maddie said.

"It's over by the phone machine. It probably needs to be charged."

"Maddie, I'm going to stay and watch for a little while," Pearl said, "are you staying, Emiko? Jane, is that all right? We'll stay out of the way."

"Yes, I'm staying. I'm helping with the registration cards," Emiko said. "Maybe I could help Maddie with whatever job she'll be doing?"

"You wanna help me? Hold the baby," Maddie said and took the baby from Pearl and handed him to Emiko. The baby giggled.

Nick smiled as Emiko appeared more than a little nonplussed. Yep, she was a single woman who had grown up as an only child. "You all right there, Ms. Emiko?"

Emiko smiled wanly.

"Nick, please pay attention, I only have a few more minutes." Maddie said. "I have a PTA meeting and then grocery shopping. I will be back later to pick up Pearl. Oh, and I guess, make dinner, help with homework, build an effing science project, taxi the kids around, and run a few loads of laundry. Other than that, I'm more than happy to help run this circus, too." She slammed the pocket doors shut behind her. A second later, she dragged open the sticky doors and grabbed the baby back from Emiko, then slammed the doors again.

The baby started to cry but the sound diminished as Maddie left the house out the back door.

Pearl cleared her throat and said. "She'll come around, honey."

"Maybe," he said and took a breath. "So, Pearl, you can help settle people inside when I pass them to you at the door. Kids on the floor, older people in straight back chairs, others on the couch. You'll see how it works. Jane? You need anything?"

"I'm good." The cat jumped into her lap, which always creeped him out a little.

"I'll work in the dining room," Emiko said as she slipped through the doors, and left them half open.

He watched Jane caress the irritating cat that hissed at him whenever he walked by. When Jane looked up, she gave him a thumbs-up.

"You're in a good mood," he said.

"It's good to be back. This feels perfect. Plus, I love having Pearl here. You can't know how much it means, sister."

"You're welcome, Sister Jane" Pearl said and chuckled.

When he finally got outside, the porch was hopping. He did his routine and told everyone what to expect, how to fill out the cards, how to donate, and so on. He called out the first five names and passed them through the front door to Pearl who was waiting. He was a little thrown to see the same dark-suited man with the foreign accent standing on the steps.

"May I help you sir?"

"I want to make an appointment with the woman, your mother?" the man said as he handed Nick another card.

"Uh, mother-in-law. Sure, we can do that, but I've got to work with these walk-ins first, Mr. Krashinko," he said and looked down at the minimalist card." Then we can work out the day and time."

"No, I will tell you the day and time now. We will come tomorrow in the morning. Perhaps eleven hundred hours. This is important meeting, you understand. And my name is Krav-chen-ko," he enunciated to Nick. "Work on that. Ciao." And he left.

Nick made a mental note of the time and hoped there wouldn't be a problem accommodating the stranger. Jane told him a million times that God accepted all people, but this guy seemed like a stretch. Should he mention his apprehension? Probably not.

He got the next group ready and then his phone rang. It was Toni.

"Hey there Nicky. It's Toni."

"I know. I have caller I.D. like everyone else in the world."

"Very funny Nicky. Listen, I wanted to touch base with you. We are all set for Sunday afternoon. Bishop Bones is all in. He has a few people who need healing that he will bring along. We've got the gospel choir and Sister Kimani, voice like an angel, who will be the soloist, Jamal the piano player is bringing a few others to fill in the music, Rovanda made more healing cloths, and Jackson put out a press release to the Christian stations in the area. We are ready to roll. But one thing, we still need a piano. You're gonna have to rent a piano."

"A piano? Where am I gonna rent a piano?" he asked.

"From the piano rental store, of course. You got this, Nicky. Oh, and Rovanda will drop off Sister Jane's dresses sometime today. You make sure she tries them both on. Listen, I gotta run. Let me know when you get that baby grand? God bless you." And Toni hung up.

God only knew how much that would cost up-front. Thank God the porch donations were keeping up or he'd be in hock to about three thousand bucks. He wondered if he could get Maddie to make some calls about the piano. No, that was a bad idea. The new girl, woman, the China doll, whatever. He'd give her that assignment. When he put his hand in his pocket, he fingered the business card from the dark stranger and realized he had already forgotten what time they were coming the next day. For another minute, he thought about the police, but then decided to set that subject aside. One day at a time.

41

WEDNESDAY IN THE FIFTH WEEK OF LENT, TWOMEY

The Lafayette Wastewater Treatment Plant has had three accidents in the past month, but the city only reported one of those accidents until now. Located on the banks of the Susquehanna River in the Southeast corner of Lafayette, the plant had approvals for multiple improvements at the beginning of the fiscal year. Most seriously in need of an upgrade were the digesters, where sludge (the organic portion of the sewage) is processed through the waste and flow metering system. The company that won the contract for this work, A&M Methodologies, replaced the distillers and digesters improperly and, as a result, the plant discharged bacteria-laden effluent back into the river, according to anonymous sources close to the operations of the plant. A&M Methodologies has had cost overruns due to a proposal rife with inaccuracies. The costs have far exceeded what other companies proposed and it's clear that agreements made under the table could be bribes. City officials could not be reached for comment.

He folded the newspaper and drank deeply from his coffee cup as he sat contentedly at the local coffee hole. It was a good start. Even if no one read past the first paragraph, they would grasp the corruption. The mayor would not be pleased, but honestly, Twomey never pointed a finger at the mayor's office per se. He also managed to keep Nick out of the article by name, but he wasn't sure how much longer he would be able to cover for the guy. Sadly, Nick was dirty as hell, even though he never meant to be. He was stupid when it came to business. Add to that his belief in Sister Jane's miracles, and it showed his inability to think through long-term consequences and fact-based realities. Nick should have known. Poor Nick would probably go to jail.

His phone rang and he picked it up without checking the caller.

"I want the name, Twomey," Chuck said, popping his gum in between words.

"Sure, sure. I'll do a follow-up and lay out the players. I think the guy was duped."

"You getting soft on me? Let's nail this guy and I mean sooner than later. We don't need to wait 'til the Aegis deadline. We got good play in the main section, byline and all. Don't ruin this for yourself."

Chuck hung up. And there was the dilemma he faced. His byline topped two strong story lines, but at what cost? He had to deliver, or he would be back at the starting gate—again. This wastewater deal couldn't have been Nick's brainchild, so whose was it? Unless Nick gave up his friend, Twomey would have to throw Nick under the bus. Either way, he had to interview Nick soon.

As he left the coffee shop and walked toward Jane's house, he saw another black Suburban parked at the corner right outside the restaurant. More army escorts? He checked the license plate, diplomatic not Army, and this time, he wrote down the number. He pulled out his "dumb as a brick" persona and knocked on the driver's side. The window powered down halfway.

"Hello there. Just thought I'd let you know you parked illegally. It's a small town and they take these things seriously," he said.

The driver was movie-typical mafia, with dark glasses, dark hair, and a dark suit. Who wore suits anymore? Two guys sat in the front and an older man in the back. The boss?

"Is no problem," the driver said, "but thank you very much." He started to roll up the window.

"You lookin' for a place to eat in town?" Twomey put his hand on the window, having assumed they wouldn't cut off his fingers in public.

"I beg your pardon?"

"Food, you know? Lunch? You are obviously from out of town, maybe you'd like a recommendation for a nice place to eat. Or you're visiting family? Or maybe Sister Jane across the street there?"

"Please remove your hand," the man said.

He did of course, waved, and smiled as the nearly black tinted window went up the rest of the way. "Just trying to be hospitable," he said to the closed window. He went inside the restaurant beneath the apartment and ordered a sandwich to go and watched the "Blues Brothers" through the window while he waited.

Heavily accented, they could be from anywhere. If he had to guess, maybe Greece or Albania or maybe a country farther north. They could be Russian, but the accent wasn't quite right. One thing for sure, there was nothing in Lafayette that would interest guys like that except for a woman who claimed she could heal people.

Belinda called.

"Arnie gets out tomorrow from the detention center."

"Yeah, so?"

"He's your son for God's sake. Have a heart," she said.

"Belinda, I am paid up for the month. What do you want?"

"He needs a place to stay. My apartment is too small."

"No."

"Come on Wade. He just needs a couch for a few days until he can get on his feet."

"Nobody gets on their feet in a few days. No. Why can't he stay with you?"

"You know, I've already got company."

"Kick the son of a bitch out."

"You want Arnie back in the pokey?"

"That's a given whether he crashes at your place or mine. I've got two rooms. You've got four. You win."

"Fine. Be that way. You know if you would have accepted him—"

"Don't put that sorry-ass crap on me, Belinda."

"I think he needs help, like a miracle."

"What?"

"Yeah, I heard about this woman. She does like miracles and shit right there in Lafayette."

"Don't be a jackass. She's a fake."

"How do you know?"

During this entire conversation, he watched the black car. Up until then, nothing had happened. The trunk popped; they were on the move.

"Listen, I gotta go."

"I'm gonna bring him to that faith healing service on Sunday."

"Oh, for Christ's sake. Do what you want." He hung up on her.

The driver got a wheelchair out from the trunk while the other man in the passenger seat got out, walked to the back of the car, and sat down in the chair. The driver assisted the older man out of the back seat; he leaned heavily on a cane.

Twomey paid his bill, said he would pick up his sandwich later, and headed up the street. He crossed over in time to intercept the three men before they reached Sister Jane's. The older gentleman was in his seventies, maybe even eighties. But Twomey had a bad feeling about all three. He stopped them at the gate with a disarming smile. Several people on the sidewalk shuffled in line to get a better look. A couple of guys stood on the porch steps prepared to carry the wheelchair up to the house if needed.

"Hello again," he said, "So you are here to visit the Sister. Unfortunately, you see, lots of people are waiting. You probably won't get in today."

The driver scrutinized him and said, "Get out of our way. We have an appointment."

"Oh, that's great. Do you have your registration cards filled out? Let me get you one."

"Unnecessary," the driver said as he casually shoved past.

"Hey, wait a minute," Twomey said and then took the opportunity to grab on to the guy's jacket which pulled open enough to reveal a paddle holster at the waist and the butt of a gun. The driver took hold of Twomey's shirt at the neck and pulled him close. The guys from the porch hollered and ran down using the name of Jesus to break up a potential fight.

Twomey raised his arms in surrender. "Hey, hey. No offense." He wasn't sure if he sounded dutifully yielding or not, but he did get at least one answer to his hunch. These were thugs, plain and simple, and armed.

Nick came out of the house and immediately ran down the steps.

"Stop, stop. Slow down, everybody. Mr. Kravchenko, right? I got it right, right? Please come in. Back off, Twomey. What's your problem?"

and then to the crowd, "Everything's all right, folks. These gentlemen have an appointment. It's fine. Sister Jane is waiting for them."

The helpers began the arduous process of carrying the wheelchair up the steps, followed by the old man with the cane, and then the driver. The old man gave Twomey a dissecting look but walked on without speaking. Twomey used their diversion to walk to the back of the house to warn Sister Jane. Whatever game she was playing or tricks she was using, it would be unwise to try and hustle these people. The stakes were much higher.

When he came through the kitchen and dining room, he found Jane in her usual chair by the fireplace mantel along with the damn cat, while new "team members" sat at the edges of the room: a tall, more sturdy version of Jane (clearly a family member), a Japanese American woman who was some kind of workout buff in a Marine Corps zip sweatshirt, and an African American woman who sat at the dining room table with hand sewing. Elevator type music played in the background and candles burned on the mantel. They had upped the theatrics a notch. A basket sat on the end table near the door that read: *"Prayer Cloths: Give what you can."*

"Twomey," Jane said and stood, "what on earth are you doing? I watched through the window and saw you accost those men. They are my clients."

"I've got news for you, Sister, those guys may look like clients to you, but they are goons. One is carrying a gun."

"Which one?" the Japanese American woman said as she stood.

"Don't be ridiculous," Jane said.

He turned to the young woman, "Who are you exactly?"

Jane answered, "This is Emiko, a friend. That's Pearl, my sister. Now, you need to leave."

"I'm Rovanda, the black sidekick," the African American woman said and waved from behind them.

"Sorry, Rovanda," Jane said, "I meant no disrespect. Mr. Twomey, I am asking as politely as I can, please leave."

"I'll go out the back," he said. Then he stopped on the other side of the dining room table, next to Rovanda. "What are you making there? Looks

233

beautiful," he lied. He sat down beside her. No way was he missing this.

The front door opened, and the three men came in, Nick followed.

Nick announced, "Everyone needs to leave the room so that Sister Jane can have a private meeting with Mr. Kravchenko and his—friends."

"I won't be in the way," Emiko said and sat near the pocket doors.

Miracle, the cat, hissed at the men and then leaped onto Emiko's lap.

"I'll hold the cat," Emiko said to Jane, who wrinkled her forehead.

Jane seemed to gather herself and turned to the men, "Please, welcome to my home, sit down. These people are part of our ministry. Please come in and sit." Twomey had never heard her use that description before. Kravchenko stood behind the wheelchair. She filled in with pleasantries. Finally, she spoke to the older man directly.

"And what is your name, sir?" She spoke to the older man.

Twomey heard the driver answer for him. "That is not important. He is our Didus, our grandfather. He does not speak English. He is not why we are here. But this one," pointing to the wheelchair, "this one, he is what you call diabetyk, yes?"

"Oh," she said, "diabetic? Yes. All right. How long have you suffered?" she asked the man in the wheelchair.

"You only need to speak to me," Kravchenko said.

"And your name please?"

"I am Kravchenko."

"Nice to meet you, but really, I'd like to speak to the person who is ill."

"He does not speak the English," Kravchenko said.

"Yes, I do," the man said.

"Shut up."

Twomey watched as she bent down to the man in the wheelchair to pray. He admired her guts. She barely registered the sinister nature of the guys. He wrote down Kravchenko's name phonetically in his notebook. The work-out junkie, what was her name? Emiko, he thought. She leaned back into her chair and started texting fast but then pulled forward again. That's when he noticed the bulge in her back. Good God, was she a fed? That made sense. If military escorts picked up Jane, they probably interrogated her. If she were valuable, she would need protection. This was her watchdog.

"Please remember," Jane said, "I cannot know the timing of your healing."

"What are you saying?" Kravchenko said. "You heal or you do not heal. Are you lying to us?" His voice sounded menacing.

Twomey saw Emiko tense, ready to pounce if needed. He rose stealthily and moved closer to the pocket doors; he tried to stay partially hidden. He switched his attention to Jane as she explained again how the healings worked and importantly, that none of them were her miracles, but God's.

The woman in the corner stood up. "Are you challenging my sister's honesty, her authenticity? Because I can tell you—"

"Pearl, please sit down. It's fine," Jane said.

"What's going on?" Rovanda whispered in Twomey's ear behind the door.

He jumped and then put his finger to her lips.

"And sir, what about you? What can God do for you?" She reached out her hand to touch the older man, who had also refused a seat, and watched the entire scene silently.

Kravchenko slapped her hand away. "We are not here for our Didus. Not yet." Kravchenko swore and said, "Let's go."

"I can walk," the man in the wheelchair said.

"Of course, you can walk. You're an idiot. Bring the chair," Kravchenko said. He gave the grandfather his arm and they walked out.

Twomey watched Nick follow the men. Outside, the crowd cheered thinking Sister Jane had healed the man in the wheelchair and he could now walk. Twomey tapped Emiko on the shoulder and handed her a note.

"Here's the license plate number, diplomat, so good luck with that, but your people will be able to track it down," he said.

"My people?" she said.

"I'm not stupid," he said.

He touched her back and she grabbed his arm. He had no doubt she could have flipped him in short order.

"OK, OK. I was just trying to prove my point. It bulges."

She put on the zip jacket she had draped on the back of her chair.

"Lord Almighty, that was strange," Rovanda said as she stepped into the living room and around him. "Let me hold this up to you, Sister, before I tack the ribbon to the hem." She held up a white dress to Jane, who stood by her chair, somewhat stunned.

He had never seen such an ugly dress, with its partially completed gold cross on the front and gold ribbons hanging from the shoulders. Would his mild-mannered faith healer wear such a thing? She would look like somebody's idea of a nun in the Follies. She glanced in his direction and he could tell she was conflicted. He shook his head at her. She rolled her eyes.

"Sister, I think you need to try this baby on. I'm not sure these ribbons are hanging the right length in the back and on the sides," Rovanda said.

"Not now, Rovanda, please. Wait, this isn't the same dress I saw before. How many dresses are there?" Jane said.

Jane's sister inserted herself, "I think you could use a break, Janey. Go upstairs with Rovanda and sit for 15 minutes. I'll tell Nick to hold off on the next group."

"Just two," Rovanda said as she followed Jane up the stairs, "Toni said you might not like them at first."

The sister watched them go and then stepped outside. He could hear her speak to the crowd and answer questions. The cat hissed at him.

"Oh, shut up," he said to the cat. Ninja girl chuckled behind him. "You must be the journalist. I read your articles. Interesting how you left open the possibility that she might be on the level."

"Uh, no, not exactly," he said. "I just haven't figured out how she does it, that's all. What did you guys find out on Monday? Something must have happened, or she wouldn't have a bodyguard."

"You make a lot of assumptions."

"I put things together. You know, like military escorts and black Suburbans, armed ninja-powered shadows. That kind of thing," he said. "I'm trying to confirm which ones are the black hats and which ones are the white.

"I see. Let me help. Guys with guns – black hats; ninja woman with cell phone – white hat," she smiled but then sneezed. "Dammit."

"The cats? Yeah, watch that one in particular," he said as he pointed to the tabby sitting on Jane's chair. "She hisses at me as soon as I walk in the room."

"She could be the canary in the coal mine. She hissed at those tough guys too."

"Very funny."

"Why are you here, Twomey? That is your name, right? Wade Twomey?"

"And yours again?"

"Emiko Fujihara."

"All right, two reasons: to drop off today's newspaper—it's on the kitchen table—interesting reading about corruption in the city, possibly orchestrated by none other than Nick Fabriani—and number two, I need to speak to said Nick. It may be his only chance to clear himself."

She shrugged. "Not in my wheelhouse. So, you're not interviewing Jane?"

"Not today. I'll catch up with Nick outside."

The door opened before he reached it and Jane's sister poked in her head. "Has anyone seen Nick? I don't see him anywhere."

"Looks like he made a getaway," Emiko said.

"You're a laugh riot," he said.

"I'm not sure what to do out here," the sister said.

"Just hand out the registration cards. Triage the sick ones; anyone nearly dead gets a red ticket and comes to the head of the line," he said.

"You seem to know the system" Emiko said.

"It's all in the details. I'll find him."

42

Same Wednesday in the Fifth Week of Lent, Jane

She closed the door to her bedroom and heaved a great sigh. It had been a long day and it was past her bedtime. And where was Nick? He left without letting anyone know where he went. Thank God Pearl was on board now. Her sister's take-charge temperament had helped herd the clients. Had she just called her clients cows?

The day continued to deteriorate when Maddie showed up at dinner time, baby carrier in tow.

"Look at this newspaper. Where is Nick? I'm gonna kill him," Maddie said as she waved the Aegis around.

"What happened?"

"I've called him a hundred times and all my calls are going to voice mail."

"Maddie, listen to me. I'm sorry, but Nick isn't here," Jane said.

"He disappeared before lunch and didn't tell anyone where he was going," Pearl added.

Maddie let out a guttural scream. "Well, he's bound to turn up eventually. I'll wait." She called home and told Mitchell to cancel his plans and babysit the other kids. There was quite a row on the phone. Afterward, Maddie plopped onto the recliner, crossed her arms, and seethed. How the baby slept through all that, Jane couldn't fathom.

Now, she was grateful for this tiny piece of privacy. As she sat and looked around her bedroom, she saw it with new eyes. Why hadn't she changed anything in the room since Richard died? Their bedroom was quite masculine with its dark furniture, cool blue colors, and flying duck pictures on the walls. Wouldn't the room be warmer in a pale yellow? She could probably get a flowered bedspread or even a quilt at a discount store. And what about sheers instead of those awful blinds? But when could she do something as mundane as shop? She could ask Toni to do it, that one loved to shop. Or Rovanda.

No, neither. If the dresses they picked out for her were any indication of their taste, she'd best wait. And that look on Twomey's face, the mockery in his eyes. She reddened even now. Why did she care what Twomey thought anyway? Why had he warned her about the men in black suits? True, they had frightened her at first; particularly the one called Kravchenko. But for some reason, she liked the grandfather, he had kind eyes. For all she knew, he was the godfather, like Marlon Brando. A sobering thought.

She tried again to put them out of her mind. She had done what they asked. Was there more to them than that? She gnawed at her lip.

Take-charge Pearl had ordered in Italian from the bistro for the four of them and managed to keep the meal going with chit-chat. Pearl convinced Maddie to stay the night and sleep in Richie's old room which Nick had commandeered as his own. Emiko barely spoke to anyone. Before heading upstairs for bed, Emiko did say, "Don't worry too much about those men. I called Baxter and he has plenty of powerful contacts. He'll take care of it. Now go to bed, I'll be right across the hall."

But where was Nick? She worried. She needed comfort food like chocolate or ice cream or maybe a shot of something stronger. Dang. Lent was still going, in fact ten more days of no sweets until Easter. What the hell? She deserved a cheat. She changed into her pajamas and robe and stepped onto the landing when she heard a huge crash. She looked down the stairs in time to see her front door fly open; someone tossed in a body. A second later, Emiko was at her door, in a crouch, weapon drawn. It was like an episode from Law and Order. Jane froze.

"Don't come down," Emiko shouted as she raced down the steps. "It's Nick." Emiko expertly checked his neck for a pulse and then ran out the open door.

Pearl came out of the Celeste's room and stood next to her, "What's happening?" Maddie stumbled out of Richie's room.

"I—I—I don't know. My God, my God, it's Nick. That's Nick." Jane recovered herself and ran down the stairs.

"I'll call 911," Pearl yelled and ran back into her room.

Maddie screamed, "Nick? Omigod, Nick!"

Both women kneeled beside Nick who lay sprawled on the ground. Maddie sobbed and continued to call his name. She lifted his head onto her lap. He was bleeding from his nose and mouth and one hand appeared black and blue, his fingers misshapen.

Pearl, phone in hand, was halfway down the stairs when Emiko reappeared at the front door. "Don't call 911. I made the appropriate medical call. He's alive. We'll have medics here shortly. Don't move him." Emiko plucked a note from Nick's chest. When her phone rang, she walked into the living room, tucked her pistol into the small of her back and scanned the note as she listened to the caller.

"I'll get paper towels," Pearl said, ever the practical one.

"Don't move him. My God. Nick. Mother, don't move him," Maddie cried.

Jane ignored everyone at that point. She prayed, "Holy Father, may your mercy prevail and heal Nick's body. Spirit of God, meet Nick's spirit, integrate broken tissue, close his wounds, soothe his pain." She stroked his hair and found more blood; she prayed again. "May his head be made whole, straighten his bones, clear his mind." She covered his swollen hand with her own, not wanting to imagine how much pain he had endured. She wept.

When she finally looked up, two men were standing in the door, apparently the medics Emiko had called in. To her amazement, Emiko stood next to them with her hand up, staying them. Maddie was silent although tears ran down her face. Jane heard Pearl saying quietly yet repeatedly, "Dear Jesus, dear Jesus."

"Are you finished Jane? May the medics come in now?" Emiko asked, her voice as steady and calm as though she was talking about bringing in dessert.

Jane kissed Nick on the head and put the sign of the cross on his forehead. For all his bad choices, his mistakes, and poor judgment, he was her son-in-law, the father of her most precious grandchildren. All was redeemable. Who was she to deny him?

Emiko helped Jane get up from the floor and passed her to Pearl and they walked over to the couch. A medic helped Maddie rise and then they brought in a stretcher.

Maddie asked, "May I go with him?"

The medics looked to Emiko for permission and she nodded.

"Mother, do you have any of those frozen milk pouches for the baby if he wakes up?"

"I do. You go on. We're fine," she said.

Maddie hurried over to her mother then and kissed her cheek. "Please forgive me." She raced after the gurney out to the ambulance.

"Where will they take him?" Jane asked Emiko

"It's a secure facility, that's all I can tell you. But you need to read this note. I think we can guess its source," Emiko said as she handed her the folded typewriter paper torn at the top where someone had stapled it to Nick's clothes.

If he dies, you will never see us again. No problem.

"What does that mean?" Pearl asked.

"They're testing me," she said. "I guess the episode earlier today wasn't enough. How Nick got in the middle of this, I don't know."

"He walked them out, remember? We didn't put two and two together. I'm sorry. That was my miss, my responsibility," Emiko said.

"Why would it be?" she said.

"I should have known. I should have predicted something like this. I wasn't paying attention. But now we need to move forward. You need to rest if you can. Both of you. I have to write my report."

"Who are you reporting to?" Pearl asked. "Never mind, I don't think you'll tell me."

Emiko smiled.

"What time is it?" Jane asked.

"A little after midnight" Emiko said.

"Pearl, I can handle the baby, but would you please take my car and go back to Maddie's house? I'm sure Mitchell has done a good job, but tomorrow morning, the kids need to get off to school."

"What should I tell them?"

"Maybe say their father was in an accident and their mom went to the hospital with him. As soon as we know more, we'll let you know."

Emiko said. "Let us give you a ride so you don't have to drive." She got on her phone.

Jane and Pearl looked at each other.

"We have hit yet another kind of normal," Jane said.

"You mean the shit just hit the fan," Pearl said, and sat closer to her sister. They held hands and leaned back on the couch.

43

THURSDAY IN THE FIFTH WEEK OF LENT, JANE

"Jane, this is serious," Emiko said. "I'm not an alarmist, but this time, I have to agree with my superiors. You would be safer at a secure site."

They sat at her kitchen table, Miracle on her lap, the other two cats eating, the parakeets twittering over all the excitement. Jane was still in a state of disbelief, but she didn't want to give up her freedom to the government. She liked Emiko and even trusted her, but she wasn't sure Emiko would be her "handler" if she moved to another location.

"Will you force me to go?"

"I wouldn't, no," Emiko said. "But we have to do something to keep you safe. Can you put the house visits on hold for the next few days? Cancel the service?"

She considered their options. She could put a sign on the door to direct people to the healing service on Sunday, but she didn't have the heart to cancel altogether. Nick, and all the other people had worked so hard to make it happen. She sipped her coffee. She missed her creamer.

"I need to make a trip to the grocery store," she said aloud.

Emiko put a hand on her arm. "Are you even listening to me? Those men have threatened your life. We are researching these guys and so far, it's not good news. You can't just go out to the grocery store."

"I know. I know. Sorry. I was thinking out loud. Yes, of course. We can put a sign on the door. We'll say I'm in consultation with the Lord."

Emiko smiled. The doorbell rang. "Don't you usually start at nine? It's barely 8:15."

"Sometimes people come early. I'll go and tell them we're taking a break," she said.

"No, I'll go," Emiko said, but Jane followed all the same.

When they got to the door, Gillespie stood at the door with Lindy in her wheelchair. Lindy looked up and smiled. Emiko stepped aside.

Gillespie cleared his throat, "Uh, sorry to come so early. Lindy was really agitated yesterday. Deztinee called me and asked me to come down. Lindy was inconsolable and kept saying your name. So, I ordered a transport van for this morning."

"Come in, come in," Jane said. She took Lindy's hand and squeezed it as Gillespie pushed his wife's wheelchair over the threshold. She settled them into the living room. Emiko asked Gillespie if he wanted a cup of coffee, but he declined.

She noticed how drawn Lindy looked since their last meeting and took both of her hands into her own as she sat on her barrel chair. "I am so happy to see you, Lindy."

"It's all right. All right. Jane. It's Jane, Danny. See. It's Jane."

"What can I do for you Lindy?" she asked.

"What the hell do you think? Isn't that what you do now? Cast a spell? Make a miracle? Part the Red Sea?" Gillespie said.

She glared at Gillespie. "I've got enough going on right now, Dan Gillespie, without you attacking me in my own house."

"No, no. Please stop. It's Jane, Danny. Hello, Jane," Lindy said

She redirected her focus to Lindy. "Hello, Lindy. Do you want to be healed?"

Lindy shook her head but leaned forward as though to whisper a secret.

"Oh, for God's sake—" Gillespie started. Jane caught Emiko's eye and she took the hint.

"Daniel Gillespie, is it? I'm Dr. Fujihara, Emiko Fujihara. I'm with DARPA. Are you familiar with that organization?"

"Of course. But—"

She heard them talking as Emiko pulled Gillespie to the side. "We've been studying these phenomena of Jane's and have discovered some remarkable results."

Once again, Jane refocused on Lindy who kept repeating, "Jane, I'm sorry; I'm so sorry."

She was unclear what Lindy needed. Sentences and phrases disconnected. Her strokes had taken so much from this once vibrant woman, the captain of the cheerleading squad in high school and a cross country and relay star in college. At one time, we all thought Lindy would make the Olympic track and field team. But Gillespie had other ideas and whisked her off to law school with him. When he moved them back home to Lafayette, they already had three children, a set of twin boys and a little China doll they adopted. Their kids were friendly with Richie, Maddie, and Celeste, but soon, the Gillespie children enrolled in private schools and Ivy League colleges. Their paths diverged. It was the way of the world she supposed.

Lindy paused and Jane asked again, "Let me pray for you. God will heal you; He can give you back your life."

"No. No. Forgive. Forgive. Forgive."

A scripture flashed through Jane's mind. She didn't know it exactly, but she remembered something about a paralyzed man and Jesus saying, 'Your sins are forgiven.' All the scribes and Pharisees were up in arms about that. And what was the last part, 'Which is easier: to say, 'Your sins are forgiven,' or to say, 'Get up and walk'?

"Lindy Gillespie," she proclaimed, "your sins are forgiven."

Lindy quieted and smiled, but Gillespie roared, "How dare you, Jane Freedle? What gives you the right? What sins? You are no saint, no apostle, no angel."

Jane stood.

Lindy reached out one hand to Gillespie and the other to her. "Listen, listen, listen. Please, please listen. It was me. It was me and Richard. It was me all along."

Jane looked down at Lindy, the woman's hands outstretched between the two of them. "What?" and for a moment, her heart went cold. Was it possible? Was she hearing correctly?

Lindy looked worried.

Jane shook her head to clear it. In that instant, she saw it: the need that drove Lindy here. Her healing was within. "You're forgiven Lindy. It's all right. I forgive you."

"Thank you." Lindy lowered her hands and then sighed, her eyes closed, and her head slowly fell forward as though falling asleep.

"What the—" Gillespie said. "Lindy?" He turned to Jane, "What is she talking about?"

Jane stepped away from Lindy's wheelchair. She looked for Emiko who was on her phone and didn't realize what had happened. She touched Gillespie's arm to get his attention. "I don't know about you, but I always suspected Richard was having affairs. I never thought they were serious. But I was afraid to rock the boat. I was afraid to know."

"That's bull pucky. Lindy would never--that's not possible. Son of a bitch."

He walked into the kitchen. She could tell, even from the back, that he was holding himself very tight. Who knew what went on behind closed doors? Perhaps their marriage was less solid than she had always assumed.

"Mr. Gillespie!" Emiko said. Jane turned; Lindy had nearly doubled over, and Emiko kneeled beside the wheelchair. "I don't feel a pulse."

Gillespie ran back; he and Emiko pulled Lindy from the chair and onto the floor. Emiko started CPR while Gillespie called 911. Jane wanted to pray, to bring Lindy back from the dead but she couldn't. She knew; this was the ending Lindy wanted, confession and forgiveness. Who was she to change that trajectory?

Emiko looked up and beseeched her to pray, to do what she had done hundreds of times. But Jane shook her head slowly and sat on the healing chair. Miracle jumped onto her lap and purred as she rubbed the cat's head. Ecclesiastes came to mind, *There is a time for everything, and a season for every activity under the heavens: a time to be born and a time to die.*

When the EMTs arrived, Gillespie stepped back against the stair railing. Tears drenched his face and mucus ran down and across his lips. He wiped his face on the arm of his crisp blue oxford cloth shirt. He turned to Jane and his face contorted with anger and grief, "If she dies, I will shut you down. Or I might shut you down anyway. I don't know you anymore. You have become deranged. You are a menace to society."

"Mr. Gillespie—" Emiko started to say, but he slapped away her outstretched hand. "And you? I'll be contacting my Senator about you and your bogus study; what a waste of taxpayer dollars." He started to the door and then came back, turned Lindy's wheelchair around and pushed it out the door.

Jane snapped out of her trance and ran to the door; the cat leaped away. "Gillespie! Dan!" she called, but she was too late. The transport van driver took the chair from Gillespie and he climbed into the back of the ambulance without a backward glance.

"She's gone. You know that, right?" Emiko said.

"Yes. It was what she wanted. To die in peace."

"But the strokes? Do you think she was capable of making that call?"

"Maybe not. Maybe I played God," she said.

"Can I get you anything?" Emiko asked.

"No. No thank you. I think I will lie down for a while."

She walked up her stairs slowly. She closed the bedroom door behind her and stared at the queen-sized bed.

Had Richard screwed other women on their marriage bed? That was crude, but that's how she felt. There was something raunchy and vulgar about imagining him with someone else, violating the sanctity of their bed, especially with a close friend. Maybe he took Lindy to a motel or a hotel in Baltimore. Maybe they went to Gillespie's summer house on the Eastern Shore. How long ago was this affair of theirs? How long did it last? Lindy went into Safe Haven almost five years ago. Wasn't that around the time Richard curtailed having any sex at all with her? She remembered that night.

He pulled off her and sat on the side of the bed. "Sorry, Jane. I guess I'm getting too old."

"Don't be silly," she said as she rubbed his bare back. He was still lean and strong from swinging all those golf clubs. "You can check with Amos. He might have a suggestion."

"I'm not going to my internist to talk about my lack of erections. God, Jane. What will you say next? That I should try Viagra?"

"I don't know. The commercials sound reasonable."

"Well, this is not that kind of problem." He got up and left the bedroom, leaving her feeling more alone and unfulfilled than ever. Happy anniversary to you, too.

She sat on her side of the bed now. After three years, she still hadn't acclimated to the entire bed. She slept on her side, on the very edge, taking up as little room as possible. No more. She stood up, whipped off the dark brown bedspread and threw it on the floor. She pushed Richard's pillows onto the floor and placed hers smack in the middle and crawled into the bed and stretched out. For a long while, she lay there and stared up at the ceiling. Richard's voice was silent. And eventually, she slept. That afternoon, bleary-eyed, she came down the stairs, amazed at how long she had slept. Emiko greeted her cheerily and said she had several phone messages to share if Jane wanted to hear about them.

"What? You've downgraded from Dr. Fujihara to secretary for a menace to society?"

"Sure. Why not? I'm a woman of curiosity and I am fascinated by human behavior and abilities. Plus, I like you, Jane Freedle."

She smiled. "That's nice to hear. Thank you. I like you, too."

"Hungry?"

"Not so much. Maybe I'll have a bowl of cereal."

Emiko laughed, "Ah! One of my staples. I'll join you."

They sat amiably in the kitchen among the cats and parakeets and Emiko sneezed.

"Let's take care of that." And before Emiko could say anything, Jane took her hand and said a very brief but pointed prayer about the allergies and whatever else Emiko was holding at arm's length.

"What did that mean?" Emiko asked.

She shrugged her shoulders, "I don't know, going with the flow."

"That last part sounded more like advice than prayer," Emiko said.

"I like Baxter, too, that's all. Now, tell me about those phone calls. I'm already feeling better." She got out the cereal, bowls, and milk while Emiko shared some of the phone calls she had taken for Jane.

"Toni called to commiserate with you about Nicky and how glad she was that everything had turned out so well. Toni added several 'Praise the Lords' which I cannot recreate."

Jane laughed.

"Toni also chastised you for being negative about the dresses. Toni said,

248

and I quote, 'those dresses were inspired by the Holy Spirit—" and then begged you not to hurt Rovanda's feelings. And finally, believe it or not, Toni's last question was whether you can pray for blemishes, liver spots, and wrinkles."

"She did not ask that?"

"She did." Emiko went on to say that Sister Bernie called to let Jane know that she and the sisters were praying for her. Maddie called to let you know that they released Nick from the hospital, and they would be heading home. Maddie also said Aunt Pearl had everything in hand at their house.

"How did Maddie sound?"

"Good. Surprisingly good. Oh, one more thing, a bit of surprise. Nick did a tell-all interview with Twomey."

"In front of Maddie?"

"Apparently. You know, don't you, that Nick did some bad things and has gotten himself into some real trouble at the wastewater plant and in his role as a city manager."

"Yes, unfortunately, I've watched Twomey's bylines," she sighed. "I need some garden time. It's such a lovely day. Do you think I can sit out on the back deck?"

"I'll let the guards know, but only for a little while, all right?" Emiko got on her phone as Jane slipped on a light sweater and walked out onto her deck.

About an hour later, Emiko opened the back door and said, "You have a visitor." She was surprised to see Twomey. He carried a small package with him.

"Here, this is for you."

"A gift? You're kidding?"

"Hey, don't rain on my parade. I was in the antique store and saw it and thought you might like it," he said. Then added, "You have any beer?"

"Lord, Twomey, you are such a contradiction of terms. No. No beer." She opened the small box and pulled out his beaded gift. "It's a rosary. It's lovely. This is very thoughtful of you, but, uh, you do know I'm not Catholic?"

"Does that matter?"

"No, I guess not. Not really. Thank you." She wrapped it around her left hand and held the cross in her palm.

They were silent for a time.

Eventually, Twomey cleared his throat and said, "I talked to Nick's wife earlier today. She said the thugs beat up Nick pretty bad; almost killed him. And you did your prayer thing and he's better."

"Yes."

"I called Nick this afternoon and got the whole story. I mean the whole story about the treatment plant and how one of his buddies set him up. And some other ethical issues."

"I know."

"He should have known better. But I have to write it, you know? I mean, it's a story."

"Yes."

"Nick's not very good in the business department, not much common sense."

"Yes, I know."

"I thought I should tell you—What? Wait. You know?"

"Maddie called me. She said they released Nick today from the secure hospital; I think it's across the river, don't you?"

"He'll probably have to do some jail time," Twomey said, "unless the goons catch up to him first." He looked directly at her, looking for a reaction.

"They don't want Nick. They want me. Because of the gift."

"That's a dangerous game to play, you know. Don't you think it's time to let go of this chicanery? Those bad guys are the real deal," he said.

"So am I. Or rather, so is God. Are you so hardheaded? What more proof do you need? Tell me, have you ever heard of someone nearly beaten to death and then released the next day by certified doctors?"

He looked away. Another silence dropped between them.

She spoke first. "Can we talk about something else? Easy stuff, like tell me about your family. Are you married? Parents still alive? How long have you been a journalist?"

"Journalist? Wow, there's a laugh. The TV guys are journalists now, you know, the ones with breaking news and all that. I'm a reporter. Once a reporter, always a reporter. Nose for news," he said, tweaking his nose. "That is, unless the nose is filled with coke or the brain is drowned in booze."

"You did drugs?"

"Are you so provincial?"

"Now there's a compliment. It's always so lovely to talk to you, Mr. Twomey."

"Sorry. Look. Do you mind if I smoke?"

"Yes."

He looked at her and laughed. "All right. Twenty-five words or less. I made a lot of mistakes, mostly drink and ponies. My wife divorced me and is bleeding me dry, almost worse than the gambling. My kid is a bum, probably an addict, currently cooling his jets at the detention center for a DUI. Correct that, he's out now for good behavior. I moved up to dullsville Lafayette, thinking I would sail into retirement. And then you happened. And the corruption story. And now I get a little moment in the sun and a chance to redeem myself."

"That was more than twenty-five words."

"Yeah, my editor tells me that all the time. Your turn."

"I think you already know everything about me. You even went back to my yearbook in that first article," she said as she wound and unwound the rosary in her hand.

"Yeah, high school sweethearts, I noticed. Sorry about the loss of your husband."

"Thank you. They call it a widow-maker, his heart attack. It's a terrible word."

"Widow-maker?"

"No. Widow. Just widow. But I suppose, eventually, there comes a time to reinvent oneself."

"And do you prefer faith healer or charlatan?" he said.

She stood up abruptly. "Why are you here, Twomey? What do you want? Another article? What will it take for you to accept that mysteries exist in this world? Believe or don't believe, I don't care, but dammit to hell, leave me alone if your mind refuses to even try to understand. You'd better go."

"Actually, I thought you liked me."

The back door opened, and Emiko stuck her head out. "Food's on. Hope you don't mind Chinese carry-out? You here for dinner, Twomey?"

"He was just leaving," Jane said while Twomey said, "Sure."

44

FRIDAY IN THE FIFTH WEEK OF LENT, TWOMEY

He lay in his bed, having slept little. He had worked on the Nick story for a couple of hours after coming home from Jane's. He didn't stay late, just long enough to eat and get in trouble again for telling her what to do. He thought she should give up the healing business altogether. At one point, Emiko kicked him under the table. He left after that. Jane was a paradox, a combination of obstinate and kind, resolved and unsettled. But she didn't come across as a liar or a con artist. What was the game? He picked up her picture from his end table and stared at it. What if he had met her back in the day instead of Belinda? Disaster, that's what.

His phone buzzed and he groaned at the screen: Chuck.

"Get your ass moving, Twomey, there's a hostage situation up at the casino off I95."

"Shit. I'm on it."

"Call in and give your story to MaryEllen over the phone as soon as you have something. We'll put it in for you."

Before hanging up, he said quickly, "Thanks Chuck."

His adrenaline kicked into overdrive. He was one of the closest reporters to the scene and would get a lot of coverage and possibly, inside details if any of his old dealer friends were still around. Unless they were inside. That was a sobering thought. He grabbed his laptop and notepads in case there was enough time to do a real story. He wondered how far out the press boundary would be. He ran through his options.

On his way toward the car, which he had to park two blocks over, he saw Emiko standing on the sidewalk outside Jane's, no bodyguards visible.

"Where is everybody?"

"Jane's spending the day at her daughter's. The guards are nearby. You're out early."

"Hostages held at the casino. And you?" he said.

"Headed to Washington; I'll be back later."

"Is it true about Nick? I mean the injuries and the magic?"

"It's unexplainable. I've told you that. You may need to suspend your disbelief. Definite anomalies present themselves in the reality structures we are used to observing."

"That's a doctorly kind of thing to say. May I quote you?"

"The quote yes, the attribution is a person close to the family." She turned her head when a man pulled up in a red sporty BMW, maybe an X2? She ran and got into the passenger seat. Except for the bowtie, the guy was right out of GQ. Twomey did his girly wiggle wave at them and headed out.

On his drive over the bridge, he got another call, surprised to hear the mayor's voice on the other end.

"Mr. Twomey, I thought we had a deal and you would not run Lafayette into the ground as a hotbed of corruption."

"Now Mayor, I thought I was pretty even-handed. I made it clear that all the facts were not in yet. Besides, I just got the back story from Fabriani. He threw A&M under the bus and has the paperwork to prove their part in the foul play. You will come out smelling fine. All you have to do is make a statement that your administration is following every lead and cooperating with the authorities."

"Authorities? What authorities?"

"There has to be an outside investigation; Nick's old school friend lives across state lines and Lafayette isn't the first city to get the blowback."

"This is going to cost us a fortune in legal fees."

"I'd be more concerned about the cost to the plant. You'll have to have that work re-done completely and there will be cleanup to the river."

"Why are you here Twomey? Why don't you go back to the city and play with the big boys?"

"I just might do that, sir. But right now, I'm headed to the casino. Did you all mobilize to help? And this is on the record."

"Yes, of course, we sent our SWAT guys to help and our two K-9 units. But that situation is really up to the Stateys."

"Right. Thanks. Gotta go," he said and hung up.

The rest of his day was all about the hostage scene. The biggest surprise came around one o'clock when the hostage negotiators got the guy with the gun to release the hostages and give up his name, Jay Martinez.

What the hell? he thought. His old doctor buddy just hit rock bottom. He ran over to the crisis team.

"Hey, excuse me. Hey. I know this guy."

"Who the hell are you?" an officer in green fatigues said.

"Twomey. Wade Twomey. Let me talk to him. Here's my I.D."

The guy looked at his driver's license and swing badge, then laughed. "You've got to be kidding. You're a shitass reporter. Get outta here."

"But he's a friend—"

"And I'm the Queen of England."

Twomey gave it up. He called in his third report and updated the story, adding what he knew about gambling addiction. He hoped Jay wouldn't do something stupid.

Later, he ran into an old blackjack dealer who told him another angle. According to Charlie, Jay lost his cash by midnight, stepped away from the table, and then came back with twice as much, but blew it. Jay's third return to the table found him even more reckless in his betting and flop sweating. When he lost that cash, Jay pulled a gun, grabbed another regular, and put the muzzle to the gal's head.

Twomey hated to do it, but he had to file the story.

Chuck gave him an "attaboy."

Twomey left the casino around four, right after the negotiators got Jay to surrender. Twomey was exhausted as he climbed into his car but then his phone chirped a reminder: he had a stupid ass high school lacrosse game to cover. The absurdity of the two events rattled his brain. At the game, he overheard several women talking about gamblers and how crazy it was that people were still in a casino at seven in the morning. Little did she know how many times he had come out of the house after sunup. That's what we did.

When he got home, he tapped on Vasquez's door and peeked in. The guy was out cold on the couch, oxygen in his nostrils. Vasquez's robe had fallen open revealing a body white for lack of sun and pocked with scars. Twomey walked in quietly and did the mother thing by covering the man with a nearby afghan. Vasquez never stirred.

45

SAME FRIDAY IN THE FIFTH WEEK OF LENT, JANE

The evening sky was blue and cloudless, so they sat outside at Maddie and Nick's. Maddie brought the small kitchen television outside to hear the news about the crisis at the casino. Before dinner, Nick had talked a bit about his ordeal, but not as much as one would think. She saw a much different Nick. Maddie filled in for him when he would go suddenly silent. Despite the healing, he moved slowly and often sat in a kind of stupor. The children were uncharacteristically quiet as well.

Maddie asked, "I'm sorry to bring this up, but is this healing service still on for Sunday?"

Jane thought Nick would jump right in, instead he deferred to her. She hesitated, then confessed, "I don't have the heart to cancel it. People are counting on me. We turned away so many people at the house because we promised them this service. Besides, Toni's church is bringing the volunteers and music for free."

"Not quite, no, not quite free," Nick said quietly. Jane thought he would say more but his mind wandered again.

"Well, in any case, it's a snowball that would be very difficult to stop," she said.

"Toni called to remind you both of a meeting tomorrow to wrap up details. Are you up to that, Nick?" Maddie asked.

"What? Sure, yeah, sure. I guess so. One last meeting," Nick said.

"I'll give you a ride over there. You can stay here tonight," Maddie said.

For now, Maddie was staying close to her husband, touching him, and helping him whenever he needed something. As sweet as it was to watch, Jane thought it was unsustainable over time. If Nick went to jail, how sympathetic would Maddie be then?

On her way home, headlights followed her. That made her nervous until she realized it was one of her special security guys. One got out of his dark car after he pulled up behind her parking pad. He walked her to the kitchen door.

"Good evening, Ms. Freedle. Did you have a nice time with your family?"

"I did, thank you." On the deck, she hesitated. "May I go in?"

"Yes ma'am, Dr. Fujihara and Mr. Baxter are inside waiting for you."

"Oh, all right. Thanks."

Emiko sat at one end of the dining room table with her laptop open and Baxter on the other end, on his phone. Jane sensed an iron curtain separated them this evening, which was unusual. Baxter disconnected his call and got up to greet her with a small hug.

"Hello there. Hope you don't mind that we let ourselves in?" Baxter said.

"How was your day with your family?" Emiko asked.

"Fine. Fine to both questions. Nick is doing well. And you?" she said to Emiko. "You went back to Washington today?"

"Yes, we both did," Baxter said. Emiko glared at him.

"How are the patients at Walter Reed?" she asked.

Emiko answered, "As you would expect, Jane. They are doing great. Many of them asked about you. It will be nearly impossible to keep this experience out of the news. Eventually, the patients will be discharged in good health and there will be lots of questions."

"So, Jane. Let's change the subject. I have a surprise for you," Baxter said. "Have a seat," he indicated one of the dining room chairs.

"Baxter," Emiko said, "I thought we were going to wait until—"

"No, you want to wait, but I know how this will go if we wait. If you want some control over the thing, we have to initiate."

"And if your idea backfires? If they divert Jane? What happens then? My project goes out the window and your influence hits zero. It's risky," Emiko said.

"Excuse me. But I'm still in the room," she said.

Baxter spread his hands and forged ahead, "Sorry, Sister Jane. How would you like to meet the president?"

"What? Our president? The president?"

"That's right."

"Is he sick?"

"Depends on who you ask," Emiko said.

"When?"

"Tomorrow. Emiko and I will go with you every step of the way."

"You know, I didn't vote for him this time. I mean, I always vote Republican, but—"

"No worries," Baxter said. "Nobody cares about that now."

Jane turned to Emiko, "What should I wear?"

Emiko smiled. "I'll help you pick something out. We can do that now if you like. Baxter can stay with his brother in Bel Air."

Baxter did a mock pouty face.

"Fine. See you tomorrow ladies. Oh, and Jane, keep this under your hat. Right?" Baxter said as he packed up his gear.

46

SATURDAY IN THE FIFTH WEEK OF LENT, JANE

They were already on I-95 in a government car when she remembered. She should have called Nick to let him know about her great adventure, but in all the excitement, it slipped her mind. She was in a daze. My God, she was on her way to meet the President of the United States. Emiko had helped her pick out a suit she had worn to Easter service several years ago. She had forgotten about the pale green ensemble tucked away under a dry-cleaning bag at the edge of her closet. They had added a bright scarf with exotic birds around her neck and beige pumps. Along with a little make up and clip-on earrings, she felt almost pretty. How long had it been since she had dressed up? Certainly not much since Richard's funeral.

Of course, back then, she had worn traditional black at the funeral and wake. Maddie had dressed her that day, but Jane had few strong memories. The day had roared passed like a merry-go-round on steroids. She remembered shaking a lot of hands and hugging a lot of necks. Only one person's words stuck with her the rest of the day and beyond, "Welcome to the club." The woman meant the widow club, the one club no wife ever wants to join.

"Oh Emiko, I should have called Nick to let him know I wouldn't be at the meeting."

"No worries. I texted them."

"Thank you. I appreciate all that you have done for me; I feel like I haven't done anything for you."

"You have done plenty. You've shared your gift, your home, and you've let me into your life. Plus, I haven't sneezed in twenty-four hours."

Jane smiled. "You don't act like a scientist. You act more like a daughter or daughter-in-law. Are your parents still living?"

"My father is ill, he had a stroke about six years ago, but my mother is taking care of him. They still live in the same house I grew up in near Oakland. I don't get to see them as much as I would like. They were toddlers in one of the Japanese-American internment camps near Sacramento."

"Oh, that's terrible."

"It's fine," Emiko said, patting her hand, "they don't remember much. I'm glad they were only kids; it made the experience less traumatic."

"I think," Baxter said, "we should talk about food. I have a bag up here on the front seat full of bagels, toppings, and coffee plus a couple of water bottles. We will be doing a lot of waiting around, so even if you had breakfast, you should shore up."

"Baxter loves his food," Emiko said.

"May I ask a personal question?" she said as she caught Baxter's eye in the rearview mirror.

"Now Jane, I know you find me intoxicatingly handsome, but I'm already taken."

"Oh, I figured that out a while ago," she said as she gave a nod to Emiko. "I am curious if you always wear a bowtie."

Emiko laughed. Baxter blushed. And then they all three laughed. Baxter handed back the bagels and they chatted about several inconsequential things. She never did find out the answer to her bowtie question.

She quieted as they entered Washington and headed down the familiar streets that took them past iconic government buildings and museums. She thought of the many trips that she and the children made to D.C. Before 9/11, a visit to the White House was more casual with less red tape. How things had changed.

About fifteen minutes later, they were at the guard gate and Baxter handed over their identification.

"Thank you, Mr. Baxter, good to see you again. Have a nice day," the guard said.

"You come here that often?" she asked.

"Maybe more often than I would like. Here's the skinny on the next few hours," he said. "We'll drop off the car at the lower entrance, show our IDs a few more times, drop off our cell phones, and eventually get to the first waiting area. I will leave you in Emiko's good hands as I touch base with a few of my colleagues. When it gets closer to the president's open window, I'll come and get you two and we graduate to the waiting area outside the Oval Office. Emiko will have to wait for us there when one of Tim's team escorts us into the Oval."

"Who's Tim?"

"He's the chief usher, but you probably won't meet him," Emiko said.

When they found their way to the first meeting room, Baxter left them. Quite a few people sat in typical waiting room chairs and settees, reading newspapers or magazines. There was soft music in the background. Everyone spoke softly.

Jane leaned over to Emiko, "I feel like I'm waiting for the dentist."

"Hmmm. I just hope it doesn't feel like a root canal."

"What do you mean?"

"Never mind. Just kidding. You know how important people can be sometimes. Be yourself and you'll be fine."

"I've been asking God how to pray. Just in case. I used to have a list of politicians that I prayed for once a week, but I've been away from that practice for a while. I feel a little guilty about that."

Emiko laughed a little too loud. People looked up.

"Why is that funny?" she whispered.

"It's not. Sorry. Never mind. I had a very catty thing to say that flew through my brain and out again."

They finally settled into an amiable silence; Jane perused the National Review™ while Emiko read People Magazine™. By late morning, she was bored. She let her mind wander to the prayer service on Sunday. Was she doing the right thing? With the house prayer shut down all week, they could have as many as two hundred people at the service. How could she pray for that many people in a few hours?

Finally, Baxter returned and said it was time to go to reception outside of the Oval Office. As they proceeded down the hallway, Baxter called it the gallery, Emiko caught a restroom sign and asked to stop. Jane followed.

"God bless you. As soon as you said the word, maybe power of suggestion, but I feel like I am going to bust."

Emiko laughed.

Jane looked in the mirror as she washed her hands. She was nervous and couldn't imagine what she would say. Should she shake his hand? At least she knew enough that she wasn't supposed to curtsy or kiss his ring. Did he even wear a ring? He was married. Oh, would she meet the first lady? That would be lovely. She had to settle down. She put on a little more lipstick and straightened her jacket and pulled at the skirt that was a little wrinkled from all the sitting.

As they went into the reception area, she began to worry anew about the president's health. Wouldn't it be top secret if he were ill? Would they want anyone to know about it? Would it be like that movie "Dave" where they would hire a stand-in? Whenever she saw the president on television, he appeared healthy and robust. What if it wasn't really him? Or, what if he was a hypochondriac and wasn't sick at all?

"Give me strength," she said.

"What?" Baxter bent down to where she was sitting. "You all right?"

"Yes. No. Oh, I don't know."

"You'll be great. I'll be right there with you. No worries."

When the man ushered them into the office, Jane kept saying thank you very much. She couldn't stop herself. She sounded addled. When the doors opened, she was unprepared for what she saw.

Many men and women sprinkled the office, none of whom she recognized on sight. The president sat at his desk and didn't even notice her entrance. Baxter walked her around and introduced her to several of the people, although their names basically flew in one ear and out the other. She kept looking over to where the president sat. Was he talking to someone important, like a world leader? No, they wouldn't let her in for that. She tried to hear what he was saying, but Baxter pulled her over to one of the gold couches that faced each other.

Then she heard the president say, "I'll call you tomorrow. Incredible stuff!" and he got up from behind the desk; she didn't realize how tall he was.

"All right everybody, out you go. I'll sign those letters later this afternoon, Allison. And Jeannie, keep me posted on that thing we talked about earlier. Thanks, hon. Go, go, go folks. This could be monumental," he said and then walked straight to her.

Baxter stood and she followed suit, although it was a lot harder to get out of the cushy couch than it was to get in.

"This is Jane Freedle, Mr. President, the amazing woman I told you about who could turn the world upside down."

She looked at Baxter and wondered what in the world he was talking about. She didn't want to turn the world upside down or sideways.

"Well, well, great to meet you at last," he said as he reached out two hands to her and shook her hand rather enthusiastically. And then to Baxter, "We'll be fine just the two of us, won't we Janet, I mean Jane, right? It's Jane?"

"Yes, thank you."

"Please, please, sit down, sit down."

"Sir, I'm sure Sister Jane would be more comfortable if I stayed with her. It's overwhelming to meet someone like you for the first time."

"Ridiculous," he said. "You're not afraid of me, are you, Jane?"

She moved her head in a couple directions, not sure which movement would be better in this situation. She looked at Baxter and pleaded with her eyes, but she could tell he would not say no to this man.

"Sure. Fine. I'll be right outside this door, Jane. All right?" Baxter said.

"OK," she said, although she wasn't sure anyone could hear her. She took a very deep breath. Her hands were shaking so badly, she sat on them. Then she realized how ridiculous that looked and pulled them out again. She grabbed one of the throw pillows and held it up against her right side. The other hand she slipped halfway between the cushions.

The president sat on the couch opposite her and looked at her steadily. "What year were you born?"

"I beg your pardon?"

"Sorry. I'm curious if we're the same age."

"Uh, 1948. December second."

"Oh, Sagittarius. I'm a Gemini. We're known for being expressive and quick-witted. Nice, right?"

"That's very interesting," she said blandly since she knew absolutely nothing about astrological signs except for the little horoscopes in the Aegis on Wednesdays.

"So, you're the miracle worker?"

"Actually, God is the miracle worker. You are a man of faith, so I'm sure you can appreciate the difference," she said and smiled. She hoped she hadn't said the wrong thing.

He looked beyond her intently; she turned to see what had captured his attention. She saw several people walking about outside. She wasn't sure what they were doing, but he tracked who was talking to whom.

"Mr. President?" she ventured.

"Sure, sure. Gotta keep your eyes on everything in this business. Where was I? Oh yes. I've heard some great stories about you. Just great. How long have you been able to do these things? That's a real talent," he smiled warmly.

She felt uncomfortable with the question. After all, she'd only been practicing healing prayer for a month, if she told him that, he might think she was inexperienced. Oh, what difference did it make? If she were to pray for this man, and if God was in it, then perhaps they should get to it. The man had already checked his watch two or three times.

"Would you like me to pray for you, Mr. President?"

"Absolutely. Of course. How does that work? Do you have to lay hands on me? That's the way of it right? We had a great group of pastors come in here last week and a whole bunch of them had to do that."

"What is your illness sir? I need to know how to pray if you are sick."

"That's classified," he laughed. "I get to say that a lot."

"Excuse me?"

"Here's the thing. I have a presentation in the Rose Garden in about twenty minutes, so we need to move this along. No hurry, really. I have respect for what you people do. I do. But this job comes with a lot of pressure. A lot of pressure. But really, I'm good. Doc gave me a clean bill."

She tried to track his intent. "But sir, if you're not sick, there's no reason for me to pray."

"Here's my take on this. I think of it as insurance. You have health insurance, right? Regular health insurance or Medicare? Anyway, I heard about that guy at Walter Reed who was in a coma for three months. You come in, you pray, and bingo, the guy jumps out of bed. I like it. That is good stuff. It's clear to me, you do your little bit and people get well. That's great, right? I need to stay strong. Not just today, but every day. It would be fantastic. You could be my daily vitamin."

She was having a flashback to Kravchenko, who implied something similar. Surely this could not be happening again.

"I don't understand," she said.

"Simple. If your prayers, or whatever it is you do, heal people, then, ultimately, a person could live forever, right? Who needs a White House doctor if I have you?"

"No. I mean, no sir. I mean, I can't accept."

He glared at her and she looked away. He was very commanding. She was out of her head saying "no" to the most powerful man on Earth.

"I mean," she stammered, "I mean the gift is not like that."

"What? You can only pray once for somebody?"

"No, nothing like that. It's not intended as an elixir or the fountain of youth. It's a grace. Yes, that's the best word I have. It's a grace."

"What does that mean?"

"It's a kind of forgiveness. A pardon."

"I don't really need that. But listen. This is a little test anyway. So here, I've got golfer's elbow. Hurts like hell. Pain goes up and down my arm. Starts here and then sometimes down to my wrist. Sometimes I need to put off signing important bills because of the pain. You know what I mean?"

She hesitated. He did not seem to understand her fully.

"Come on, Sister Jane. That's what Baxter called you. I like Baxter, he's a good man. But you don't want to make him look bad, do you? Besides, you came all this way. If this works, I'll give you a great review. You'll get great ratings. We both will. Business will be booming."

"It's not a business."

"Honey, everything is a business."

She stood and walked over to the other couch where he sat. He held up his right arm and she touched his elbow tentatively. She gave him the proviso warning that healing did not always happen instantaneously.

He laughed, "Yeah, like Congress."

She prayed quickly. She could feel that his pain was real and there was no check from God or blankness in her spirit. She had worried she would hear a silence, but instead, a peace came over her and she was content with the moment. She stepped away from him.

"Thank you so much for the opportunity to meet you and pray for you. Perhaps I could get an autograph?"

But he wasn't listening to her. He worked his elbow and moved it around in all kinds of directions. He stood and did some trial swings with an imaginary golf club.

"Wow. This is fantastic! Look at this! Do the other one," he said as he nearly skipped over to her and put his other elbow in front of her. "Do you know how many strokes this will shave off my handicap?" he chuckled again. "Wait 'til Todd gets a load of this?"

He stood expectantly in front of her, so she took the other elbow in hand and prayed again. It was not a very well-thought-out prayer. The entire interview and prayer had not gone anything like she had imagined. What did she know about this president or any other president for that matter? All of them were faces on television and pictures in the newspaper. Sometimes the news spoke of these men glowingly and at other times, not so much. In the end, he was just another man who had suffered and was now free of the pain. She had done the right thing. It was not for her to judge.

"Sir, I'm glad you feel better. It has been an honor to serve you in this way. I will continue to keep you in prayer. But I think it's time for me to leave now." She started toward the door where she came in. At least, she thought it was the same door. The room had several doors from which to choose.

"What's your name again?"

"Jane. Jane Freedle."

"Let's keep this simple, OK? I'm the President of the United States. And seriously, you can't say no to me." He walked over to his desk and hit a buzzer. A door to his right opened and the same lovely secretary came in and stood near the door. "Allison. This is Jane Freedom. She will be staying at the International until other arrangements can be made."

"Wait!" she said. "Please, a moment. I have an important event tomorrow. Hundreds of people are involved," she said, while hoping the Lord would forgive her for this lie. "I can't cancel it." She moved swiftly to the door and yanked it open. Baxter stood right there. She looked at him and then turned to the president. She raced past Baxter. Behind her, she heard the president bellow.

"Baxter, get your ass in here."

Baxter closed the door behind him quickly. She stood in the reception room; people stared at her. She couldn't find Emiko. She finally heard her name.

"Jane!"

She saw her friend at the far doorway and walked as quickly as she could, and eventually ran into Emiko's arms.

47

SAME SATURDAY IN THE FIFTH WEEK OF LENT, NICK

It was the last planning meeting before the healing service. Jane's dining room table sat eight people comfortably, so the rest of the attendees stood around the edges of the room; they passed cookies and coffee around. He was glad Toni agreed to run the meeting. He didn't have the heart for it anymore. He looked at his hands again and moved his fingers to insure they weren't broken. He wondered why the memory of that night caused them to ache.

His last two days had been surreal, from the terrible beating to waking up in a hospital with only a few aches to show for his experience. Last night, as he tried to sleep, the memories returned in flashes: three of his nails pulled from their beds, several of his other fingers bent until they broke in half, the smell of his skin as they burned him with smoldering cigarettes, and the razor blade cuts to his skin. He cried out. Thank God, Maddie was right there. She turned on the bedside lamp and held him, talked him through it, and waited for his trembling to subside. He knew it was phantom pain, like a missing limb, he knew this intellectually, but the pain persisted. He had considered canceling the service after all, but Toni and Rovanda were dead set on continuing and surprisingly, even Pearl and Jane seemed willing to see it through. Toni wanted him to testify about his experience. That was not going to happen.

When the team asked about his ordeal, he offered few details. And when they asked about the healing, he didn't remember anything after they threw him into the car and dumped him here. He tried to explain about the phantom pain, but they lost interest. Toni started the meeting.

"Thank you everyone for coming round this afternoon. I think it's a shame we couldn't get into the high school sooner for the decorating and heavy lifting."

"It was too expensive," he said, but no one seemed to hear him.

"But where is Jane, our star of the show?" Toni asked.

"Maddie and I got a text earlier this morning that Jane had to go with Emiko to an important meeting in Washington, D.C. That could be anything. But honestly, I think we can finish the plan without her as long as she has a handler to bring her onstage at the right moment."

"I'll be in charge of that," Rovanda said. "But I want to say one other thing. You know Jane doesn't like either one of her dresses. I don't want to fight her on this, but I've put in a lot of work on them."

"I know you have. I don't understand Jane sometimes," Toni said. "I think they're beautiful. Show them to everybody, you have them with you? Rovanda does amazing work."

"Why does she need two?" someone asked.

"Well, she's got to change at intermission," Toni said.

They spent the next ten minutes showing off the dresses, one white and the other light blue, both with big gold crosses across the chest and ribbons that flowed from the shoulders. He went out to the kitchen for another cup of coffee. He felt very jumpy but couldn't figure out why, like another shoe was about to drop. When he got back to the table, they were discussing the drapes, the rented palms, and the extra up-lights.

"Here are the receipts for these," Toni said as she passed a stack down to Nick.

"What? But I thought—"

"We really should have set up some of this sound equipment today. It's going to be tight tomorrow," the worship leader, Marcus, said.

He turned to Marcus. "I know, but didn't you guys need that equipment for your service in the morning?"

"Oh, we can't use that. We rented some stuff that's scheduled for delivery by ten. I'm leaving our service early and bringing a couple of guys with me to run the setup and sound checks. Would be cool if you could bring in some lunch for the brothers."

"Yeah, sure. I guess so," he said.

He was beginning to feel that familiar anxiety when things were going bad. It always crept up from his gut. He thought the church folks had donated everything to the cause. He never asked, of course. That was part of his problem. He never seemed to ask the right questions at the right moment.

Toni spoke. "Nick? Are you listening? I want to remind you that Bishop Bones will expect a stipend tomorrow. I think he would prefer cash."

"Like, what are we talking about," he asked.

"Oh, I don't know. Like any guest speaker, maybe $500."

"What?"

Everyone stopped and stared at him like he was somehow being disrespectful of the bishop.

"Let's see how the donations go tomorrow, all right? I'm sure we'll all be fine," he said, although he didn't feel as confident as he tried to sound.

"Honey," his mother spoke, as she put a hand on his arm, "it's going to be great. I'd like to sit at the table out front, to take the tickets and donations, but I'll need a cash box. Would you like me to get the change for that? I could go to the grocery store and get some singles and fives."

"That would be great, Ma. Are you feeling OK? You look tired. You get over that flu from a couple of weeks ago?"

"I'm not sleeping, that's all. I can't seem to get enough. Then at night, I wake up like I can't breathe," she said.

"Have the Sister pray for you," Rovanda said.

"What? Pray to help me get to sleep? That's silly."

"We can pray for you right now," Toni said. They all held hands around the table, several people laid their hands on Rosalie's shoulders and back while Toni prayed. Nick noticed again how different her prayer style was from Jane's. Toni's voice did a lot of swooping in and out, as she called on the power of God to cast out the enemy that kept his mother awake at night and beseeched Christ Jesus to pour out his breath of life on Rosalie. He thought they had finished praying when another woman spoke up and then another and another. Finally, he heard his ma's voice quietly say, "amen." Toni sighed. "I love it when God shows up. Amen? Amen. Now let's go over the Order of Worship." She passed out papers and began to review everyone's responsibilities.

He stopped listening. Instead, he thought about his phone interview with Twomey and how he had finally confessed how Zach had squeezed him into signing off on the wastewater plant contract. Nick's father had always called him a knucklehead. Too true. He had tried to show everyone that he could be a success; instead, he had a string of failures behind him. When Zach had approached him about the contract, it sounded like a win-win. Everybody would make a little money on the project. It was only a few thousand, but it had helped them get through Christmas and the down payment on that car for Maddie. But now, it wasn't a win for him at all. And he could see, the healing service was turning into a money pit as well. Maddie was right. She was always right in the end. Poor planning, no budget, and once again, he was in over his head. Jackass.

The wastewater plant fiasco would send him to jail. He didn't have the heart to tell his mother. His phone rang with a new song, "One is the Loneliest Number," a real Goldie Oldie.

"Hey Maddie," he said into the cell.

"Hi. Just checking in to make sure everything is OK."

"Yeah, we're fine. Won't be much longer."

"What's wrong. You don't sound right," she said.

He wiped his eyes. "No, no. I'm good. Thanks. See you later." It kept happening, the sudden tears, like a little boy lost. Sweet Jesus, how would this end? The only thing holding him together was his wife. Wasn't she the one who had always held the family together? But once he was behind bars, would she walk away and take the kids with her? Who knew? After he told his story to Twomey yesterday, she surprised him.

"Thank you for not holding anything back, for not exaggerating or blaming anyone else. That means a lot," she said and then hugged him.

He had surprised himself. His near-death encounter with Kravchenko had scared him nearly senseless. He supposed the truth seemed appropriate.

The door opened and his worst nightmare walked in the door as though he had conjured the man out of thin air. The brother, Sasha, was with him, and they both had weapons drawn. Nick dropped his coffee cup and it shattered.

"Hello Nicky, my old friend. We came to see if you were in good health. What do you say Sasha? He looks good, yes?"

"Amazing," Sasha said and then crossed himself three times.

"Now, please everyone, please hold up your little handy, ah, excuse me, you call them cell phones. Please hold them up and Sasha will collect them." Kravchenko emptied the basket of cloths on Jane's end table and gave it to Sasha for the phones. He read the little sign about them being prayer cloths blessed by Sister Jane, took a handful, and put them in his pocket.

"And where is our delightful Sister Jane? My grandfather wants to see her again. You see, he would like to stay in good health."

"She's not here," Nick said, and sent up a little prayer of thanks. The phantom pains started shooting up his arms from his hands. He went to the table to sit down.

"Please, no walking around. Everyone just stay where you are," Kravchenko said, and then he signaled Sasha to check upstairs.

Nick heard Toni and a few others mumbling in prayer. It didn't help his pounding heart. His mind raced to the possibility of more torture and he almost vomited.

"So, Nicky, you don't look so good, maybe you should sit down. So, you have a little meeting here today? Is it someone's birthday?" Kravchenko casually tapped the muzzle of his gun to Marcus's head as he leaned over and plucked a cookie from a dish on the table.

Nick stood up. "Please. Don't hurt anyone. Please. We are having a meeting. That's all. Tomorrow is the healing service. Sister Jane will be on stage to heal many people. You can bring your people there. No charge." That was not the smartest thing he had ever said, but the only thing that came to mind.

"And these people? This one here, very pretty," Kravchenko said as he touched Toni's hair. He turned toward Sheila who had started to weep. "Not necessary to cry, please stop."

"These are Jane's friends," he said. "They are here to help. Guys, this is Mr. Kravchenko and his brother, Sasha, who tried to kill me the other night." Sheila began to pray, "Lord have mercy" through her tears.

"Nicky, Nicky. We are old friends now. You may call me Dimitri. Besides, we didn't try to kill you. Instead, we tried NOT to kill you. Much more difficult in our line of work."

"Very funny. You should try stand-up comedy," his mother said.

"Ma, please don't," Nick said.

Sasha came back down the stairs shaking his head.

"Sit down Nicky, you bore me." He stepped around the table. "And so, this is another Babusya? This is our word for grandmother."

Rosalie stood up, "You bet your sweet ass I'm a grandmother and this is my son and if I had my gun with me, you'd be dead."

Kravchenko laughed; he signaled Sasha to take Rosalie.

"You let go of me you son of a bitch. I may have to say five hundred Hail Marys for that, but it's worth it. You are worthless slime—," her voice continued until Sasha covered her mouth as he dragged her out the door.

"Why are you taking her? She's not even part of this?" Nick leapt up.

"Sit down! We want the Sister, the miracle worker, of course. We make you a very easy deal. We take Mama of Nick. Tomorrow, we call you on this special phone and after your big party, we make exchange." He tossed a cheap phone onto the table. "We tell you where. We tell you when."

"Omigod," he said.

"No worry, Nicky. We are very good to our women. She is OK. No problem. But, of course, if there is a problem? We make it quick." He started to leave and then turned. "Oh yes, please, no police. No big guns. Or," he pointed to his head with his weapon, "we go bang bang to Babusya."

As soon as the car pulled away with a screech of tires, the room burst into everyone yelling and crying. He heard them argue over whether they should call the police.

He stood and screamed at them, "No police. It won't do any good. Are you trying to kill my mother? Didn't you hear him? These aren't idle threats. These are killers. And it's my fault. It's all my fault." He ran to the door and closed it, then leaned against it. He felt his body slide down to the floor and he wept. He couldn't stop.

"I should have died. I should have died."

48

Same Saturday in the Fifth Week of Lent, Twomey

He spent most of the day writing and re-writing, working through the final version of the mess Nick made in the city manager's office. He wasn't sure if he was trying to give Nick a break because of Jane, or what. Vasquez said he was going soft. Maybe he was, but what was the point of beating the thing to death? Nick would go to jail, had already lost his job, and more than likely, would lose his family. What else was there for Nick to lose? He remembered that feeling. Once he had started lying about the money and then added payday loans, Twomey had created quite a shitstorm. Maybe that was it. Maybe he wasn't all that different from Nick when he was that age. Twomey knew a lot about being an asshole.

He promised Nick the story wouldn't hit until the Monday after the healing service. Not an easy task with Chuck breathing down his neck. His other problem was explaining away Nick's beating and Sister Jane's prayer for his healing. The fact that Emiko, his ninja warrior, had whisked Nick to a super-secret site, probably over at the VA, meant something. But what? Maybe it was the feds who had some sort of miracle drug. But why would they bother to use it on Nick? In the big picture, Nick was a nobody. Unless they were hiding the secret to Jane's powers over there. Did she have powers? Come on Twomey, you're losing it.

His phone pinged. He picked it up and read the text. It was Vasquez: *Come.*

Twomey stopped what he was doing and headed down their shared hall. He quickly donned his gloves and booties. Vasquez was on the settee; he signaled Twomey to come over. Vasquez faced away from the door to the view out the back window of rooftops and another very blue, cloudless sky.

"I think this is it," Vasquez said. "Carry me to my bed. I am unable to walk the distance."

Twomey followed all of Vasquez's directions to get him comfortable in the bed: the oxygen, the purified water, the coverlet, the pillows, the music, the cell phone.

"Let me bring Jane to you," he said reflexively.

"The absurdity."

"What do you have to lose?"

"My dignity."

Twomey stood next to his bed wondering what to do next. He looked around the room; he had never been in this room before. It was bigger than he expected. The furniture was like the rest of the place, modern with cleared surfaces. No knick-knacks. Although he did see a couple of pictures in frames on a dresser; he walked over to get a better look.

"My parents and my lover. All have departed into the mist."

"No afterlife then?"

"Piffle."

"The paintings?" Most of them mounted on the walls, but the last two merely leaned against the furniture.

"A series completed. A journey concluded."

They were silent for a bit as he examined each painting. He remembered Vasquez working on the nearly all-black one and would have assumed it was the last in the series. Instead, the final painting was an explosion of some sort, like the big bang on top of a series of overlapping shapes, not buildings per se, but structures. Pure drama.

"Read to me," Vasquez said.

"All right. I have a copy of the <u>Scheherazade and the 1001 Nights</u>. You wouldn't want to miss any of those. I have the book next door."

"You should remain in journalism and flee comedy. It doesn't suit you. The book I'm reading is here, on the nightstand."

He picked it up and read the title, "<u>On Death and Dying</u> by Elisabeth Kübler Ross. Nice light reading." He opened the book randomly. "Should I start here? The chapter on hope?"

"No. Read the previous one on acceptance."

"If a patient has had enough time (i.e., not a sudden, unexpected death)

276

and has been given some help in working through the previously de-
scribed stages, he will reach a stage during which he is neither de-
pressed nor angry about his 'fate'…"

He read on for about thirty minutes until Vasquez slept, his breathing
slow and shallow. Twomey wondered if the man would make it through
the night. What was Twomey's role in this man's death? He didn't know
him. Not really. But the idea of Vasquez dying alone did not sit well.
Twomey left the apartment but assuaged his guilt by telling himself he
would check in periodically through the day and night.

In the hall, he took a quick look across the street and was surprised to see
the now-familiar black suburban peel away. What the hell, he thought.
He dialed Nick's phone number; it rang once before someone answered.

"Who's this?" he said

"Help me. Go to Jane's. Please help," a woman's voice.

The phone went dead; he heard swearing in the background, a man's
voice. His only option was to go over to Jane's to find out what happened. It did not sound good if it involved the thugs.

When he got to Jane's house, a small crowd of people was there. He
didn't know most of them. Three of them sat with Nick on the couch
praying while a few others appeared to be cleaning up. The African
American woman he met the other day came up to him.

"May we help you? This is not a good time."

Nick looked up and lunged at him. Several women screamed.

He held up his arms defensively. "What are you doing, Nick?"

A couple of guys pulled Nick off him.

"This is your fault, too. You son of a bitch. If you hadn't written those
articles, they never would have known about Jane. And Ma would have
died peacefully." He sobbed and the men wrapped him in their arms.

Twomey could have said a few things to remind Nick that it was his idea
or that his articles were more debunking than advocating for the Sister,
but he chose to be silent.

"They took Jane?" he finally asked.

"They took Rosalie," an overly dressed blonde said. "Nick's mother. We
were going to call the police, but the terrible foreigner said he would kill

277

her if we did. Oh, dear Lord, protect your daughter."

"Nick?" Twomey said.

Nick sat in Jane's chair. "They want Sister Jane. Since she wasn't here, they took my mother and said they would make a trade tomorrow."

"Where is Jane?"

"I don't know. With the Asian woman, I think. They've been gone all day," Nick said.

"Her name is Emiko. She was nice," the black woman said.

Twomey turned to her. "Who else is in charge here? You? What's your name?"

"I'm Rovanda and this is Toni, Jane's sister-in-law on Richard's side."

"Are you the terrible reporter who wrote those awful things about Sister Jane?" Toni said. The room grew quiet.

"I'm the good reporter who knows what to do next. The best thing is for everyone to go home. There is nothing more to do here. Nick will be all right. I'll call his wife. I've seen and talked with these black hats and, in this case, the police will be no help. Emiko is some type of government agent. She will bring in the feds."

"Whaaaat?" Rovanda said, "Oh my dear Lord."

People began murmuring in agreement and asking for God to intervene.

Nick said, "He's probably right. Nothing else will happen today. Please pray for my mother."

They slowly gathered their things, spoke encouragingly to Nick, patted him, and proclaimed the will of God would be to bring his mother home safely. Soon, it was just the two of them.

"You too, Nick."

"What do you mean?"

"Go home to your wife. Tell her what happened here. Tell her you love her. And, if you're lucky, she'll stay or wait or whatever it is she may need to do."

"I should have died. They would have left her alone then. It's all my fault. I don't deserve to live."

He handed Nick some napkins from the dining room table so he could honk and wipe his face. There wasn't much else to do.

"Look, guy, you're at the end of your rope. This is where the higher power stuff comes into play."

"I didn't think you believed in God."

"When you're this low, everyone believes in God. Go home," he said.

"What will you do?" Nick asked.

"I'll keep an eye on the place. You call your wife."

"They took all our cell phones."

"Whose phone is that on the table?"

"It's the phone they said they would use to contact me tomorrow, to set up the exchange."

"OK. Give me your wife's number. I'll call you or have Emiko call you when they get back.

Finally, Nick left.

Twomey stood on Jane's porch. Over the years, many strange people and circumstances had floated in and out of his life but nothing like this, from an eccentric dying neighbor to a professed faith healer to some seriously unnerving bad guys and dysfunctional family members and not to mention, a very hot federal agent. But Jane was the real quandary. He liked her. But did he believe her? Did he believe his higher power could do this?

He went home to check in on Vasquez, grabbed his laptop, and came back to Jane's to wait for the next act of this drama. Eventually, Jane and her ninja would show up. Where the hell did they go? And why?

49

Same Saturday in the Fifth Week of Lent, Twomey

The first sign that Jane was back were two army types who came in to sweep Jane's house, one from the back door and one from the front. He raised his hands in the air until they asked him to produce his driver's license. The front door soldier called it in to someone and Twomey got the OK; the same guy went upstairs to look for more danger. Twomey stayed put at the dining room table until Emiko and Jane walked in the front door.

Jane looked exhausted and ashen. Emiko was in a black pantsuit, and Twomey would have bet good money she was carrying. He rose to greet them.

"Hello, honey," he said. "How was your day?"

Jane looked puzzled. "What?"

Emiko stepped between him and Jane. "She's had a hard day. Let it go. Whatever it is that you find funny right now is not appropriate. Go home." She turned back to Jane. "We'll sort everything out. I promise. I trust Baxter and you should, too. Please try to rest."

Jane nodded. They began to walk up the stairs together, Jane leading.

"Wait a minute. We need to talk," he said as he stepped to the stair handrail.

"Not now," Emiko said. Jane kept walking.

"Yes, now. Don't you get it? Something big happened here. Didn't she get Nick's phone call?"

Emiko turned to him. "I turned off Jane's phone. What is it?" She held up her hand. "No. Don't tell me. Let me get her settled and I'll come back down."

He threw up his hands and walked back to the dining room. A few minutes later, Emiko strode into the room, pulling a lot of attitude behind her.

"What could be so damn important, Twomey? The last thing she needs right now is one more thing to worry about."

He wanted to cop an attitude, too, but couldn't muster it up. "Well, when the Sister turns on her phone, I guarantee you she will be down the stairs before either one of us can stop her with enough worry to fill a stadium."

"Why?"

"The black hats came back and took Nick's mother; they plan to exchange her for Jane tomorrow."

"Shit. When tomorrow?"

"Don't know. Maybe after the service. They gave Nick a throwaway phone."

"Oh shit, shit, shit," Emiko said; he saw her pull out her phone to call in support.

Jane ran down the stairs and into the dining room in her terry cloth robe and matching slippers, held her cell phone in front of her and said, "What's going on? I have more than a dozen calls from Maddie but most of the messages are telling me to call her. I tried to call her back and all the calls go to voice mail. For God's sake—"

"It's not good news. Nick's mother has been kidnapped," he said.

"Rosalie? Oh, dear Lord God." Jane went back to the living room and slumped onto the couch. "It's all too much. I—I don't understand how this can be happening. I'm in the Twilight Zone or something. And all of it from one small prayer for a cat; the world is caving in on top of me."

As though on cue, the tabby, who seemed to trail Jane like a witch's animal guide, appeared out of nowhere and jumped into her lap. Jane buried her face into its fur. Emiko was still on the phone in the kitchen and then both his and Jane's cells chimed.

"Twomey," he said into his phone without checking for the caller.

"You still have access to that wacky faith healer?" It was Chuck, of course. What timing.

"Yeah. I'm with her now. Why? I mean, it's not a good time," he said as he got up and stepped into a corner of the dining room.

"Twomey! Are you listening? The Post got a leak from the White House

that your nutcase was there today and healed the president."

"He was sick?"

"What do I know? You get her story before all hell breaks loose, that's all I care about," Chuck said.

He took another look at Jane who had already hung up her call. She looked like she might burst into tears at any moment. Emiko passed him, sat beside Jane, and spoke to her quietly.

"I don't think I can do that," he said. "What time is it anyway?"

"I don't give a shit what time it is. Don't be a jackass. This has been your assignment from the get-go. Do your job or we'll cut our losses and pass it along. It's national news, Twomey! You have thirty minutes to get me copy with quotes. Get her side of the story. Now!" Chuck disconnected. In the old days, Chuck would have slammed the receiver down. That was one thing Twomey didn't miss at all.

He stood in the doorway of the dining room and watched Jane for a minute. Finally, he said, "Is it true? Did you see the president today?"

Jane threw her phone onto the floor and stood up, "Oh for God's sake!" The cat leaped onto the floor and then up to the mantel.

He stepped toward her. "Give me the story Jane. I'll make sure it's done right. This place will be crawling with reporters at the crack of dawn. Give it once, and I'll take care of the rest."

She strode right up to him. "What's with you? Which is it, Twomey? Are you a good guy or something else? Quit with the puppy dog eyes and smooth words. Say whatever the hell you want. I don't care anymore. What about Rosalie? Do you care about her at all or just your damn story? That could be life or death while the only thing that happened at the White House was the president improved his golf game."

Emiko came between them. "This was classified. How did you find out?"

"It was a Washington Post leak. My editor wants the follow-up."

Immediately, Emiko was back on the phone. As he stepped around Emiko to face Jane, he heard the name Baxter again. Who the hell was this Baxter anyway?

Jane stood stock still, breathing slowly. He stood in front of her and gently took her hand.

"I'm sorry. But I need this."

"Oh, well. By all means, let me keep you in inches. On the record, I prayed for his golf elbow, and he predicts his follow-through will be better than ever and he will shave several strokes off his handicap." She took a deep breath. "My husband died on a golf course. Did you know that? That's all I know about golf or want to know." She looked at the ceiling. "Oh crap. So, off the record? The President demands I become his personal healer. Tell me, Mr. Twomey, crack reporter, who is the deluded one? Me or him? Honestly, just make up the rest. It doesn't matter. I'm going off to points unknown tomorrow. Too bad I don't speak Russian or Albanian or Ukrainian or whatever the hell those people speak. It doesn't matter." She walked away and up the stairs.

He went back to the dining room table, picked up his laptop, and moved toward the front door.

"Where are you going Twomey? Don't write this story. Don't do it," Emiko said to his back.

He kept walking. "I have to."

50

PALM SUNDAY IN THE SIXTH WEEK OF LENT, JANE

As was her habit, Jane stood at her kitchen door and looked out to the back yard. This time, reporters and news vans filled the lane behind the house. Soldiers walked the perimeter of her yard and kept everyone out. Emiko tapped her on the shoulder and offered coffee. She turned, thanked her, and saw Baxter at the kitchen table along with another man whose name she forgot. She didn't care.

"Should we review the plan, Jane?" Emiko asked.

"Which part?" she said.

"The exchange part with Mrs. Fabriani," Baxter said. "You know, we recommend you cancel the service; it might make things a little easier."

"No," she said. Not long ago, she would have jumped at the chance. Now, it was her last hurrah. No matter what Emiko and Baxter said, she had a bad feeling about the exchange. In any case, one jailer was like another and sick people were everywhere. What difference did it make?

"Jane," Emiko said very quietly, "you will not be leaving the country. We will protect you and Mrs. Fabriani. I assure you, but you must promise me that you will let us know if Kravchenko contacts you and where they are setting up the exchange. We told Nick the same thing. We will be there. You are not alone." Emiko gave Jane her cell phone, "Your daughter called. I told her you would call her back when you had a moment."

Jane was a walking paradox. Sure and unsure, afraid and unafraid. There had been a few days when all seemed well with the world and with her God. She had understood what God wanted her to do and she had surrendered to the task. But this? Was God in this? She wasn't sure she could go through with it. Her hands trembled, worse than ever. Perhaps she could pull a Richard and collapse with a heart attack. What would they call that type of instant death: not a widow maker since there was no widow, an orphan maker? That sounded so much worse.

Still in her slippers, she padded over to the dining room table to call Maddie. Perhaps she should call all her children and say goodbye. The idea of never seeing her children or grandchildren after the exchange crushed her heart. And yet, Rosalie needed saving. All three cats sat on the table, they too, felt the danger to their beloved human. She stroked them, one by one. Since Miracle had been at most of her healings, she decided, right then, to take the cat with her to the auditorium.

"Hi Maddie. Thought I would check in and let you know we are good here," Jane said.

"*That's good.* Did you need to speak to Nick? He left for the auditorium a while ago. *Listen, I'm sorry I didn't call you back last night. Nick and I were up late talking.*"

"Are you two all right?"

"*I don't know, Mom. I really don't know.*"

"And thanks for that," she said.

"*What?*"

"Calling me Mom again."

The line was silent for a moment. "*We'll be on our way to your house shortly,*" Maddie said.

"Oh, don't come to the house. It's crawling with the press. I'll see you at the auditorium."

"*All right. Pearl sends her love. She's going to help with the kids.*"

"That's great. Maddie?"

"*Yes?*"

"I love you."

"*I know, Mom. I love you too. And please forgive me.*"

"For?"

"*Not believing you. But even more, kind of blaming you for Daddy's death. I'm so sorry.*"

She stilled. "Oh. It's all right now. I blamed myself, too. You'll be all right. All of you. See you later."

She called Richie and Celeste, but neither one of them answered. Perhaps it was for the best. She left messages.

She looked up to see Emiko at the front door. Jane hadn't heard a bell or a knock.

"You shouldn't be here," Emiko said to the visitor. "Nothing should have appeared in the press."

Twomey. He was a persistent rascal.

"It's my job," he said.

"You are no friend," Emiko said.

"And you are? Who got the government involved in the first place?"

And then Baxter, who had followed Emiko into the dining room, bolted to the door, his hackles up and ready for a fight. "Back off, asshole."

"You see the fruit of your work," Emiko gestured to the chaos outside.

"Jane!" Twomey called as Baxter tried to push him back out.

"Baxter. Emiko. Let him in. It's fine. Please," she said as she stood.

Reluctantly, they pulled back from the door.

"Can we talk for a few minutes, maybe alone?" Twomey said while giving her handlers a cocky look.

She lifted her hand (who was she, the Queen of England?). "Just give us a few minutes, please. It's fine. I could use a distraction."

When they pulled the pocket doors shut, she sat with Twomey on the couch. He appeared nervous in a way she had not seen before. Usually, he was in command of every situation.

"Look," he started, "you are breaking every logical explanation I have ever believed. I'm not a scientist or anything, but I do have a respect for gravity, if you know what I mean."

She started to speak, but he stopped her. Miracle sat on the end table next to Twomey and inexplicably, didn't growl at the man.

"But now, I'm just off-balance. I've got a neighbor across the street. He's quite the eccentric, but he's also dying of a rare disease. I know about death. I've seen a lot of people die, back in high school, I drove the car that killed my entire basketball team. It was my fault. As a young father, I watched two of my babies die before they were even a week old. I watched guys in Vietnam die. Later still, I watched my best friend die. Shit happens. I've done a lot of watching. But you've got me so far off-

286

kilter, I even suggested my neighbor come to see you. How messed up is that? Truthfully, between you and me, I don't want to watch another person die. Pretty shitty reason to call on a faith healer."

"Are you saying you believe me? You believe I can help your neighbor?"

"What? No. I mean, maybe. No. Just forget that. You've got bigger problems." He paused and looked down at the floor. He took a breath. "Listen. The foreign guys, the black hats, they are as real and as bad as bad gets. You need to stop whatever it is you're doing—real or not real. The big players have noticed you and it's dangerous. Either they'll kill you, or you'll end up in a golden prison where they may treat you like a queen, but with no rights or freedoms."

"I know. Believe me. Do you know who they are?"

"Didn't Emiko tell you?"

"They don't want to scare me more than I already am."

"I can only guess. Maybe Malina, sort of like the Mafia. They started in Odessa. Their license plates were diplomatic ones from Ukraine, but that doesn't tell the whole story. Did Kravchenko tell you what they want?"

She tapped her knee to call the cat to her lap. "The same reason as the president. They want their leaders to live forever."

"Does it work like that?"

"Maybe. God can do whatever God wants. But hey, if I'm a fake, no worries, right?"

He grunted. "And Rosalie?" Twomey asked.

She tipped her head toward the dining room, "They have a plan." The cat jumped to the recliner and then to the mantel. Jane stood up.

Twomey also stood and she took his hands into her own.

"I shouldn't like you Wade Twomey. You have been a pain in the neck."

He kissed her lightly on the forehead and then slipped a note into her sweatshirt pocket. "Don't read that until later."

The pocket doors slid open and Emiko said, "It's time."

"See you at the service," Twomey said.

"You're coming?"

"Wouldn't miss it."

287

51

SAME PALM SUNDAY, THE SIXTH SUNDAY OF LENT, NICK

As Nick drove up to the auditorium around ten in the morning, one or two television vans had already parked on the side street. Along the front walk was a line of the sick that stretched from the door of the music hall to the corner. But worst of all, across the street from the auditorium, was a crowd of protestors who carried signs like *"Evil is here,"* *"God will not be mocked,"* or *"Burn the witch."*

"Holy shit," Mitchell said to his friend, Jeff. "Look at all these people and those crazy-ass signs."

"Watch your language," Nick said.

Jeff whistled. "Look at that one, the big red hand that says, *'The Work of the Devil.'"*

Nick drove past both lines of people and pulled around to the stage door and parked Maddie's SUV. He pulled out his cell phone and called the custodian, who had promised to let them in. If this many people were here now, what would happen closer to the time?

"Dad? A couple of guys are running this way with a big camera and microphone."

"Let's get inside as quick as possible. Guys, stay away from the press, no matter what. I'll do all the talking," he said. "Grab the chair and the boxes out of the back as well as those two palm trees." He tossed the keys to his son. "Lock it up when you're done."

"Excuse me, sir. Sir!" a guy with a microphone yelled and waved and ran toward Nick just as the janitor opened the door. "Wait, please. Do you work with Sister Jane?"

"Look, we have a lot to do before the service," Nick said. He could tell the camera was already rolling, and in the distance, others were coming this way.

"Did you expect this kind of a turn-out? When will Sister Jane arrive? We'd like to set up in the auditorium. We won't be a distraction," the reporter said.

"No, I don't know, and no. No cameras in the service."

"What are you trying to hide?"

"Nothing, for God's sake."

"Were you with Sister Jane when she met with the president?" this question from another out-of-breath reporter. He now had two microphones and a cell phone waving around his face.

"What? No. Good God Almighty."

"Will Sister Jane be living at the White House?" another one asked.

"Are you concerned that she might fail to deliver?"

"No." Nick tried to close the door, but one reporter blocked the door with his foot.

"Do you have a statement about the protestors across the street?"

"No comment," he said and then changed his mind. "We can't make people believe what they don't want to believe."

"What will you do with the profits from this event?" the reporter jammed his cell phone into the space between the door and Nick's face.

Nick managed to push the man's hand and foot out of the door opening and jerked the door shut.

"Dad, we have one more load to carry from the car," Mitchell said behind him in the hallway.

"It can wait until this entrance clears," he said, and walked down the corridor, through double doors, and onto the stage area. After several phone calls, he had finally convinced Principal Reynolds to allow some early morning deliveries of loaners from a local furniture store. They all belonged to the Lafayette Chamber of Commerce. Nick and the boys moved the two love seats, end tables, and lamps into a cozy setting in the middle of the stage surrounded by artificial plants. He propped the store's sign on the floor facing the audience. Mitchell dragged in Jane's chair that Nick had picked up early this morning. He expected the sound and lighting guys to arrive soon. He sent the boys to the lobby to set up tables and chairs for volunteers.

He sat on one of the love seats with his laptop to review his to-do list. He put the lottery bucket on the floor beside him. His hands ached, but when he looked down at them, they looked normal. He sighed. He'd have to go outside soon and talk to the crowd about filling out cards. He texted Toni to bring more buckets or baskets. He leaned back and closed his eyes. Tired, so very tired.

If he could turn back the clock, he would, right then. Everything in him wanted to run away. Last night, he had asked Maddie if she would file for a divorce. He had hoped she would say "Of course not, I love you." Instead, she said, "I don't know yet." No surprise there, asshole. Who wants to be married to a guy on his way to jail? How would he face his kids? He bent over as if struck in the stomach and covered his face with his hands.

And then, what about Ma? If only he had let her be. Wasn't dying in a hospice bed better than this? She had to be terrified. And for what? She might survive the exchange, but they could lose Jane. And if Kravchenko got wind of the feds being involved, he would kill them all. Emiko had called him last night and explained the plan. She told him to trust her people; she promised no one would get hurt. He checked the cell phone from Kravchenko. No messages. He was living in a terrible spy movie.

"God help me. Forgive me," he said out loud. For a second, the silent auditorium echoed his plea until the stage doors crashed open and Toni's church guys rolled in to set up the sound and lights.

"Nick! Help us out, will you? We barely got through the crowds out there. Glory to God! We're seeing revival," Marcus called out. "Toni and Rovanda are right behind us. They're being interviewed."

"No, no, no. What are they thinking? The last thing we need is more press. We have too many people now." He jogged down the hall and poked his head out the open stage door. "Toni! Toni!"

She turned and waved. He thought she looked like Dolly Parton in her fringed, light blue jumpsuit. And Rovanda wasn't much better in a tight purple suit and a hat festooned with red satin roses and white feathers. He looked down at his striped shirt, tie, and khakis. Was he underdressed? Thankfully, the musicians looked like musicians. Let it go.

Finally, the two women scurried over to the door, calling out "Praise the Lord," to the cameras and "God bless you."

"I thought we agreed to keep the press out of the service?" he said.

"Oh, I guess I forgot. Isn't it exciting?" Toni said and hugged him.

"God is good all the time," Rovanda said and all the guys carrying in the equipment echoed, "All the time, God is good."

Before he knew it, they were all singing a praise song. He headed back onto the stage to get his laptop and the bucket of registration cards. Toni stopped him.

"One little hiccup. Bishop Bones won't be able to make it. But he said he would keep us all in prayer," she said.

"That's too bad," he said, quietly giving thanks that he had just saved five hundred bucks.

"I can do the introduction," Toni added.

"All right. I'm going outside to pass out the registration cards. I printed up the online ones, can one of your people cut them apart out in the lobby? I need someone to sit out front, now that—uh—Rosalie, my ma can't do it." He looked away, having teared up.

"It's OK, Nicky, we got this." She stepped to the edge of the stage and called out to the people milling at the back of the hall. "Twilene, honey? We need you to sit at the front table with the donation box. Where are my ushers?"

He heard a few voices as men and women in black and white moved down the aisles. He turned around and saw the musicians speeding through the setup. He felt so out of place on the stage that he grabbed his laptop and bucket and headed up the left side aisle toward the front doors. Two of Toni's men guarded the door, kept back the crowd, and let in the church folks. Despite only six singers and about the same number in the band, an awful lot of church people had arrived. He stopped at the front table.

"What was your name again?" he asked the girl.

"Twilene Jenkins, Praise the Lord. Isn't the hand of God mighty?"

"Yes. Yes, it is," he answered, hoping that was enough. "But listen, these are the online registration cards. Pink for wheelchairs, white for all the rest. You'll be collecting the cards from outside along with any donations. The cards all go in the buckets, the donations in the box. If any of your church people want to be in the bucket for prayer, they need to fill out a registration form like everyone else. All right?"

"You must be Nicky, right? We were so sorry to hear about your mama. Satan snatched that poor woman. But we believe God's holy light will keep her safe. Yes. We prayed for her this morning in service and there was a mighty outpouring of the Spirit. God is able. Amen?"

"Thanks. Yes. Sure. Amen." Right now, he needed to pass out the cards to the people standing outside who hadn't signed up online. He saw Mitchell and Jeff on their phones next to the men's restroom. "Guys! Come here. Help me pass out these cards. Ask if they signed up online, if yes, then they don't need to register again. We will draw cards randomly during the service. No red tickets, no preferred treatment. Everybody the same today. Only the people in line now can get cards. Period. Oh, except for wheelchairs. They get the pink cards. Once you run out, tell them to go home and wait for the next service."

"When's the next service?" Mitchell asked.

"I don't know. Maybe never," he said.

"Daaaaad," Mitchell whined. "Have you ever been to Wal-Mart on Black Friday? I'm not telling them they can't come in."

"All right, all right. Never mind. When you run out of cards, come inside. I'll handle the rest."

When he and the boys went outside, they started at the front of the line. He had 740 white cards and 50 pink cards. Those, plus the 200 online forms, would max out the space. The last thing he needed was the fire marshal to show up. As he worked his way down the line, the complaints became more frequent about parking and how they were saving spots for sick friends or family who couldn't endure standing in line.

"Sorry," he said, "only people in the line now can get registration cards. You want to help your friend? Give them your card. That's how it works."

At one point, a woman in line unfolded a sign she had been concealing under her jacket. It read, *"These are the End Times. Sister Jane is the Spirit of the Devil working miracles. Revelation 16:14."*

"Repent, for you serve the devil himself," she said, almost spitting at him. The people around her stepped back. She looked so normal in her Orioles jersey and baseball cap that read *"Jesus Saves."*

"Ma'am, I'm going to have to ask you to step out of line for the people who want to be here."

"It's a free country. What are you afraid of? That we will uncover the black truth of Satan's minions?" Then she started babbling and pointing at his heart. Funny how he knew this to be tongues since being around Toni and her peeps. But he'd never heard it sound so hostile.

"Ma'am, you are disturbing a peaceful assembly. If I must, I will call the police."

"Go ahead, you Satan worshipper. Listen, all of you. This Sister Jane is a demon disguised as a believer!"

He looked around, saw concerned faces and heard mumbling among them. He checked his watch; there was only an hour to go before the doors opened. He had to shut this woman up. How many more were hiding in the line, bent on disrupting the service once they were inside? He stepped away and called the local police. As soon as he hung up with dispatch, his phone rang. It was Maddie. *"We're on our way."*

"All right, we'll meet you at the stage door in the back."

"The crowds are insane here."

"You haven't seen anything until you see what's here. I'm sorry, Maddie. I didn't think. Or didn't expect. I don't know."

"What's done is done," she said. *"I want to protect my mother now."*

"OK. Sure. See you in a minute."

The sign woman was still in line, standing defiantly. He called the boys over and gave them his cards. "Just keep going until you run out; I'm going inside. They're on their way."

He had tried to say it quietly, but someone picked up on it, and the next thing he heard was a message whispering game, "She's coming, she's coming, she's running."

He sprinted past the line to the front door where the two usher/bouncers let him in. Several people stopped him on his way through the lobby and auditorium, questions about toilet paper, tissues, extra restrooms, extra microphones, water for the band and singers, and reserved seating. By the time he reached the stage door, two cars had parked at the curb.

He ran up to Jane's car. "Wait here until I wave you in. The line is all the way around the building." He had to avoid a stampede. A sharp pain crept behind his eyes.

He ran into the building and called all the available guys to come out and create a screen or tunnel for everyone in the cars. Maddie and the kids, along with Pearl, were in the first car. He thought Richie and Celeste would show up, but apparently not. Too bad. Sister Jane and Emiko, along with a couple more suits were in the second car. What was Jane carrying?

He stopped her just inside the door. "Uh, Jane. Tell me that is not what I think it is."

"All right. I won't. I brought my guitar now that I'm a superstar."

"What are you going to do with a damn cat? Makes you look like a witch with her animal guide."

Toni and Rovanda came running up then and dragged Jane down the hall toward the dressing room.

"You just called your mother-in-law a witch," Emiko said.

"Whatever. I'm a little stressed, OK?

She sighed. "Listen, Nick, all you need to do is remember the plan. You get the phone call, or a text message, and you tell me, or Baxter, immediately, so we can get our people in place at the location. Immediately, you understand?"

"All right. I get it." He started to walk away.

"Nick, have you even met Baxter?" Emiko said.

He turned and shook hands but said nothing. This was the guy who had caused the White House mess. How was that going to work out even if they saved his mom?

Baxter said, "Nice to meet you."

"Said the scorpion to the frog," he said under his breath.

Emiko put a hand on Baxter. "I'm sure you have a lot to do, Nick. Don't let us hold you up."

The music started, which meant the doors would open soon. He left them and ran down the corridor toward the front doors to make sure the ushers understood who could enter the auditorium. His worry was unwarranted. Someone had found extra baskets for Mitchell and Jeff to help collect the cards along with the lady ushers.

As he walked through the crowd and back into the auditorium, he admired the stage. Even with all the equipment and furniture, they had only filled half of the stage. But he had to admit, the overall effect was fantastic. The baby grand looked very classy. The guys had also set up a large freestanding screen for the lyrics and raised it on platforms behind the drummer. The rest of the musicians stood on smaller risers on the floor while the singers arrayed themselves down front. The scene pulsed like a rock concert. Maybe this event would work out after all. Maybe they would raise enough money to pay for everything, and he wouldn't go further in debt. Maybe.

As he watched people file in and find seats, the back area, intended for the wheelchairs, was jammed. He had to think. They could carry the wheelchairs down and put them in front below the stage but that could be a safety concern. Then it came to him, they could put them on stage. They were the most dramatic cases anyway.

"Excuse me," he said to one of the usherettes, "I don't know your name, but I'm Nick, Sister Jane's manager—"

"God bless you, son; we've been praying for you and your mother all morning."

"Thank you. Listen, I want to move all the wheelchair folks to the stage. Access is around the corner to the left, through the door, and down the corridor. No steps. Please let the other ushers know." He turned to the people already situated, "Folks, I know this is inconvenient, but please follow me. You're gonna get the best seats in the house." They cheered.

He made way for the wheelchairs back through the auditorium doors and along the corridor, through the stage door, and onto the stage. The procession interrupted the musicians, but no one seemed to mind. He showed them how to park in a huge semi-circle on either side of the band and down toward the front. The idea worked. They might even have room for two or three rows if necessary.

He checked his watch. Only ten minutes to go, and few seats remained. He would have to face the folks outside once they reached capacity. But, for the moment, he stood on the side of the stage and took in the full weight of the thing he had created. Despite everything, he couldn't call it all bad. A lot of these people would experience a miracle today. Of that, he was sure. And no matter what anyone said or did, no one could take that away from him, Jane, or the people God would select from the buckets of cards. This would be a day to remember.

"Nicky."

He turned as Toni walked toward him. "We'll start the service with a familiar song. This music is just the warm-up. Then I'll introduce the Sister. Do you want to say anything?"

"Me? No. No. But thank you. It's great. Get the audience to scoot in toward the middle. No empty seats. By the way, you did a great job here."

"Thanks. God is our co-pilot, don't you forget it," she said and kissed him on the cheek.

She strode back to the singers, her fringe flying as she raised her hands to God while Rovanda belted out a song about the army of God. She had a great voice.

He'd better go outside. The burly ushers had shut the front doors and stood outside; arms crossed. No one else could come in. He tapped on the door to alert the guards and slipped out. God, give me the words to say.

"Folks. Hello! Folks. People. Please, please step back from the doors. Please. That's right. Thanks so much. Thank you. Step back, that's right," he said as he gestured for space around him. As he did so, a couple of town police came up to the doors to stand with him. "We are so grateful to you for reaching out to Sister Jane. We know many, many people need God's help. But she is only one person. Even those who are inside may not receive that one-on-one touch. There are simply too many of you. But please, understand, we plan to continue this—this—," he was at a loss for the right word. Then he blurted out, "crusade, that's right, we are all on a crusade for healing. We are taping the service, and we will post it to Sister Jane's Facebook page. Please go home now and join us in prayer for Sister Jane."

At the same time, the anti-Jane protestors across the street chanted, "Break the chain of Sister Jane."

"But we've been waiting all morning. My sister is dying from cancer. Please let us in," a woman said.

"I understand. Believe me. I am sorry. We have no more room," he said

"How can you call yourself a man of God and turn sick people away?" another woman said.

"She's a witch, that's why!" yelled a woman who crossed the street toward them. "They'll take your money and fill their pockets to spread heresy and blasphemy. Listen to us," she gestured for her friends to yell louder, "Break the chain of Sister Jane."

He turned to the police and said, "I don't know what else to do."

The officer said, "We'll call in some sawhorses from Public Works. We'll take care of this."

He shook hands with the officer and slipped back inside the building. As he opened the door to the auditorium, the sound of a thousand people singing was nearly deafening. Despite all their efforts to limit the number of people who came in the door, several stood along the side aisles and in the back. Some of the younger ones sat on the floor in front of the stage. The wheelchair folks and their loved ones made a dramatic statement on stage. The place was on fire for God, except for a few stoic men and women here and there, he assumed they were agents. They stuck out like a fly on a wedding cake.

At the end of the intro songs, Toni came down to the front of the stage and encouraged more hand-clapping and shouting to God.

"Glory. Glory to God. Give Him a clap offering. He is here. God is here. Amen? Amen. Give Him praise," she cried lustily. Slowly, the music settled down into a soft background, and Toni spoke earnestly to the crowd. "We are all here to glorify God. This is not about Sister Jane; it's about the mercy and grace of God. She told me to tell you that. She is a messenger of hope. Don't listen to the naysayers and haters. Sister Jane is a woman of God." The crowd roared.

"Now, we will be taking an offering for Sister Jane's ministry. We are so grateful to Brother Nick; give us a wave, Brother."

He waved and smiled as though he had done this sort of thing all his life.

"Many more people are here who need the touch of God. Amen? Amen. So, as we worship God in song, please be generous. God will bless you for it, for we all know, God loves a cheerful giver. Let's pray—"

He didn't hear the prayer because Mitchell and his friend came up to him with five buckets of cards. They had multiplied like the loaves and fishes' story.

"Mitch, go find your mother and sit with her, or sit backstage." Naturally, they delighted in the chance to sit on stage, so they turned around and left for the back way.

As he walked down the aisle to the stage, he almost ran into Twomey. "How'd you get in here?"

"I have connections to the family," he said and smiled. "You hear from the black hats yet?"

"How'd you know about that?"

"You told me."

"Oh," he said.

"I'll see you backstage."

Someone hushed them from behind.

"And now," Toni was speaking again, "let's all lift up our hands and reach out to the stage and send out the blessings of God to our one and only, Sister Jane!"

52

SAME PALM SUNDAY IN THE SIXTH WEEK OF LENT, JANE

She looked at herself in the dressing room mirror and barely recognized the reflection. Everything she saw was a Toni creation: her normally straightish pixie cut was curly and poufy on top, her heavy make-up made her look like a mannequin (especially the red lips), and the sparkly clip earrings already hurt her ears. She would have cried, but for the inevitable damage it would cause to her fancy eye make-up and no one around to fix it.

Miracle sat on the counter in front of her. "What do you think?" She asked. The cat meowed in a tone that wasn't particularly encouraging.

She remembered the night Pearl had made her up for the prom. When Richard came to the door, corsage in hand, he laughed.

He said, *"I'm sorry. I — you just look so different. Great. I mean you look great."*

She had held back the tears, but she also vowed never to wear make-up again. She had kept that vow except for special occasions when she added a little rouge and tinted lip shine.

"Why don't you wear more make up?" Richard used to ask her frequently.

"Because it makes me feel like a fake. I knew a woman who got up early every day to put on make-up so her husband wouldn't have to see her without it. Is that what you want?"

"You take offense at everything I say. You should build up your self-esteem."

If only she had stood up to that kind of talk. If only. But here she was again, letting someone else determine what she should look like. Why had she allowed Toni to do this? An hour ago, she didn't care one way or the other. But now she did. She felt like a phony.

She stood up to get the whole effect of the white dress and its gold lamé cross embroidered to the front, and the long flowing ribbons from her shoulders. It could almost be a wedding dress, or was it a gown for a martyr's final walk?

Someone knocked and called out, "Ten minutes, Sister."

"Thank you."

She revisited those flights of fancy she had had a few short weeks ago of healing great crowds of adoring fans; how she would sprinkle gold dust upon them, and they would arise with a shout. And although she had already experienced amazing healings, they were never that dramatic. She prayed in a simple way; was that God's way? Her reflection in the mirror was the fantasy. She had to stop this circus. Somehow. Sister Bernie said she could stop anytime, but everything had gotten so far out of hand. Her persistence was hurting people, like Rosalie and Nick. And now, people accused her of being a witch or in the hand of the devil. Insanity.

Perhaps the best way to stop was to be unsuccessful. She could fake it, and not pray at all. No one would heal, and they would leave her alone.

"What do you think about that choice, God?"

No answer, of course. Face it, failure on that scale would make God look bad. His name was the headliner, not hers.

What if she just sent them home? But that wouldn't solve her problems with the scientists, or the military, or the president, or the "bad guys."

Could she disappear? But then, what about Rosalie? Would Kravchenko murder her? Was she willing to test his resolve? She remembered the bloody Nick on her doorstep. No, there was no doubt the bad guys were willing to do harm.

Miracle meowed again. She looked at the cat in her mirror and then herself. She said out loud, "This is not me. Who am I trying to please?" The cat batted at the ribbons as Jane removed the dress and white pumps. She felt better already. She put her jeans back on and the navy-blue sweatshirt Misty Renee had given her for Christmas that read "*Best Grandma Ever.*" She put on her sneakers. She brushed through her hair and wiped off most of the make-up and lipstick. She could have done more with a sink. She pulled off the earrings.

A tap came to the door again, "It's time, Sister Jane."

"Thank you. OK, God. This is me, Jane. Remember, I'm with you."

When she opened the door, the church volunteer, Hazel, she thought, appeared stunned.

"Sister, weren't you supposed to wear the white dress?"

"Yes, but God told me to change clothes and I didn't want to argue with God, would you?"

"No, ma'am. And the cat?"

"Oh, I almost forgot. Thank you." She turned back to the dressing room and called Miracle to her. The cat jumped into Jane's arms without hesitation.

No one noticed Jane's entrance until Toni made the big introduction, "Let's all lift up our hands and reach out to the stage and send out the blessings of God to our one and only, Sister Jane!"

She walked out into the lights and immediately saw Toni's mouth drop open. She tracked Toni's exchanges with Rovanda and the other women on the worship team. And yet, the crowd stood and cheered. The audience didn't care what she wore. As she walked past Toni and Rovanda, she mouthed "I'm sorry" and kept walking until she reached the front of the stage. Toni ran up behind her and gave her the microphone. Jane fumbled with the mic and cat for a moment.

When she spoke into the mic, it made a terrible feedback sound. Toni came up again and showed her how to hold it and where to stand. Jane felt Toni stay nearby. Was that supposed to be for moral support? She stared into the crowd, then stepped back and said, "I don't think I can do this."

Toni grabbed the microphone, "Let's pray, people. Lift up your voices to God and give our sister strength to do this work." Toni's voice lilted in a mass of tongue speaking as did the singers behind her. The band began to play in sync with their praying.

A low roar arose from the audience as people joined the frenzy. She wanted to put her hands to her ears, but she had the cat in her arms. What the hell was she thinking? She looked behind Toni and saw Nick sitting on the steps of the stage, his head in his hands. Twomey leaned on a wall backstage, shook his head and looked down at the floor. On the other side of the stage, Baxter embraced Emiko. All wrong. And the sound kept building.

"Stop! Please stop!" She screamed. She grabbed the microphone back from Toni. "Stop. You must stop now, please. This is not right." She began to weep. "Go home. You should all go home. I have made a terrible mistake."

The auditorium quieted quite suddenly.

"I'm sorry," she said, and turned to leave. She stopped mid stride. "Oh my God." All around the stage, men, women, and children sat in wheelchairs; they had come for a miracle. They had defied reason. Could she do any less? "Oh my God, what a fool I am."

Miracle meowed in her arms. She laughed.

"All right," she said to the cat. "I get it." She turned toward the audience once more and brought the mic to her lips.

She cleared her throat. "I'm sorry. This is all a bit overwhelming. Her voice was like paper. "Let's try this again. My name is Jane Freedle. I am here, yes, but the important thing is that God is here, too." The crowd rose and cheered. "Please, sit down. Let's just sit down." She turned to Toni, "please sit down, everyone," and she indicated all the people on stage.

"We love you, Grammy," Misty Renee yelled as soon as the roar died down. "Nice sweatshirt."

Jane laughed and so did the crowd. "My granddaughter gave me this shirt last Christmas. I love her very much. I love all my children and grandchildren. And, I can see now, God has given me a love for all of you, too." Applause yet again.

She looked around for a place to sit down and only then realized what Nick had done: created something like her living room, right there on stage, including her barrel chair. She hadn't even noticed it missing from her living room this morning. She walked over, put Miracle on one of the end tables, like at home, and sat in her chair. She took a deep breath.

"Let us begin by putting everything in God's hands. I understand Nick will call the names and we will pray together. I only have a few reminders. I have no control over the time it takes to manifest a healing. We must all trust God. When God heals you, please go to your primary doctor as soon as possible for verification." She hesitated, but then continued, "One word of warning. If God does not release me to pray for one of you, I will tell you. In the past, the only time this happened was when a woman came to me who wasn't sick."

"You're a big fat fake," a woman yelled from the back of the auditorium. It was Minerva James. "You're in league with the devil. These people are being sucked in by the thousands of demons filling up this place."

Although some people tried to shush her, it took several ushers to wrestle her out as she kicked and screamed. A kind of agitation floated through the room.

"All right, folks," Nick stood and signaled the band to play quietly behind him. "This is how it's going to be. You have all filled out cards and we will pick them out from the buckets. Pink cards are for the wheelchair folks and white cards are everyone else."

"One more thing," Jane said, "Neither God nor I will show preference for age, or race, or illness. No one will ask you about your faith or lack of faith or whether you attend a place of worship. We are all equal here."

Scattered applause sounded a discouraging note.

Nick picked a pink card from the wheelchair bucket. He read out, "*Matilda Raymond, age eleven, cerebral palsy.*"

Jane turned as a woman, probably the girl's mother, jumped up and cried out, "Here." Nick helped her wheel Matilda's chair up to Jane.

Jane thought about the four hours that stretched before her. Even at a record speed of eight minutes per person, she couldn't heal more than thirty people in four hours. What were they thinking? But then, little Matilda sat in front of her. She wanted to talk to the girl, to ask her questions, to talk to the mother, to wrap the little girl in her arms, to hold her, and tell her how much God loved her. But there was no time. She prayed. Nick tried to hold the mic up to her mouth, but she batted it away. "That's it?" the mother asked, clearly disappointed that Matilda didn't rise and dance around the stage.

"God is present, this I know. Healing is coming."

They wheeled away.

The next name Nick called was someone from the audience: "*Angelo Palamieri, sixty-two, severe arthritis.*"

This was taking too long. Jane sprang from her chair and met Mr. Palam-

303

ieri at the stairs. She walked with him toward the couches and asked him where the pain was the worst, she touched those places and prayed as they walked. Suddenly, the man went to his knees, shouting and praising God and Sister Jane. Nick ran up to him and the man spoke into the mic about his terrible pain and now it was gone. The place went wild with shouts of praise to God. But Jane didn't listen to any of it.

No time. No time. So many sick. She had to move faster. In the next fifteen minutes, she ignored Nick and his buckets and walked down the line of wheelchair people as quickly as possible. She asked their ailment and then prayed. She touched them when she could. Sometimes, she heard herself laugh. Once, tears welled up and ran down her cheek. Sometimes, the person got up from the chair and at other times nothing was apparent. She would turn to the caregiver and say, again and again, "Trust God. Healing is coming."

She finally had to take a small break. She stopped to look around. She saw Miracle sitting on the lap of a little girl. She smiled. Maybe it was the cat that had the gift. She was so thirsty. She found a water bottle on an end table. She stood and drank deeply. As she lowered the bottle, she saw Twomey offstage; his arms still crossed, he leaned against the stage wall. He waved gently. She turned the other way and saw Baxter and Emiko still offstage to her right. Baxter gave her a thumbs up.

She heard Nick call up five people at a time from the audience now. Had she done all the wheelchairs? She couldn't tell. The stage was a circus of people talking, praising God, and singing. She sat back down. She saw Maddie come up on the stage to help move people offstage, to create a traffic flow. What a surprise.

Jane lost track of time. She became less like a person and more like a channel of energy, an energy she couldn't have stopped even if she wanted to. The need was so great. And perhaps, because there were so many people, or she was working so quickly, she could feel a transfer from God within her to the person. No, not just the person, but to the infinite abyss that was that other human being. At that moment, she figured out what she had never understood before. The Spirit of God wasn't just going out to the unhealed part of the body at all, at least not in most of the cases. No, God's Spirit was reaching into the soul, the very core of the person who was suffering.

All the physical healings were manifestations of the Presence of God's indwelling, like water filling an empty cup. She recalled Jesus's first miracle, when he turned water into wine. That's what it felt like to her, pouring Spirit into these people and Spirit transformed them within. Each person needed a new wineskin to hold the new wine. She wanted to stop and celebrate.

Then she heard the name Twomey, it stopped her short. But when she looked up, it wasn't her Twomey at all, but a young man standing with a rather flamboyantly dressed, black haired woman. Had Jane just called him "her" Twomey? What was that about?

But no, this was Arnie Twomey and his mother, Belinda Brown. The young man's sickness was drug addiction.

"He's clean now, 'cause he's been in jail, you know?" Belinda said, "I'm just so afraid he'll get caught up with bad people again."

"Mom," Arnie said, "let me talk. See, it's like a drumbeat inside. Right now, it's a low thud inside my chest, but eventually it will get louder and louder."

Jane looked past them to Twomey off stage. Yes, he knew this boy and woman, but he wouldn't look at her. She was sure he didn't expect this.

"Let's pray." She looked into Arnie's eyes and said instead, "God forgives you. Your father forgives you. You are set free, in the name of the one and only Holy God, his earthly son, Jesus, and the Holy Spirit who dwells with us forever."

Arnie looked back at her, unsure.

"It's all right. You look like your birth father. He's here, too. Did you know? Over there." Arnie turned, and walked straight to his father, who hugged him.

She wanted to watch longer, but people kept coming, some sat on the couches and some on the floor, like at home.

It was late in the day when she saw a woman walk up to Nick, fully shrouded in a black burqa along with a boy who was holding a bandaged hand to his chest. Tears streamed down the boy's face, the bandage blood-soaked. She saw Nick pull out the phone, the Kravchenko phone, and read the message. Oh God, she thought, it's happening.

Nick said into his microphone, "We have one last healing. This is an emergency. Peter Kravits, knife injury." She saw Nick try to signal

Emiko and Baxter.

The crowd murmured, but the music picked up a little as the boy walked to her; the small woman followed. It must be close to six o'clock. Was the crowd grumbling because the woman was Muslim? She let that go. No, it was the time of day. So many missed having their names called to the stage.

"Nick, just a minute," she said. She held up a finger to the boy and woman and walked over to Nick. "Please announce that I will thank everyone at the door."

"You can't do that," Nick said as he covered up the microphone.

"I will. They will each leave with a blessing from God. It may be the last time I can do that. Make it so," she said, "Or I will take the microphone myself."

When she returned to the boy, the agitated woman looked around and behind her.

"Please, don't be afraid," she said, "you are safe here."

"My uncle says you must heal my brother. Please, lady, right away." When Jane heard the voice, she realized the black-clad woman was not a woman at all; it was the voice of a young man, maybe a teenager.

Her heart pounded. What did Kravchenko do to these boys? She held out her hands to the boy. "Please give me your hand, Peter."

"He speaks very little the English," burqa boy said, then turned to Peter and spoke a command in their language.

The boy looked at her, and hesitantly reached out his hand. She took it gently and began to unwrap the bandage slowly and carefully. She could tell the boy was in terrible pain. Inside the gauze, she found two fingers severed from the hand next to a note. She put the note in her pocket without reading it. She wanted to swear. Oh God, she thought, who would do such a terrible thing to a child, just to send a message? The bigger concern was whether the damage to the boy's hand was outside the boundaries of God's willingness to heal.

"You heal," burqa boy said, "you heal now."

She wept. She could tell the boy was about to faint. She put her hands over his eyes. He looked white as a sheet. She spoke to burqa boy, "bring him a chair. Now."

In the background, she heard Nick, Toni, Emiko, and Baxter arguing about her plan to stand at the exit to bless each person one final time. She saw the Kravchenko phone pass hands.

She returned her focus to the boy. She could only do what she had done in the past. Pray for God to heal. Nothing more. She held the two fingers, the pinky, and the ring finger, and gently pushed them up against the stumps. She closed her hand around the bloody mess. The boy yelped. "It's going to be all right," she said to him. Then she looked up at burqa boy, "What is your name?"

"Oleksiy."

"Fine, please wrap our hands together with the bandage. Can you do that? Loosely, not tight."

He nodded and then covered both their hands with a swath of the bandage. His hands shook.

She said, "Peter."

"His name is not Peter. It's Pietro," Oleksiy said.

"All right then. Pietro, look at me. Open your eyes and look at me." Oleksiy translated.

She drew his eyes to her by will, and then she surrendered the outcome to God. She did not close her eyes but looked for God in the boy's eyes. Before she began to pray, she asked Oleksiy to speak her words so that the Pietro would understand them.

"Lord God, I know you are here. You can do what no human can do. You can fill Pietro with the light of your love, and you have the power to reconnect the sinews, the muscles, the blood vessels, and bone. You are able. I believe; I believe where Pietro here may not believe. But it doesn't matter. You are who you are. And I thank you."

Her mind turned to the world of senseless pain that people caused one another, not only physical pain, but emotional agony, all for lack of God within. And it was true, that it didn't matter if a person appeared to be good or bad or if he or she made good or bad choices. Healing was a spiritual process, a mystery. She thought of Lindy, who had died under Jane's prayer and forgiveness; but, in the end, healed and at peace.

Pietro stared at her. She asked Oleksiy, without averting her eyes. "Who did this to Pietro?"

"We suffer for family and country."

"God, please give Pietro the full use of his hand to be used for good, to continue to make music. All right, Oleksiy, remove the wrap."

Pietro closed his eyes. She opened her fingers to reveal God's work. She wiped away the blood. He didn't flinch. And she saw: the hand was whole. She touched Pietro's face, "Now you may look, Pietro. God has returned to you what evil tried to take away. Go back to your instrument and play."

Oleksiy spoke up again, "How did you know he plays the guitar?"

"God saw his sorrow and knows his future. Plus, he has a musician's calluses."

Pietro hugged her; Oleksiy pulled him away. Then he commanded the boy and, afterward, spoke in the same tone to Jane, "You follow directions. No police."

"I understand," she said.

They turned to go, at first toward the way they came, but Oleksiy saw the suits standing with Emiko and Baxter. He grabbed his brother, and they ran toward the back of the stage. She doubted they would get away. It wouldn't matter. They had served their purpose.

Emiko and Baxter came out to her. "What happened here?" Emiko asked.

"Just another healing, Emiko. I've got to go to the front door."

"That's not safe, you know," Baxter said.

"I'll be fine."

Baxter took her arm and Jane looked at his grip, harder than he probably intended, but enough to show her that menace could manifest even among the good guys. Were there any genuine good guys?

She heard Nick instruct the crowd to stay in their seats until Sister Jane made her way out to the lobby. Nick gestured for her to come now.

"Are you arresting me," she said to Baxter.

"Let her go," Emiko said. "We'll be close by."

Jane watched the two exchange glances, and finally, Baxter released his grip. She turned and strode toward the place where Nick and Toni waited for her. They and two other ushers led the way. Twomey slipped in beside her.

"I saw you pocket the note. Let me see it."

"It changes nothing, no matter what it says," she said. She turned and saw Emiko and Baxter not far behind them. She reached out to people on the aisles. "God bless you," she said, over and over.

"Please give me the note," Twomey said.

She grinned at him, "What? You're getting all polite on me?"

"Hell no," he said.

"Before I leave the country, I want to visit your apartment."

"Are you propositioning me?"

"You're incorrigible," she said. "No. Your friend. I want to meet him."

"He could already be dead," Twomey said.

"I'll take my chances."

"There's an access door at the back of the restaurant to the inside stairs. I'll be sure it's open; you can go through the restaurant, pass the restrooms, and then up our stairs. But when?"

She stopped when they reached the lobby, "I don't know. Soon. Before eight." She handed him the note without reading it. And then, Nick pulled her to the front door. Toni and the guards kept the crowd in line. In the background, she heard the haters across the street chanting, *"Break the chain of Sister Jane."*

53

SAME PALM SUNDAY IN THE SIXTH WEEK OF LENT, NICK

Jane returned to her house to rest for an hour or so. Nick helped with the teardown and gave money from the offerings to Marcus to share. Marcus looked at the cash and then gave it all back to him. "God has other plans for this cash."

When Nick got to Jane's, Emiko and Baxter told him about the note and the rendezvous site to exchange Jane for his mother. Somehow Twomey got the note first, which made no sense. In any case, Emiko and Baxter wanted Nick to come to the rendezvous point with them and comfort his mother afterward. The Kravchenko text message had merely said to pass the boy with the knife injury to Jane immediately. When he saw the blood dripping from the boy's bandage, Nick had felt queasy. Kravchenko was a monster. Later, he almost tossed his cookies when they told him what Kravchenko had done to the boy. The guy was insane. A terrorist. What if he killed them all at the rendezvous? Nick felt like he was moving through quicksand.

Maddie hugged him hard when she heard he was to go along to support Jane and Rosalie.

"Don't be a hero," Maddie said.

"No worries there."

"The kids love you. Come back. We'll work things out," Maddie said.

It was the most hopeful thing he had heard from her since his big confession the night before. Would she forgive him? There was no time to ask; they called him to Jane's car.

"Put this on," Baxter said. "Emiko already put one on Jane."

He took off his shirt and pulled on the bulletproof vest. It was heavier than he expected.

"I don't think this is necessary, Baxter. Injuring me would defeat their purpose," Jane said.

"Accidents happen," Emiko said. "It's insurance, ok?"

"You're so calm. I'm ready to jump out of my skin," Nick told Jane.

She had no chance to answer. Baxter took charge.

"Jane, you sit in the back with me. Nick, you drive, and Emiko will sit up front with you."

The two of them didn't even appear armed, but he knew that couldn't be true.

He understood, intellectually, there had to be sharpshooters hidden along the way and at the meeting point, but since the meeting place was a tunnel under the C&O tracks, how could anyone hide in there?

He reviewed the plan in his head. Kravchenko's people would drive a car (probably the black suburban) into the tunnel entrance on the Boston Street side and blink their lights. Rosalie would climb out with Kravchenko and stand by the car. Then Jane's car would pull into the opposite entrance on Denton and blink their lights. Jane, Emiko, and Nick would stand beside their car with the doors open. Emiko had stressed that to him, "Don't close the car doors." Jane and Rosalie were to walk toward each other into the space between the cars.

Emiko patted him on the arm. "Everything will be fine. Jane will be safe. Our priority is to grab Rosalie and then we'll retrieve Jane from the Kravchenko vehicle after it pulls away from the tunnel."

While the four of them waited on Denton Street for Kravchenko's arrival, he couldn't bear the silence.

"So, Baxter," he turned in his seat to catch Baxter's eye. "Where do you work? How do you and Emiko know each other?" He tapped her on the knee. "I got it right this time, your name?" She smiled wanly.

"We were in Special Forces together," Baxter said. "She bailed to go back to school, and I went into government service when my duty ended."

"I did not bail. I thought it was smarter to let them pay for my education," Emiko said.

"Yeah, what about that offer from NSA?" Baxter said.

"And what about your chance to go to the CIA?" she countered.

"You just like having letters like PhD after your name."

"At least I don't have to kiss ass at work," she said

"Hey, guys, I was just making conversation. Guys," Nick said.

"Don't worry, Nick," Jane said. "It's a lovers' quarrel."

"Jane." Emiko said.

Baxter laughed. "That's the plan."

Lights blinked. Baxter and Emiko went professional in the blink of an eye. Nick stared out the windshield, frozen.

"Nick, snap out of it. Jane, are you ready?" Emiko said. "Please remember everything we told you. We will have you back in your bed tonight."

"Thank you for everything. It's been a pleasure," Jane said.

He did not like the sound of that. Baxter didn't seem to like it either.

"Jane, please don't do anything outside the plan," Baxter said.

He watched as she turned to Baxter and smiled. It was a little too Mona Lisa for him, but there was no time to argue. Baxter told him to drive slowly into the tunnel.

At first, everything seemed to go as planned. They opened all four car doors. He stood at the driver's side door and Emiko on the other side. Jane walked around Emiko and toward his mother. Baxter hunkered down in the back seat. But then, as the two women walked toward each other, he heard his ma yell to Jane in the tunnel. She appeared to shuffle as she walked. Had they hurt her? He wanted to leap forward and help her.

"Don't move," Emiko hissed.

"Jane," Rosalie said, "don't try to save me. Understand? Let me go."

"I don't understand. You're going to be fine," Jane said.

"I'm not," she paused, and then she made a few more steps. "It's like Lindy. I understand. I'm ready. Save yourself."

He knew what that meant. Lindy Gillespie died. She wanted to die. "Mama, no!" He moved away from the car and toward his mother. Ma collapsed. The doors of the Suburban flew open. Shots rang in the tunnel. Then he fell but didn't know why. His leg burned.

"Dammit to hell," Baxter yelled as he rolled out of the car and dragged

312

Nick backward.

"Ma. It's my ma," He said. Baxter dragged him behind the car; he saw Emiko crouch low and shoot at the black car. Once Baxter started shooting, Emiko ran and tackled Jane who kneeled next to his mother. Then the real shooting started. He couldn't see everything, but the noise was deafening. As quickly as it started, the noise stopped. He looked around from the back of Jane's car and saw soldiers in heavy military gear surround Kravchenko's car.

Jane yelled, "Let me help her."

"Not now," Emiko said, "she'll be picked up and taken to the hospital."

Baxter and a guy in uniform pulled Nick up and pushed him into the back seat; Emiko and another guy dragged Jane into the car as well.

"You're not listening to me," Jane said among other things. He stopped listening when he saw his blood-soaked pants.

"Oh my God, I've been hit," he said. A soldier quickly tied something around his thigh. It really hurt now.

Emiko and Baxter jumped into the front seat, and the car backed up and peeled away.

"You should have let me pray for her. You had no right to prevent me from helping her," Jane said.

"Our job is to keep you safe, Jane" Baxter said.

She was still angry. "For what? What difference does it make? I will be a prisoner one way or the other. I could have saved her."

They were silent for a while, then Emiko turned to Jane, "What did she say to you as you walked toward her?"

Jane didn't answer.

"She said to let her go. Didn't she?" Emiko said.

"But if they hurt her, like they hurt Pietro, I could have helped."

"You surprise me, Jane. I thought you said the gift wasn't really about you at all?" Emiko said.

He groaned as they took a sharp turn.

"Nick, what is it?" Jane asked.

"He was shot in the leg," Baxter said.

He thought he remembered seeing Jane reach out to him, but then Emiko said, "Here Nick, let me give you something for the pain"

Everything went black.

54

Monday of Holy Week, Twomey

He sat at his worktable and stared out the window toward Jane's house. They still came to the house, those who hadn't heard that Sister Jane had died the night before. They would open the little black, wrought-iron gate, and trudge up the steps, only to lumber back down again after reading the note on the door. Over the next couple of hours, he saw a stream of well-wishers and he figured, by the end of the day, they would cover the porch in flowers. He looked down at his screen again, at the story that would ultimately expose the entire Sister Jane phenomenon, and hopefully, bring the hysteria to a screeching halt. Then, he guessed, the flowers would stop, the weeping would stop, the drive-bys would stop. This was the power Jane had bequeathed to him. Neither of them knew if it would work. Yesterday, after the healing service, Jane had stood at the front door of the auditorium to greet and bless every person who wanted one. When Twomey walked up behind her, she told him to go home and sit with Mr. Vasquez, she would meet him there. He wasn't sure how she would manage it, but he believed her. She would come.

"Remember, I'll unlock the access door inside the restaurant from my side, but lock it back after you walk through," he said into her ear. She nodded.

He had returned to the apartment, unlocked the restaurant's back door and then checked on Vasquez, who, for all purposes, looked dead. Twomey sat in the reading chair and waited.

She arrived about ninety minutes later with the cat carrier and a bodyguard in tow whom she asked to give her privacy to pray over a dying man. The guy insisted on waiting for her in the living room of Vasquez's apartment and reminded her of the time. Twomey closed and locked the bedroom door. She set the carrier down and sat in the reading chair and looked at Vasquez for a long moment.

"Why'd you bring the cat? You know he can't be around them."

"That was before today," she said.

Whoever this woman had been, she was no longer. This Jane was a warrior, a holy woman, and a force to reckon with. She touched Vasquez's arm and spoke directly to him.

"Mr. Vasquez, I don't have much time. I need you to wake up for a moment. Mr. Vasquez?"

His eyes fluttered and then slowly opened. He took in the room, the woman, and Twomey at the foot of the bed, to whom he spoke, "You have become quite capricious, Mr. Twomey."

"That's all right. Most people think I'm an asshole."

"That too."

"Mr. Vasquez," Jane said again, "Do you want to live?"

He turned his head on the pillow to look at her. "I've worked hard to accept death," he said.

"But can you accept life?" Jane said.

"I find that question boorish in the face of my condition," Vasquez said, his voice raspy and barely audible. "It is not life itself that is undesirable; it is the quality of life." He closed his eyes.

"I am going to take that as a yes," Jane said. And without flourish or drama, she prayed for Vasquez's restoration. A minute into the prayer, Vasquez opened his eyes again and stared at her. He did not try to speak; he watched and listened. After the "amen," she said, "I believe you are my last client."

She turned to Twomey, "I don't know where you are anymore on the scale of believing or not believing in what I do. That doesn't matter. It may serve us both better that you don't believe. In any case, I need to ask you for a favor."

"Jane, I've seen too much, on both sides of good and bad. I watch you, and while I'm watching, I'm stupefied, like a kid watching a magician. But my head knows there are laws of nature that cannot be broken. I'm sorry to say that in front of Vasquez—"

"His healing is not affected by your opinion," Jane said.

"Here, here," Vasquez muttered.

"Go back to sleep, Mr. Vasquez. You will undoubtedly feel better in the

316

morning," then back to him, "I don't care about that, I told you. But in a few minutes, I'm going to the exchange location with Nick, Emiko, and Baxter, to save Rosalie. Supposedly, it will all work out, but I know better. After tonight, one way or the other, nothing will be the same."

Twomey sat on the edge of the bed. He wasn't sure where she was going with all this. Despite everything, he liked this feisty Jane. She wasn't his type really, none of the blatant sexuality that had always lured him in his younger days. He reached for her hand.

She stopped talking.

"You're right about one thing," he said, "whether the mafia gets you or the feds, you'll be out of circulation. It's like the water engine. You're an alternate technology that could disrupt the status quo. If your handlers are smart enough or powerful enough, however, they may be able to protect you."

"How?"

"I don't know. It's the stuff of movies and fiction: witness protection, that kind of thing. They could whisk you away, call you a dead woman, and that would be the end of that."

"But, my family, my home?" She turned away as tears welled up in her eyes.

"Look, I don't know. I'm sorry."

"Well, I have a plan, just in case. I want you to write about me one last time but discredit me completely. Call me names. Call me a charlatan."

"I've already done a fairly good job of questioning your authenticity. Your story gets problematic because of all the witnesses, the people who believe, they keep popping up with miraculous evidence. It would be like Vasquez rising from the dead."

"I'm not dead yet," Vasquez said.

"I know. I'm saying, it's these kinds of incidents that make it hard to call you a fake outright."

"Well, come up with something! Go into my house and take all the registration cards and letters; destroy them. Contact the Center for Skeptical Inquiry; they have an open case on me to discredit me. Interview my pastor's wife, she's a psychotherapist and said I was unusually religiously preoccupied — in other words, certifiably insane."

317

Jane stood. She had become agitated. He rose to meet her and took her into his arms. She resisted, but then she wrapped her arms around him and laid her head on his chest. After a while, she chuckled.

"When Misty Renee was little, she used to love the old Disney movie called *Lady and the Tramp*. That's what you and I remind me of, a sheltered woman and a streetwise ruffian."

"I believe that dog was a mutt, which is about right."

There was a knock on the bedroom door, and they heard Baxter's voice, "Jane. We've got to go. What are you doing in there? Why is the door locked?"

"I'll be right out," she said, "I'm praying for someone."

He pulled away from Jane just enough to look down into her eyes. Then he said, "I have a post office box, number 5575. Can you remember that number? Can you?"

"Yes, but why—"

"I don't know. Just in case. You know, you send me your address one day or something. You tell me you're alive. You send me a Christmas present. When it's safe. When you are safe. Did you read my note?"

"I did. I liked the poem. Did you write it?"

"Hell no. I stole it off the internet. I just think you're brave.

"Thanks."

"Jane!" Baxter said through the door, clearly frustrated.

"I have one last favor."

"What? You know I will do it if I can," he said.

"I want you to keep Miracle, the cat."

"No."

"Twomey. Please. They'll look for her. The bad people. You know, the crazy people out there who might think she is more than a cat."

"Jesus Christ," he said and winced. "Sorry to swear."

"It's all right, that's a good name to call on. I'll take that as a yes. Good-bye, Twomey," she said.

She unlocked the door, and Baxter escorted her out without a word, the bodyguard followed. He looked at Vasquez, who had fallen asleep.

That was just yesterday.

The phone shook him from his reverie. Chuck, of course, *"Where is that effing copy? All hell is breaking out on this dead faith healer."*

"Don't you ever sleep, Chuck? Maybe eat breakfast, take a shower, normal things like that?"

"Quit throwing horseshit and answer my question."

"Sixty minutes."

"I'd better see it in thirty. Or less." Click.

And so, he wrote the article/obituary for Jane Smythe Freedle, irrational woman in her senior years, distraught by grief and loss, who had managed to create an environment of collective delusion, and so on. He faked what he could about the death and even stretched it to "caught in the crossfire" of rival gangs. As far as her healing abilities went, he wasn't as corrosive as Jane would have liked, but then, he hadn't expected Baxter and Emiko to remove her so quickly. At least, that's what he hoped had happened. He was sure the article would land slightly below the fold on the front page, "Sister Jane is Dead." About an hour after the story hit, there was a tweet from the White House that called Sister Jane's visit to the White House fake news.

Later that day, beer in hand, and laptop propped on his chest, the cat lay beside him as he stretched out on his couch. He watched the latest news about another mass shooting in Arizona, when he heard a familiar tap on this door. He didn't move to open it but waited. Vasquez entered and stood in the doorway. He wore no gloves. He was still in his black t-shirt and sweats, the clothes he had chosen for his death bed. He looked thin, but otherwise, his skin looked completely normal, flushed even.

"Where is she?" Vasquez asked.

"Gone. Sister Jane is no more. Do you remember, she told you that you were her last client?"

"But why?"

"The world couldn't handle it. Holiness, I think."

"Now that it's too late, you believe?" Vasquez said.

"Do you?"

They both stared at each other for a moment, then Twomey said, "You look good."

"Yes. I'm going to take a shower."

"Then what?"

"I'd like to take a walk. Outside. Would you like to accompany me?"

"I would," he said.

55

EASTER SUNDAY, TWO YEARS LATER, JANE

She sat on her little porch and rocked. She had always dreamed of a house in the mountains, and here she was, breathing fresh sweet air on a clear day, marveling at the beauty of Mt. Rainier in the distance.

She had loved her time at the Iona Community and grown fond of the simple life and daily schedule. She remembered asking Sister Bernie, long ago, if she should become a nun and they had both laughed. And yet, in some ways, she had become a nun. Almost. Her exact title was an associate and only one or two people in the community knew they were providing her sanctuary. Nor was she Jane any longer, but Lydia. That took a while to remember. But the most difficult part of the plan was losing her family, particularly her beloved grandchildren. Baxter told her she could never go back. He had called in a lot of favors to slip her out that very night. And then, he and Emiko disappeared from her life as well. She had a single official contact person, a woman she had never met who occasionally called her to check-in, but since Jane was a good and obedient client, as far as Agent Brown could tell, those calls came less and less frequently.

Jane never mentioned to the agent what she knew about her family and friends. Pearl retired and moved into the family house for a season, but then sold it and downsized to a condo. Maddie took the cats, Bart and Simpson, while Hang and Richie took the parakeets, and soon after that, Hang had a healthy baby boy. Pearl and Maddie had looked for the tabby, Miracle, but never found her, much to their sorrow. Nick was convicted and jailed for a year, then got off early for good behavior but Maddie didn't take him back and they divorced amiably. He got a job as an insurance salesman and took a portion of his inheritance to pay for Maddie's tuition to become a social worker. That made Jane happy. The grandkids were doing fine.

Toni and Rovanda started the Sister Jane Society and taught people

321

how to pray for healing. What were they thinking? Gillespie had filed a suit against her estate for his wife's death but then died of a massive stroke and the family dropped the case. Her twin brothers died within six months of each other in Florida. On Twomey's side, his son went to tech school to become an electrician and his ex-wife, Belinda, married a man who won the lottery. Twomey retired. She knew of all these things because of P. O. Box 5575 in Lafayette and her post office box in Seattle. The only news she received from the agent was a photocopy of a Washington Post wedding announcement for Dr. Emiko Fujihara and Archibald Baxter.

She stood up as a car pulled down her long driveway. And there he was. The "tramp" carried a rectangular bag and a small flat package as he walked up her porch stairs.

"Hello. Any chance an old guy could get a cup of coffee?"

"Maybe. Depends on what peace offering you bring?"

He stepped on the porch and handed her the package. She opened it carefully and exclaimed.

"Oh, it's a Vasquez. It's stunning."

"His work is different now, but he wanted you to have one."

"And what is this?" She pointed to the bag.

"Remind me never to drive cross-country with a cat again."

He let out the cat and she sauntered over to Jane and rubbed her leg. Jane knew she was grinning from ear to ear as she held the cat in her arms.

"Please tell me that the return of this cat does not mean you are back in the 'you know what' business," Twomey said.

"Well, there's a man in Canada I've heard about and would like to visit."

"God help me."

"Exactly."

End